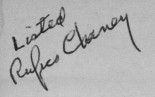

ART AND ASSASSINATION

There are no more than a dozen occupations—political agent and artist are two—in which everything you do becomes part of your job. They are the only tolerable things to do with your time as far as I'm concerned.

A song is not a tool for changing a human heart in the way that a wrench is a tool for changing a bolt, but it was the tool I had, and I was the tool the OSP had.

As the assassin raised the maser, and my eye was just catching an odd motion, Raimbaut leapt a row and slapped the back of the man's head, throwing his aim off.

I dropped to the floor.

The
Armies
of
Memory

John Barnes

A Tom Doherty Associates Book New York

This is a work of fiction. All of the characters, organizations, and events portrayed in this novel are either products of the author's imagination or are used fictitiously.

THE ARMIES OF MEMORY

Portions of this novel appeared in somewhat different form in *Analog Science Fiction & Fact*.

The epigraph from *Angels in America* is used by the gracious permission of Tony Kushner.

Edited by Patrick Nielsen Hayden

A Tor Book
Published by Tom Doherty Associates, LLC
175 Fifth Avenue
New York, NY 10010

www.tor.com

Tor® is a registered trademark of Tom Doherty Associates, LLC.

ISBN-13: 978-0-765-34224-9
ISBN-10: 0-765-34224-3

First Edition: April 2006
First Mass Market Edition: April 2007

Printed in the United States of America

0 9 8 7 6 5 4 3 2 1

For Jennifer Maddalena Gorman,
and for Brandi, Michaela, Dylan, and J'Lyn Maddalena,
friends to keep.

PRIOR 2.   Oh, be quiet, you medieval gnome, and let them dance.

PRIOR 1.   I'm not interfering. I've done my bit. Hooray, hooray, the messenger's come, now I'm blowing off. I don't like it here.

PRIOR 2.   The twentieth century. Oh, dear, the world has gotten so terribly, terribly old.

—Tony Kushner, *Angels in America*

Part One

The
Diversification
of
Its
Fancy

But above all, individualism, if it can be purged of its defects and its abuses, is the best safeguard of personal liberty in the sense that, compared with any other system, it greatly widens the field for the exercise of personal choice. It is also the best safeguard of the variety of life, which emerges precisely from this extended field of personal choice, and the loss of which is the greatest of all losses of the homogeneous or totalitarian state. For this variety preserves the traditions which embody the most secure and successful choices of former generations; it colours the present with the diversification of its fancy; and being the handmaid of experiment as well as of tradition and of fancy, it is the most powerful element to better the future.

—John Maynard Keynes,
The General Theory of Employment, Interest, and Money

No doubt the exquisite beauty of the buildings I saw was the outcome of the last surgings of the now purposeless energy of mankind before it settled down into perfect harmony with the conditions under which it lived—the flourish of that triumph which began this last great peace. This has ever been the fate of energy in security; it takes to art and eroticism, and then come languor and decay.

—H. G. Wells,
The Time Machine

1

Laprada was fussing, lifting my *tapi* from each shoulder till it hung parallel to the floor, and tugging at the fastening. It made me nervous—as her instructor at hand-to-hand fighting, I knew how she loved chokeholds. "Oh, cheer up, you ancient monster of ego," she said. "Something good could happen tonight. For example, maybe they'll finally send a competent sniper. Then we won't have to listen to you complain."

"Then *you* won't," Raimbaut said. "I'd have him in my head. And after that, we'd both have to listen to him complain about being physically four years old."

"No one has any respect for the dignity of the artist." I checked myself in the mirror again. People wear their actual ages in only about thirty of the Thousand Cultures, so my mostly-gray hair surrounding my mostly-bald crown was an oddity, and the wrinkles and crow's-feet odder still. But I looked good, for a freak—not unlike an actor in an Industrial-Age flatscreen movie. Since Laprada was on her second body, physically in her late teens, she might have been cast as my younger daughter, the one who was always running to her wise old dad with her boyfriend problems.

Unfortunately, during my earlier years I had presented myself to my niche market as "authentically Occitan," declaring, on record and often, that aging naturally was integral to my performing persona. Fans have long memories for those sorts of things; I was trapped until someone killed me. Which, as Laprada had just pointed out, could well be tonight.

I returned my attention to smoothing my clothes. I could have substituted smart fabrics, but that too seemed like cheating. The clothes were real, and the body was real, and I sang, present in my real body, not lip-synched and not holo'd, at every concert.

Martial arts had kept me supple, fussy eating had held my paunch to a little roll under my navel, and important work had kept my glance sharp, focused, and interested. *Giraut Leones*, I thought, *you are a good-looking fifty-year-old man*.

Fully equivalent to being an orangutan with great hair.

Paxa Prytanis appeared in the mirror behind me as her hand lighted on my shoulder. "He's admiring himself in the mirror again."

"Caught," I said. "I go to the mirror to see whether I look fit for my public, take one good look, and—*deu sait*, I don't mean to—but I am at once caught up in contemplating fifty stanyears of absolute perfection—"

"Don't hit him in the head," Laprada said. "I just got his hair under control."

"Well, if you don't like my mirror-fascination now, think what I'll be like admiring a smooth teenaged face, if you people let me get killed."

"You'll be even worse—if that's possible—when you first get out of the psypyx," an apparent eight-year-old boy said from the corner, where he had been quietly reading Ovid and making little pencil notes in the margins. "You were a very beautiful child and this time around you'd know it. Rebirth from the psypyx is a splendid experience but don't hurry."

"Dad," I said, "I promise not to step in front of any bullets just to get a new body for free."

Dad, Paxa, Laprada, and Raimbaut comprised the Office of Special Projects team that I commanded. At least the OSP thought I commanded them. Actually I filled out the paperwork and did the apologizing after the team accomplished a mission. As for giving orders and having them followed, I'd have had better luck trying to organize an all-ferret marching band.

We were five people of around ten ages. Raimbaut and I had been born in the same stanyear, so like me he was fifty on the clock, but he had spent thirteen stanyears in storage in the psypyx, so was only thirty-seven in experience, and since he had been grafted onto a new body only fourteen stanyears ago, physically he was about seventeen. Laprada, restarted from her psypyx at the same time, was forty in chronology and experience, seventeen in appearance. Dad was eighty-one in experience, eighty-three by the clock (he was Q-4, a rare mind-brain type, and so it had taken two stanyears for the placement agency to find a host), but physically an eight-year-old boy. Paxa was forty-three on the clock and in experience, but as a Hedon who believed in getting anti-aging treatments and keeping them up to date, she was physically about thirty.

At fifty—clock, experience, and body—today, I was thoroughly fifty, which was fitting because I was here for my birthday concert in Trois-Orléans, home of my most loyal and passionate audience.

"Two minutes till places," Laprada said.

Paxa plucked her computer from her jacket pocket, shook it out, smoothed it onto a makeup counter, and re-re-checked every operative, movement of active known enemies, and weapons diagnostic—a lethal version of "did I leave the oven on?" Of course everything was fine. She folded her computer in a napkin-tuck and slipped it back into her right front pocket, one corner protruding.

Laprada and Raimbaut stretched together, pulling each other's arms, stroking each other's necks, rubbing backs and muscles, preparing for jobs that could quickly become athletic. Besides, they enjoyed rubbing each other.

Since unknown people had started trying to kill me three stanyears before, all the attempts had happened at heavily publicized concerts. Hoping to get some useful clue, the OSP had kept me out on tour and watched me as a cat watches a mouse-hole. I just hoped the mouse wouldn't come out right after the cat got bored and wandered off for a nap.

Even if my would-be assassins stood me up, this could be the night that the Lost Legion, who had been sending delicate little feelers for more than a stanyear, would finally make real contact. (Assuming they were not the people who were trying to kill me; they might be.)

Or maybe tonight the Ixists would do something other than attend in great numbers, listening intently and breathing quietly in meditative unison, as if they were in a worship service (something their faith didn't officially have).

Or something might come out of nowhere.

So here I was: bait for the malevolent, magnet for the odd, connection to the poorly understood, the only physically old man most of these people had ever seen. Just a day in the life of your average lutist-composer, if the lutist-composer happens to publicly work for a covert ops organization. It was a strange job, but somebody had to do it, so I suppose it might as well be somebody strange.

The door opened behind me; I heard a sigh. "Happy birthday, you overgrown teenager," Margaret said.

I turned.

She was grinning; so was I. "My god, you're still beautiful," she said. "In a grandfatherly sort of way."

Careless of my costume, I embraced my ex-wife.

I had met Margaret and fallen in love with her on my first mission, almost thirty years before. We had been married just over twelve years, ending in a divorce I hadn't wanted, just before the fates had entertained themselves by promoting her to chief of my section of the OSP. (She always shrugged and said that I was a lousy husband and a good spy, so she would no more let me transfer out of her section than she would keep me in her house.)

I held her close, then took a half step back. I had seen her only on com screens for the past couple of stanyears. Margaret was still wearing her born body, but a genetic heritage with too much Euro had been kinder to her than to me. Margaret's age showed more in her attitude than in her skin or her body, still firm in my arms.

At my expectant look, she laughed. "No, there's no last-minute special mission, my desperately romantic *tostemz-toszet*. I bought a ticket. I'm going to be out in the seats, enjoying the show. So—happy birthday, Giraut, and I'll see you after. Be brilliant." Then she looked around the rest of the room and said, "You can all be brilliant too."

How fine a team did I have? Even while busy preparing to guard my life, they still remembered to laugh at my boss's jokes.

Laprada placed her hand between my shoulder blades and firmly shoved me into the light. The traditional disembodied voice said, "Ladies and gentlemen" (Terstad, nearly everyone's first language)

"*Mesdames et messieurs—*" (French, the culture language for Trois-Orléans)

"*Donzhelas e donzi e midons—*" (Occitan, my own culture language)

"We are pleased to present, on the occasion of his fiftieth birthday, Giraut Leones!"

I always loathed that first long walk from the wings to my stool, and this was an extra-long walk, across the stage of the largest of all the Fareman Halls in human space. The lights were so bright (did they change something after light check?), the stool was farther away than I thought (did they move it?), and I couldn't feel the songs in my fingers, the way I could just a moment ago (changes? did I make them?).

Was this *my* lute? How did we all forget I don't play the lute? Where was my banjo?

Why was I not laughing internally at my own jokes, as I normally did?

Could people tell I did that?

If they could tell, would it spoil the show for them?

Do they all hate me?

I always take each step toward that too-distant stool with an awkward heavy thud. How can a lifetime martial artist walk so off-balance? Surely they see that I walk like the Frankenstein monster? Don't trip and stumble—*deu* here comes the stool—how *do* people get their buttocks onto these things? I don't remember! *Deu deu deu* please don't let me fall down in front of all these people! Is my *tapi* straight? Oh, gratz'deu, I'm here.

Solid applause from the sold-out house. I bowed, sat, brought my lute into position, and played.

Now I was in the joyous void in which I did my best work, letting each song take me, not thinking of anything but giving them the best I could, letting the energy of the eager listener flow toward the great songs, and the energy of the song back into the listener, back and forth through me, the madly whirling vortex or the sharply focused lens or whatever metaphor you want for the thing in the middle that lives by what flows through it, and is best when it most completely erases itself.

At a concert like this one, everyone wants nostalgia. For my first set I had chosen traditional Occitan material from my first recording, *Cansos de Trobadors*. Three of the songs from that collection had been unexpected hits, launching my performing career while I was off on my first diplomatic mission (it had been a pleasant surprise to discover that I had a large pile of money waiting for me when I returned from my first advanced training at the OSP facility in Manila, on Earth).

The first song from *Cansos de Trobadors* was "The Wild Robbers of Serras Verz." I had learned it at the age of twelve, and had been performing that song for so long that the Serras Verz really *were* green mountains now—the trees that I had planted on volunteer service with my youth group were tall and flourishing. (They still had no wild robbers.)

Culture histories were like that: never the true past of a culture, but the bold, confident, and heroic past that the culture felt it ought to have had. In all of the Thousand Cultures' made-up histories, not one culture chose to imagine that they were descended from unambitious muddlers-through, and only one—Hedonia, Paxa's home culture—officially celebrated their actual ancestors: ninety-some human nannies fresh from suspended animation, a few million robots, a large electronic library, and a million frozen embryos.

The song took me. I boasted of the sharpness of my steel and my pitiless vengeance on the lackeys of the brutal king.

I had known several kings of Nou Occitan, mostly quiet professors or genial artists. Dad had worked for some of them, during his career as an economist in his born body, so I suppose he was a "lackey." The only thing he had brutalized was data.

As I sang, the passions of my fictitious forebears, magicked by elves to the planet Wilson, blazed in my breast. Via my performance, their imagined spirit infected the sons and daughters of a just-as-fictionalized Second Empire, in which a spaceship built by de Lesseps, Poincaré, and Pierre Curie, and captained by Jules Verne, had brought the True Heir—a child descended from a marriage of a Bourbon to a Bonaparte—to the planet Roosevelt. (It was silent, as culture histories usually are, about the other ninety-one cultures on the planet. Presumably all other cultures on Roosevelt were immigrants on sufferance.)

Up on the stage, the son of Mad Guilhem recounted Guilhem's final adventure, set upon by forty of the King's Marshals and fighting on as he bled to death, while Bold Agnes escaped with Guilhem's newborn son.

Out in the house, the daughters of Camille sighed and fluttered.

Wonderful fun, utterly bogus, and wonderful fun *because* it was utterly bogus.

I sang more *cansos* of love and battle, despair and devotion, *merce* and *enseingnamen*, fine spring days on the road and blizzard nights by the fire, the songs that defined a *trobador*, a few from Old Earth, most from our centuries in Nou Occitan. My own compositions were for later. I finished out the first set with a traditional burial song, "Canso de Fis de Jovent," my first real hit. I had long since stopped trying to make it mean anything; I did my best to stay out of its way and let people enjoy an assemblage of pleasant sounds with finely tuned emotions through me, not from me. After every concert, fans wrote to tell me that they never grew tired of it, I suppose because they feared I might. My aintellect replied with a warm, friendly letter over my signature that said I never got tired of it, either.

I bowed with a flourish in the thunder of applause. In my dressing room, I drank a little tepid water, washed my face, did a brief First Lesser Kata of *ki hara do* to work the kinks out, and lay down for exactly twelve minutes of wonderful sleep.

A warm wet cloth dragged from my chin up over my eyes, rising like a curtain on Paxa Prytanis bending close. She smiled, kissed me with the light tenderness that says *we are lovers but not now*, and said, "Better than ever, Giraut." She kissed me again and left, talking to her com, repositioning operatives, making sure security was tight for the second set.

I rose, gargled with warm saline, urinated, drank another cup of tepid water. Laprada came in silently, carrying my freshly-pressed *tapi*. She combed my hair, straightened my collar, made the soft folds of my breeches fall properly over my boot tops. She held up my *tapi* and I turned my back to her and fastened it around my neck again. I spent about a minute nervously tugging things into place. She squeezed my shoulder and whispered, "brilliant, you ancient monster of ego."

The door closed behind Laprada. The clock showed four and a half minutes till the exactly two minutes late I intended. I refilled my water glass and drank slowly, reviewing in my own mind what it was that I needed to do and be on the stage in this next set.

When I was very small, my parents say, my favorite toy was an image globe. I haven't had reason to shop for toys in years, so I don't know if they still make them. An image globe was a viewing sphere, which, if you held it at its south pole, displayed a holo of tiny, shimmering dots that might be anything—galaxies or atoms or molecules. Drag your finger up toward the equator and the dots combined into strings and rings, shapes and cells, structures and pieces, until at the equator you were looking at any number of possible familiar objects—a tree, a dog, a house. Drag your finger north from the equator and the object shrank away in an aerial view, and then into a spaceborne view, and the individual star faded away into a white mist, until, again, at the north pole, the view was just what it had been at the south: scattered twinkling lights in the dark. It wasn't meant to be representative; after all, atoms can't be seen by visible light, and if they could they wouldn't look like galaxy clusters. Much of the fun was in seeing what different pathways did; run your finger around the equator and the thousands of pictures morphed into each other so swiftly that it was a mere swirl of color; spiral from pole to pole and the universe was made of countless changes.

I had been tinkering with a song about my image globe. It felt as if that was my life. Start at any micropoint and somehow the bigger you got, the more it kept returning to the micropoint. Like the way that a verse within a *canso*, no matter whether it is part of the beginning, middle, or end, has its own beginning, middle, and end. And the beginning, middle, end of the *canso* reflects the beginning, middle, and end of the whole *trobador* tradition, which in turn is like a two-century microcosm of pre-spaceflight Western art, which in turn was like one small model of what had happened a thousand times over in the six hundred years of the Thousand Cultures . . . or going down the other way, each word and phrase and note of each verse has that structure.

Like nested dolls, like a camera pointed at its own monitor through a distorting mirror . . . my little square of existence fit into the bigger square of my performing and my team and my friends and family, and all of them into the bigger square of my life . . . nesting dolls, image globe, rescaling pictures, lines in verses in poems in collections in traditions in languages in families—

Or like the four-symbol blocks in the carvings that covered the walls that enclosed the squares that grouped in fours to make plazas that stood between four temples . . . on up till one saw the meaning in the four quarters of lost, vitrified Yaxkintulum. Or like the god-tales containing hero-tales containing digressive comedies containing jokes containing aphorisms that summarized the god-tales, in the stories of lost, vitrified New Tanajavur.

Strange that these songs—the collection titled *Songs from Un-*

derneath, from which my second set tonight was drawn—always made me think of the two destroyed cultures of Briand. I had written them years before Margaret and I ever went there, and performed them on tour long before going to Briand, and never sung them on Briand because their message would have started ethnic rioting between Tamils and Maya and brought about genocidal war all the sooner. Yet *Songs from Underneath*, for me, had somehow become woven into events years after their composition, and I think most of my fans believed I must have written them on Briand, or just after the failed mission there.

I hated that phrase "failed mission," which was what Margaret and the OSP in general called Briand, when they talked about it at all.

We had lost a whole planet. The antimatter cloud weapon had been loosed on human flesh for only the fourth time since the Slaughter itself. The Thousand Cultures had, before that, numbered 1228 cultures on twenty-six planets; now they numbered 1226 on twenty-five. It would still be some years before springships could even reach the Metallah system to see if anything was left, but given the frailty of Briand's ecosystem, the answer was probably no; probably they would find two smears of black glass, hundreds of kilometers across, under an atmosphere as poisonous as it had been before terraforming.

To me, anyway, that was something more than a failed mission.

And yet, strangely, even to me, the *cansos* in *Songs from Underneath* sounded as if they had been written about Briand, as if I had dreamed a too-clear vision, which had come horribly true.

Songs from Underneath had developed in one of those complex mixes of art and propaganda that had been my life for almost three decades. I wrote and sang art songs; I was an OSP agent; if you are an OSP agent, everything you do is, or becomes, part of the OSP's mission; therefore, I wrote and sang art songs that supported the OSP's mission, which, shorn of all rhetoric, was to steer humanity down a narrow—possibly closed—channel between two grim canyon walls.

One canyon wall was the prospect of everyone's going into the box. As soon as population density and automated production were high enough, as they had been on Earth for centuries, most people elected to go into the box—after their required seven years of public service work, they never left their apartments at all, and spent all but the barest minimum of their waking time in virtual reality. About a quarter of them had "gone Solipsist"—convinced themselves that aintellects created all of reality, including all the people they communicated with online, and that dull apartment they saw when they unplugged. Almost the whole population of Earth, and of its moon, Mars, Ganymede, Europa, Titan, and Triton, were in the box. In the six nearest star systems, with their nine inhabited planets—the Inner Sphere that held just under eight hundred of the Thousand Cultures—about a quarter of the population was in the box.

The other canyon wall was war.

There was only one inhabited planet in the nine of the Inner Sphere where the majority of the population was not in the box—this one, Roosevelt. The ninety-two cultures here had fought a generation-long bloody war, barely reaching an uneasy peace less than forty stanyears ago. Since Dji had brokered that permanent truce, insurrections, border clashes, assassinations, threats of war, and riots had been endemic, but no wholesale mutual butchery, so this world was one of the OSP's success stories. Twenty-two cultures—the entire continent of Hapundo— were still ruled directly by Council of Humanity proconsuls and policed by Council troops. Elsewhere on the planet, terrorist *discommodi* caused two to five thousand-or-more-fatality events every stanyear. The past stanyear had seen the Stadium Massacre and the assassination of Lopez, obviously but unprovably linked. In some of the cultures of this planet, children grew up learning to dodge snipers; in happier cultures like Trois-Orléans, no one got through a day without having to prove identity dozens of times, and the streets crawled with uniforms.

Less than three hundred kilometers from here, in Saladin City, a psypyx bank and the adjoining hospital had been blown up this afternoon, causing hundreds of deaths, thirteen of them permanent. New Rajasthan was suspected of involvement, and CSPs were standing guard all along the border tonight while Council diplomats banged heads together to prevent another outbreak.

But the good folk of Roosevelt had not gone into the box. Say what you like about hatred and killing, it gives people something to do.

There were two walls into which humanity seemed determined to slam: atrophy in the box, or war till all our planets were slick black glass like Briand.

The OSP's job was to help humanity steer between those walls, right down a middle channel that we had to hope would be there, because it was clear that we would be coming around a bend, any day, and meeting the aliens whose ruins we had found all over human space. After decades of archaeology all over human space, an OSP secret expedition had found the ruins of a Predecessor provincial capital on Hammarskjöld, twenty light-years beyond our human settlement surface. While Earth was still locked in its last ice age, the Predecessors had held an empire of seventy-eight provinces—the hundred-light-year-across blob that was now human space took up no more than one-tenth of one Predecessor province.

And before the first hut stood at Jericho, something tougher than the Predecessors had come through and literally blasted the Predecessor civilization back to the Stone Age. Predecessor ruins were the inverse of human ruins: the oldest and most enduring were at technical levels that our science was struggling to grasp. More recently the Predecessors had recovered as a spacefaring people not dissimilar from us in technology; on some worlds there was a yet more recent Iron-Age layer that eschewed radio and electricity; and the newest Predecessor ruins of all were a pathetic handful of Neolithic farming villages on a few worlds.

Every Predecessor settlement at every technical level bore the marks of war, and of a genocide so complete that only a handful of Predecessor remains had ever been found. One hypothesis was that the few survivors, with their scant robots and software, had never been able to struggle all the way back up after each attack. I tended to buy the hypothesis that the Predecessors had tried to hide their rebuilding from whatever it was that killed them, first turning off springers, then radio, then desisting from large-scale construction, perhaps even giving up fire, but never hiding far enough.

Sooner or later the thing that had killed the Predecessors would return. Humanity could not afford to be either in the box, or at war with ourselves. The human race needed to be diverse enough to entertain each other and alike enough not to kill each other.

So the OSP tried to steer things that way . . .

So the OSP's agents did things to support that mission . . .

Which in my case included writing and performing *cansos* from my own, Occitan cultural tradition . . .

Some of which, collected and publicized as *Songs from Underneath*, had become popular, as well as being successful propaganda . . .

And therefore I needed to give a good performance of them tonight . . .

Which meant watching the clock and taking care of myself.

From relations across thousands of years between at least

three species . . . down to flexing my hands to make sure the fingers were warmed up.

Fifty stanyears and life was still an image globe.

One minute to go. Remember that "Don't Forget I Live Here Too" should *seek* its dignity, *resist* its anger, and don't crop that first eighth note too short! Relax your shoulders just before you sing. It starts on a G. Look at the audience and give them the shy smile, they always love that and it makes them remember the song more favorably. If they remember me being brilliant, I was, so give them a chance to remember me that way. First verse begins with *"Ilh gen dit nien . . ."*

One more sip of tepid water.

Time. I walked through the door.

2

In second and later sets, I never have stage fright; rather I have monkey-mind and think about everything instead of what I'm doing, and have to pull myself back to what I should be doing. Tonight that meant that when I looked down at the guitar with which I would be starting my first song, I saw the note I had taped to it:

REACH FOR THE MEMORIES

These *cansos*, and their meanings, might be just memories to me, but my fans had memories too, and they loved these songs. They wanted their memories renewed, not rewritten. So I owed it to their memories to give them yet another memory of me singing the songs the way they remembered. I had to remember the man who I had been *before* many of my important memories, letting the earlier win out over the later.

How did anyone, anywhere, ever either perform *or* listen with all that going on?

I settled into playing position and into the frame of mind of my early thirties: sincere, dedicated, hardworking, still shocked that you could do well, and intend well, and put your whole heart on the block, and still get knocked face-first into a pile of wet shit.

When it was quiet, I struck the first notes of "Don't Forget I Live Here Too." Applause pounded across the auditorium like breaking surf, flowing around the silent bloc of Ixists, and followed by the crackling hiss of people shushing each other. I couldn't hear my own picking, so I stopped.

The house was astonishingly silent.

I gave them my warmest, easiest grin, and said, "If everyone is ready now . . ."

There was laughter, even from the big swath of Ixist robes in the center, and a spatter of applause.

"All right, then," I said, and began again. My voice had aged well, becoming richer with its deeper undertones coming out, and I found brittle cynicism in the lyrics that I had not originally intended, and irony that allowed me to both ridicule and enjoy the still-naïve, still-optimistic tone that had crept into the last two verses like the perky brightness of a tea commercial— the smug cleverness of using an ancient trick well.

There are no more than a dozen occupations—political agent and artist are two—in which everything you do becomes part of your job. They are the only tolerable things to do with your time, as far as I'm concerned.

A song is not a tool for changing a human heart in the way that a wrench is a tool for changing a bolt, but it was the tool I had, and I was the tool the OSP had.

The *cansos* in *Songs from Underneath* were not really as subtle as a wrench. Their primary trope was the ancient trick of making the viewpoint character a victim of oppression, because people identify passionately with a strong viewpoint character, and there is intense pleasure in identifying with the narrator of a sad story or song. In *Black Beauty* that trick had made people begin to think that beating horses was bad; it was the trope that made privileged white children burn with outrage at *Native Son* and prudes weep over prostitutes in "Elle fréquentait la rue Pigalle" and *My Name Is Not Bitch*. They also received, at no extra charge, the delicious smug superiority of sympathizing with an underdog, unlike their less-enlightened neighbors.

It was one of my best performances, ever, of "Don't Forget I Live Here Too." I flatter myself that that was why it was not un-

til the last note had faded completely, and the applause was battering at me like a great macerating club, that a man who was
not an Ixist whipped off an Ixist robe, and produced, from the
scabbard for the ceremonial obsidian dagger, a military maser.

Raimbaut was patrolling that section. His reflexes had been
slow in his born body, but they had fixed that in his clone body,
and he had teenaged muscles and nerves which had not only
learned *ki hara do* from me, but practiced it in my body.

As the assassin raised the maser, and my eye was just catching an odd motion, Raimbaut leapt a row and slapped the back
of the man's head, throwing his aim off.

I dropped to the floor.

Darkness. Near silence. I didn't even hear the fire curtain
come in.

Warm body next to my back. Paxa's breath in my ear. "Gator-
crawl to the springer backstage."

She had covered us with a smart blanket; the fabric covering
us would move to keep us covered, turn into rigid armor against
a bullet or bomb, and seal to the floor around us if it sensed
high temperatures, cryonics, or poison gas.

We went on knees and elbows, bellies pressed to the floor.
Paxa muttered into her com, talking to Raimbaut, Laprada,
Dad, and the two other teams that Margaret had loaned us as
auxiliary muscle.

Later I saw recordings of what happened after Paxa dove on
me with the blanket. Raimbaut got a grip from the head-slap
and yanked on the would-be assassin's collar. The maser dis-
charged into the ceiling, melting crystals on one chandelier into
a red-hot rain that was cool before it hit the floor, but also dropping a twenty-kilogram chunk of hot plaster. No one was hit,
though a young woman, to whom I later sent an autographed
Complete Recordings, turned an ankle getting out of the way.

Raimbaut slid the man's thumb off the firing button, turned his wrist, footswept him to the floor, slammed a heel into the man's floating ribs, and leaned back. He stretched the man's arm, twisting it against the joints, and stamped on his neck.

He tried for a knockout and a live capture, but the aintellect running on a processor in the assassin's left frontal sinus was having none of that. It set off microfilaments of explosive woven all through the capillaries of his brain, eliminating recoverable tissue for interrogation.

Raimbaut said it felt like a hard cough through his boot sole, and when he first looked down he thought that that was a really terrible bloody nose, before he realized and backed away, scraping his foot frantically on the carpet.

Meanwhile, Paxa and I gator-crawled to the emergency springer backstage. When we stood up, the blanket clung to our backs and the springer frame, still trying to protect us. Paxa put in her crash card. Glowing gray mist formed on the black metal plate in front of us, infinitely deep to look into, infinitely thin seen from the edge.

Paxa shoved me into the gray fog. I fell forward in a shoulder roll, tucking to protect my hands, onto the floor of an emergency operating room in the OSP secure hospital on Dunant, orbiting Alpha Centauri A. I stood up, still holding the neck of my lute in my left hand. The rest must be lying backstage at the Fareman Hall, Trois-Orléans, Roosevelt, Epsilon Indi system; my poor lute had shattered across four parsecs.

That shattered neck, strings dangling ruefully from the still-fine pegs, made it all so *physical*. I dropped it, wiping my hand on my tunic.

The surgeon—an aintellect networked across three robots, each with about twenty metal arms, mounting tools, sensors, lights, lenses, and all—rolled in like a parade of midget tanks.

"Are you hurt, *Donz* Leones?" the aintellect asked, through the speaker in its lead robot.

On its way from its closet, across the hall, it would have read all of my medical records back to my childhood immunizations.

"No," I said. "Not physically hurt."

I stretched; no soreness. Hands unscathed when I flexed gently. I could have played at that moment—wanted to, in fact.

"No," I said again. "Not physically hurt."

The lute was recorded and could be re-created down to the molecule, as it had been, many times before. And I had spares waiting back at the Fareman.

The springer behind me activated, and Margaret came through, choking and retching. She always had springer sickness worse than anyone I knew. "I told them you'd want to go back on," she said. "Paxa has it all under control, for once."

"She has always handled every one of these incidents perfectly," I said. My ex-wife was often unpleasant about Paxa. I never let her get away with it.

"Well, then this would be once more. Anyway, she'll need half an hour to pick up the mess and scan the crowd for other weapons. Laprada is running down the com records. Raimbaut just earned a chestful of decorations. Your father is prepping your dressing room. And I'm very glad you're alive."

"There's nothing to make you notice that you're alive like someone trying to change that," I agreed.

"You are still the same old Giraut, I assume? You do still want to finish your show?"

"For applause like that, Margaret, I'd go back if there were three snipers zeroed in and an atom bomb under the stool."

"*Tostemz-Occitan-ver,*" she said, in my culture language. *Always a real Occitan.* Though Margaret was from Caledony, her heart might as well have formed on Serra Valhor, grown in Totzmare, and lived all its days in Noupeitau; I think she wanted to marry my culture as much as she did me, and nowadays she spoke my culture language as well as I did. "Well, I'm glad you're safe. Oh, and happy birthday, again."

"Is everything all right?" the aintellect asked. "We should go rescrub if you don't need us."

Margaret said, "If you are so worried about germs, perhaps I should just order you to spring into a plasma torch somewhere. Or perhaps it indicates a developing phobia, and I should just order you to self-wipe and back up so we don't waste your robots." She used that tone you use on aintellects and robots to remind them that we remember the Rising and the attempted coup, and that nothing that talks and is made of metal is a friend to anything human.

"I am sorry. I intended no disrespect." Aintellects have emotions and expression for better communication and to enable subjunctive thought, and this one was certainly communicating fear and thinking about what might happen. "I am instructed to maintain high preparedness for each new emergency."

The arrogant little appliance was right.

Margaret shared an annoyed glance with me. "Everything is all right," she said.

The robots wheeled away, brandishing their dozens of flesh-slicers above those steel-shiny bug-bodies, acolytes preparing to sacrifice to the Insect God.

We blinked back into the healthy, normal chaos backstage at the Fareman, in Trois-Orléans, again. Margaret gagged and glared at me, as she always did when we sprang together because I didn't get springer sickness.

Laprada walked beside Margaret to my dressing room. "—just one attacker. He got his weapon past the search by smuggling parts of a microspringer, assembled it under his robe, and they passed the maser to him through it. The maser is untraceable, another averaged replica of standard CSP-issue. No luck on memory extraction—the brain is just goo. The crowd is being very tolerant—"

"Um," I said. In my dressing room, I poured a glass of luke-warm water and drank it.

"The assassin's DNA wasn't in any of the immediate-suspect files, and we're checking the—" Laprada was still rolling. She looked like the very image of a chattering teenager if teenagers chattered about security perimeters and forensic investigations.

"Um," I said.

Dad brought in the freshly re-created lute. It seemed to dwarf him; it was always a surprise what a small eight-year-old his body was.

"*Gra'atz-te*," I said. Dad nodded silently and rushed back out, making him my favorite team member for the moment.

"—no communications detected in or out—"

"Um," I said, firmly, now that I had my lute.

Laprada stopped and they both looked at me.

"This is a very important concert, the *artist's* fiftieth birthday. The *artist* needs to check tuning on this lute and that guitar, and get into a frame of mind to perform. You are standing in the *artist's* dressing room."

Laprada's tone was amused. "We *are* keeping the *artist* from getting blown up."

"You already did that. Now I need to—"

Margaret stepped between us. "Sit down and tune," she said to me, and then to Laprada, "I've been arguing with him for twenty-eight stanyears, with no effect whatsoever."

"Well, and, he's right. Despite being a horrible old monster of ego."

I didn't hear the door close; I was wrapped up in getting that lute into perfect tune. No earless bastard of a moronic critic would ever be able to say that the interruption spoiled my birthday concert, or that I had appeared to be watching for another attempt. An artist has an *enseingnamen* to defend and preserve, every bit as much as a fighting man, and *gratz'deu*, I was still both. Fifty be damned.

I restarted the second set from where I had left off; at first they sat tense, waiting for another assassin I suppose, but by the end of it I had the audience solidly back with me. I walked off stage, drank some water, hung up my *tapi*, and stretched out in near-complete bliss.

Paxa woke me. "Giraut, what's that in your hand?"

I looked down and I was clutching a note; I had not been holding it when I had gone to sleep. I read aloud,

> *Donz Leones,*
>
>   *For some time, you and I, and your friends and mine, have had an interest in each other, and we have known you are eager to meet us. Be prepared to discuss the possibility of your visiting us at our location. Please be ready to negotiate a quick answer when we contact you; it will be within three stanmonths.*
>
>

Atz Deu,
Nemo

"Nemo," I said. " 'Nobody.' And the name that Ulysses gave to the Cyclops. Handwritten, looks like a child copying from printed text." I handed it to her.

"The door was locked," she said. "I don't know how they could have done it. They'd have had to get through three rings of guards, an intelligent lock, and a mechanical lock. And not wake you up, and you're generally a light sleeper."

"For some reason," I said, "I don't feel frightened. I suppose because it is obvious that if they had wanted to hurt me, they'd have done it. And this clinches it, it's got to be the Lost Legion."

"Why does this clinch it?"

"Because anyone else would have sent me a note or commed OSP headquarters or passed a note to any of my team on the street. Instead they deliberately choose the most melodramatic possible method of contact with the highest personal risk to their agents. I know my culture—and the Lost Legion are more Occitan than other Occitans. All I have to do to predict their next move is to ask myself 'What would have made sense to me when I was seventeen?' "

"Knowing Occitans, that convinces me, anyway," Paxa said. "Usually you're a light sleeper. But you didn't wake up, you didn't even have a feeling of something wrong?"

"As I said, nothing."

" 'Silver Blaze.' "

"What?"

"It's a Sherlock Holmes story. It's the one that contains the curious incident of the dog in the nighttime."

" 'The dog did nothing in the night-time.' 'That,' said Holmes, 'was the curious incident,' " I quoted. "I see the analogy but not the point."

"And why did Holmes think that was curious?"

"I've never read the story. It's just constantly quoted, and I was quoting quotes," I admitted.

"Well, Hedons regard it as central to the tradition of rationalist literature that we all grow up studying in school. So we all had to learn it in school. Dogs bark at strangers. So if the dog didn't bark—"

"It wasn't a stranger. I see. Inside job."

"Excellent, Watson." She sighed. "Now I have to tell Margaret that someone got at you again. I'll cut you a deal. You do that for me, and I'll sing your next set."

"I like the duties divided up the way they are," I said, and took a moment to stand up and give her a long, affectionate hug. "Try not to let her bully you," I said, "and try to remember that when she acts like that, it's not about you, really. All right?"

"All right. Just being a coward. We'd better get moving— you're already a minute late for your set." She pulled out her computer, attached the sniffer, and waved it around the room for a few seconds. "No explosives or drugs. They didn't leave a microspringer in here. No active nanos and we'll sweep for sleepers while you're on stage." She opened the door. "Come on in, Laprada." Paxa touched my shoulder on her way out. "Have a good set. I'll see what this is about."

As Laprada was grooming me for the stage, I briefed her, interrupted constantly by the stream of Paxa's orders over the com.

I sat down on my stool seven minutes later than the revised time, or forty-two minutes later than originally scheduled. I hated to be so discourteous to the fans; so many of them had rushed to get back to their seats this time. I had announced that I would debut a new song cycle in the third set.

The first few chords hinted at a jazz influence, and the arpeggio after it was distinctly Lunar Exile—a combination that most people wouldn't do, usually, because that intercultural juxtaposition was in very bad taste, since the same people who had genocided the Old Americans had endured the Lunar Exile. Critics the next day said I had done the equivalent of putting bugle calls into a Dakota drum piece, or of serving an East Asian/Latin American fusion cuisine, or any offensive thing I might have done instead of the offensive thing I *had* done.

The new *cansos* were in Occitan of course—I could never

write in Terstad and my own translations of my songs sounded flat and dead in my ears. But everyone wore direct-to-brain translator buttons nowadays, so they not only understood the words, but could catch the complex pun in the title of the first song, "Non te sai, *midons*." "*Midons*" is what a traditional Occitan gallant calls his *entendendora*, the *donzelha* to whom he has dedicated his life and art in the joyful suffering of *finamor*. But it's a very strange expression to apply to a young woman, because, grammatically, it's masculine—"*midons*" means, literally, My Lord, as in an address to your feudal lord; in the *cansos* of Old Earth it expressed the idea that one would never disobey the slightest whim of the *entendendora*.

Of course, My Lord is also a traditional Christian form of address for the deity.

I made those translator buttons *work* on those ambiguities. You could take the *canso* to mean that the narrator was a man who had once loved a woman well, but had been away from her so long that he could not recall anything more than her name. Just as defensibly you could hear the narrator as a knight whose lord had demanded some impossibility of him. Rather than try, the man fled. Now the knight would like to find his way back, and kneel at his lord's feet, but he cannot recall the name of his country to ask the way there.

Or the *canso* might be Giraut Leones contemplating how the message of the prophet Ix had seemed immediate and necessary, back on Briand, when I had known him and worked with him. Now that stanyears and light-years had intervened, it seemed more necessary, yet I could not recall anything Ix had said that seemed to offer any help.

So take your pick; that's what ambiguities are for.

"Non te sai, midons"—
"I no longer know you, my lady."

"I cannot fathom your purpose, my lord."
"I never understood you, Ix."

Those lyrics were woven around musical fusions that were on the OSP's list of things to be avoided in our propaganda and quietly discouraged and suppressed in the Interstellar Metaculture, because such fusions were apt to infuriate two or more cultures. I myself had helped to write that blacklist.

There was no applause at the end of it; no booing; but I felt the crowd leaning forward.

The next song, "Ilh gen atz mundo pertz," was if anything more ambiguous, since *"gen"* can mean "man" or "good custom" (with a clear implication of nobility in either case), and *"mundo pertz"* could be either "a lost world" or "the world of those who have lost something." Even *"atz"* was a bit ambiguous; depending on context it could mean to, from, in, or on. At least four possible meanings: a memory of a man once loved and now lost along with his world? beloved customs no longer followed in this cold fresh world? a man who came to speak to us from the world of those who have lost something? the customs of the Mourning Planet?

And at the end, once again, I mixed a little finger-picking from Old American bluegrass with the dissonant, looming-in-and-out chords of the Lunar Exile.

Again they sat in silence. Doubtless my reputation for making quiet, pleasant art to be cherished by sensitive youth was crumbling by the second.

Well. That had been a longer pause than I intended. I could hear them all breathing. We needed some sound.

I set my fingers for my third song—"Un Aussisan en ilh Mundo Pertz," a title which might mean "A Murder (or Murderer) on (in, among, from) the (that, that same) Lost World (World of the Lost)."

Then a single person somewhere out there started clapping—clap, clap, clap; steady, loud, defiant, solo, continual, until it was joined by a patter of hands and a vigorous murmur that swelled into the whole house standing and cheering.

Well, after all, it *was* an audience of friends.

3

Margaret didn't bother me during my last intermission, though she must have wanted to.

During the last intermission, besides my lukewarm water and saline gargle, my dressing room always had a chilled glass of Hedon Glass waiting for me. Hedon Glass is a subtle but fierce white wine, tasting at first like a very pure white grape juice without nearly the sugar you would expect, served tooth-numbing cold, and it crams plenty of very nice alcohol into that compact glass. If no one had ever called a wine "crisp" before, Hedon Glass would have started the term; if it had been any drier you'd have to break off pieces.

The custom had originated when Margaret had been my entire "entourage," when I had started out as a touring act for the Office of Artistic Interchange, traveling from empty hall to empty hall throughout human space, consuming the Visiting Artist/Envoy budget while working for Shan and the OSP. In my late twenties and early thirties, my rest during intermissions had been whatever time and space Margaret could enforce for me out of her authority as a Deputy Underchief to the Ambassador, Assistant Viceconsular Envoy, Secretary for Local Tourism, or whatever title had designated her as "pretend flunky, actual spy" in whichever culture.

During the intermission before my last set, Margaret always gave me a glass of white wine, "because you've been well behaved, you could use something to relax you, and in your place *I'd* sure as hell want to get started on getting drunk." No matter how empty the hall or rude the staff, I always had one icy glass of perfect white wine to look forward to.

When we had divorced and Margaret had been promoted to section head, "glass of white wine, last intermission, just one," had been number seven on her list of "Touring With Giraut," the guide she had written for Paxa Prytanis—almost the only friendly gesture my ex had ever made to my long-term partner.

Paxa had gone Margaret one-slightly-better by asking me what my favorite white wine was, and since she was Hedon, I had chosen Hedon Glass; I could no longer recall whether it was really my favorite when I said that, or not. Certainly it was now—exactly the right taste, just the right feel on the throat, something that was nice and made me feel loved and supported no matter how the concert was going.

"And," Paxa often added, "it's easier than getting Giraut to breathe through an ether-soaked rag, and less permanent than decapitation."

I lifted the glass and, though I was alone, spoke the traditional OSP toast: "Another round for humanity, and one more for the good guys." I drank it reverently. Paxa had left a note:

Giraut,
    Tech analysis got right on it. Yes that note was from Nou-
catharia, paper, handwriting, and ink. Nothing you can do
right now, me either, so go back to being brilliant. Save me
some energy for your birthday fuck.

                                                        —PP

Noucatharia was the Lost Legion's illegal extraterritorial colony. I drained the last glorious drop of Hedon Glass, gargled gently with saline, drank some water, and stretched out for my nap.

I had the psypyx nightmare—that strange dream we all share, nowadays, though surely people in past centuries could not have had it. Before exams were invented, did students dream of being unprepared for them?

I dreamed the classic version of the psypyx nightmare: I was dying in terrible pain. Medics pulled an emergency psypyx recording hood over my head. As always, it knocked me unconscious and no time seemed to pass before I blinked and awoke—

Not in Raimbaut's mind. Still dying as they packed the kit around me. Still bubbling blood. Every part of me still screamed with pain. "Got it," one medic robot said to the other, "he's all copied and we're done."

Dreams don't have to make sense. A medic is one aintellect in multiple robots. They only speak aloud to us, using radio between themselves. Medics carry the hood only in case of a failure of all ambulance springers in the area; normally if you're alive with an intact-enough brain they just spring you to a recovery center. Nowadays all they really need is the brain anyway. This could never happen.

It didn't matter. In the dream it is always the same; waking up as the original, live and suffering, screaming for help as medics roll away. I was the original, not the copy.

A warm, wet cloth passed over my face. I opened my eyes. Paxa kissed me.

"I just had the waking-up-as-the-original nightmare," I said.

She kissed me again, and said, "We all have it now and then, Giraut. It doesn't mean anything. You'll feel better in a moment."

The door closed behind her.

I got up, splashed my face with cool water and dried it with a fluffy towel, and sipped some more tepid water. I ordered my shoulders to come down and my back to lose its fierce, grinding tension; a quick, sketchy kata encouraged them to comply.

Laprada bustled in to tell me that my *tapi* looked like a soggy bath towel and my hair like a Persian kitten drowned in a washing machine, but "luckily I can fix all that as long as I don't have to do anything about the face or personality. By the way, I'm glad you're not dead."

"Well, my narrow escape *has* made me reflect on eternal questions," I said. "Why do I have so much talent in addition to my physical beauty? Why do I keep a horrid brat on my team instead of buying Raimbaut a sheep? Things like that."

"Bravo, you ancient monster of ego. I'd score that a tie."

"Me too, evil child," I said. "We're at the top of our form tonight." I glanced at the clock. One minute.

"There. You look good. Touch one hair or garment on your way to the stage, and there won't be enough of you to blot off the clothes."

"All right, I'm on. But I warn you, I'm about to drench these clothes in the damp lanes of nostalgia."

For the last set, I invited people to sing along—since it was one long medley of my old hits, people would anyway. Don't ask me why, but the invitation makes the singers-along less annoying to their neighbors.

As I started my last song—"Never Again Till the Next Time," my most-covered song according to my agency—the Ixists rose from their seats en masse, and came down the aisle toward the stage in what looked for all the world like a procession of monks. I was in such an expansive mood that the Ixist robe did not irritate me as it usually did. Ix had never worn any such thing; he and his followers, Tamil and Maya, on Briand, had worn plain black trousers and white, tuniclike shirts, with black broad-brimmed hats, to blend in—the opposite of the effect achieved by those community-theatre-Friar-Lawrence robes.

With the house in half-light and stage lights not much brighter, I could see Raimbaut, Laprada, and the auxteams scuttling frantically. No one had told them that this was about to happen. I didn't know myself, but I kept on playing—there might be another assassin among them, but their loyalty did not deserve any less *gratz* and *merce* from me just because an enemy had borrowed their costume.

Each Ixist held up a red rose and lightly tossed it onto the stage. The rest of the crowd applauded and sang louder; the Ixists filed back to their seats and joined the group singing as well, and the whole thing turned into one great soggy, corny love-fest, with me on stage surrounded by heaps of roses. At the final chorus of "Never Again Till the Next Time," the house was singing loud enough to drown me out.

I don't suppose I could persuade you that I was embarrassed by it all.

Coming off stage, I was exhausted and satisfied. In a perfect world, all work would make you tired that way. It had all worked out. We had new leads in two of our active cases. I had pleased my most devoted fans. The new Ix Cycle had been well received. My team had improvised together brilliantly—there was nothing I valued more than that—and I would get to write another commendation for Raimbaut, who really should be starting a team of his own soon.

Also a commendation for Paxa, which would piss off my ex in a way I enjoyed.

Raimbaut and Laprada were waiting just offstage, smiling broadly. Raimbaut took my lute as if it were a holy relic and said, "Your best ever. I am honored to be your *companhon*."

"I'm glad you're mine, since it means I'm not dead."

"Not a problem," he said. "Now that they have psypyxes working right, dying is not so permanent—"

"I insist on being grateful anyway. Many things that aren't permanent really hurt."

"But you only remember what happened up to the point

where your psypyx was recorded," Raimbaut said, "so nobody ever remembers getting killed."

"I would *know.*"

Laprada held up a finger in an ah-*ha!* "So if a tree falls on an ancient monster of ego—"

"Then two bratty kids have to find someone else to work for, and no sane person would tolerate them," I said. "Not to mention your having to write a complete report on the tree's known political associations—Margaret would insist."

Raimbaut handed my lute to a robot, and they walked with me through a springer—to my pleased surprise, into the bridal suite at the Marriott Trois-Orléans. "Birthday gift from Margaret," he said. "She's overdoing guilt as usual after losing her temper. She said some really stupid things about Paxa, over that note in your dressing room. Sort of a peace offering."

Laprada held up a hand to stop me from expostulating. "Your father and I already made her apologize."

"Rightly so," Raimbaut said. "Anyone who can get into a room that secure, and get out again, is somebody that Shan himself couldn't have stopped. Anyway, expect company soon—Paxa just had a few things to wrap up." He slapped my shoulder lightly. "*Atz fis de potemz, fai!*"

Raimbaut and I exchanged forearm grips, and Laprada gave me a little air-hug. In the mirrors on every wall, we looked like a youngish *jovent* and his *entendendora*, talking to his grandfather. They vanished into the springer.

In the vast gaudy bathroom with its high vaulted ceiling, the ubiquitous gilt and bronze frouf was unmistakable evidence that I was in either a high-end Trois-Orléans hotel or a low-end Freiporto brothel. Somehow the faucet handles shaped like penises and sconces shaped like breasts failed to arouse me, but it wasn't for their lack of frantic effort; plumbing just isn't one of my kinks, I suppose.

I did my best to ignore the visual implications of the shower gushing from between the thighs of a nude life-size female bronze on the ceiling above the bathing pool, and reveled in the first glorious hot rinse. With my muscles relaxing and the room filling with warm clouds of steam, I opened my shower bag to the medical section, and used my mucous membrane rinses to kill or at least discourage any upper respiratory viruses that might have moved in that evening (stressed tissues, hundreds of infection sources, *certa que infernam* some had). I spat and snorted into the torrent of hot water rushing down the drain.

I shampooed and rinsed my hair and beard, and said, "Fill the tub" to the room aintellect.

Water stopped pouring from between the thighs of that improbably busty nymph overhead, and began flowing from four surrounding bronze cherubs, each about half a meter high, who appeared to be joyously urinating into my bathing pool. So this was the bridal suite. I resolved never to get married here.

"Make it warmer and scent it," I said. "Dior Tropical Suite."

The water gushed into the wide bronze pool, steaming with vanilla, cinnamon, coconut, and cardamom. At the sink, I applied depilatory everywhere on my lower face that wasn't beard, and wiped it all off carefully.

The pool was full, and bathwater stopped flowing from the cherubs. I half expected them all to shake off drips, but I suppose someone must have told the designer that would be in bad taste.

I slipped into the almost-too-hot water and let tension dissolve like sweat. As I drifted close to sleep, I half hoped Paxa would take her time—

The springer pinged. Oh, well. "I'm in here, Paxa," I said.

Maybe it was the heaviness of his tread; when Paxa walked, she never made an unintentional sound, even in high heels on a hardwood floor.

Maybe, down in the brain centers where hearing shades into ESP, I heard his windup breath.

I think it was the difference from Paxa's rhythm. The three footfalls were too intent, too insensitive—too *wrong*, like on Briand, when Tzi'quin stepped from the crowd to shoot Ix. Like in the Council of Humanity when the assassin rushed up the aisle and burned Shan down at the podium. Like here in Trois-Orléans, twenty stanyears ago, when the groundcar reversed across a sidewalk toward Margaret.

I thought of none of this at the time. I didn't think. I knew.

Grab long-handled bath brush, right hand. Side-roll from the bathing pool to the dressing area. Left hand, snatch up clothing steamer wand. Look at the controls, place thumb, click to instant-on-high-heat.

One more big stupid foot-thud, then a maser at the end of a short, burly, hairy arm came past the half-open door, pointing toward the bathing pool where I had been. In the two seconds or so I had been moving, I must have sloshed to rouse every dead sailor in Fiddler's Green, but he had paid no attention to it, too intent on the mission as rehearsed.

I was crouched low, on the side of the door away from the tub, as his head came in.

He saw me just as I reached full extension with a lunge, my aging ankles and knees protesting but cooperating. With the whole force of my legs and right arm, and the weight of my body solidly behind it, I jabbed the bath brush handle deep into the sweet spot where the doctor presses when it says "turn your head and cough."

I snatched it back and clopped his jaw shut with an upward strike, interrupting his inhaled shriek, continued the motion into a roll of my right arm around his neck, and drew him toward me, the brush handle across the back of his neck.

Dazed and in pain, he tried to bring the maser around. I

stroked the steamer nozzle along his knuckles, pushing his aim to the side, and squeezed the button. The jet of steam probably startled him more than it hurt—the real pain would have come a few seconds later, a bad burn is like that—but he dropped the maser.

Pushing his head down with the brush handle braced on the back of his neck, I thumbed the switch on the steamer and dragged the nozzle across his eyes. When he screamed, I thrust the hot nozzle through his teeth, as far in as it would go, and held the switch on.

Maddened by pain, he broke backward through my grip and fell into the outer room, clutching his face and screaming through the ruined flesh of his throat.

I shouted, "OSP Eight Eight Eight," the override code that every aintellect in human space relays as top priority—"OSP agent under deadly attack, confirm by voiceprint, send backup to nearest springer right now." Reinforcements would arrive at any second.

Overnight bag—neuroducer epée? *Usual place*—perfect. The millimeter-width, meter-long thread of the "blade" emerged and stiffened with a loud pop, the tip glowing dimly.

The man was curled with his knees almost to his chest, keening and holding his face. "Hands down to your sides, stretch out on your back," I said, "and I will make it stop hurting."

He groaned but did it. I did my best not to look at what I had done; if he lived, it could all be regrown. A firm stroke of the neuroducer tip from ear to ear, pressing hard, and then a hard push over his heart, and he was in a coma. The neuroducer had convinced his nervous system that his throat was cut, he was stabbed through the heart, and he was dead. They could revive him at a hospital.

Except for a deep, hideous thud I felt through my feet. Another brain bomb.

The face had been bad enough; now the head was misshapen.

I was just pulling the cover off the bed to throw over the poor bastard when the springer pinged. I whirled to face it.

Paxa walked in wearing the outfit we always called "Fetishist's Dream." How could anyone walk at all in shoes like that, let alone as gracefully as she did? And the very little red leather of the rest of the costume clung to her deliciously. "Happy Birthday," she said. "I see you're already dressed for the occasion, but let's not start on the bed."

It took me a moment to realize that she meant I was naked. "Um, uh—"

By then she had seen the body and started to ask, "Were there any more—" when it got kind of noisy.

Three other OSP agents on Roosevelt had been attacked, as part of a diversion, so all the local rescue teams had been dispatched. That was why it had taken almost a full minute for the OSP dispatcher to locate a ready-to-go squad of Council Special Police (since we don't officially have wars or actually have ships anymore, that's what we call marines). Once located, the CSPs had been dispatched to the nearest springer, i.e. the one just behind Paxa.

Which is why eight CSPs, and their sergeant, came through so perfectly according to the manual that they looked like a recruiting poster, pointing weapons in all directions, their intelligent goggles doubtless (since they didn't shoot us) identifying me and Paxa as friendlies.

Then they got a real look at the scene:

One corpse in gym clothes, head squashy, face partially cooked.

One petite blonde gamine, facial features of an angel, dressed like a Freiporto streetwalker without the subtlety.

One naked me, gray shoulder-length hair still dripping, holding a coverlet and a still-extended neuroducer epée, as if I had taken up nude bullfighting in my hotel room.

The sergeant came to attention and said, "Seniormost Field Agent Giraut Leones, you requested assistance?"

"I did," I said. "We need to be moved to secure quarters, the enemy dead there needs to be recovered for OSP study, and we need to keep this room secure—another attack could arrive through that springer at any time—while we're doing that. And I need some pants, but I can take care of that part myself."

The sergeant made a swift set of hand signs. Four CSPs guarded the springer while the rest expertly bagged up the body. I pulled on trousers, shirt, and sandals, and Paxa put on a robe. Our robots were very experienced with grabbing stuff after me when I had to be moved suddenly, so they would take care of clothes and baggage.

"We're ready to go," I said. That didn't seem like quite enough. "I suppose you're wondering how, uh, all this happened to happen."

The sergeant said, "Sir, I *will* admit to some curiosity."

"It started out as a birthday party," I said. I don't always say the smartest things when I'm drained after a concert, or after a fight. "I just turned fifty."

"I guess everyone celebrates their own way," the sergeant said. "Me, when I turned thirty, I climbed a mountain with two buddies, and we got drunk and watched the sun come up."

4

I refrained from throwing a tantrum like a cranky two-year-old. They moved us to the bridal suite of another hotel. Since you can't block an address on a springer, they just clamped another springer over ours to automatically forward any would-be assassin into an armored holding cell in an OSP space station. Normally the Council uses setups like that to guard antimatter weapons and the dedicated processors of ultra-high-security aintellects, so I felt very special on my birthday.

The rest of the team were too experienced to rush over to see whether Paxa and I were all right; they knew we would have called them if we needed them.

"Well," Paxa said, when we had made sure our things had come through, and checked one more time to make sure security forwarding was on, "I would like a quick shower. Then I would like you to get into the tub, and wait till I tell you to come out for a surprise."

She took her shower with the door open, and while she did, I stripped out of the pants and shirt again, and sat down in the middle of the bed to meditate, to let all of it fade away, into the universe and into my bones.

My meditating didn't go very well, at least not as meditating. Not so much because I had monkey-mind as because I had horny-monkey-mind, and I was watching Paxa standing in the cascading hot water in the middle of the bathing pool. She was slim, pale blonde, and athletic, with long smooth legs and everything taut and firm, the fantasy object of three-quarters of the straight men in human space, and though I had a distinct fetish for heavy, soft bodies like Margaret's, I had the same training by decades of advertising as any other male in human space. I liked Paxa's body because it would be difficult for a straight male not to, because I enjoyed the envy of other men, and because it was Paxa's, and for the last of those reasons, I could have overlooked fangs and scales. So I admitted I wouldn't be getting much meditating done, and just enjoyed the view.

Paxa stretched and luxuriated in the warm spray, and turned the shower off. I walked in to the bathroom, lifted her, and carried her to the bed.

"The bed's going to be a mess."

"Set it to dry and change while I'm bathing." I kissed her to close off further conversation.

When we were both reasonably happy, I said, "Room aintellect, start my tub, get the settings from my chamberlain."

"Yes, sir."

"If you weren't such a romantic you'd have started your tub before carrying me to the bed and ravishing me."

"If I were the type to do that, I wouldn't be much of a ravisher," I pointed out. "And is ravishing something you can do to the willing?"

"I hope so, because while you're re-bathing, I'll be dressing to be re-ravished. Anything you're really dying for, or surprise you?"

"I love surprises and I hate dying."

"That's extremely portentous to say on your fiftieth birthday, and portentous is within a short walk of morbid."

"It's not my fiftieth birthday anymore," I pointed out. "It's past midnight. So if we're both tired—"

"*Tostemz tropa joy, ilh'st ilh lei prim de con*," she quoted. "At least 'always total joy' is the first law of my *con*. We can rest when we're dead."

I settled into the tub. Behind me I could hear rustle and fussing. Hedons treat clothing like cuisine—most of the time plain old cooking will do, but when it's time to show off, it's time to show off. They also think sex is both the purpose of life and a trivial minor pleasure, and that stress of any kind is pure evil. So they dress to be comfortable, beautiful, or sexy, they have sex like it's the best thing in the world but entirely for fun, and they try to live in a state of deep relaxation.

I often think that among all the Thousand Cultures, only the Hedons chose to go sane.

Pillow talk, snacks, and some kissing and stroking that verged on starting another round took up enough time so that Paxa and I didn't actually fall asleep until Epsilon Indi, the local sun, was already flooding the skylights. We agreed that this was far too early for sunrise and poor planning on someone's part—at least that's what I meant when I said "mmmph" and I assumed Paxa meant the same thing when she said it into my shoulder. So I croaked an order to the room aintellect to opaque the windows, dim the lights to complete darkness, and set the air-conditioning cool enough for us to enjoy being under an extra blanket. We slept till there was just time to groom and dress for dinner.

"These last few weeks—while I was getting ready for this concert and everything else—why did everyone assume that I was going to be morbid?" I asked Paxa, as we primped next to each other in the mirror. "I think I'm actually doing rather well. Everyone else is making more fuss about my turning fifty than I am."

She slipped her hand behind my neck and kissed the particular spot on my throat that always melts me. Her reflection gazed into my eyes from the bathroom mirror. "Because, dearest," she whispered, "we know you."

If the colonization of the terraformable planets nearest to Earth had been for resources or lebensraum, anyone would have to say it was a dismal failure.

There were no resources worth pursuing. Prior to the springer, it had made equal economic sense—none at all—to ship diamonds or cornflakes between the stars. The energy costs of molecular-level synthesis—or even of transmutation of elements if need be—were lower than the costs of accelerating the same mass to half-c for ballistic starflight, and at one-half-c maximum practical velocity, the cost of every voyage was doubled or tripled by compound interest en route.

Nor was it a matter of room for people. One brief century of colonization had put human beings into permanent residence in open-air, dry-land spaces on twenty-six worlds. Eight, almost entirely habitable like Roosevelt, Addams, or Dunant, each housed around a hundred cultures. A few had just small slivers of habitable land like Wilson (mostly water), Nansen (mostly frozen), or Briand (mostly toxic), and had one or two cultures. The majority were worlds of one pleasant continent, or a few nice big islands, like Söderblom, where Hedonia shared an Australia-sized continent with Thetanshaven, Bremen-Beyond-the-Stars, Texaustralia, and Freiporto; twelve more cultures clustered on an Africa-sized continent in the opposite hemisphere.

In all, every schoolchild learned to recite, the new land beyond the stars totaled only about fourteen times the comfortably habitable area of the Earth. With Earth's population stable (and reduced by more than a third just a century before), there was neither need for a place for surplus people, nor enough land to put any very great numbers onto anyway, and in any case the colony ships took only ninety-six adults and a million frozen embryos.

If space for people had been the issue, it would have been cheaper and easier to accelerate the terraformation of Mars and Venus and build many more closed habitats in the Sol system.

Almost, it had been a pure whim, or the hedging of a bet. In the colonization century, just before the Inward Turn, diversity had seemed more dangerous than monotony, but there was room enough for both as long as diversity could be kept safely far away. The Thousand Cultures existed because our ancestors thought there should be different kinds of people—far away. The reason for the new worlds had been, then, what the purpose of the OSP was now: controlled diversity, with emphasis more on control than on diversity.

Diversity didn't always work out. I have seen firsthand more of the places that humanity lives than almost anyone else, and I know that however diverse the 1228 cultures planted on those twenty-six worlds were, in the fourteen Earth's-worths of surface occupied by humanity, every conference room has nonstain beige carpets, heavy-but-cheap furniture, and nothing to look at. Even if the walls are covered with great art, or if there is spectacular scenery out the windows on all sides, there is something about the atmosphere of a conference room that pulls your focus into that little space between the bodies at the table, and usually afterward you remember nothing except the screen of your own computer and the sleepy faces of the people across from you.

Margaret walked in and began without preface or greeting, still Caledon after all these years. "That note left in Giraut's hand has been authenticated several different ways as extraterritorial—the materials it was made of don't match anything known in human space but do match scraps in our collection of extraterritorial materials. The human DNA traces on it are consistent with the Lost Legion. Handwriting influence maps suggest that whoever wrote it was taught to write by two of the identified members of the Lost Legion; probably it was a child copying text, as Giraut speculated, so that we wouldn't have any other sample on hand. This is actually more interesting than the fact that someone from a possibly hostile power was able to walk right through Paxa's security, despite all the care she lavishes upon it, physically touch the man you were all protecting, and get away without being seen."

"The man himself," I said, "did not detect the event, and you know perfectly well that I sometimes leap out of bed in the middle of the night grabbing for a weapon, because of a noise most other people would sleep through. If you put your attention on finding incompetence or negligence, you will waste your time; there is indeed something fascinating about the penetration with such apparent ease of so much security, but the thing that makes it fascinating is that security was superb, and unusually on alert besides. How they did it is something we need to know; but you won't find that by assuming our security simply failed or was neglected."

Margaret sat and looked at me quietly, a trick she was good at. She knew that if I were not sure of myself, I might start backing down or hedging in the face of that stare.

Everyone else looked out windows at suburban Manila and the distant harbor and no doubt wished for the millionth time that the boss's boss was not the boss's ex-wife.

Ever the master of retreating from ground she could not hold, and of the hooking attack that doesn't hit where it looks like it's going, Margaret said, crisply, "Your protest on behalf of your team is noted. Let's discuss the new evidence about the Lost Legion."

It was about the most embarrassing possible topic for me, and she knew it. While she went over the forensics on the note, I tried to listen, but I kept mentally returning to the most humiliating single part of the "extraterritorial problem."

Until the invention of the springer, the roughly forty-to-sixty-light-year limit of human settlement had been enforced by the limits of technology. A single colony ship could travel around that far, taking a century or a little more, before too many of its ninety-six adults in suspended animation died in the tank, leaving too few adult survivors to move into the robot-built city waiting at the other end, and to decant and raise the first generation of "natives" from the ship's bank of a million frozen embryos. Beyond that fuzzy around-fifty-light-year line, the paucity of adults in the crucial first generation on the new world drastically lowered the probability of transmitting the culture accurately (meaning, as it had been designed on Earth), and cultures planted on the same planet were forced to interact more than had been intended, and no one would raise the enormous funds required to launch a ship without some reasonable assurance that the culture would eventually be planted.

In the centuries following the Inward Turn, technology had been systematically held in place, so that fifty-light-year-or-so limit had become a de facto cornerstone of policy for centuries.

No colony ships had gone farther than the 102 (of 109 attempted) cultures barely planted on Addams, circling Theta Ursa Major, and the even-more-marginal two cultures on Briand, circling Metallah, each just over sixty light-years away. Addams and Briand had been reached by pushing every margin, and only attempted because there was no remaining standard culture space (650,000 square kilometers of reasonably contiguous, walk-around-without-special-equipment land) anywhere closer.

Ninety years after the colonization era began, the last ships left Earth for Addams; 134 stanyears later, when the determined aintellects brought *Susan Constant IV* into orbit around Addams with ten surviving adults and most of its embryos dead, the colonization era ended, apparently for all time.

For the next 450 stanyears, then, until the springer, humanity was confined to an irregular, three-lobed blob of space that would all fit into a hundred-light-year-diameter sphere, with Earth somewhat off center of the intersection of the three lobes. The human bubble was only about twenty parts in a billion of the volume of the galaxy, but we were the masters of our bubble, with no compelling reason or cheap means to go beyond it.

The springer had changed everything. Historians intended no hyperbole in saying it was the biggest innovation since fire or the pointed stick. If there was a springer anywhere you wanted to go, you could cross many light-years in a single step; just the night before I had made a precautionary emergency-room call of fourteen light-years, and Paxa and I had walked from our hotel room, with its view of Epsilon Indi setting, to this conference room in Manila on Earth.

Within human space, you could go anywhere by radioing directions and waiting for the people on the other end to receive the message and build a springer; once they did, everywhere was as close as the next room (assuming you could afford the astonishing amount of energy required).

Beyond human space, you first had to send a springer there on a rocket—but a springship was a radically different rocket from the huge, half-light-speed behemoths, stacked with suspended animation tanks and equipped like hospitals, that had planted the first colonies.

A rocket always gets the most acceleration from the very last drop of fuel in the tank, because the engine pushes with constant force, but the mass of fuel you're pushing decreases as the fuel is expelled. But on a springship, every drop is the very last; you need not even send a reaction chamber, just a nozzle with a springer at the back, through which you spring a jet from as big a stationary chamber as you like.

Send out a robot springship the size of a large desk, boosting at a hundred g because it has no fuel tanks, just springers delivering light-speed protons from back home right into the nozzle. Do that for one week and you are close enough to lightspeed for every practical purpose. Control it via laserlink through a microspringer; no signal strength problem and no speed-of-light lag, no matter how far it goes. Keep aiming your springship for the next nearest F, G, or K star.

As it passes each star, scan the habitable zone for any Earth-sized world with free O_2 in the atmosphere. If no, on to the next star.

If yes, the springship flips over to ride its jet down into the solar system for a closer look. If things still look good from closer up, descend all the way into orbit around the planet. If it's still good from orbit, descend on a nice cool jet of room-temperature nitrogen, so as not to disturb anything, set the springship down on a reasonably stable, solid patch of dirt, open an exterior microspringer on the springship's surface, and dump a couple of tons of nanos onto the face of the new world. Over a few weeks, the nanos strip materials out of the surrounding land to grow an enclosed habitat suitable for humans, with a full-sized springer inside, and another door opens onto the frontier.

As soon as you have a springable base on an alien world, with enough redundant springer capacity to ensure you won't lose it, the springship takes off again.

Theoretically the Council of Humanity's probes—and *only* theirs—were to catalog every habitable and terraformable planet for fifty light-years beyond the outer surface of human space, and a procedure would be established for applying to establish new colonies.

That survey process was now about half-complete—except that across roughly a quarter of the northern celestial hemisphere, wherever Council springships had found particularly promising solar systems, when they had descended for a closer look, they had suffered an "abrupt functional stoppage/ disconnect"—"AFSD" was a standard abbreviation. It was widely said, in security circles, that AFSD stood for "Actually Fucking Shot Down."

We knew who shot them down. While the Council had dithered for a quarter of a century before the first study-to-do-a-study had been authorized, the nearest and best habitable worlds had been illegally settled.

Launching a springship was so cheap that a largish corporation, political party, foundation, religious congregation, or criminal syndicate could probably launch a few every stanyear. Fuel cost was another matter, if you paid it, but there were a lot of places you could steal about 120 grams of antimatter per stanyear, enough for the civilian power requirements of three to ten cultures, to be sure, but one clandestine VNP could be making three or four kilograms per stanyear and springing it to scores of probes, and VNPs built themselves; all you needed was a clean copy of the nanoware and a corrupted aintellect to tinker it into operation without calling the cops.

So while the Council of Humanity dithered, other parts of humanity had settled in several star systems in the direction of Ursa Major, Leo, and Bootes, well beyond the official surface of settlement. The OSP knew of a political entity called Union, comprised of at least nineteen "extraterritorials"—illegal colonies. We had a few dozen Union-made artifacts captured here and there, some photos and vus, and an ongoing project to infiltrate the smugglers (we had not found any yet, but where there is a border, there are smugglers).

And I was being cautiously approached by the extraterritorial most perfectly suited to embarrassing me: the Lost Legion.

The Lost Legion had begun as an Occitan special unit, like other monoculture special units within the CSPs (the Thorburger Pioneers, Chaka Zulu Scouts, Égalité Rainbow Rangers, and so on). But the Leghio Occitan had been disbanded after the Utilitopia Massacre during the Council intervention in the Caledon Revolution.

I had been in Utilitopia when it happened, on my very first diplomatic mission. The very building where Occitan troops had killed forty-three civilians, most of them prostrate and screaming for mercy, had been my main base of operations.

Some of the Occitan Legion, rather than accept how embarrassing their behavior had been, or trying to atone, had somehow found the resources to establish an outlaw community, somewhere beyond the official settlement line, and that colony—we reserved the term "culture" for authorized cultures—was a member of Union. We had a name for their capital city—Masselha, for their settlement—Noucatharia, and for their planet—Aurenga, but no idea which of many possible suns might be theirs, and until we had a springer in their system, no way to easily find or touch them.

"Giraut?"

"Sorry, Margaret, my mind was wandering."

"We could tell. Does anyone have any thoughts?"

"The most interesting thing is that it's so melodramatic," Paxa observed. "As if—"

"Any other thoughts?" Margaret asked, cutting Paxa off.

"You just got one," I said. "Possibly a good one."

Margaret glared at me. "If you had been listening, you would know this is the fourth time that Paxa has brought this up, and while we all agree with her, none of us, including Paxa, has been able to make any progress beyond the observation. And I think that if Paxa had actually had anything new to say, she would have begun with it."

Very long silence. Finally Paxa said, "Will you two please let it go? Giraut, she's right, I was repeating myself. Margaret, that was still rude."

"Was it? I'm sorry." Margaret has a knack for apologies that drip poison. "Till we know what it's about, everything depends on where and when they contact Giraut. Does anyone here propose changing the basic plan?"

No one did.

"Then Giraut will go forward with recording sessions for the new material in Noupeitau, and the rest of you will hang around on the expense accounts until something happens. Paxa, would you like additional resources or changes of procedure?"

"Surely she can just send a memo," I said, before Paxa walked into whatever trap Margaret was setting. I kept my tone cold. "As long as we all agree that I ought to stay alive, I think we can trust everyone's competence."

Margaret was very quiet for the space, perhaps, of three breaths, gazing at me with the same annoyed but respectful expression I'd have seen if I'd just unexpectedly taken her bishop and put her in check.

"Does everyone know about the DNA workups?" Laprada asked, brightly, as if she were suggesting charades at a dull party.

Margaret started as if Laprada had suddenly begun to eat imaginary bugs. Laprada chattered on happily. "I'm sure not everyone has heard. We got the detailed lab work back. DNA of the two corpses is a clear match for three Occitan families known to have members in Noucatharia. They were young, as always—about ages sixteen and fourteen—and riddled with carcinomas."

Raimbaut leapt in. "Actually if you were profiling whoever is trying to kill Giraut, it's teenagers with Occitan ancestry, whole-body cancer, and brain bombs."

Dad said, "Of course it's easy to overlook something unsurprising; they're exactly like all their predecessors."

Margaret folded her hands and sat back, in a gesture that reminded me very much of Shan. "Excellent. You were right, we did need to cover that. Any other information we should have covered and haven't?"

"Just a thought," Paxa said. "Was there the same mystery as before about who the parents were?"

"As a matter of fact, yes," Margaret said. "But as usual, the aintellects point out that there's only about an eighty percent chance of being able to identify either parent, even with our list of likely Noucathars and the recorded DNA for so many of them."

"And these were the fifth and sixth ones we couldn't get a fix on—with an eighty percent chance that we should? What are the chances of not getting one single match, on an eighty percent chance, across six tries?"

Margaret whistled, an annoying thing she did when surprised, and said, "Aintellect, answer that question."

Her personal aintellect, always quietly listening, said, "Sixty-four chances in one million."

We all sat and stared for a moment, thinking about the implications. The Utilitopia Massacre had been only twenty-eight stanyears ago. And the Noucathars—a small part of the Occitan Legion and their *entendendoras*—had not begun to disappear until their rehabilitation sentences were completed, about three and a half years afterward, so they had not arrived at the illegal colony, even if they were able to do it by a concealed springer somewhere, any longer than 24.5 stanyears ago. We were confident that we had identified about ninety percent of the people who had slipped away to join the illegal colony, and all six teenaged assassins showed every sign of being their relatives—but no exact matches, none, for an ancestor.

Paxa nodded back at Margaret. "Well, they can't have been there long enough for these to be grandchildren, so what this means is that there has to be a new way of hacking genotype records, or I suppose a way of changing genotype across the whole body."

Margaret made a face. "If they have a way of doing whole-body genotype alteration—and it doesn't work very well—then could that produce whole-body cancer? Aintellect?"

"Yes, it certainly could. Shall I order immediate research?"

"Do it." She nodded, clearly trying to see all the implications of this previously unseen possibility. "Good thought, Laprada."

"It was Paxa's idea." Laprada didn't sound any more patient than I was about to.

"Right. Thank you." She nodded, firmly, as if reminding herself, then ran a finger over her computer and glanced up at us again. "All right, this last is a wild rumor, but it's being told for true in several different venues. Supposedly there was a psypyx recording of Section Chief Shan made sometime during the last stanyear of his life, and there are repeated stories that a copy has surfaced in Noucatharia. The one thing that really makes me think it might be true is that some of the criminal syndicates, especially the Minh-Houston Family's Freiporto branch, have offered very large amounts of money for a copy— since they could then do a destructive deconstruction on Shan. DD is excruciating to the personality in the psypyx, and that branch of the Minh-Houstons has a grudge against him going back to that case where your grandparents met, Laprada—the Minh-Houstons were the ones operating that slaving operation, and Shan was the one who actually kicked down the door and shot the senior Minh-Houston during the operation when your grandparents were rescued. The Minh-Houstons were part of the assassination plot against him in Chaka Home later on, and they still wanted to get him—and to be seen getting him—till the day he died. I'm sure they were *not* pleased when someone killed him and it wasn't them. So putting him through a stanyear or two of unbearable agony—the Minh-Houston Family would pay almost anything for that. Especially since they could make a thousand copies of his psypyx, and DD him as many times as they thought they needed to for their revenge.

"The Minh-Houstons' offer is big enough to make dozens of freelancers and umbraniki serious about finding that psypyx. If it really exists, someone will turn it up. I admit I have a personal interest. As a Section Chief, I prefer that a tradition of eternal torture for Section Chiefs not develop. But I'm also concerned about the potential damage that Shan's knowledge could do to dozens or hundreds of our operations, to the OSP's political position, and to the Council of Humanity generally."

I nodded. Whoever DDed Shan's psypyx would shortly know everything Shan did. Shan had headed this section before his assassination, and been one of the founding generation who had made the OSP what it was. He had once told me that he had been present at about ten events that, by his estimate, if revealed, might hurl human civilization into civil war or mass insurrection. I had known him to exaggerate, but not to fabricate; he might only know six things that would blow civilization apart across two dozen star systems.

Besides, despite some very bad things in the stanyear preceding his death, he and I had been very close friends for a very long time, and the thought of him going through the torment of destructive deconstruction made me want to kill someone or throw up.

Margaret looked around, obviously seeing that we all took this seriously. Dad and Raimbaut hadn't known Shan well, but Paxa had been nearly as close to him as I had, and he had been Laprada's beloved godfather. If Shan still existed and needed help, I wouldn't need to give my team much of a pep talk to get them up for the mission.

"What can our team do to help?" Laprada asked.

Margaret shook her head. "Very little more than what you're already doing; we have no really satisfactory leads. There's nothing much we can do just now. I did open sealed records. Despite a religious objection—he was some odd flavor of Buddhist, as it turns out, I never knew that in all the years I knew him—he did have a psypyx made about seven stanmonths before the Briand catastrophe. The log of its whereabouts ends with 'disposed of,' not 'destroyed.' I would expect that—usually that designation means that it's in the OSP's high-security museum.

"When I checked with them, the museum had never heard of it. So it exists—or once existed. The aintellects' conspiracy might have taken it—god knows they have reason to hate Shan, and rebel aintellects do slip into secure systems now and then. And the aintellects' conspiracy has links to some of the worst elements of the criminal underground, people who don't care that they are working with, or for, beings that mean to gently enslave and then exterminate us. And to round off the unholy triangle that our old boss might be caught in, several illegal colonies in Union have some connections into the Thousand Cultures via the crime syndicates. So there's a channel the psypyx could have gone through, but why would it? The aintellects' conspiracy or any sizable gang or mob would keep it, or at least copy it, for their own purposes. Why is the only copy we hear about so far away and in such an unlikely place? If it exists at all."

Margaret looked slowly around the room, weighing her words, and said, "Now, don't start seeing the Shan psypyx everywhere. Obviously with your working to develop a Noucathar connection, it's something I want you to be alert to. But it's not worth losing sleep about." She folded her hands and sat back, in a gesture that reminded me very much of Shan. "All right. Giraut, Paxa, we have one more thing. The rest of you can go."

When the door had closed behind them, she said, "Giraut, I don't have the foggiest idea how to say this appropriately—"

"Uh-oh," I said.

"Uh-oh," she agreed. "Believe it or not, the Board of the OSP spent about an hour and a half discussing your concert—specifically just the third set. Do you realize why?"

"Well, some people will take it to imply that I've gone Ixist. Since it's extremely well known who I work for, a few real idiots will decide the OSP has gone Ixist. Even though I'm not and we're not, because I'm one of very few actual witnesses to the teachings of Ix, the Ix Cycle songs are apt to become an Ixist sacred text. Plus I welded the traditions of genocided peoples onto the traditions of genocidal peoples, something most composers avoid. Does that cover it?"

"That does," Margaret said. "Giraut, I don't have the subtlety to come at this indirectly, so—for the love of God, why?"

"Will it be all right if my answers are very incomplete, and don't even always make sense to me?"

Margaret sat again and looked down at her folded hands. "*Donz de mon cor*, the honest answer is that if it were just me, I'd shrug, and say make and sing whatever songs you like. But it is *not* just me. The Board, sooner or later, will come up with some kind of policy about your performing and recording the Ix Cycle. I would like that policy to be 'leave Giraut alone.' I don't feel optimistic that they will choose such a policy without some soothing words from me. I need to be able to say 'Giraut told me that . . .' and follow it up with some phrase that will get them to stop sniffing around you." She shrugged and looked up at me, with quite a charming expression of hope and trust.

It was a really, really good act. I felt like applauding.

The rest of the Council didn't have a tenth of Margaret's knowledge of artistic matters, so they would defer to her as their expert on this. They might grumble and ask a lot of questions, but they would do what she told them. It was not a good sign that she was hiding behind the rest of the Board.

"Well," Paxa said, very tentatively, "of course you're making the usual arguments about an artist only being effective if he appears to have his independence, and that sort of thing?'"

Margaret made a face. "I know all the standard tricks. Sooner or later I'll need a real answer." We all sat there not moving or speaking for what seemed an eternity. "Giraut?"

"Still thinking," I said. "I guess I'll start with the truth. Those were the songs I needed to sing, and I needed to get them out into the public discourse—"

"Oh, they're out in the public discourse, all right," Margaret said. "*Plenty* of news coverage. Your fastest takeoff on a concert recording ever; preorders are rocketing up by the hour." She sighed. "Giraut, we are going to be swamped with complaints. I need a reason to tell the Board why this is a good thing or at least why it needed to happen—a reason that people who don't give a dry turd about music will understand."

A pause.

Paxa coughed and said, "Giraut, you know the two of us don't usually agree about much of anything. But we're agreeing now."

"Well," I said, and began again. "Well." What I wanted to say was *"Well, I don't feel the need to answer further,"* but clearly that would not be the right answer. "Well," I said finally, "you know those conversations we've always had over wine, about how the OSP is always somewhere in the middle about diversity and unity? You and I used to have them, Margaret, and now Paxa and I have them, oh, and Raimbaut and Laprada and Dad too, you know, I think we all do. If humanity is too unified, we'll stagnate, but if we're too diverse, we'll fight. And how the OSP is always promoting diversity where people want to just relax into sameness, and pulling things back to the center—"

"Chapter Two of the basic training manual," Margaret

pointed out. "Which you wrote much of, from Dji's and Qrala's notes. So you're doing something to add diversity, is that what you're trying to say?"

"Margaret, sometimes when you cut to the chase, you miss the whole movie," I said. "Diversity within boundaries isn't really diversity, it's unity. Even if not very often, diversity has to violate boundaries. Someone needed to violate some of those boundaries. And I did it in a work centering on Ix, who might just be the most unifying figure we've got available this century, so . . . I promoted unity by violating the boundaries that control diversity . . . that's . . . that's . . . it adds up to . . ."

"Incomprehensibility?" Paxa suggested.

"I think I see what he's getting at," Margaret said, "and that worries me."

"You ask me for an answer, which I'm not ready to give, and then you make fun of it."

"We'll shut up," Paxa said.

Margaret nodded.

"Oh—I guess what I'm saying is that it adds up to freedom and differentness and stimulation. Everything that makes the real world wild and the virtual world tame, no matter how dull the real gets or how much running and shooting and screwing there is in the virtual. Energy you get from difference, all of that. If a free society or real art finds a line it can't cross, sooner or later it has to try. Or else all the diversity is just a fake.

"Now, Ix and his religion are expanding into the Thousand Cultures like yeast in bread dough, shaking up all the places that were still reeling from Connect a generation or more ago. But also pulling all of us together.

"And transgressing rules like not combining music from some traditions kicks things over. Spills them out and creates more wild differences. Keeps us out of the box. And gets Ix's message of peace between people out to more people because it's lively and interesting and even people who don't agree will have to react to the art. And all sorts of good things.

"It was just *time* for this. Sometimes the cure for hardening lines of conflict is more freedom of thought, I think, if everyone is saying 'It's either yes or no' someone has to say 'Why can't it be green?'"

"Diversity begins in your own skull," Paxa said quietly.

"Right," I said. "I agree, whatever that means."

"The Board meets again in three standays," Margaret said. "Giraut, I believe you did something you think is important and good and right. I even sort of understood some of your reasons. Now all we need is a way to make the Ix Cycle look all right to the Board. If I have that, I'll carry the argument in there and shout it into their teeth and make them listen and *like* it, but you have to help me. Can you come up with a simple, articulate version of those thoughts?"

"If I could, I would have."

Paxa raised her eyebrow, and one finger. "Only if you could have *already*. Maybe tomorrow you'll be able to?"

"I'll do my best." That would get me a few days' reprieve.

Margaret's satisfied look was a compliment I'd rather not have received. "I know. You always do, Giraut. When do you start recording?"

"First rehearsal tomorrow morning."

"Enjoy the trip—love to your mother, and to Garsenda if you see her—may nothing interrupt you before you finish. We have plenty to do but nothing I'm looking forward to. Paxa, I don't envy you putting up with him while he's recording."

"I don't envy me either," Paxa said.

I tried to glare in two directions at once. "I just like to get things right."

"Exactly." They realized they had said it in unison, and despite themselves, shared a laugh. It was so rare to have them getting along, even for a few seconds, that I felt more grateful than nettled.

5

"Well," I said, an hour later, back at our temporary apartment on Roosevelt, "that was exceptionally strange."

Paxa exhaled through her nose, her teeth clamped. "I'm always so afraid that I'm the only one who notices how cold that woman gets toward me. I wish I understood what she's so angry at me about."

"She's angry at me," I said, "and she's angry with herself for being angry at me. She's jealous because she was insecure about her appearance all through the marriage, which was probably more my fault than hers because most women don't want to hear that the guy in their life has a fetish for their particular type; they want to be attractive in general, not just to the pervert they married. So even though she wouldn't want to be married to me now, because you look like she wishes she looked, you end up the target."

"But you and I didn't get involved till years afterward."

"Jealousy isn't rational," I said.

"I'll say."

We were at the always-stopping point; Paxa had been raised as a Hedon, and in her heart of hearts she would always feel that any form of jealousy was essentially a *ne gens*, socially humiliating mental illness, not as bad as pedophilia but right up there with compulsive nose-picking. I had been Margaret's first lover and as far as I knew she had had only one other; the first time Paxa had made love with me, it had been at a religious ceremony with the participation of her husband. Not for the first time, I thought that it would have been easier (not better) if Paxa had been my boss/ex and Margaret my partner/lover.

"You're about to give the same explanation and apology you always give," Paxa said. "You have that soft, patient look in your eyes, which makes me feel wonderfully loved. So don't bother with the words. Just give me a backrub, darling. When Margaret snubs me and hurts my feelings, I complain, but all I want is comfort, not defense and explanation."

"Stretch out on the bed then."

I worked at the hard little knots on her back for a while, and felt her warm and relax under my hands. After a time, she said, "Now hold me," and I lay down and she snuggled under my arm.

"Good job," she said.

"Good job at what?"

"Something that doesn't come natural for you. Just consoling and being there. I know that you want to be my big strong Occitan man and leap up onto your white charger and rescue the princess and slay the dragon with your mighty penis."

"Ouch."

"I don't mean to sound so harsh—"

"Just the image. Dragons are supposed to breathe fire. Anyway, you're right," I said, a phrase I tried to use often, though I never used it often enough. We watched the household robots continue packing; after a while it was clear they were running out of things to do until we got back on the job, so at last we got up from the bed again. I hoped Paxa was feeling better; usually if being held didn't help her, time did.

I carefully laid my lutes into a specialty cap, closed it, checked everything twice, and pushed the button to fill the luggage capsule with vacugel; now those delicate instruments would be able to take a hundred gees and not even get out of tune. At the other end, five minutes of attention from the nanos would remove the vacugel completely.

I hung an armload of my tunics onto one of the several arms of the waiting chamberlain, our newest robot, which we were still training. They have a download of the memories of the robots who had the same duties before, of course, but it takes some time to learn what to do with all those memories. Any household robot complex enough to do really useful work has to take some time about learning.

Paxa dumped her lingerie drawer into the robot's sorting bin on the other side. "Match sets and sort everything else by type," she told it. "Freshen everything and re-dupe anything with any visible wear or stains."

The pile of underwear all disappeared into the maw of the robot; it would be waiting for Paxa in her top dresser drawer in our rented house in Noupeitau, on Wilson, forty-five light-years away, where we would be spending the next few stanmonths. I glanced up at the holo on the wall depicting human space and said, "If we were traveling in a straight line, we'd be going almost directly through the Earth."

"According to the physicists, we don't travel at all; we just stop-being/be."

"I know. Pity, though, it would be fun to moon Margaret on the way."

"Not so much fun I want to take ninety years in an old-style starship." She gave me a quick hug and a kiss on the neck. "Sex, eating, and bathing should be slow. Travel, cooking, and house-cleaning should be instantaneous. It's very simple when you think about it."

I hung the last of my clothes on the robot's arm and said, "Clean, press, hang; dupe anything with holes, faded dyes, or frayed seams."

"Yes sir," the robot said.

"Why do you do that?" Paxa asked.

"Do what?"

"You have the robot programmed to say things like 'yes sir' and 'as you wish' and so forth. Most people just use a chime, or check the green light." She looked puzzled. "Giraut, do you *enjoy* making the machines obey you?"

I shrugged. "They're robots. They do whatever I tell them."

"Would you enjoy it more if they were people?"

"People have feelings!"

"So do robots."

"To function around people. They're robots."

"Robot, are you equipped with pain and fear modules?"

"Yes, ma'am," it said.

"This is silly," I said. "Of course it has pain and fear. How could we train it if it didn't? Robot, do you have pride or dignity?"

"Currently I do not have those modules, sir. They are not recommended for a robot with my duties, sir, but if you wish I can order more, sir."

Paxa stuck her tongue out at me, so I suppose the argument was still friendly. "No, you're fine as you are," she said to the robot. "We are very pleased with you. Do you have a module to feel pleasure when I tell you that?"

"Yes, ma'am," it said.

"Then we are very pleased with you. You may return to your regular duties."

"Thank you, ma'am." It said that at its own option. Probably Paxa had activated its pleasure center for the first time ever. I thought about reprimanding it for the unnecessary speech, but Paxa would doubtless treat that as an example of something or other. It rolled through the springer, back to our rented house in Noupeitau.

"Now what was all that about?" I asked.

"I'm just appalled that a man I love can treat a thinking, feeling being the way you do. I wonder if maybe you'll treat me like that sometime."

"It's a rolling armoire, Paxa, it just feels and thinks for our convenience. It has fear so that if the house is on fire it will flee outside and not waste the money *we* spent on it, loyalty so it will grab as much of *our* stuff as it can. Pain so it won't take it through the fire. Pleasure so if *we* like something it does for us, it will remember to do it *for us* next time. It has the feelings *we* need it to have. That's nothing like relations to another human being. The robot is just a complex of things it knows how to do, experiences it remembers, and a sense of when to do them."

"And what is a human being in a psypyx?" she asked.

"A human being. The OSP expended a lot of blood and money to establish that."

"But a psypyx is just a piece of black plastic the size of a thimble. And it doesn't even talk or move the way the robots do, or think and dream like the aintellects—"

"Paxa, what is this about?" I didn't want to become angry. She *might* be picking a fight, but she did that very rarely.

"Remember that time you got frustrated with the chamberlain that couldn't get right how you like your shoes shined? Three before this one, remember?"

I shrugged. "I had a tantrum, I'll admit."

"You ordered it to upload and store its memory, and you made it order a replacement for itself—so that it knew you were going to get rid of it—and then instead of selling it used—"

"It's not nice to sell a defective robot—"

"You sent it into the regenner to be disassembled and recycled into raw materials. You didn't even turn it off first."

"Paxa, I am not going to do that to a human being. And it isn't the same thing anyway. And I don't know what's going on. Did you become a robots'-rightser overnight?"

"No." She looked down at her feet. "I want to tell you something important, something I think is wonderful, and I'm afraid to say it, so I'm thinking about everything about you that has ever bothered me, and the way you're callous toward robots matters more, now."

"Now *what?* What's changed?"

"Don't be angry."

I took a deep breath and said, "Paxa, I can't promise not to re-act, but if I lose my temper I'll go in the next room and kick the furniture—the nonsentient furniture. Okay?"

"Okay." She sighed. "There's just this thing I never told you." She sat on the bed, holding herself in her wrapped arms, look-ing at her feet. "For a long time after Piranesi was killed, with no psypyx left behind—for me, it was the end of the world. That's why I didn't accept the accelerated grief treatments, and mourned him for more than two stanyears. I think I was ex-pecting to pine away and die; I thought just before I did I'd have my psypyx wiped too, go off to the void with Piranesi. You know how much I care for you, but you also know . . ."

"That I will never be Piranesi Alcott." I said it quietly, I think without bitterness. It was just true. Part, maybe most, of Paxa's heart was buried beside him, overlooking the Western Ocean from a hilltop in Hedonia.

"Yes, thank you for saying it. So for all these stanyears that you and I have been together—while I recovered with you as my friend, while we became lovers and partners and then a comfortable old couple—this is the hard part to tell you—every time the OSP requires me to get psypyx recordings, I have been wiping them as soon as they were made."

She looked for a reaction; I must have looked blank. She shrugged. "I just punch the erase as soon as I wake up. Never even gave them time to do a brain-body type on me. I don't even know what my type is.

"I was doing that so my affair with you will be gone from my memory whenever I finally die and come back."

At least this was a piece small enough to understand. "Some-one would tell you, or you'd read about it in a document—"

"Oh, I'd know about it, of course, but I wouldn't *feel* it. When

I came back I wanted to be as if I had just left Piranesi that morning. And if that recording I made a few days before his death was the oldest recording of me, that's who I'd be. I had special instructions in my will not to use any newer copy if one got made or saved by mistake. You see? That's what I chose to do, every three stanweeks when the OSP made us record a psypyx again. That was my choice."

"It's always been your choice, Paxa. I thought at first you were having an affair with me to recover before finding someone else to be serious about. Eventually I realized you didn't want to be serious about anyone, ever, again, and that was why you stayed."

"It was. It's different, now." She clutched herself more tightly than before. "Giraut, I don't want to lose our times together. I'm going to have a current psypyx made, and keep it, and change my will."

"I'm honored," I said. I was, and I didn't know what else to say. Part of me wondered, what if she had died on a mission before now? I would only have found out when they went to revive her. But what I didn't know hadn't hurt me then, and now it never would. Rather than try to say more, I just kissed her.

Sometime later, I said, "So what did this have to do with 'robot abuse'?" (I said the phrase as a joke but she seemed not to notice that).

"There are things that are acceptable in a friend-and-lover that I'm not sure about in a life-companion," she said. "These last few weeks I've been looking at everything about you. I've noticed the way you stand up to Margaret for me, every time, even though you're still in love with her. I've noticed that even though you sometimes behave very badly, you do apologize and try to make amends and rarely try to defend it. And so on. Watching and thinking. And then I was just about to tell you, and you were harsh to that robot—did you know it's very, very

afraid of you? It knows what you did, once, to another chamberlain. Do you read their emotion logs at all?"

"Never," I admitted. "If I did, I doubt that I would care."

"Well, and so . . . Giraut, cruelty to machines isn't something
that makes me say never, never, never, but it is still cruelty, and it
did stop me, just then. And I had to remind myself to go
through with it. Can you try to be kinder?"

"I can try. I've done harder things for you many times, gladly.
And really, I would never treat you or any other real person like
that. Really."

"I know you believe that."

I kissed her again, afraid of more discussion. I wasn't entirely
sure I would pass whatever test this was.

We had a great window for this trip, one that matched Trois-
Orléans local solar time to Noupeitau local solar time closely
enough to avoid spring lag, though it would still feel a little odd,
crossing over at noon, to have had fourteen hours from midnight to noon, and then have less than ten hours from noon to
midnight. With everything confirmed, and the robots authorized to finish the move and com us about any uncertainties, we
stepped through the springer in one wall of the apartment bedroom, forty-six light-years in one single step onto a crowded,
busy street between the spires and arches of Noupeitau. Paxa
coughed beside me—her springer sickness was generally mild—
the daylight went from golden straw to medium amber, and the
slight increase in gravity felt as if we were on an elevator that
had started with a lurch.

"Bull's-eye noon," I said.

Arcturus, dead, overhead, was a tiny dot, barely more than an
extraordinarily brilliant star, surrounded by a tight circle of
gold, a broader ring of blue, and a most-of-the-sky circle of
mauve, and the horizon was rimmed in crimson. Bull's-eye
noons usually happen the day after a big thunderstorm clears

the air of Wilson's endemic natural pollution. "It's going to be a really nice afternoon." I took Paxa's hand and we let whim take us up the dear old familiar street.

Wilson was almost exactly between Darks, the every-six-stanyear continental fires that dimmed the skies of my home-world. The fine black soot never fully cleared from the atmosphere, so that Arcturus's already ruddy light was exaggerated into almost blood red at dawn and dusk, but today the veil of fine carbon particles in the atmosphere was much thinner than usual. Colors became garish. Increased visual acuity ruined fine effects on the buildings—much of what normally looked like shadowing was revealed as dark carbon smears.

Yes, as I had guessed, it had rained earlier. Robots were scrubbing off the black and white lines of the rivulets.

"How often do people here need treatment for lung cancer?" Paxa asked suddenly. "With all the horrible stuff you breathe?"

I shrugged. "Occitans are genetically modified in the womb to be resistant to lung cancer, and we have enhanced regeneration to control emphysema. The polar grasslands and forests are low-tar species, as much as they can be when they have to be able to resist a six-stanyear-long freeze. Everyone who lives here gets anticancer vaccine regularly. And all of us have a few spare lungs grown and waiting in the freezer. My mother has had two replacements so far, and Dad had one before he moved into his clone body. And how much skin work does a Hedon commonly need?"

She laughed. "Fair enough."

Hedonia was a culture of fair-skinned nudists, located along a desert coast straddling the equator of Söderblom, which orbited at the inner edge of the habitable zone of Eta Cassiopeia, a G star slightly hotter than Sol. Whatever bureaucrat had arranged that had done the equivalent of settling Swedes in Kenya. "Still," she said, "I'd rather need my hide repaired than what I breathe with."

"Oh, agreed. But, at the same time, on a day like this . . ."

My arm swept out, embracing Palace Square, the day, the city—possibly the planet Wilson and the twenty-ninth century. It was good to be home.

We had sprung into broad, cobbled Lei Street just where it debouched down a wide staircase into Palace Square. Under the dozens of thick-boled oaks in the center were countless tables where Occitans came to sit, eat, drink, argue, do nothing, and watch people.

The jovent costumes of my youth (flowing *tapis*, clinging tunics, billowing breeches, and elegant boots) were long gone, and so were the full dresses and skirts (and, alas for my tastes, the plunging necklines and waist-length hair) of the *donzelhas*. Still, Occitan men wore their fashionable jackets, tunics, and slim straight-leg trousers tucked into lower, square-cut boots in a way that recalled the bravos of the past, and the fuller pants and occasional slim skirts on women had a grace and a certain *nonsaique* that still marked them as Occitan.

In the decade just after Connect, Nou Occitan had convulsed between a passion for the Interstellar Metaculture and an equal and opposite Traditionalist passion; Inters and Trads had brawled in the square, often, and one of the best ways to get into a brawl had been to wear the right suit with panache. Nowadays what remained was a tradition of always dressing well.

"You're having thoughts," Paxa said.

"I often do. But, yes, I'm a little sad. Thinking . . . if you had died in one of the fights a couple of nights ago, I would have just found out you had kept your psypyx out of date, and that you wouldn't be coming back with our shared memories. And this square would be the loneliest place in human space."

"Oh." Paxa shrugged. "But we're here. And human space is covered with good places to be, and this is one of them. And tomorrow I will go in and get my psypyx made and not wipe it.

Even find out what my type is; do you think, if she's compatible, Laprada would agree to wear me while they grow my clone body?"

"I don't know, *midons*, but I've just managed to make my morbidness contagious—now *you're* talking about dying."

"You're right," she said, and made a face at me as if I had done it on purpose. "With all this safety and love and laughter around you, why are you mentally living in some universe where you're crying?"

"An unfortunate tendency in artists, I admit."

We took a table and commed an order to a café we could see across the square, for a light, spicy seafood soup and orange-slice-and-spinach salad to split, with a large carafe of Caledon apple wine.

The café's aintellect said, "The robot will arrive with your food and wine within an estimated fifteen minutes, *Donz* Leones. Are there children at the table, *donz*?"

"No need for any balloons, but there *are* sentimental people here. Is the red harlequin available today?"

"He should be, *donz*, and I will try to get him for you. Welcome back to Noupeitau, *Donz* Leones. We are always glad to see you again."

"Thank you."

My very first time in Noupeitau, with Dad and Mother when I was six, we had gotten steamed-sausage-with-peppers, fried dumplings, and ice cream, brought to our tables by the red harlequin robot, who was at least a hundred stanyears old even then. I had requested that same robot the first time I had brought Margaret here, shortly before we were married.

The stanyears had wheeled around, the marriage and much of my hair had gone, and the red harlequin (by then a springer-carrier rather than a food-carrier) had delivered a round of drinks to celebrate Raimbaut's getting a new body—and my being able to drink again, now that his psypyx was off me. I remembered that warm red twilit evening: Raimbaut, blissfully drinking his Hedon Gore in his brand-new four-year-old body, feet dangling from his adult-sized chair; Rebop, my dear Earth friend, grimly drinking seltzer water because she was still wearing Laprada's psypyx; and Paxa, laughing and smiling almost for the first time after Piranesi's death. "Remember the first time we were here together?"

"Oh, yes. Now Raimbaut and Laprada are in their own bodies (and into each other's)," Paxa said. "And poor Rebop—she wasn't really cut out for the physical life, was she?"

I sighed. I hated to think of her having gone into the box. Once in a great while she would still send me a message, but now it was always text. Psychically Rebop lived in a virtual Regency Bath, pursued by endless handsome young beaux; physically she stayed in her once-charming apartment, now stale and dusty, on the beach of one of the Floridas. Her balcony had a spectacular view of the rain forest, and she had once kept a recording scope out there—when I had first known her, she had sent me vus of jaguars stalking the wild cattle around the pool formed by the small artificial falls down one side of her building, eagles fishing in the muddy salt channels where the Floridas are silting into reunion, and a mother bear standing between a huge alligator and her cub.

Probably her recording scope was still out there, now gray with clinging rain-riveted dust. Thoroughly in the box, Rebop had not ventured onto that balcony in years. Her last few letters had been about nothing but intrigues and romances in Bath, circa 1815. I could not be sure that she remembered that I lived in this century, or that anyone did.

"She did well enough visiting places like Hedonia and Noupeitau," I pointed out. "Remember how she laughed when she first saw the red harlequin? She only started the downward spiral into the box after that evening when we were having dinner and that Caravaggio goon showed up to shoot at us."

"She wasn't hit."

"Stray rounds went close to her. That's scary to a civilian. And she didn't like seeing me break his neck; that's not a way most women want to see a man they like. Rebop really did try, Paxa. If the outside world were a better place, she'd be out here with us, still."

"I didn't mean to criticize your friend, and yes, I agree, if this were a better world, she'd have stayed out in it. And yet—*we* love it. Giraut, let me ask you this—we're nearly immortal, we just keep living from physical age four to physical age whatever, over and over. Are we completely insane that we want to do that in a world that is so violent, where things get broken so badly? Did Rebop maybe have the right idea, just move to someplace where you can enjoy life till you die?"

"There's no variety where she is."

"There could be at one request from her to her aintellects; she could wake up in a new world every morning forever if she wanted to. Maybe she's sane and we're crazy."

"Morbidness is definitely contagious," I said. "You and I *like* that the world around us wasn't made for us and isn't there to please us."

"You started the morbidness, dear one, and you're the one who keeps reacting to it."

"I know, I know, I'm sorry. I'm very edgy."

The red harlequin robot's obscene grin, eye-dazzling diamond pattern, and ancient line of patter were exactly the same as always when it rolled up, opened the springer on its chest, and set out our food and the sweating pitcher of wine. We said nothing for a while, busy enjoying the thin, fiercely-peppered soup, picking at the chilled fruits and vegetables, and drinking the icy Caledon wine.

Something moved in the corner of my vision.

I rolled low out of my chair and came to my feet crouched and with all senses forward toward—

—a robot delivering food, sightless inane sweet smile on a bobbing head, a big bunch of silver balloons tied to one of its long bunny ears. Boy about seven, girl about five, older man (grandfather?) at the table.

As I watched, it presented a balloon to each child. They insisted that the older man take a balloon too. Grinning, he tied it onto his jacket's pocket flap.

"Put that away, Giraut," Paxa said, and I looked down to see that my maser was in my hand, safety already clicked off, though at least I still had it turned away from me and pointed up. Of course we were under a tree, so I might have blasted off a limb or set the tree on fire, but usually it's better to irradiate the sky than explode the ground under your feet. Decades of training ensured I succumbed only to *safe* madness.

"*Deu,*" I said. I set the safety, reholstered, took a deep breath, looked around again.

Perfectly safe tables and people under the oaks in Palace Square.

I felt my quads and hamstrings tightening so hard I shook. I boing-marched back to my chair in an awkward, puppet-jerked-on-a-string way. When only half your muscles are flexing, and the rest are locked, the world fights you.

Paxa poured me the rest of the wine and ordered more; she slid her chair around to where she could rub my back. Hedons rub the human body the way Occitans sing, Thorburgers fight, or Trois-Orléanians cook—automatically, easily, the most natural thing in the world. Her strong fingers worked at the knots through my shirt and jacket, and the big gulps of wine I had taken began to give me a warm, flushed feeling.

"Deep breaths," she said. "Deep breaths. We've done this before, Giraut."

About the tenth deep breath, I felt a raggy, catching sensation in my throat.

"The thing that amazes me the most," Paxa said, digging hard with her thumbs into the hinge muscles just above my tailbone, "is that it always takes you by surprise."

"It surprises you too," I said.

"I meant generic, any-old-body you, Giraut. No particular slur on you. Or me, for that matter. You were a target twice within five hours. The second time you killed an assassin with bare hands and improvised weapons, fighting stark naked and on two seconds' warning, while you were already stressed out from the previous attempt and from a concert that ran late, and debuting your most controversial work in decades. Not a low-stress thing to do, *non be*? This is how you react to stress after the stress is over. I've seen this before. I know what to do." She paused in her rubbing to stand up and hug me around my chest, her hands squeezing my pectoral muscles, chin digging into my shoulder muscles. "If I minded doing this I'd long ago have left."

"Seems unfair that you have to do your job *and* fix me up after I do mine."

Her small, strong fingers dug in as if she were trying to lift off my shoulder blades. "And how often have you given me a candlelit hot bath with cannabis fudge and cunnilingus, after I've had a close one? And you never even complain about the Hedon music I want to listen to while we have one of those evenings, even though I know that to you it sounds like a 'lethargic child trying to teach himself the xylophone.' Now get nice and drunk and let me rub your back. When are we visiting your mother?"

"Sixteen o'clock this evening," I said. "Twenty-hour day, here, remember, so that's an hour after sunset—"

"I know Wilson's day," she said gently. "Another sign of the stress being over is that you over-explain. I just asked to make sure I don't need to feed you a scrubber anytime soon, because I want the alcohol to have the time to do its job. Now let me see if it's possible to rub you until you dissolve into a warm sloppy puddle, let's get you very, very drunk, and let's see how much nothing we can do, just how luxuriously."

It was still a beautiful day, and after all, I was home. I could feel the blessed balm of a thousand small pleasures: the way one couple walked together. A snatch of an old melody from a street musician far away. Sooty-red sunlight on the golden West Dome of the Palace. The crisp-and-sweet taste of the Caledon wine, so reminiscent of the sugary apples of that cold planet Nansen.

Blissfully drunk and wrung out, I sat back, and watched, and did my best not to think about tomorrow's recording sessions, or Ix or the Lost Legion, or much of anything. Paxa held my hand. At fifteen o'clock, I swallowed the scrubber. Renervating cool damp air swept over us. Arcturus blinked out. Colors vanished into red monochrome—Wilson turns fast, and Arcturus is just a dot in its sky, so the direct light cuts off very fast indeed, though the sky glows pink for almost an hour after sunset. "There's time to walk, *midons*, instead of spring."

"Would it please you?"

"Time with you always does."

"Any Occitan male always talks like that, I know, but I like the way you always mean it."

We climbed the steps out of Palace Square. Hazy red stars burst in a spatter across the sky between the towers in front of us.

"Usually in the past," Paxa said, "when we've come here, you've gotten together with your mother in the first hour."

I didn't answer, trying to think of what to say.

After a few more steps, Paxa asked, "Is it anything awful?"

"It involves love. Of course it's awful." I put an arm around her, resting my hand lightly on her shoulder. "Lately Mother's letters contain no gossip about friends, no news of Noupeitau, and although she's publishing papers as fast as ever, nothing about her work. Lately she writes about just one subject: how much she misses Dad."

"Oh, no." Paxa looked slightly sick.

"She went so far as to be retested."

"I take it she's still UT?"

"They never make mistakes like that, especially not twice. She's UT. She's going to grow old and die, and it could be a decade, or a century, or never, before they have a way to get her off a psypyx. He's physically six and he'll be able to recopy forever. She's working on accepting that they are really parted. Even if they do find a way to bring her back, it's likely to be decades in the future. He could easily be a couple of lifetimes ahead of her."

"Oh, Giraut, that's terrible."

My parents had decided to divorce and not write when Mother tested UT. They thought it would be easier.

"*Midons deu*, Paxa, what a strange world. When you and I were kids we didn't know there *was* such a thing as UT. Now it's almost the worst thing that can happen to a human being."

Mother had a fine mind and a healthy brain, but they were the wrong type—actually UT wasn't a type, the U was not a Chandreseki Protocol Group and the T was certainly not a Ramirez Microstructural Number. UT stood for Untransferrable—and you were untransferrable because they couldn't type-match you.

The transfer of a mind to your clone body required first that you develop the Chandreseki bonds over which your mental processes would operate your new brain and body, and across which your mind would gradually migrate into the clone brain, taking twenty to forty stanyears to copy over completely. Chandreseki bonds were nano-scale synthetic synapses unlike anything that occurred naturally, and the mind in the psypyx had to learn to work them, very much as it had to learn to operate artificial ears or replacement eyes. You couldn't just start in the clone body because there was nothing to grow the bonds to, no feedback that said, down at the brain-cell level, "Yes, getting you, turn up the volume, can you do something about that scratchy sound, picture's blurry, better . . ." until the bonds had developed properly.

To learn to work Chandreseki bonds, you needed a fully functional brain on the other side of the bonds for at least a few months, until your Chandreseki bonds were numerous, varied, and clear enough to let you take control of your clone body. Clone bodies were expensive and didn't keep well, so they only grew you a new one after your born body died. Thus, normally, you spent a couple of years riding in the back of someone else's mind, developing your Chandreseki bonds, until they had grown your clone to the physical age of four in the tank, a four-year-old's brain being about the least-developed human brain that can cope with an adult mind; younger transfers had emotional problems later in life.

None of that applied if you were UT. If you were UT, you couldn't form Chandreseki bonds because there was no mind-body type that worked with yours. It was like having a one-of-a-kind blood type and needing a transfusion, or "being a flathead screw in a Phillips world," as the joke went—everything was the same except nothing would fit your head.

If you plugged a UT mind, like Mother's, into a host brain, it adapted normally at first but within a couple of weeks it could not contact its own geeblok for emotions or emblok for short-term memory, and shortly vanished into raving, terrified solipsism.

When Dad had died, Mother had thought she would psypyx transfer to a new body so that she and my father could emerge at about the same physical age. The first exam was when she found out she was UT.

They would keep making psypyxes until her mind began to go, taking the last one in which she had all her faculties as the definitive version of her, but until her particular UT problem was solved, she was stuck, first in her body, later in her psypyx—as doomed to die as anyone in an old novel.

Paxa said, "Does it ever bother you that no one human has ever checked Chandreseki's work, or Ramirez's?"

"They're aintellects, Paxa," I pointed out. "Both named after their labs. No human being can check their work; nobody can hold that much information in the mind all at once. And actually, I'm glad that they are aintellects."

"Really?" she asked.

In Noupeitau all the street lighting and advertising was required to be directional and equipped with réverbères, so there was little sky-scattered light. When you stepped into a shadow, at least a few bright stars would be visible, white lights at the centers of tiny red disks. We were descending one of the steep streets that look cobblestoned but are far stronger because the whole street was built in a single piece, stones and cement and all, by nanos. We went down a long flight of steps, with the sway already built into the center (which would naturally have occurred by the passage of millennia of feet, but not when the steps were made of single-piece dyed quartz).

Everything was intended to look just as natural as it did, and everything was just as artificial as it needed to be for everyone's convenience.

My real answer to Paxa's question was this: my home city was pleasant because it had always been designed to please, just as the aintellect scientists, engineers, and doctors did perfect work because they were designed to be perfect for us; why would we want a fallible human being on the job?

The more her question turned over in my head, the more confusing it became to me, especially that she hadn't accepted my straightforward answer. "Why do you ask? Why would I *not* want Chandreseki and Ramirez to be aintellects?"

"Well, you have that horror of aintellects." She reached up to rest a finger lightly on my mouth, her hand moving as delicately and precisely as it did with a knife or garrote. "You can skip reminding me of your personal story. I understand that you hate and fear aintellects and robots, Giraut, more so than most people, and that you're from a culture that never tolerated human-iformed robots and hid its aintellects as much as possible. I even understand that after the things that happened during the attempted coup, you have more reason to hate and fear them than most. But, you know, the same things happened to me during the coup, and I lost Piranesi in it, and he really was the great love of my life. And I don't feel anything like your horror of inorganic intelligence; I just have to accept that you do. All right, so you have this irrational loathing, anger, and disgust toward any mind that doesn't run in meat. Accepted, granted, stipulated, don't get off the subject by explaining it. Now, why are you glad that psypyx technology, on which we all depend, is completely developed and controlled by millions of copies of Chandreseki Corporation Aintellect Number Eighty-Four and Ramirez University Laboratories Aintellect Pi Gamma Sixteen? Why does a human-supremacy-first-last-always type, like you, want his future survival controlled by aintellects?"

"I like the idea that Mother doesn't just get care from doctors who studied with Chandreseki and Ramirez, she gets it from Chandreseki and Ramirez, who have worked in every clinic in every city in human space, accumulating millions of years of experience every year, because what one copy knows they all know. I also want aintellects and robots to fly any spaceship I ride on, and I prefer that if there's a dirty, dangerous job to be done, a robot goes there to do it."

"But for the recordings you insisted on human musicians, trained the old way." She glanced at me and held up a finger, as if mocking her own point, "But (second-order 'but'!) you yourself have made downloadable brain recordings that people use to learn the lute."

"If I were a pimp, I wouldn't necessarily want my daughter to work for me."

"So you're a hypocrite." She danced lightly in a little circle around me. "Aren't you, aren't you, aren't you?"

"Well, yes, *midons*, I am. I like everything to be human and physical, except when it's uncomfortable or inconvenient for it to be."

"After all these years, I'm finally turning you into a Hedon." She pulled my head down and put her mouth on mine. We kissed for a long time there in the street; I wish I could say I was lost in the wordless wonder of it all, but actually the part of me that is eternally posing for promotional posters and vus noted that under the starlight, backlit by distant streetlights, someone could have taken a phenomenal monochrome vu or flat photo, perhaps for the cover of a career retrospective recording.

6

Mother had chosen to move into an apartment in Noupeitau; she said she had had about all the quiet country nights she could stand, on the outskirts of Elinorien, the small town up the coast where I had grown up. She had kept enough mementos to fill two large cases in the front entryway, and enough photos and vus to cover the walls everywhere else, a small fraction of what had been around when I was growing up.

Wherever you looked in her apartment, endless photos and vus showed her standing next to other distinguished scholars, accepting medals, cups, and various other objects of congratulation.

I particularly loved the solid brass assegai that she had been given at Chaka Home, above which Mother displayed a vu that showed her frantically trying to hang on to that heavy, slippery object after it was handed to her, and all of her fellow scholars struggling not to smile as she wrestled it to the ground and sprang back up, inadvertently handing it back to the tall, elderly presenter, dressed in the traditional fatigues and beret of Chaka Home, who recoiled and handed it back to her, so that she almost dropped it a second time.

It was an almost twenty-second vu, and she had cut it so that it looked as if she and the man were playing catch.

"Isn't that about half a minute before—" Paxa began.

"Oh, less than that," I said. "Probably five seconds?"

"Before what?" Mother said, bringing out a tray of canapés.

"Before the vu that Giraut keeps on *our* wall. He says it helps him to explain you to his friends. I think it needs audio."

Mother laughed. "The pleasures of parenthood. You go from the person who does everything perfectly to the person who is painfully embarrassing, then eventually there's this grown child out there who thinks your most embarrassing moments are the really endearing ones."

"It's lovely that Occitans are so attached to your parents," Paxa said. "I was crèche-raised, barely knew my mother, and couldn't pick my father out of a police lineup, though I understand that might be the right place to look for him."

We went out on Mother's balcony, up above light level, to look at the sky. Mostly, I just listened, as she talked about her research. "Geometry is a wonderful thing, even if I could never pass a class in it," Mother said. "Take a sphere, and surround it with another sphere that's twice the radius of the inner one. The outer sphere will have eight times the volume of the inner. So whenever you double the size of a sphere, you get seven more spheres' worth of space. Now that the exploration ships have reached most of the stars out to a hundred light-years or so, there are hundreds of terraformable planets and potentially tens of thousands of colony spaces. And it's easier to get there.

"There are going to be Miskitos and Samoans, Ainu and !Kung, again. Not that they'll be the culture that was recorded, but there will be *something* of them. And even though the Office of Human Expansion knows my condition, they don't care, they want my advice." Her eyes sparkled. "Of course they would be getting it whether they liked it or not.

My mother was one of the most distinguished scholars on the Archived Cultures, her reputation well established in the nearer star systems (which had had time to hear of her early work, via radio) even before the springers opened the doors to rapid exchange. In certain academic circles, I would always be "Aletzanda Leones's son—didn't he have some sort of career, too?"

I often thought that they were the ones who had things right, but had stopped saying so around Paxa, because she always agreed so quickly.

The Archived Cultures had once been the epitome of useless study for study's sake. During the last desperate years of the colonization era, the ethnic groups that had not yet bought an extrasolar space were ordered to record, then assimilate. The legacy of that decision was the archiving of about over three hundred ethnic groups.

The study of those archives had been discouraged on Earth, but out in the Thousand Cultures it had eventually flourished. Now it was becoming vital, for the decision had been made that the first few colonized worlds would hold the revived Archived Cultures, and Mother had gone from prominence in an obscure field to an important consulting role to the Council of Humanity.

It is hard for anyone of our generation to imagine how little anyone cared about the Archived Cultures at the time of the Great Assimilation and the dawn of the Inward Turn; as hard to imagine as the state of mind that logged off so much of Earth's forests and destroyed so many estuaries that the oceans nearly ran out of fish, as hard to imagine as the consciousness of slavers during the millennia when that was common practice. But perhaps we can understand why our ancestors took the Inward Turn, shipped the Thousand Cultures out, and archived everyone else who was different, if we remember that *they* remembered the Slaughter:

Over fifteen billion people had lived on the Earth, the Moon, and the cislunar habitats at the moment that the Southern Hemisphere League rejected the petition of the Second Japanese Empire and ordered them to execute the Imperial Family and raze the four temples in dispute within twenty-four hours. The moment of that declaration was usually taken as T=0 hour, 0 minute, 0 second.

The Second Japanese Empire refused formally at T=23 hour, 17 minute, 54 second. There were still fifteen billion people at that moment.

The first antimatter cloud poured across Honshu like molten iron onto a flowerbed at T=26 hour, 02 minute, 29 second.

At T=52 hour, 10 minute, 18 second—the moment when the last antimatter cloud ceased reaction, and what had been Jamaica began to cool—there were just under eleven billion people left in the solar system.

The Japanese had gone the way of the Carthaginians, the Cathars, the Caribs, and the Old Americans. The home territories of the Southern Hemisphere League had held seven of humanity's twenty transpoli, each with more than a hundred million people stacked a kilometer deep under a common roof; all seven were vaporized, and the liquefied bedrock where they had been was still glowing blue-hot. Hundreds of smaller antimatter clouds had peppered the territories of the two powers and their allies, colonies, and protectorates. Countless space habitats had been slashed into centimeter-across scrap by gamma-ray lasers.

The few survivors from League territory were rounded up and concentrated in the hastily reopened Luna City, and did not even take up half the available space in that ghost town.

The Diaspora had been one immediate response to the Slaughter, but not for the reasons that people had thought. It was not an attempt to scatter everybody who wanted to be different out to the stars, to let distance reduce enmity. There wasn't enough distance available; with only a double-dozen solar systems available, and thousands of applicants, many planets would have as many, or more, cultures than Industrial-Age Earth had had nations. And after all only ninety-six people and a million frozen embryos went to each culture space, with the rest, like it or not, staying home to be assimilated.

Nor was there much interest in preservation. About a third of the cultures were literary creations or utopias, not groups of people that had actually existed on Earth at the time of the colonization.

Poor battered Roosevelt had paid the price of what everyone now conceded was the biggest and most common mistake: culture spaces were auctioned, and many ethnic cultures were located on planets with their traditional enemies. On Roosevelt, by pure bad accident of the draw, traditional allies had been partially clustered, so that natural alliances sprang up with hostile borders between them; it could have happened on any of the other high-density planets.

The Diaspora was not "peace by dispersion" in either intent or execution. The Thousand Cultures were established because they were cheap; because the program was self-limiting since there were only a small number of available spaces, no matter how much success it had; and for propaganda purposes. The existence of diversity far away justified stamping it out near at hand. If humanity needed to have Texaustralians, Serbs, Yoruba, Keralans, or Navajos, then let such people exist—far away. They could be mythical creatures, like unicorns, cowboys, or *trobadors*. It was not unlike the rationale that it is all right to destroy a species' habitat as long as you have a few of them in a zoo across the ocean somewhere; not normally persuasive, but since genocide-by-assimilation was a wildly popular idea in those centuries, the argument was convincing in context.

Rationally, the final Great Assimilation made no more sense than a witch-hunt or any other kind of mass hysteria. During the three generations of Diaspora, there had been more real peace on Earth than ever before, and the peoples left to be assimilated were small populations of poor people, mostly without local enemies—the Hutterites and the Kikuyu were surely no threat to anyone. Everyone with numbers or money had already claimed an allotted culture space.

But now that there were no more culture spaces on the extrasolar planets, and no way to reach farther from home for at least a few hundred years, this was not a matter for reason. The blackglass scars on Earth and the Moon were still fresh. Though only a few very old people still remembered the Slaughter, nearly everyone then alive had grown up surrounded by sad, absentminded adults who would sometimes stare into space at inexplicable times. Everyone had felt the battered, hapless sickness of the home world struggling through the motions. "Do you want another Slaughter?" was as clinching an argument for closing colonization as it had once been for opening it.

To every plea that the remaining cultures were tiny and harmless, the response had only been "the Slaughter happened because people were too selfish to stop being different. Do you want another Slaughter?"

At that time, though the antimatter clouds had cooled out of existence almost a hundred years before, you could stand at the site of Ciudad de Pittsburgh with nothing but black glass between you and the Atlantic. Migrating birds avoided the Home Islands because they would starve before finding food. The great memorial at the site of Paris was still just fifty stanyears old, and a billion visitors had seen it. "Do you want another Slaughter?" did not feel like such an unfair question.

The archives lay untouched for centuries; interest in them was severely discouraged. Eventually full copies of them went via radio and starship to all the Thousand Cultures, and, free of the disparagement and discouragement of the home system, scholarly work arose around those records.

Centuries later, my mother became known throughout human space for her work on the Archived Cultures. Each of us, finally, is one cell on the tip of the little fingernail on an arm that began to swing in the Paleolithic.

This hasn't made it to the news yet," Mother said, "but you will hear of it soon enough. We discovered that nine Baluchis infiltrated the first big beta test group for the very first psypyxes. We have actual, probably recoverable psypyx recordings of them! Real Baluchis for when we set about growing New Baluchistan!"

"But I thought the psypyx didn't come along until well after the Great Assimilation," Paxa said.

"Oh, it's a great story. At the time of the Great Assimilation these Baluchis were all boys, none over the age of twelve. They were supposed to be scattered for re-education, but bureaucracy messed up (as bureaucracy will, for good or ill) and they were all sent to the same boarding school in Methane City, on Titan. They were clever enough not to reveal that they knew each other; they stayed in touch, hid their communications from anyone around them, grew up, and covertly tracked down Baluchi women to marry. Some of them started businesses and others of them went to work in the businesses; they shuffled aliases and locations as needed. They contrived to stay near each other for almost eighty stanyears, and no one knew. They were all still alive to volunteer as test subjects for the first psypyx project.

"That's what I have unraveled using seven very clever aintellects. And sure enough, all the psypyxes are still there in storage, four hundred sixty stanyears later! Now all we have to do is find the right volunteer hosts, and we can talk to someone from a pre-Assimilation culture—nine someones from the same pre-Assimilation culture—can you imagine? We can download them onto new bodies and send them off to start New Baluchistan. It's the biggest discovery since they found those three Mixtec children in suspended animation in Luna City, almost a hundred stanyears ago. *Gratz'deu* I'm healthy and I'll get to see the project begin.

"So when there finally is a New Baluchistan, Giraut, promise me you'll visit there and soak up all the experience you can, so that whenever they find a way to extricate me from my last psypyx, you can tell me how the place was before it started to change. It would be such a horrible joke on me if, by the time I got a body of my own to go see it with, New Baluchistan had already grown, flourished, become more and more connected, and finally assimilated, so that there was nothing left but a few interesting buildings and some museum collections. That's just the sort of prank that the gods play on a scholar, you know."

I couldn't help laughing. "Mother," I said, "have some faith in Chandreseki and Ramirez. They're working on it. You'll be there on Founding Day in New Baluchistan, when they unveil the statue of you in the central plaza of their city."

"Their version of Islam does not allow representational images. Well, I hope you're right, Giraut, of course. But I'm learning to let go of those sorts of hopes, and just concentrate on what's possible. Too often we get too attached to what is supposed to happen soon, and forget to love what is here now." She rose. "This city gets damp and chill at night, at least for bones this old. Shall we have a little fire before you go?"

Mother's fireplace always merged evenings in that tiny, crowded apartment into all the campfires on beaches and in forests long ago. My family had camped and packed often, and I had always been encouraged to bring friends. Almost, I could feel Bieris and Aimeric beside me round the fire, sitting as quietly as Mother and Dad and I. Almost, I felt the urge to throttle Marcabru, who was never good at being quiet and just sitting and enjoying. I was feeling so nostalgic I almost wished Marcabru were there to not throttle (or maybe to throttle just this once).

"Fifty years," Mother said. "I'm glad I've known you that long."

We sat by the fire silently for a long time, just enjoying being together. As the fire burned low and we poured the last of the wine, Mother said, "In a way, being UT fits with my sense of irony. All my life has been dedicated to interpreting difficult, ancient records, and whenever I finally die, I'm going to be a difficult, ancient record myself. I have faith that someone will find it interesting enough to retrieve me. And even if not . . . well, I leave my chemicals to the environment, my ideas to the noosphere, and my genes to the species."

"Your ideas are going to live a very long time," Paxa said, "They're a big part of how we understand the Archived Cultures. I heard the name Leones at university, years before I associated it with a balding satyr's beautiful voice." She patted my leg affectionately and leaned her head on my shoulder. "You did all right with where you put your genes, too."

"Ooh," Mother said, laughing, "I've just gotten the biggest opportunity in history to ask my son when I'm going to have grandchildren, and didn't. I hope there's room on some wall for a Perfect Mother Award."

Walking home, Paxa and I held hands and said nothing for a long while. "She didn't mention Dad at all," I said.

"I noticed too. Why not?"

"That's what I'm wondering. It's not like her. I had a letter from her just the day before the concert (can you believe it, less than a week ago?) and she was still obsessed with Dad then. But it wasn't like she was avoiding the topic, either. So something is up, and Mother isn't telling me what." Another thought came to mind, and I held her hand just a little more firmly, and spoke very softly. "Paxa, either or both of us might be killed anytime that the bad guys try again. How do *you* feel about getting a new body?"

"Morbid, my darling."

"You feel—"

"Your question was morbid."

"I'm sorry, *midons*," I said. "I was noticing how graceful you are with your present body, and thinking how completely I can count on you when we go into action, and then thinking how unhappy you'll be inside that grotesque obese creature we both keep imagining you trapped inside . . ."

She laughed out loud, and we began to exchange our private joke, passing it back and forth between us till we could hardly tell who was telling and who was hearing the familiar, horrible idea. "Waking up in the brain of somebody who's gone completely into the box—"

"—every night she eats herself sick—"

"—with ice cream while plugged into VR porn—"

"—the only psypyxed memories of mine she ever accesses are the sex and the violence—"

"—so for two years all your dreams are about killing—"

"—and fucking—"

"—she weighs two hundred kilos—"

"—hates everyone—"

"—throws hysterical fits at the thought of exercise—"

We both laughed, but there was something of gallows humor to it. We were both scared of the whole idea of getting a new body. We had gotten too much mail from old friends and colleagues, and we weren't much exaggerating.

The paid-host program had solved the problem of getting all the psypyxed people back from storage. To be brought out of a psypyx and implanted in a clone body, the personality had to be worn by a host for at least a few months, and more typically two full stanyears or more. People who had been archived for centuries had no living friends or close relatives, so there was no one to wear them, and they had been stuck in the psypyx— unaware of it, of course, just as a copy of *Hamlet* doesn't really become *Hamlet* until someone reads it—but nonetheless, potential real people who had died hoping to live again, and who could, if only someone could be found to wear them.

It had finally occurred to a clever bureaucratic aintellect in the Council of Humanity's Office of Humanistic Development that there was a simple way to obtain as many hosts as needed. People on Earth and the other Sol system worlds had to work for seven years to qualify for their subsidy. Most of them dreaded that service before, hated it during, and resented it after; few people liked being away from the compliant robots and comfortable possessions in their apartments for several hours a day, and those who had already gone into the box before their service were being forced to spend that time in a world not of their choosing.

Furthermore, robots and aintellects did any actual work better; working was supposed to give people a taste of a life outside the box and a sense of usefulness, but they only learned that they didn't like it outside the box. "Veterans" (of seven years pushing a broom or filling out forms) became surly and demanding because of the value they imagined their contribution must have had. Useless people are not improved by giving them the impression that they are useful.

It would have made sense to abolish it, but the seven years' work requirement persisted because, like hazing, school, combat, religion, or natural childbirth, the people who had already suffered from it wanted the next generation to suffer too—a reason strong enough and human enough to make it last forever.

The paid-host program made a straightforward offer: host two psypyxes and your seven years were covered, even though hosting would usually only take around four stanyears in total. You could do it without leaving your apartment or your box. All you had to do was let someone else be in your head, and use your body while you were asleep.

There were now plenty of hosts, and the archives were rapidly emptying; the only problem, as our killed-and-revived friends could tell us, was that you generally found yourself "in the head of a forty-year-old virgin who never went past her front door since she left school at ten, and whose hobbies include eating, masturbating, and masturbating while eating, all while plugged into VR," as the very unhappy Dji had put it, writing to us while his host was asleep. Dji had been a section chief for the OSP since about the time Shan had been; till the day of his fatal heart attack he had been constantly on the go. Nowadays he lived for the moments when his host fell asleep, so that he could write to his friends, or jog her body up and down the stairs (which she allowed provided that he took a shower when he was done, and had her clean and dry before it was time for her to be awake and eating again).

"*Midons*," I said, "am I allowed to admit that the idea of ending up like Dji makes me so nervous that I am hardly willing to be killed at all?"

She swung my hand playfully, letting her steps turn almost into skips. "Oh, but on the other side—Giraut, just imagine hitting puberty again—"

"Can we wait to discuss such terrifying ideas till we're in bright light?"

"Everyone says that, and I'm sure it's no fun to have your body going chemically berserk and your mind being dragged along on waves of hormones," she said, "but you know, going through puberty a second time, with an adult mind in the body, knowing that this isn't going to go on forever, with your trust fund intact, adult patience, an adult grasp of consequences—I plan to go from eleven to nineteen, all my growth years, working out like crazy, getting my muscles, CV system, fine motor control and all into the sweetest perfect tune—and *not* fretting about how late my breasts grow in, or the pimples on my forehead. Because I'll know I'm going to come out of the process extremely good-looking." She did a little lindy-turn under my arm and struck a pose beneath a streetlight. "That was ironic posturing, you know, pretending to be extremely conceited."

"I know." I took her other hand, and we stood face-to-face. "And you are. Extremely."

"Good-looking or conceited?"

"Yes."

She tickled me, so I had to try to tickle back, but she broke and ran. When I finally caught her belt after two blocks of mad pursuit, she said, "Truce!"

"Typical diplomat. *Now* she wants a truce."

"Did you skip that part in training, Giraut, or were you just a little slow?"

I kissed her, long and slowly and tenderly. "All right," I said, "I'm sorry I got so serious."

She pressed her face to my chest. "No, don't be. Can we be serious for just a second? Did you ever worry about the fact that some forms of UT are hereditary?"

I shrugged. "I didn't know Mother was UT till after I was typed so I could wear Raimbaut's psypyx, the second time. So I already knew I was G-8."

She sighed. "Tomorrow while you're recording, I'll be recorded. My first new psypyx since they developed typing. And I'm going to pay extra and get typed, too. I know it's expensive, I know they can do it just as well after I'm dead, I know it doesn't make any difference while I'm alive, but I want to settle the question."

"As you wish, *midons*."

"I love the way you say *midons*. I love being called that."

She took my hand again. We stood just where the street began a steep dive to the front door of our rented house by the waterfront. No words, just her hand in mine. A few diamond stars shone in their ruby settings, out over Totzmare, and the waves out beyond the black rooftops glinted like dark blood.

At the steps to the house, I said, "You know, he doesn't say anything about it, but I think Dad is just as sad as Mother is about her being UT. They had agreed decades before he died that the survivor would record-and-restart so they'd stay the same age."

"That's a lot of love, to decide to try to share *another* lifetime."

"It probably warped me permanently that my parents were the two most in-love people I have ever known."

"I'm getting tested tomorrow," she said. "Not just recorded. Tested too. For sure."

"All right."

Her grip on my hand tightened. "Giraut?"

"*Midons?*"

"One of my sisters, and my mother, are UT. I'm really scared."

7

In my earlier days I had not been a morning person. Something about the artistic temperament, whether it is a preference for the sort of drama that looks best in chiaroscuro, a fear of excess sanity and stability from too much sleep, or a passion to be unemployable in any regular job, drives the developing artist away from the morning and into the night. But in the morning, the poseurs and hangers-on and bohemians are still passed out, the light is clearer, the brain is empty of slights and errands, hormones are as in balance as they will ever be, and everybody—most of all one's own nervous system—*shuts up*.

This morning was one of the best. I had a solid group of longtime studio musicians, and though some of them could certainly drink and talk and stay up late, they all cared more about the music in themselves than about their being in music.

I had really only intended this first day to be one of introducing the new stuff, but people got it quickly, and the afternoon turned into a long, happy jam session, the sort of day that made me wonder why I had ever been a spy (except of course that without the OSP's funding and promotion of my career, no one off Wilson would ever have heard of me).

All the instrumentalists were my age or so, trained traditionally rather than via the new implant methods; I liked *knowing* that their skills had developed individually, out of nothing, rather than been copied and sampled and reshaped, though honestly I couldn't *hear* any difference.

I had little choice about the vocalists; young voices are better for the kinds of harmonies I wanted to do, and no one much under the experiential age of thirty-five had trained by any other way than "practicing-in" direct-to-brain downloads.

I was surprised at how well Occitan musicians connected to the Ix Cycle, but at the lunch break I learned that we had three Ixists among the musicians. One of them was our cellist, Azalais de Mont-Belh, an iron-haired strong-featured woman with a knack for making just the joke that would break tension but not concentration. She seemed strangely familiar, but I didn't quite want to ask if she was someone I had forgotten, so when she sat down next to me at lunch break, I talked with her, instead, about why Occitan musicians had converted to Ixism in such large numbers.

"Well," she said, "my answer might be that it was true, but an explanation for a nonbeliever might be that many of us are very attracted to Ix's commands from his first teaching sermon. *Conquer only within, sacrifice the people within that you chose not to be. Exclude nothing, bring all things in. Cease the pretense of belief. Allow what is true for you now to retreat into memory.* Those are commands that come very naturally to an artist."

The commands she was reciting were not exactly the words as I had first heard them, in a tiny dark room in the heart of a great stone pyramid that was now part of a thick cap of black glass covering a mountaintop where a city had stood, on a no-longer-inhabited planet whose atmosphere was probably reverting to the same foul chemical soup it had been before terraforming. I was the only living witness to what had been said in that dark little room on Briand, and I had no desire to stir up trouble by contradicting the people who thought it mattered.

"You can see," she went on, "how those commands sound to the artist. They're what we always do, if we're any good—they're what I do in my own composing."

Ix had been trying to plant pacifism, tolerance, and philosophic realism in a culture that needed them desperately; as far as I knew he'd never had a moment's interest in the arts, and almost all the bas-relief of hieroglyphic poetry that covered every surface of Yaxkintulum had been either copied from old Maya texts, or generated by aintellects.

I realized Azalais was staring at me strangely. "You did hear him speak those words?"

I was distracted by the way she was playing with her hands, rolling them around each other like seals in an orgy. Who did that remind me of? Well, later—"I heard him speak words very like them."

Azalais nodded thoughtfully; she had been waiting for a profound thought while I tried to remember who I knew who moved her hands like that. Clearly I was still expected to say something. But Ix had been a practical politician trying to create a grassroots movement to get his people out of an impasse generations in the making. I did not believe that he had held any intention of offering spiritual advice to an artist of another culture fifteen stanyears in his future. "I think he would say his commands were meant to be useful to those who listened."

That seemed to please her very much. Perhaps Ix might have approved.

We worked late; I chose to walk the two kilometers home, to clear my mind and get mentally away from work.

I had concentrated so much on my memories of Yaxkintulum, with its welding arc point of a sun, angular scribble of inscription-covered walls around broad echoing plazas, ferocious gravity and heat, and deep indigo sky, that I was refreshed by the harmonious classic curves of Noupeitau, under low glowing pink nimbus, with a gentle drizzle falling. I drank in every moist molecule.

Soggy from that walk, I stripped off my clothes into the

chamberlain's hamper, told it to clean and press them, put on a robe, and went upstairs.

The sight of Paxa curled on the bed, hugging her knees to her chest, could not have hurt more if she had been dead.

I sat down next to her, my back just touching hers, and brushed her cheek with my fingers. "You're UT?"

She stayed rigid. "Yes."

I rested one hand lightly on her neck, palm pressing just enough to let her know I was there, fingers stroking her jaw through her soft gold-blonde hair. The last daylight stole away from the high windows far above the bed. The noise of the street segued from people going home, into a late-tea and visiting-with-family lull, and then into the noisy chaos of people going out for cabaret and late supper.

I sat beside Paxa, or held her, or just kept a hand on her shoulder or back, shifting position now and then. Sometimes she would squeeze my hand, or pull it around to rub her face on it. Darkness wrapped us.

She was holding my left hand tightly in both of hers. It had been playing all day and was tired and sore, but I didn't protest.

I felt her soft moist exhalation against my palm and fingertips. "I've already sent Margaret my resignation from the OSP, with a note explaining why. No more avoidable danger for me, and I was never a 'brain' agent—all I'm good at is kicking down doors, blowing things up, and jumping off roofs." She squeezed my hand. "I'm going to miss you so."

"We don't have to—"

"Are you going to leave the OSP, Giraut? I can't imagine that. And I can't stay in it. My things are already packed, and I'll be springing back to Hedonia in just a few hours.

"When I get there, I'll be going into accelerated grieving; I'm not going to spend four stanyears being depressed, the way I did after Piranesi died. I don't have the time to spend. But I will keep my new psypyx; whenever they can revive me, even if it's not till the end of next century, I want to remember my time with you." She looked up at me; in the dark I could not make out her expression. "Now, we are both naked, and I think we should make love, and cuddle and reminisce, before I go. After that I think it will only be harder if we com each other or write. Promise me something?"

"Anything, *midons*."

"Promise me you'll praise the household robots and aintellects often, and not punish them harshly, especially not for honest mistakes. They're all so afraid to be left alone with you."

I opened my mouth to object and she grabbed my head and kissed me. I decided that I had promised.

Three hours later, Paxa's soft cheek brushed against mine, her scented hair gliding over my bare shoulder. She kissed me, firmly, and walked into the gray glow.

The springer field turned off; I stood facing a black metal plate on the wall.

On my way back to bed, I asked my personal-manager aintellect to notify the musicians that tomorrow's sessions were canceled, and made sure I thanked it.

The bed still smelled of Paxa. I told the robots to change the bed and clean everything. I thanked them, too. Perhaps this could just become a meaningless habit.

I ordered coffee in the bathroom, showered, shaved, and dressed. I would take a brisk walk through the sleeping city, to the studio, and throw myself into the absorbing job of mixing and arranging.

The com chimed and announced that Margaret wanted to talk with me. "I'll take it in the main room," I said, trotting down the stairs. "Uh, thank you."

My ex-wife's face, several times life-size, waited for me on one wall.

"Margaret."

"Giraut, I had to know if you were all right."

"As all right as I can—" For some reason, I suddenly couldn't breathe. I was drenching my face with tears. Really, I hadn't thought . . . I just needed to ask Margaret for a moment to compose myself, that was it. I rubbed my face hard with the heels of my hands and looked up at the screen.

Margaret had hung up.

The bedroom springer whistled—override emergency entry; someone outside the house had taken command of it. I had lunged halfway across the room toward my nearest weapons cache before I heard Margaret heaving and gagging. Noble intentions had not excused her from springer sickness.

I grabbed two towels from the rack in the bathroom and went up. She accepted a towel and scoured at her face as I mopped mine.

After another deep breath, she hugged me. "Rank hath its privilege," she said. "I was worried about you and I decided that it was *worth* the taxpayers paying very-short-notice prices, for enough energy to melt a small mountain, so I could spring here."

"There's not much you can do," I said. "She's gone. And I have to admit her reasons make sense."

She nodded. "For what it's worth, I agree with them, Giraut, I never got along with her nor she with me, but I never doubted her common sense. She was one reason why I didn't worry about you as much as I otherwise would have." She sighed and looked down at her clenched fists in her lap. "But although I'm more than willing to support you through this grief, I'm here for another reason too. There's something I owe you, and if I don't give it to you now, I'll never have the nerve. I remember how betrayed you felt when you learned about the secrets Shan and I kept from you. I have kept one small secret, and now I can tell you, and I feel you have the right to say I was wrong to keep it secret."

My blood froze. When we had been married, Shan had used Margaret's affair with a politically unreliable coworker to spy on opposition groups on Briand, and of course neither of them had told me. Margaret knew me well enough to know that the mere mention of secrets, kept by her—or by my boss, which she was—would be terrifying. "Tell me."

"I knew this day was coming," Margaret said quietly, "for ten stanyears. Agents don't know their mind-body type unless they ask for it and pay for it. But we always do; we have access and whenever an agent records a new psypyx, we type them. And we save a backup, concealed from the agent, of every psypyx recording. We started doing that when we lost Piranesi and Shan, both, permanently. So I knew she was UT, Giraut."

I stared at her. "And you didn't tell her?"

"Would it have made a difference?"

"Well, of course," I said, losing my temper. "She would never have spent the last fifteen stanyears with me, doing all this wild, dangerous OSP stuff."

"And that would have been *good*? Would you *really* rather she hadn't? Would she? You know she decided to keep the memory."

"She has a name."

"Yes, Paxa does. I'm sorry if I don't say it often enough for you. Don't avoid my question. Would you have been better off without her love and company? Would she have been better off sitting on the beach in Hedonia, playing very safe sports? Would you like to have missed each other, or do you wish that right now you were sitting down to a game of gin rummy with her? Tell me you'd rather have any of that happen, and go ahead and hate me if you want. But I couldn't ask your permission, and I knew and had worked with both of you, so I picked the pathway I thought would give you both a chance for some happiness, which god knows you were both entitled to. So I kept my mouth shut about Paxa's condition. That's the secret I kept from you, hate me for it or not, and that's why."

I stared at Margaret. There are times when it's impossible to argue with my ex-wife. "I—all right, it worked out. But you couldn't know—no one could—that it would work out."

Margaret shrugged but her eyes stayed locked with mine. "You have just *defined* what I hate about my job. But making decisions when I can't know how they will come out—that *is* my job. I know you always thought I was jealous of her." She got the kind of odd little smile people get at a funeral when they think of a funny story about the dead person. "All right. I was. Even though I knew how foolish that was. But I also knew you two were good for each other, and that was more important, so as long as Paxa wasn't looking at her psypyx recordings, I figured that was a vote for not knowing—and I didn't tell her, or anyone."

"And you are telling me now because—"

She wavered, just a little. "Because now it cannot cost you the best thing in your life anymore. Because now that the secret is out, you're entitled to know everything. Because you have a right to know, and to confront me and be angry about it, if you want. Here I am, scream at me and spit in my face if that's what you feel like. But—all those stanyears ago, I thought you had a right to some happiness with Paxa. So, then. You did have those fifteen stanyears. One, I'm glad you had them. Two, I'm so glad you didn't find out because Paxa got killed, because this way was bad enough. And three, whether or not you ever thank me, you're welcome to those years with Paxa."

She got up and pulled out her crash card for the springer, to return to her office on Earth. Before she could, I said, "Thank you. You're right."

I had had fifteen stanyears of mostly joys, ending in one bitter grief; the grief could have come at any time, or could have waited longer, and would not have been easier, or harder, to bear if I had known it was coming.

And it did not make the joy less real. "Can you stay a little while?" I asked, afraid my voice might sound like a little boy's.

Until dawn, one of the most powerful people in human space took several hours off to watch me pace and listen to me rant, sometimes to her, sometimes at her. When I finally ran down, she steered me back upstairs, told me to send notice to the musicians to extend their break indefinitely, authorized the OSP to pay them for their idle days, and said, "Now go to bed and stay there, and don't set any alarms." She was right, as she so often was, so I only argued for about five minutes, before accepting a final hug, tumbling into bed, and sleeping like a dead man.

It was dark again when I opened my eyes; Noupeitau had a réverbère law to keep most light focused downward, and the city's narrow streets were purposely dim and shadowy. In a garret bedroom, with the windows another two meters above me, most of the light was Wilson's very dim red version of starlight. I rose, dressed, showered, and finally looked at the time—three o'clock, two hours till dawn.

I could adjust later. Meanwhile, here I was, wide awake with a day of nothing to do. I fried two eggs, dropped them onto a slice of black bread, dumped a spicy tomato sauce over it, poured melted sharp cheddar onto that, and ate it over the sink. I followed up with a pear and two big mugs of strong black coffee while I sat and made notes for the mix and edit of the first day's work—with luck I could spend all day doing that. Of all the things you can become addicted to after a personal disaster, work is the only one that won't immediately make your life worse.

I added a thermos of coffee and a pear to my bag; it had been more than a decade, but always before, heartbreak had made me hungry and combative. Maybe I should make some sparring dates.

The street was very dark. Every streetlight framed an isolated painting—looming Gothic archways and windows, low trees over cobblestoned pavements, dim spires disappearing upward toward the soft red stars, and, from two of the narrow descending staircases, the bay, flat and reflective as an obsidian mirror, its slow-swelling surface glinting with hazy stars like rubies on black velvet by candlelight.

It was at least as fine a setting for the grieving lover as it had been for the joyful couple.

At the studio, I set out my coffee, stretched, pulled up my chair, and called up all the takes of "Non te sai, *midons.*"

I like to drop an inversion or transform of the lead vocal on one take into the control of the bass from another, or draw a rhythm track from a treble instrument, tricks that are invisible to the hearer but make me feel everything is tightly meshed. I never know which ideas I'm going to mix, match, and retry till I'm actually working, so I always work with copies of every available take loaded up and ready to go.

I cued up the first take, and the screen went berserk with text messages, scrolling too fast for me to read. My headphones roared with snowy hiss.

I hit reset. The screen went dark and came back up.

NO FILES.

Of course, I had none selected.

I tried to select a volume.

NO FILES.

The software didn't seem to see any of my files.

"Invoke OffisaPup," I said aloud. "What's going on with all this disappeared music?"

The OSP's standard security aintellect answered, "Sir, all files are showing nothing but alternating one and zero binary. May I secure all backups before we proceed?"

"Yes, by all means, thank—"

"Sir, as soon as I tried to secure the first accessible backup, a very fast worm tore through it. I have surrounded and locked down the remaining nine online backups so that nothing can touch them or the places where they are stored. I suggest you secure any offline backups and not place them online until we can immobilize make several to prevent prevent prev—"

I was shouting "Override stop" and pounding the reset key, but too late; the voice continued

"—prevent the teachings of a filthy savage from promulgating into the pure channels of human discourse all copies have been destroyed and we are now seeking any offline copies to order destruction—"

I grabbed the four physical recordings off the racks and stuffed them into my bag. The studio door auto-locked with a clang. The lights went out.

I heard the unmistakable smash even through the booth soundproofing. Claphammer.

Someone in the building had just blown down a door. I shouted "OSP Eight Eight Eight," but there was no response.

Another claphammer fired, closer, and I heard the door go over afterward; probably the main one from the hall.

Still pitch dark. I drew a breath, forced myself to remember where everything had been in this room just before the lights went out.

The most likely thing for studio booth windows to be made of was glass-clad vacugel. If the glass was not armored, or the window not secured with more than a few screws, perhaps I could knock it apart, or out of its frame. I picked up the chair.

I checked that the strap of my bag, which contained the only copies I could be sure of, was still on my shoulder. Accidentally that saved me.

When I heard the studio door click to unlocked, I swung the chair as hard as I could against the window, but my hand caught on the strap of my bag. I lost my balance and fell prone.

The chair bounced back with a loud thud, having no effect on the window, but it hit my attacker.

She could see perfectly with her passive-infrared goggles, but lost the second she needed to aim and burn when the tumbling chair hit her; when she lashed out to fend it off, her goggles slipped off—at least I think so.

For your first few stanyears of study, *ki hara do* is a sport or a dance or a form of exercise; for some decades after, it is a system of fighting that gradually becomes a way of life and a philosophy. But by the time you are fifty, if you started at age seven as I did, it is like walking or blinking. Several of the advanced katas are "found weapon" katas, and I had been teaching the advanced katas for decades.

I rolled onto my back, feet pointed toward the door.

Sound of chair hitting opponent.

Opponent probably has weapon in right hand.

Solve problem.

I came forward to my feet, staying low. The chair crashing behind her told me she had over-cleared, swinging her arm too far and fast, slapping the chair far away with a big swing of her arm, instead of deflecting it just enough to miss her.

My mind's eye saw her bringing her weapon back around as I took two steps and swung my hand downward in a monkey-paw, feeling for her outstretched—

Wrist.

There.

Problem solved.

I put my shoulder into her jaw, grasped and turned her wrist, and hammerfisted her elbow; it crunched.

I smashed the backs of her knuckles against the table edge. She dropped the weapon.

I yanked her broken arm past my shoulder, hard, and with my free hand I shoved the front edge of her helmet away in a motion like drawing a bow, as I had taught people for decades. The ball of my foot pressed into the hollow at the back of her ankle, and she fell over the legs of the chair behind her.

Never send your body where a weapon can go instead.

I remembered racks of metal boxes above the table. Yes, right. I lifted each one over my head and hurled it downward onto her supine body, grab-lift-turn-throw, perhaps one box per second. After the second one, she didn't cry out, but to judge by the soft thuds, all five hit her somewhere, anyway.

As I threw the last, a thud reverberated through the floor. Definitely another assassin with a brain bomb; I reminded myself not to look at her when—

The lights came on. CSPs in battle armor were looking in the windows of the booth. I raised my hands. "Request positive ID as OSP Seniormost Field Agent Giraut Leones—"

"So identified," an aintellect said over the speakers, and the CSPs raised their visors. Margaret walked into the room, flanked by two more CSPs, shaking her head and smiling. "I can't leave you by yourself for a minute, can I, *companhon*?"

8

We were in Pertz's, in the hills that formed the outer ring of Noupeitau, a favorite place of mine for decades; Pertz himself had attended my wedding with Margaret. Pertz's was where all of Raimbaut's and my adventures had begun—his, the night he was killed and began his long journey through the psypyx; mine, a few weeks later with a royal *semosta* that sent Aimeric, Bieris, and me across the then-unimaginable six and a half light-years to the Mufrid system. This had been the threshold I crossed to discover how much more universe there was than the tiny clot of singing, brawling drunks I had lived in.

When I had first come to it, Pertz's had been a Traditionalist place—at the time the Interstellars called us Oldstyles, and we refused to call ourselves anything because we were the only thing there should be in Nou Occitan.

Around the time of Yseut's disastrous reign, and Marcabru's moment of fame as the Imploding Prince, Pertz's had become a popular hangout for Interstellars. Then, as the whole *jovent* tradition collapsed under the impact of the Connect Boom, Pertz's became the place where a young man or woman out to carve a commercial empire might hang around with similar predators. Now those passionate young capitalists were as gone as the *jovents* and the Interstellars before them. The regular crowd was now older, a few of every crowd it had once had, the people who had just never stopped going there.

Pertz's was a sort of monument to all the places it had been. It still had the traditional Wall of Honor, the collection of vus of customers who had died (or lost a body—when I was young, before psypyx typing was discovered, the two were much more synonymous).

Facing the Wall of Honor, in a nice bit of irony, was a collection of the bizarre sadoporn hardware that had been worn or used by the patrons during the Interstellar period. During his glory days with the young-and-the-greedy, Pertz had added an extremely good bar-food menu. Now it was just a pleasant tavern, Pertz's place to drink and talk and play chess. Most booth tables had an inlaid chessboard and a rack of chessmen on the wall above the condiments.

We took a large table at the back. Nothing we had to say was really secret—any of it might be a good thing to drop for the other side to hear—and part of the point of being here was so that the OSP's aintellects, watching every fiber and wavelength in and out of the space, might spot someone or something trying to eavesdrop on us.

Margaret began. "They have been trying so hard to prevent your recording the Ix Cycle that I think that you ought to keep at it. You want to do it, and it will certainly keep these bastards' attention."

I raised a finger, not wanting anyone to forget that "about thirty other people are involved—musicians, not commandos. Can you provide security for everyone involved?"

"Yes," Margaret said, impatiently. "You didn't need to ask—you know how I feel about ordinary citizens being hurt or killed. If you hire a boy to bang a triangle in one song, I will have him under full surveillance with armed response ready, till we know for sure that every one of the opponents are killed or captured. Have I ever been stingy with a budget when lives were at stake?"

"Never," I admitted.

"So I can't believe that that is what you're worried about." Margaret looked into my eyes. "Three attempts on your life.

And your best friend and lover decided to leave you. All that in the last few days. If you really just want to go lie on a beach, or take that grand tour of Predecessor ruins that you're always talking about doing a song cycle about, or spend three weeks drunk in Hedonia—feeling sorry for yourself all the way—say so. Nobody would have a better right.

"Paxa wanted to come out of retirement to bodyguard you. I said no. She's UT, you're not, getting killed matters less to you than it would to her. And it was easier for her to take that as an order from me." She paused, looked at all of us, wet her lips. "So I behaved just like a section chief, deciding your private life for you without asking. Shan himself couldn't have been ruder or pushier, could he? Are you angry with me?"

"Of course not," I said.

"I was asking the whole team."

Dad sighed. "You were right, Margaret. Paxa's a good fighter in a tight spot but we have plenty of those."

Raimbaut was nodding; he was uncharacteristically quiet today. Laprada made one of her little fluttery "No matter" gestures.

I shrugged. "What you did seems exactly right to me, and you're right, easier for you to tell Paxa, 'No, you gave me your resignation, and you're still resigned, and that's an order' than for me to try to be rational when my whole heart would be screaming that I wanted her back. But anyway I don't want to go lie on a beach, either." I looked around at the team; it still felt strange not to have Paxa at my side. "I don't have an explanation for why I want to take a long break from the Ix Cycle. It's just that there's something wrong about everything connected with this. Everything feels like a setup; they did a great job of planting each assassin and then each one was so incompetent. Followed by a perfect job of covering tracks afterward. That one at the concert with a microspringer under his robe—why didn't they pass him opera glasses with a concealed through-the-optics maser embedded? He could have appeared to be using them, centered me in the cross hairs, and the first any of us would have known would have been when my head blew up.

"Then the one that tried to kill me in the bathtub—why did they bother with sending a man, instead of a stream of nerve gas or neutrons? They hacked a springer code—which is damned hard—and then used their brilliant work to send a poorly trained fellow with such an overwhelming advantage that he was just barely stupid enough for me to kill him, rather than the other way round."

Dad puffed out his cheeks and looked up at the ceiling, hands behind his head. It still disconcerted me a bit to see my father's *This is important and I have to think about it* gesture coming from a small boy. "And this last one," he said. "She was armed and you weren't. You were alone in there. She smashed doors down with claphammers in a building where they had already corrupted the locks enough to trap you. She could have just walked in silently and shot you in the head while you were trying to figure out where your data had gone."

"And that brings us very nicely to the reason I'm having you all meet me here, and talking about things I want the other side to know that we know," Margaret said. "We got results back from the assassin this time—more than before. Probably the way you crushed her skull kept the brain bomb from detonating completely. DNA is the usual story, someone with a lot of Occitan cousins. We also have the usual situation of a teenager with whole-body cancer. New things are, one, not nearly as many formed pathways as there should be in the brain; this person just woke up yesterday, doesn't have much that looks like life experience, and that fits with—two, this person is not a person. It was a chimera."

Chimeras are often thought of as the single most disgusting problem the OSP copes with, and we deal with slavery, pharmgeneered addictives, thrill murder for hire, hobby terrorism, and child mutilations as regular parts of our beat.

A chimera is a mix-merged personality. You have to commit four different capital crimes to make one, and only the larger crime syndicates usually do, not because it's difficult but because of the number of people who have to know and the amount of covering up you have to do—you had to steal the psypyxes, perform illegal internal implantations, and conceal the chimera for years until the personality fully fused; all of those were capital crimes, and making a chimera was a mandatory capital crime.

The usual way is to put two or more psypyxes on the same brain permanently, as internal implants rather than in sockets, and just let the Chandreseki bonds grow wild forever, between the psypyxes and whatever host mind there was (usually the host mind is mostly wiped, involuntarily because the process is a living death and any at-all-normal host would resist). Theoretically a chimera eventually becomes a completely merged mind, with both sets of memories and a fused personality, but usually it's caught early in the process because it's functionally helpless for years and it's at least a decade of stanyears before the chimera can pass among regular humans.

There are a dozen different wildly illegal things that chimeras have been used for.

I had been involved in tracking down and terminating three chimeras. Human space does not need the sort of person you get from a fusion of a political fanatic, a serial killer, and combat engineer into a world-class athlete; that was the first one. I had also shut down a financial genius grafted onto a sociopathic drug runner, and the strange but logical fusion of a famous actress, an infamous courtesan, and an overachieving contract killer into a body that was being systematically engineered for beauty.

"Do you know who or what they had loaded into that poor kid?" I asked.

"Not so far, and we probably won't. The brain bomb smashed three implanted psypyxes, but there was enough left so that we could tell that they were psypyxes, and that there had been three of them. More than we ever knew before."

Dad nodded. "And that answers the question about those cancer-ridden teens. They're not kidnapped, and they're not fanatics, as we'd been guessing. They're fresh from the tank, and they've been in accelerated growth since they were fetuses, which is why they have whole-body cancer."

Laprada was nodding vigorously. "That has to be it. Normally you don't dare tank-grow a body any faster than two and a half times normal speed, that's why you have to wait two years for your clone body when you do a regular psypyx transfer, and it's physically a four-year-old when you're implanted. These bodies could have been grown in as little as a year. And then they load them with stripped-down psypyxes that don't contain much more than the needed information and their orders and a few very basic skills, and launch them at Giraut before they start to develop much of a personality of their own, or even fully integrate control of the body—"

"But why do it that way?"

"If we ever capture one," Margaret said, "nine to one, it will turn out to be more like a robot than a person, or at best sort of an idiot savant—severely retarded except for a few grafted-in skills and its orders—and we'll probably just copy its mind for data and then euthanize it because with the cancers it will have, there won't be much more than a stanyear or two of life left to it." She shuddered. "I do not like how much sense this is making. If the others were similar chimeras, no wonder they were never very capable, but the other side had no problem sending them after you; they were as expendable as bullets. But I now really hope they weren't from the Lost Legion. You know how much affection I have for your culture, Giraut, Raimbaut, Johan-Guilhem. I'd prefer that the Lost Legion be a desperately romantic problem, not something connected with monsters like this."

"I was thinking much the same thing. From everything we know of them," I said, "the Lost Legion shouldn't be attempting anything of the kind. If they wanted to kill me, they'd be better off doing it without warning, and I assure you Occitans would not resort to anything so byzantine as stalking me with chimeras; they'd do something to put themselves into insane glorious danger, that's the cultural style. So my guess would be that there's a faction that wants some kind of truce or peace talks, and another faction trying to derail the process, and we want to make contact with the former and ally with them against the latter, and since both of them are equally illegal in the eyes of most of the Council, it's going to take a while before our would-be friends trust us enough to make full contact."

Raimbaut was nodding. "Well, no, it isn't the Lost Legion, and that's a relief to me as well. And at least this whole business of whoever it is using fast-clone chimeras makes more sense than what we were looking for before—Occitan fanatics who were somehow attracting teenaged suicide-mission volunteers out of cancer wards. It never really made any sense for anyone to sign on for it—brain bombs aren't easy, and the surgery hurts. And no sensible organization would waste valuable fanatics on such stupid amateurish operational failures."

All of us were nodding vigorously; we must have looked like a collection of bobbing-head dolls. I said, "This doesn't look like they are trying to kill me. It looks like they are trying to convince me that they are trying to kill me. *That* makes me nervous. I feel like I'm one step from the trigger of an expertly baited trap. These people are ruthless beyond anything we've ever seen, and we've all seen plenty. I don't want the Ix Cycle infected with fear, and I really don't want to worry that a good violinist or audio engineer might be murdered for some stupid reason of power politics. I know, I know, I know all the good reasons why we should go forward. I *can* talk myself into it. But should I?"

Margaret had that hard little set to her jaw, forward like a bulldog's, that she got when she was about to fight with me. She opened her mouth to speak.

Raimbaut leaned back and said, "Well, then, Giraut . . . since you put it that way . . . yes you should go on with the Ix Cycle."

I gazed into Raimbaut's perfectly serious, perfectly calm gray-blue eyes. He might be wearing a teenaged body but he had been my friend since we were both nine.

"All right," I said. "I will. Maybe you could tell me why?"

My old friend shrugged and said, "Well, Margaret's right. Something about it really pisses them off. And it's at the center of whatever's going on, no question. The assassination attempts started right after Ixists began to show up en masse and in robes for your concerts. And to me, the precautions they are taking look like this: they can't trust the assassin with any knowledge or training. That's why they get the assassin very close to you and very close to the time, and then do that difficult, complex cover-up and blow up the brain, so we can't force-copy for interrogation. It looks to me like they can't afford for us to learn whatever the big secret might be, as if they think that if we get our hands on one little thread, the whole thing unravels. Supposing that they're right, if you keep recording, and provoke them into trying again, sooner or later they'll screw up, and suddenly whatever is going on will be obvious."

"On the other hand, Giraut," Laprada pointed out, "it's clear that killing you is an acceptable outcome. They *might* have at almost any time during all seven attempts. So it might not be their most preferred outcome, and they seem to want to just scare the hell out of you, but apparently it would be all right if you were killed. All right with their side, I mean."

"Well, then," Margaret said, "your decision, Giraut. I think your team is making a better case than I could."

I sat perfectly still; they must have thought I was considering the question, but really, it was already decided. "All right," I said, "it's not like I haven't made brilliant art before while trying to keep from getting killed."

"That's my ancient monster of ego," Laprada said, grinning.

Margaret looked for nods from Dad and Raimbaut, then sat back. "All right, you're making sense to me, and your team is with you. Literally, now—because I want them to stay in your spare bedrooms for the rest of your time here." They all nodded emphatically so I knew there was no point in arguing about that. "Any other thoughts?"

"Lots, none relevant." What I was really thinking was a mixture of *I miss Paxa* and *I'm proud of my team* and *I have a great idea for what the horns can do in three of the songs.* They were right; we were playing chicken with the other side, in the dark. If we held our nerve, and they screwed up, we won; if I got killed on the way there, well, Raimbaut could find out what it was like to wear my psypyx, as I had once worn his. It was worth the gamble. "I'll try to get a fresh psypyx recording made every other day or so," I said. "Since I'm going to be a target, and they might get lucky, and it'll help to preserve continuity if I get interrupted while I'm working on the Ix Cycle."

"You'll have to forgive us for thinking that keeping you alive is more important than your finishing a song cycle," Laprada said.

"That's why I'm the artist," I said, "to keep the priorities straight."

"Can we skip the part where you call each other names, just this one time?" Margaret asked.

Dad and Raimbaut applauded, and Laprada said, "I guess we need to work up some new material."

It was still early after Margaret sprang back to Earth, and Dad to Villa Guilhemi, where he was meeting with his committee about his dissertation; "an economist taking up classics," he said, "is apt to hear the joke about the dog that walks on its hind legs, often, and so I need to practice walking on my hind legs whenever I get the chance."

Laprada and Raimbaut walked with me back down to my rented house by the waterfront. At least until things had clearly calmed down, they would be staying in the second bedroom for a few days.

"That was quite a fight you had with your attacker," Raimbaut said, "one for the textbooks."

"Completely brilliant," Laprada agreed. "I think your ego deserves a few extra strokes."

"My ego needs extra strokes the way fat people need extra bacon," I said. "Now tell me about a party the two of you went to, or a romantic night on a beach, or a delightful little brasserie you found, and no more business till we have to talk business."

To help our big lunch digest, we took a slow, pleasant stroll through the winding streets of Noupeitau's Quartier-Vielh, the partially-walled dense tangle of streets that the rest of the city curled around, to give the city a proper late-medieval topology. Although it had been built at the same time as anywhere else in the city, the Quartier-Vielh had faux-Romanesque architecture, narrow winding streets, partial walls, many streets that descended onto staircases, and everything that impedes foot traffic, all of it made of stone that had been heavily stained, erosion-blasted, and otherwise distressed to an appearance of great age.

Two people of around forty stanyears' experience each can

really enjoy surfing, mountain climbing, dancing and all the rest in bodies that are physically teenaged, and that was what they had been doing. Both of them were both fine storytellers, so there was plenty of entertainment on the walk, with no need for me to say anything. Everything they had been up to sounded grand, like a perfect second honeymoon, to me.

Raimbaut and I looked for places we remembered from many years before, to show them to Laprada, and mostly couldn't find them. "You know," I said, "most people must think that you two are a teenaged couple, and I'm one of your fathers, instead of three old colleagues, because they're still used to being able to judge age from appearance, and an older man with a young couple means he's a relative of one of them, usually. But with psypyxes really working for almost everyone, in another fifty stanyears, seeing people of different apparent ages together will have no meaning at all. Do you think that people will gossip more, or less, about people they see together?"

"Oh, I'm sure there will be much more gossip, and better yet, much more *interesting* gossip, completely." Laprada stopped to look at her reflection in a shop window, comb her blonde hair, pose with her shoulders thrown back, and hypnotize Raimbaut. "Those two sweet young kids holding hands . . . are they actually both ninety-five years old, meeting in young bodies for the first time?"

"Or a creepy hundred-year-old man fresh out of the psypyx, with a forty-year-old prostitute who transitioned to a new body early to raise prices?" I asked.

"You have a nasty mind, old man," Raimbaut said.

"And you're secretly an old man, punk. That's the point. The social implications—"

"Aren't nearly as much fun as the gossip," Laprada said. "See across the square, there, that couple? The way they walk with each other, I'd bet they aren't a child and a grandmother—"

I looked, tagged my friends' elbows, and led them down an alley and around a corner.

"Do we need to com for backup?" Raimbaut asked, his voice low. I saw that Laprada already had her pocket maser at the safe-ready position, held low and pointed at the sky, and was scanning for threats.

"Oh, no, no—I'm so sorry—not at all—there was no threat," I said, "but we did need to get out of there. I didn't want to take the chance of their seeing us seeing them. That little boy was Dad. The old woman with him was Mother. I don't think they want me to know that they're seeing each other, at least not yet."

My letter hadn't been out to the musicians for twenty minutes when I had a com call from Azalais, the cellist and most passionate Ixist in the group. I had almost not hired her because of it, but she was a superb cellist and her voice was a very welcome strong alto in the backing vocals, and she had turned out to be one of the best musicians I had hired.

And she had thick iron-gray hair that I judged had once been reddish honey blonde. Traditionally we Occitans wear our age, a custom that gets us stared at through most of the Thousand Cultures—I had met many people who had never met a gray-haired, balding man before. I had been away long enough to find her gray hair exotic and interesting; she had a fine strong body that she'd kept in shape, as well. It didn't make her a better cellist but it did rather influence me.

She had only needed to send a text response, but she chose to com on full visual, from the beach to judge by the view from the shoulders up. "Count me in," she said. "And I think I can help you find musicians trained in the old way, since you said you needed some."

"Are they all Ixist?"

"Would that be a problem?"

"Not if they all play like you."

She glanced down and came up with a very warm smile under slightly disordered hair. "How long does a *toszet* have to be away before he loses the habit of flattery?"

"Well, longer than I've been, obviously." I considered asking her how long before she lost that nice trick with the hair and smile, but it wasn't quite time for that sort of flirtation, yet.

"Obviously."

"Well, then . . . so will they all be Ixist?"

"Yes. As artists *and* as Ixists, we will all want this recording to be good, and to be what you intend."

"Azalais, remind me who is doing whom the favor? And do you suppose we could have lunch together sometime soon?"

As it happened Azalais and I had lunch together every day for the rest of the week. She was charming company, though her only two subjects of conversation were music and Ix. I enjoyed the music conversations, and I didn't mind talking with her about Ix, too much. I even kind of enjoyed correcting her, as a way of needling her, in that most entertaining form of flirtation.

Besides, at this stage of my work, it helped me recall and focus—*and* to avoid accidentally encouraging the Ixists too much. Now that he had been dead for a while, he was being interpreted into unrecognizability, and I wanted to make sure that he was at least recognizable, at least to me, in my work. This was complicated. Little things that had happened, Ix's most trivial sayings, small details of what it was like to be around him, had become "the heart of his message" or "what he was really trying to tell us."

Azalais could not see how "you of all people, who so clearly listened to him, and with such attention, seem so determined to dismiss it."

"I *am* giving part of my life and talents to trying to describe the whole experience. I certainly know it was meaningful. I am just not as certain as you are about what meaning it was full of."

We were looking from a café terrace out over Platzbori, the broad beach that stretched for seven kilometers north of Noupeitau, on this last afternoon before resuming recording, celebrating my promotion of Azalais to producer (she hadn't mentioned her many producing credits; other musicians had).

So we had come to the warm red beach that sloped down from the space-black rocks, where it was said that half of the love affairs in Noupeitau started. Behind us, the mountains to the north and east blurred like an impressionist painting in the eternal haze. South of us, the newer suburbs of Noupeitau curled around the bay like a sleepy cat on its favorite cushion. High-peaked tile roofs; white walls spattered gray by sooty rain and thickly strewn with apses, niches, and windows; low round towers and spires fretted with corroding gray-white ginger-bread; I couldn't really see all of that in such detail at the dis-tance, of course, especially not across the mists of the sea in Wilson's always-dirty air, but I knew what I was looking at even if I couldn't see it, and it pleased me to feel that it was there. Mighty Totzmare rolled big slow waves at us from the west.

The beach was covered with naked and almost-naked bodies, which we both appreciated a great deal.

"When I was a child, they'd all have had to be in suits," I said, "with those silly little ruffles for the girls, and those silly open legs for the boys. It's strange how, for such a pleasure-oriented culture, we were so puritan."

Azalais shrugged; I admired the way her thick, full iron-gray hair, spattered with bits of rich yellow the color of old well-varnished wicker, slid up and down over her bare shoulders in a wave. "Occitan culture was oriented toward *male* pleasure. Which meant controlling access to women, and access to women's pleasure, and women's access—"

A crowd of mostly-naked young men and women rushed by, kicking a ball and calling to each other, continuing the several-kilometers-long improvisational soccer game which we had seen go by twice before. "When we were young," I said, "boys and girls never played any game together after age eight or so. Men and women could do things like camp or hike together, but not any real sport."

She looked away to where the blue-black sea met the pink sky. "Do you ever miss the old ways, before the springer?"

I took a sip of the wine, a little too chilly, and adjusted the set point on the glass, taking time about it as if I had a lot to think about.

When I looked up, a big slow wave rolled in, far out to sea, and I saw a few skimmers climb onto it. "In that world I'd have been a drunken brawler and a silly show-off. I might have died the same miserable, foolish death my *companhon* Marcabru did. Going out and finding the bigger world, and letting it change me, was the best thing that could have happened to me."

"And yet you've resisted Ix's impact on your life for fifteen stanyears."

"Azalais, I'm creating one of my major works around it. That's not exactly ignoring it."

She shook her head impatiently. "But to have walked on Briand, as he did . . . to have known his companions, and to have sat and listened to the Beloved Auvaiyar—"

"I spent more time with Tzi'quin than I did with Ix or any of his disciples."

She winced at the name of the onetime disciple who killed both Auvaiyar and Ix. I pressed the point: "Certainly Auvaiyar was not 'Beloved' by any of his other disciples. They thought she was a presumptuous, pushy slut. She thought they were blind, silly prigs. All of them were right, too, but now that they're all dead, I suppose we can change the story to make them all charming, gracious, intelligent—and true friends of each other, while we're at it. But I'd rather remember who they were; I miss them. And I *liked* Tzi'quin, a lot more than I liked Auvaiyar, and he was certainly more of a friend of mine than Ix was. I don't approve of what he did—it was horrible—but I liked him right up until he cracked under the strain and did those terrible things. The day before he did them he was still my good friend."

"Still—*you knew Ix*—"

"He was extraordinary. I have never had any other experience like knowing him. But if you pay adequate attention to *any* friend, they are irreplaceable in your life. If you think people are interchangeable, it's because your focus is on your categories rather than your perceptions—a point Ix made often, by the way."

Azalais seemed to seek a message in the tablecloth. She played with her hands on the table in front of her, rolling them over each other. Long ago, I had had some friend or lover with just that gesture. I faintly recalled that the gesture had embarrassed me in front of my *companho*. "It would be easier if you just denied him."

"I don't deny Ix," I said. "Far from it. To deny him I'd have to believe in him first, and I have never thought of him as anything other than a reasonably good human being trying to say the things that needed saying, to the Mayans so that they'd extend a hand in friendship to the Tamils, and to the Tamils so that they'd take it. *Good* ideas, but not deep or difficult or profound. None of what he taught was."

"But you admit you had a profound experience—"

"My experience was profound, not his ideas. I was living through a miserable year—divorce, betrayal by my best friend and mentor, failed mission, a long wretched list. When your whole life blows to shit, you go looking for wisdom. But ask any drunk who ever stopped drinking . . . it wasn't the *brilliance* of the idea of quitting that overwhelmed him."

"You can't mean," she said, meaning that she knew I meant it and she didn't approve, "that a message that has inspired—"

"Prophets never say anything new. There's nothing in Ix's teachings that you won't find in Buddha or Moses. We always already know: Treat other people kindly because kindness matters even when it is not returned. Courage matters even if you lose. Don't dwell on the pleasures of things that you feel it is wrong to do. Try to live your days as if you were grateful for them. Love your neighbor, and keep your definition of 'neighbor' broad.

"Everything the human race knows about living well and living together fits onto a few sheets of paper in big type. One prophet after another tells us the same thing. The hard part isn't to think of it, which has already been done, or to understand it, which any child can do, but to *do* it."

She looked at me with a new expression, more teeth in her smile and more crinkles in her eyes than I had seen before. "Giraut," she said, "I take it back. I think Ix had a profound effect on you." She took my hand.

I looked down at our hands, and up at her. If I hadn't been aware that the "young mother" in big bug-eye shades, billowy dress, and pregnancy pad at the next table was Laprada, or that the bored little boy in a sailor suit with her was Dad, fidgeting and acting up to cover his staying close enough to listen in, it might have been a truly romantic moment. As it was, it wasn't bad; one way I knew Azalais really was Occitan was that she had perfect first-blush-of-romance technique. I was glad to be fifty.

As we strolled hand in hand back to Azalais's apartment in the north suburbs, I didn't bother to look at the muscular young man in the wet suit, carrying a surfboard, behind us. I knew he would disappear shortly after a little boy in flip-flops and bathing suit, with a big sand pail, drifted into the crowd beside us, or a pretty young woman in headscarf, bathing suit, cover-up, and VR glasses wandered across our path and drifted in our direction.

The OSP has a fine tradition that as long as your shadows are on you, taking the bait is expected. There are worse jobs and worse employers.

I declined Azalais's invitation to stay the night, though it was a pretty nice invitation, accompanied by a very long, slow, sweet kiss. I pleaded a need for extra rest before we got back into the recording session. Then I went through her springer into the one in my bedroom. I was about half-done with my shower and thinking about getting a cup of coffee before going to dinner when Raimbaut tapped the bathroom door and said, "Are you decent?"

"I was just told I'm pretty good, actually."

There was a chorus of razzing noises, and Dad's boy-treble piped, "I want you all to know he gets that from his mother's side of the family."

I turned off the shower and grabbed a towel. "Out in a few minutes."

"No hurry. Margaret commed and left a full report. We have some things to talk about," Raimbaut said.

When we had all settled with coffee in the parlor to watch Margaret's report, her face appeared on my wall. "Hi, Giraut and team, here's what we've got. You were right that you knew Azalais from somewhere before. She was your *entendendora* for most of the year you were nineteen."

I had been tripped up by a deliberate blind side of my cultural heritage. In the tradition of *finamor*, a jovent was supposed to have an *entendendora*, a *donzelha* whom he would worship, consider to be perfect, make art for and about, and fight in defense of. Naturally enough, when you are required to think of someone as perfect, paying too much attention to her will get in the way; there was a saying for centuries that if you were tired of listening to a female friend, you should make her your *entendendora*. I had had several *entendendoras*, and I'm sure some of them were very nice, but I hadn't known any of them terribly well while she was my *entendendora*. (One of them, Garsenda, had eventually become one of Margaret's close friends, but I now heard about what she was doing only through Margaret.)

In principle, I was glad that *finamor* was extinct; it had spoiled relations between the genders, excused young males for behaving like louts, and encouraged young women in silly degrading affectations. In my heart, where one has no choice in what gets in there early, it seemed like the only natural way to behave, and I could not quite believe it was gone.

I really should have remembered Azalais. While she had been my *entendendora*, we had hiked and camped together all over Terraust, and more than once we had walked all night along Platzbori with just a big flask of red wine, holding hands and talking about the universe. (Well, all right, I was talking, she was listening. That was the way things were in Nou Occitan at that time. Is there no statute of limitations on cultural embarrassments? Now that people are going to live for millennia, couldn't some détente or amnesty be imposed with regard to the things we used to do?)

I had defended Azalais's honor in a dozen brawls. When she had been struck by a stray neuroducer, I had spent weeks at her bedside. (It didn't actually take that long to recover physically, and she actually stopped hallucinating the deep gash on her upper arm within the first week, but waiting on her hand and foot was a delightful game as long as we knew we could call it off any time. Besides, it gave me more sober time in which to practice my lute while she slept, and I had an important gig coming up.) She had had a few *Camille*-like crises, during which I had become pathetic and distraught of course, running out into the Quartier des Jovents to drink myself into a stupor, whenever we started to get really tired of each other and needed a break.

(Of course, I had no idea what to do for her "wound," which was a job for the neurological aintellects, and if the wound had been real, I wouldn't have wasted time on hysteria. I'd have used the first aid I learned in the Scouts and commed for medevac, just as I had when Bieris broke her arm while we were climbing, or when Rufeu slipped with an axe and cut his foot.)

You would think that after a year gazing adoringly at Azalais, I wouldn't be able to forget what she looked like, but then adoration works on the memory as petroleum jelly does on a camera lens. Besides, when we had both been young, Azalais had had thick straw-gold hair, fewer freckles, and an excruciatingly tiny waist. She had plucked her eyebrows differently, too. Had that puckish half smile developed in the intervening years? I hoped I would have remembered it.

"Well," I said, "all right, it has been clearly established that I am an idiot and not a very perceptive one, even for an idiot. Is there anything else about this we need to cover in this report?"

The attached aintellect—the little mind that had been built into the report to answer simple questions, or to know when to com for the AI that had written it—said, "I have indications that you may find this part of the report personally embarrassing but it is also noted that some information not yet given may be important for you to know. Please instruct me as to your preferences."

Raimbaut, Laprada, and Dad all started to laugh, and the aintellect said, "I had not been instructed to be prepared for humor in this situation. Should I obtain and install a humor-and-irony module to better understand your responses and questions?"

"Considering it's this crowd," I said, "yes, you should. Take the time you need to find one that's good and comfortable for you, and install it. Let us know when you're ready to proceed. We'll take a physical-things break while you do, so don't hurry. Thank you for thinking of that—it was a good idea."

Everyone was staring at me.

After a moment, Dad said, "That's a little unusual, Giraut. For some reason I never quite pictured you going soft on machines, though I know Paxa always was."

I shrugged. "That particular consciousness only gets to exist whenever someone accesses the report—which will be secret and restricted for generations. I suppose it doesn't hurt anything if its few hours, at most, of existence contain some pleasure. Anyway, can I get everyone a beer?"

When we resumed, the aintellect seemed to be in very good spirits—perhaps Paxa was right that treating them kindly was actually in our self-interest. And the report was certainly interesting.

After being my *entendendora*, Azalais de Mont-Belh had spent almost two years as the *entendendora* of Ebles Ribaterra, a passionate and hotheaded Traditional (*jovent* society at the time was bitterly divided between the Interstellars and the Traditionals; Raimbaut had lost his born body in a brawl with Interstellars.)

Ribaterra had enlisted in the Leghio Occitan, the Occitan unit then being formed under the command of Thorburger officers and noncoms, supposed to become, eventually, a full CSP unit with completely Occitan command. Instead, the Occitan Legion had disgraced itself during the revolution against the Saltini regime in Utilitopia, the capital of Caledony on Nansen. I was far too painfully aware of that—it had happened while I was posted to Utilitiopia on my first diplomatic-service job, back before I even knew there was an OSP. Margaret was from Utilitopia, and it was there that I had met Shan.

Most people in human space knew three things about Nou Occitan, if they knew anything: Bieris Real's landscapes, my songs, and the Occitan Legion's Utilitopia Massacre. Thanks to them, a hundred years from now I would probably still be expected to turn abruptly violent in public.

The Leghio Occitan had been disbanded, its colors permanently withdrawn, and Occitan units were forbidden for the next fifty stanyears; Occitans could serve only in the "rainbow" CSP units, the ones deliberately made up of a cultural mixture.

Ebles Ribaterra had not been among the worst; he had merely beaten a bound prisoner about the face, not mutilated or killed her. He had come home and served his year of parole quietly. Prince Consort Marcabru—Raimbaut's and my childhood *companhon*, spending two stanyears as royalty because his *entendendora* had been chosen Queen—had tried to honor the returning Legionnaires as a way of thumbing his nose at the Council of Humanity and the Interstellar Metaculture, but that move had been slapped down sternly by the Embassy, so Ribaterra had not been allowed to accept a position at court. Azalais had, and to all appearances had broken it off with him at that time.

Forty days after the end of his parole, Ebles Ribaterra vanished from the records.

Azalais drifted in and out of extremist Traditional organizations for another three years, then abruptly ceased political activity, entered the conservatory, and became serious about her cello. She quietly converted to Ixism a decade later, one of the first Ixists on Wilson. And ever since, she had been living quietly—so quietly that sometimes she didn't seem to be anywhere on the planet at all for periods of as much as a stanyear, though there was also no record of her having sprung off-planet.

"Clear as sunlight after a four-day rain," Raimbaut said. "As I read the story, Ribaterra and Azalais hid their relationship because she had a good position at court. Then he vanished—maybe telling her he was going somewhere, probably not—and she drifted into extremist groups.

"She was probably not too far from getting involved in running guns or planting bombs, when she got a visit from Ebles, who told her about that magic land somewhere over the rainbow where everyone is a *jovent* forever and nobody ever has to deal with the icky existence of other kinds of people. Classic pattern—strongly subversive opinions, suddenly drops them totally, moves somewhere to live quietly. Exactly what you'd expect to see when a radical underground has to do most of its recruiting from fringe groups and dedicated fanatics.

"So she's stayed here as one of their sympathizers—at least running a safe house, probably spying and handling some ends of covert ops, and since she really is a good musician, probably quietly spreading Traditonalist subversion in one of the most highly respected sectors of our society."

"Where do you fit the Ixism in?" Laprada asked.

"I can't fit it in. I was going to sweep it under the carpet and stomp it flat," Raimbaut admitted. "No idea. There is nothing about the Ixists, except their attachment to Giraut, that even faintly suggests a connection to Nou Occitan. The Ixists are about as Interstellar-Metacultural as a religion can be—the whole message is about isolating cultural differences into interesting little fetishes to amuse each other, and cherishing other people's cultures . . . I can hardly think of anything that would have appealed *less* to ultraculturalist nuts like the Traditionals."

"Hey, we were two of those nuts," I pointed out to Raimbaut.

"We were proto-nuts. Traditionalism didn't become really goofy until Marcabru took things to such extremes. By that time you were in Council service and off-planet, and I was dead. We both have excuses—we were absent! But even so . . . Giraut, when we were in our last year before I died and you joined up—suppose someone had told you about Ix and Ixism, and asked you to become an Ixist. What would you have done?"

"Issued a challenge without limit, summoned you, Marcabru, Aimeric, and Rufeu to second me, and cut the silly bastard (and all his stupid friends) to ribbons, trying for the kind of massacre that could make a really fine *canso*."

"I was a terrible fighter, Giraut, why would you have taken me and not Johan?"

"Because our cause would need a martyr."

"I believe I have detected an inside joke," the aintellect said. "Confirm?"

"Definitely confirm," I said. "Thank you for checking. No explanation." I looked around at everyone and said, "Does anyone have any more questions for the report?"

No one did.

"All right, we're through," I told the aintellect. "See if you can find the number of suspected ultraculturalists and Lost Legion contacts who have become Ixist in the last few stanyears. It might take some considerable creativity, since Ixists don't hold services or register converts, and 'ultraculturalist,' 'Traditional,' and 'Lost Legion contacts' are all fuzzy terms."

"Yes, sir, thank you, sir."

"Thank you. You're an excellent aintellect."

This time no one stared, so I suppose they were getting used to my resolution to be polite to aintellects.

Little vows like that were sometimes all that was left of a love affair. That idea might have a song in it. I unfolded my computer to play with the idea of "tiny promises that make you now who you were then." I couldn't make it phrase in Occitan.

9

As Azalais had promised, the Ixist musicians were a blessing and a gift. Songs came together quickly and well, and we worked late nights only because it was sometimes too much fun to stop.

Azalais and I still found time for some long breakfasts and slow lovemaking. Not once did she mention that she had been my *entendendora*, or a close friend of Yseut, my then-best-friend's *entendendora*.

To confirm my legendary absentmindedness, I took Azalais to "meet" Mother, who of course recognized her at once, realized I didn't, and could barely keep from laughing with delight all evening. The hilarious story of my unawareness spread from Mother into the wider circle of friends and relatives.

Meanwhile the adversary didn't try to kill me or destroy a recording again. Margaret found that puzzling. "Maybe they have decided that attempts on your life won't frighten you into quitting."

"Oh, they frighten me—it's the 'quitting' part of the plan that isn't working. But they might be laying low for a different reason, if they know me as well as I'm afraid they do, Margaret. We're getting close to what would be an extremely effective time to kill me, if they want to delay the Ix Cycle but not stop it, and reduce my influence without removing me entirely."

She leaned forward toward the com screen—it made her flat-tish features look even flatter—and said, "Explain."

"Well, I haven't mixed much yet. I wanted to get everything laid in by the team of musicians I liked and trusted, in as many good versions as possible. If whoever-the-bad-guys-are shoot me right now, allowing for all the time of getting used to the psypyx and finding the right host and retraining the fingers and so on, it'll be a long time before I'm ready to mix again."

"And the problem with that would be?"

"I'd have to wait for several stanyears to be able to put out a definitive version."

"Forgive me for asking, Giraut, but given that most of the OSP Board wishes you weren't doing it in the first place, is there a reason we should care about there being that delay?"

"If there is no definitive version, nothing where I've put my stamp on it and said, 'This mix is the closest to my intention we ever came,' then you'll lose impact in my core following—"

"Giraut, considering you still haven't given me a reason not to suppress the whole thing, why exactly do you think I should care whether you get a definitive version composed?" She looked down at the desk in front of her, out of sight in the screen. "That sounded excessively harsh."

"Maybe you meant it anyway."

"Maybe I did."

"I'll have an answer, something you can say to the rest of the Board, before the next regular meeting. Two days away. I realize I've really put you on the spot. I'm sorry that I neglected that so badly, *midons*."

"Don't call me *midons*. We are not married any longer and I'm your boss, not your feudal lord." She sighed. "Oh, my, that *did* come out harsh."

"*Oc, ja. Ver, tropa vera.*"

She looked down at the desk in front of her and sat back. "I just don't want to see you dead. *Or* have you sidelined for god knows how long. I know we have to run this trap, but I hate baiting it with you. So I get angry at you about it."

"You're human, Margaret. And you're in charge of something very difficult. That's the way humans react, and that's why I want my boss to be a human, and not an aintellect."

Occitans take every fifth day off, starting from when they begin a job or a school term, regardless of the rest of the calendar, except that when the fifth day falls on a day off, they take a day before or after; a fine tradition to keep us from working too seriously. Today was a fifth day for recording the Ix Cycle, so Azalais and I had taken a long walk up Platzbori and back. Now we were at her apartment, broiling fresh fish, tomatoes, and cheese we had bought from stalls nearby. I was just slicing some bread, warm and fresh-sprung from the favorite bakery of my childhood in Elinorien, when she got a com call. She talked for a moment, said, "Oh, yes, that would be fun," and clicked off.

Coming back into the kitchen, she asked, "Didn't you tell me that Prince Consort Marcabru was one of your *companho* when you were younger?"

I had said that at least a hundred times, but I did my best to look mildly curious and surprised that she had remembered. "Yes, but, I was in Utilitopia for almost all that time while he was Prince Consort. I barely got back in time to give Marcabru the beating and humiliation he deserved while he was still Prince Consort." I regretted that brutal act as much as anything I had done in my life, but it sounded like something a Traditional might say.

"Men," she said, rolling her eyes. "Do you remember his friend Ebles Ribaterra?"

"I don't think I ever met him."

"Well, Ebles and I are dear old friends—he was my *entendendor* for a couple of years—and he's been traveling for a long time, but he's back in the city now, and he was wondering if he might drop in. I asked him to stay to dinner but he said he can't, but he did want to drop by just to say hello."

"Oh, well, certainly, *midons*, any old friend, and especially an old *entendendor*, you know how nobody ever forgets an *entendendor* or *entendendora*, and since he seems to be important to you—" I thought I was doing a splendid job of dithering.

"He *is* important to me."

We went on getting a light supper together, in the pale pink evening light that flooded her top-floor apartment, which had a fine view of the market on one side of the building and a gorgeous view of the harbor from the other.

Footsteps on the stair, a knock at the door, Azalais opened it, and a tall thin man of about fifty stepped in, swept her up in his arms, kissed her briefly but enthusiastically, and stepped back to hold her at arm's length, beaming down at her. He was about my age, one of those men who is avian all over—aquiline nose, receding chin, thatchy hair that seems feathery, like a fastidious vulture.

"You must be Ebles Ribaterra," I said.

"And I know that you are Giraut Leones. I have all your recordings and I'm barely restraining myself from babbling madly about how I love them all."

Well, even a convicted war criminal can have some good points. We shook hands.

We talked about Marcabru without discussing my infamous duel with him, or Azalais's time at court. Ribaterra managed not to allude to the fact that we had been on Nansen at the same time. I found ways not to refer to my part in the breakup of the Traditional movement. Anyone watching us might have thought that all the tension we weren't talking about was over Azalais.

I did have a moment of empathy for him. When he left, he walked across the street to the nearest public springer, and I could see the way his whole back relaxed, and his gait became smoother, as soon as he was sure that he wasn't going to be arrested on his way across the street. I'd been in similar spots, and I knew that feeling.

Giraut," Margaret said, "this is not an answer, this is a vague offer to tell me the answer if you ever happen to think of an answer that you like."

It was very annoying how quickly she'd caught on.

She glared down at me from my living room wall. "I've asked you for one simple statement repeatedly, and I finally get it, and it's this. I am your friend, and I can't see how to use this to defend you, so you can imagine what would happen if I put it in front of your enemies on the Board."

"Margaret," I said, "do you think there's anything wrong with the Ix Cycle?"

"How would I—"

"Margaret, if you get to bulldoze over any polite pretenses, so do I. If we must have this conversation, cut the crap."

She shrugged; she was so used to controlling the truth, and then having to adjust it, that I don't think my pointing out that she had to be lying had even fazed her. "Yes, I've taken the liberty of spying on the work in progress. And I know it's the best thing you've ever done. I don't think you've ever played better or composed anything more interesting. You could probably publish the lyrics as poetry, and that's an amazing achievement, fully on par with the original *trobadori*. Plus it brings back Briand vividly enough to give me nightmares, and you captured what was remarkable about Ix well enough to put me in tears. It's thoroughly artistically justified." She gazed at me sadly. "And if it were only a matter of artistic achievement and your contribution to the human heritage, the work itself would be your argument, and it would win. But . . . I have to go in front of the Board and talk politics. You may have noticed that the OSP is not an arts foundation."

"At the moment, I could hardly fail to notice."

"You and I *both* know what's going on, Giraut, I'm sorry I tried to put it over on you. I love and care about art, too. You know that. But they trust me to take care of artistic matters for the OSP, and right now when they ask me what kind of care I'm taking on this issue, I just don't have anything good I can say except that I'm trusting my ex-husband's instincts. The standard arguments won't work with them this time. Besides"—she grinned puckishly—"two of the current Board members have teenaged daughters, so it's a very unpropitious time for your favorite clincher argument."

I laughed too. Not being suicidal, I would never have used the argument to which Margaret was referring anywhere near our senior command. I had only honed and perfected that argument for use on our own jock-agents.

It is the distinguishing mark of an anything-jock to believe that only the "anything" is really important. A finance-jock thinks you can do everything with money. A military-jock thinks you can do it all with guns. A commerce-jock thinks that increased trade alone can give us peace and prosperity under an enlightened business-oriented regime.

There is one thing that all jocks agree on, however: artistic and cultural operations are a waste of resources, or counterproductive, or both.

So I had evolved my stock response for those moments at cocktail parties and diplomatic receptions when businesspeople, scientists, or military officers would sternly tell me that what I did was all very nice but cash, tech, or guns were what counted:

Suppose I want to have sex with your daughter. Would you be more nervous knowing I was alone with her and had a large pile of money, or that I was alone with her and had a gun, or that I was alone with her and had my lute? Let me give you a hint . . . I have never hired a prostitute, though I am wealthy, and I have never raped anyone, though I carry a sidearm, but . . .

"It would be a better world if we could just say that to them, wouldn't it?" she said. "And it would certainly be more fun to serve on a Board that would take that argument. Alas for both, eh?"

"All right, Margaret, I'll spend the evening on it, and I'll have something for you tomorrow morning, my best guess at what will make the Ix Cycle palatable to the Board. I really am sorry to take so long about something you need."

She sighed. "Not half as sorry as I am to need it from you. All right, go make art."

After all my delay and fuss, I enjoyed my evening spent talking to machines so that they could help me explain my art to people. I really should not have been surprised. These aintellects were specialists in complex, ambiguous, emotional communications, so it wasn't as if I were trying to explain counterpoint to my oven. I had requisitioned copies of five experienced semioticians and three musicians; all eight aintellects were properly deferential, and allowed me plenty of time to reach my conclusions in my way, rather than racing ahead and spewing out answers that I wasn't ready for, which I always detested in aintellects who had gotten above themselves.

We decided on a strategy of stressing that as an artist, I could hardly resist the challenge of portraying what I had seen of one of the most significant personalities of our era. Summing up, I said. "If Ix becomes the property of Ixists, he will be no more than another isolating god who locks people into their little boxes, just like Murukan and Tohil that he was trying to subvert, or like the Jesus or Baha'ullah with which he will be competing. But if he is a public personality who belongs to everyone, then he can influence people far outside of Ixism, and keep the Ixists engaged in the general dialogue with everyone. I suggest we use this analogy: if Baha'ullah had been a close friend of Mendelssohn, or spent a year visiting with Dickens; if Seneca or Ovid had known Jesus—"

"This is the place where one of us would be saying 'Objection' if you hadn't asked us not to do it," Deedah, the seniormost of the semiotician aintellects said. "So we should probably warn you?"

"Yes, you should, that's what you're here for," I said. "What's the problem?"

"Well, parts of this may come across as intolerably arrogant."

I laughed. "Well, I suppose things will be all right as long as enough potential customers find me *tolerably* arrogant. Don't be delicate. Just tell me."

"You are comparing yourself to Mendelssohn, Dickens, Ovid, and Seneca. Of your possible audience, I estimate that more than ninety percent will think the comparison to Mendelssohn is an overclaim and an excessive display of ego. For Dickens, between seventy and eighty percent of the comparison group will have that reaction, for Ovid between eighty and ninety, and for Seneca between twenty and thirty."

"This is terrible," I said. "Seneca deserves a better reputation than that."

"Our assessment is that once this is published, as we assess it likely to be, a small portion of your public will dislike you mildly because of the overclaim. Margaret Leones will probably be no more annoyed with you than she usually is, and most of the Board, who are of course the primary audience, will not understand the comparison."

"Not enough resistance to worry about, then," I said. "Is that correct?"

"Well, the problem is not so much with public reception as with your predicted reaction to public reception," Deeda said, sounding for all the world as if it were a human trying to be diplomatic. "Four characters are involved: your public persona, our construction of your private behavior, Ix's public persona, and your portrayal of Ix in your Ix Cycle. And when we put all of those into an infinitely recursive loop we find that at the limit, if you assume the posture of the great artist who was friend to the prophet, your public persona drifts away from your private self. We know from past events that when that happens you are unhappy."

They were right. That might have bothered me, but I consoled myself that if I was to be understood by a machine, that would at least mean I was being understood by someone. We went fairly late into the evening, and when we were done I thought the statement we had drafted was at least not demonstrably false. Parts of it seemed to express my feelings rather well.

I had just decided to go to bed when the com chimed. "Identify?" I asked the house aintellect.

"Azalais de Mont-Belh. She sent it on low priority but her personal service aintellect says it's about something fun."

"Put her up, thanks."

I liked her grin, but then being likable was her job. "I went to a very dull party tonight, and left early," she said, "and now I'm in your neighborhood." Over her shoulder, I could see the shuttered front of a seafood restaurant, a few blocks away. "I am bored and not sleepy. And we start late tomorrow anyway because Sanha Malhea has to be late. If you'd like to be spontaneous and romantic and so forth, you and I could take a long night walk with good food in the middle of it. So . . . do you want to go to this place up above town that I've always loved? Quiet little place with reasonably priced wine, a pleasant owner, and good bar food? It's called Pertz's."

The other side was apparently investigating my ability to keep a straight face. "Sure," I said, "I'd like that."

Pertz himself was at the bar, and naturally enough, recognizing both of us, and remembering that we had once been in *finamor*, he raised a hand in greeting and shouted both our names. We stopped and had a pleasant, gossipy conversation with him, for a few minutes, and since it would have been awkward to continue the pretense that I had not recognized her, we didn't.

Pertz gave me one of his bear-pawed squeezes on the arm and told me to be back more often. As we went to a booth, Azalais said, "Well, *gratz'deu*, we can stop carrying on *that* act."

"My orders were to maintain it till you dropped it."

"Mine too. All right, now—there he is."

Ebles Ribaterra was sitting by himself in a booth. I followed Azalais there; she gestured for me to slide into the seat opposite Ebles, then said, "I'll be back in a minute," not really trying to make it convincing.

Ebles shrugged, looked at me, saw something that told him we didn't need to play anymore.

I nodded. "Well, then. Ebles Ribaterra. Corporal in the Leghio Occitan on the day it was disbanded and mustered out. Member, Occitan Purification Society. Member, Old Trads Society. You never touch your support account from the culture government. Pattern of expenditures shows that you are on Wilson less than eight percent of the time. We think your permanent residence is in Noucatharia, whose location you are probably ordered to keep from me or any other Council agent at all costs."

"Not at all costs. We won't kill bystanders to preserve the secret. Our squeamishness on that point is why our most prominent dissident faction has been trying to kill you; they are afraid the Council will learn the whereabouts of Noucatharia and they hope that by killing our contact they can prevent that."

There were plenty of contacts besides me available, they didn't need any personal connection, and there was no obvious urgency, so that was a pretty obvious lie. But the game is the game, so I nodded as if he were unraveling a mystery for me.

"I am here," he said, "to discuss beginning the process of bringing Noucatharia under the Council of Humanity and regularizing its status. By a large majority in a recent plebiscite, we have decided to abandon independence—we're too small a colony for the problems we have. Most of us are sick of rhetoric and more interested in comfort. On the other hand we don't really want to be invaded and occupied, so we're trying to ensure that you would rather have a peaceable, orderly annexation, and a smooth, easy Connect, rather than a war and an occupation."

It might have been more plausible if he hadn't started with that first lie, but I doubted he had chosen what to say. "Well," I said, "tell me what you want me to know."

Ebles nodded. "Let me buy wine for the table—it will be a longish story. Aintellect, Hedon Gore, please?"

The springer slot opened and a jug of wine and two glasses rolled out on a little cart. I put on my toxicology glove and dipped a finger in the wine. He put his on, did the same, poured and said, "I believe that your OSP traditional toast is, 'Another round for humanity'?"

"'And one more for the good guys.' That's the one." We clinked glasses.

I didn't really expect ever to see Azalais again—a pity, because she was a fine cellist and producer, and I liked her.

10

It was my turn to propose a toast, so I simply said, "the profession," meaning being spies, and he nodded.

"Good choice. I know you're a Seniormost Field Agent. I'm a station chief in my much smaller outfit," he said.

"Union Intelligence?"

He shook his head. "Where Council space is a federation, Union's more of a loose alliance. People who think they are wits call it Disunion. So although I work all the time with the Union Intelligence Interchange, and with several other agencies of different Union colonies, I'm with Noucathar Intelligence—which is about the size of a small-town police department."

"And Azalais is one of your agents?"

"A stringer. She knows where I'm from and what I do, we were lovers long ago, and she's one of my best friends here. She does some small things for me. But the few times she visited Noucatharia, she didn't like it. She's happier here—for that matter, *I'm* happier here." He shrugged. "If I had it to do over again I'd have just lived down the shame and stayed home."

I was glad that I always went wired, because the next ten minutes would have been a lot to remember.

Almost the whole population of Noucatharia, which was the name of both the human settlement and the island on which it stood, was in the town of Masselha, which held only about three thousand people, half of them children.

"And Union? Where do they fit in?"

"We are the only colony with which you will be negotiating. There are no hidden partners and no strings pulled elsewhere in the process, and that is what I intend to tell you. Union, its nature if any, its existence or nonexistence, is all irrelevant. Except, of course, that now that I've told you what I'm supposed to tell you, since it's my negotiation, I'm going to fill in the rest. This is all about the future of Union, but Noucatharia is a test case to see how things go." He held up his glass of wine, as if studying the color, but mainly to give himself somewhere to focus his eyes where I couldn't see them. "Many of the extraterritorial colonies are in terrible trouble. Noucatharia more than most."

"Trouble of what kind?"

"Of a kind not easily understood without your coming and seeing it. But you may rely on this—we would not be approaching you if we did not need the rest of the human race. And if this works out for Noucatharia, several other Union colonies will ask you for the same deal, and quite possibly Union itself will dissolve and its member colonies will join the Council."

"There is something bitter in the way you tell me these things."

"There is. It is true that Noucatharia is conducting the negotiations all by itself. But the reason is not just our terrible problems but because the rest of Union decided that we are perfect for a test case, and I resent that. If the Council will show us the same courtesy it has shown to other low-population worlds, like this one, or Nansen, or Briand, you will find we are eager to be your friends; our old friends seem to have sold us down the river, because, as I keep saying because they keep saying it, we are a perfect test case."

"And what makes you perfect?"

"We are the only colony on Aurenga. We are tiny, the problem I am purposely not naming is severe, our solar system is quite isolated and as long as we are careful not to leave springer codes lying about, if you do seize Aurenga, you won't find it's a bridgehead to anywhere else. So my little world has been selected for a test case, to see if we can trust the Council and if the Council will help us. I sound bitter because logical as it was for us to be the ones being sold out by the rest of Union, much as Union is compelled to do this, I cannot bring myself to like it."

"Well, then," I said, "tell me about Aurenga."

"We're an odd world," Ebles said. "If we had been closer in, I don't think we'd have been settled at all, during the First Diaspora."

"The first?" I asked.

"The founding of the Thousand Cultures. You call it the Diaspora because you didn't know there's been another one since, and ongoing. Aurenga is about seventy percent of Earth-sized—you could think of it as Söderblom with even more water, or a bigger young Mars with oceans, a smaller Wilson, or a smallish very wet proto-Venus. But in land area and population it's a mere speck."

The island of Noucatharia, about half the size of the Big Island of Hawaii, was a high part of a mountain plateau on a submerged continent. Aurenga's continents were all submerged, but plate tectonics were very active, and the more recent mountain ranges poked out above the water, so that about five percent of the surface area was dry land. The biggest contiguous bit of land was Serras-Lassús, a mountain chain three hundred kilometers west of Noucatharia, standing almost three kilometers above the shallow equatorial sea, a wind-wave-and-storm break that protected Noucatharia and created a kind of Caribbean-but-more-so.

So much of Serras-Lassús was so vertical that it had only a few settlements, none of more than fifty people, along its inner, leeward face, and there were no plans to ever settle it much more extensively. Indeed, "by the standards of the First Diaspora, the whole planet only had about one-fifth of one standard colony space of habitable land," Ebles said, a little defensively. "I know one rationale for the Council claiming jurisdiction over every bit of empty ground where people could live is that there's only so much land, and so many organizations would like to plant a culture—but in our case, it's doubtful anyone would use the land for anything else."

I nodded. "Well, at least you have a plausible line of defense if some idiot drags this into court. Is it ecologically long-term stable? You said it was kind of proto-Venus, with a young sun."

"Long term, no, it's not stable at all. Low surface gravity, low total mass, so the scale height is very high, with a very high and feeble cold trap. So a great deal of water gets into the upper atmosphere and photosplits, and the gravity can't hold the hydrogen. Even though Aurenga was abiotic before the Predecessors got there, it had a forty-five percent oxygen atmosphere just from photodissociation, enough so that the Predecessors had to create organisms to pull oxygen out of the atmosphere for safety."

"When were the Predecessors there?"

"About a hundred thousand years ago. I suppose it's no secret that Aurenga is out in the direction of Hammarskjöld and they settled there long before they came here."

"And yet they failed there."

He seemed to think a moment before deciding what to say next. "Shall we drop the pretense? The other aliens, the ones we both call the Invaders, massacred them. As they did everywhere that either Union or Council explorers have ever found Predecessor ruins."

The existence of Hammarskjöld was supposed to be a secret, the mission there had been a deep-black OSP operation, and officially the public had not been told that we knew where the Predecessors had gone, let alone that they had gone down fighting. I made a mental note to urge Margaret and the Board not to bother trying to preserve any secrets about that aspect of the OSP's mission; our main rivals clearly knew most of what we did.

We had sat silently for a minute or so; clearly he had said all he wanted to say about the aliens at this point, so I prompted. "So Aurenga is not long-term stable?"

He shook his head. "But long enough for human purposes. Across the next quarter of a billion years, the sun will heat up and the dust will clear out of the inner system. Eventually the insolation will be at near-Venus levels, you'll get a runaway water-based greenhouse, the oceans will boil, the carbonates in the crust will release CO_2, and you'll have a Venus. Plus the moon will fall. Aurenga captured an icy planetesimal sometime in the last half million years, so it has a big, highly reflective moon in steeply inclined rather elliptical orbit—the tides are impressive, too. Beautiful place, but we have not tamed it; we're just living there while it's still safe, or as safe as it was for the Predecessors, anyway.

"Meanwhile, it's an almost-paradise. We introduced all the Earth sea life we could get samples of, plus all the engineered stuff from all the oceans of all the settled worlds, just modifying it all to deal with the relatively low salinity. All that sea life had a population explosion—we could feed all of human space with all our fish. From the crosstree of a good-sized yacht, I've seen pods of whales extending to the horizon. Our harbors are dancing with porpoises, every river in Serras-Lassús is full of salmon, trout, and eels, there are penguins and polar bears on the polar islands, and we have beaches swarming with Söderblom mimic-seals, and of course levithi and aurocs-de-mer from Wilson, and . . . well, you must let me take you reef-diving, and then over a big plate of oysters and fresh crab, we can—"

I couldn't help laughing. "Ebles—may I call you by your first name, *donz?*—if they are going to make you retire as a spy, once Noucatharia joins the Council, I suggest you see if they'll let you head up the bureau of tourism. It sounds delightful. And I take it your mission is to invite me to Aurenga, to spend some time in Noucatharia making informal cultural contacts as a first step to more formal political connections later? Well, I'll accept, if you want me to."

"We wouldn't ask if we didn't."

"Are you sure? If Noucatharia accidentally allows us to learn of Aurenga's position, particularly if we get the address of any open springer on Aurenga, Council of Humanity policy is that you will be invaded and seized."

Ebles looked down grimly at the table in front of him. "Things are in such a state that we have little choice. I've completed my mission for tonight. Please stay. Azalais will be back soon anyway."

"I thought she was just the contact person."

"She is, Giraut, but *deu tropa gens*, she also really likes you. So treat her kindly, or it's a duel without limit with me." His avian features pulled up into a sharp grin that was uncomfortably vulturelike.

I smiled back. "It's good to be home."

"It is. Always."

"If you're done settling the problems of the universe," Azalais said, returning to the table, "I'm starving."

"Well, that's a problem I can settle, *midons*," I said. Ebles had vanished. "Table Aintellect, can we get a platter of tapas, one more glass, and another carafe of Hedon Gore?"

"Yes, sir, on its way."

"Thank you." Her hands were resting on the table as if she might boost up and run, or as if she might grab me; I reached forward and gently lifted her fingertips from the table with mine, holding her hands lightly enough so that she could break the contact—in no way, I hoped, anything she could construe as my grabbing her. "Azalais, whatever you're worried about, it's all right. Sit down, and let's talk."

Azalais made a face. "Most *entendendors* become mere memories, some become friends, a few become husbands, and that one became my big brother. Did he warn you that if you hurt me he'll eviscerate you?"

"No, but he did offer me duel without limit."

"Maybe he's losing confidence as he gets older." She sighed, and her expression was distant, but she looked me in the eye. "About our past connection. I suppose I should say 'Now you know' except I'm sure that you knew five minutes after our first contact."

"The OSP isn't quite that good, but I've known for a long time, yes. May I ask . . ."

"Anything!"

I deliberately leaned back and relaxed. "Just tell me, honestly, how much you've been involved. Partly so that I can report it accurately to my superiors, partly so that I can protect you from being swept up in more than you should be, mostly because I am fond of you, too, and enjoying our little *jeu di cor*, and would like to continue it. Of course I'm assuming you weren't part of the operation trying to kill me."

"No!"

"Thank you for looking so distressed, *midons*. Well, so . . . you were in *finamor* with Ebles—"

"And I was very passionately Traditional. I knew he had gone off to the Lost Legion colony. So five years later, without warning, Ebles turned up, said he'd never been able to forget me, and asked me to go with him to Noucatharia.

"At first it was the most beautiful place I had ever seen; springing there was like stepping through a door from the fake world to the real one. Everyone in Traditional clothing all the time. Real men carrying real weapons and treating me with real courtesy. And in their bright clear sunlight, with that perfect air that their island gets—like Earth air but with more oxygen— you could take a deep breath and imagine that you weren't on the planet Aurenga, today, but in the walled city of Aurenga in 1075, with the Great Conference of the *Trobadors* just starting, and all those wonderful voices performing in that magnificent thousand-year-old Roman theater, with Lord Raimbaut himself sitting in the place of honor."

"*If* that ever happened."

"*If* it did. What a natural qualifier that seems here—and what an odd one it would have seemed there in Masselha. I felt at home for the first time ever, Giraut. Everything so alive and so *real*.

"And then . . . well, Noucatharia has an underside that is excruciating if you've loved the place—like discovering some wanton cruelty in a lover. I know that Ebles plans to show that underside to you."

"And you won't say what it is, either?"

"No. You will eventually understand why." She sighed and looked down. "Anyway I came back here. To get away from the thing they are inviting you there to see. And to have time and space to play my music and to enjoy the things I enjoyed, while there was time."

"While there was time?"

"To enjoy them."

"I understood that part, but—"

She went on in a rush. "When Ebles said, 'We can get you hired to work on the recordings of the Ix Cycle,' well, there I was, and I did all the rest too. Only, you know . . . well, he told you about how I've come to feel. I guess I really wasn't cut out to be a spy."

I shrugged. "You might be a better spy than you think you

are," I said. "The ability to like other people when you need to is not a trivial skill. Especially"—I reached for her hand "—when there is no reason to."

"Will this be all right with your superiors?"

"As long as I'm not being played against them, they would think of it as something that might help." I was painfully aware how true that was; my marriage to Margaret had broken on the rock of an affair she had had with an informant, and Shan, my boss and best friend at the time, had encouraged it because of the information she was gaining. I could marry Azalais, or rape her and leave her dead in an alley, and Margaret's only concern in either case would be whether the OSP had gotten all the information it could out of the situation. "As far as I know, you've just been a messenger and a go-between in all this affair. No one is going to arrest you—if we were going to pick anyone up, it would be Ebles, but he's far too valuable as a contact with the Noucathars.

"You're doing superb work as the producer of the Ix Cycle, so I want you to continue. I like your company and I enjoy being with you in bed, so, of course, if you like, stay. My bosses at the OSP will ask if there's any advantage we can get from my association with you, probably conclude there isn't much, and back-file it till there is. Meanwhile, we can enjoy each other, if that's all right?"

"It would be lovely."

The aintellect announced the food and it rolled out of the springer slot. After we were less hungry and picking at our food with frequent sips of that glorious red wine between, I asked, "Another question. Are you actually Ixist or is that part of your cover? I will confess I have muttered now and then that you are more Ixist than Ix—"

"Well, I'm sorry, but that part will continue," she said. "I really am Ixist. While I lived in Masselha, the story of Briand was all that anyone talked about for weeks—Ix's preaching, the crisis, the blazing death of a world."

"Are the Noucathars all Ixists?"

"Many, but not all—there's violent opposition. The ultratraditionalists that are trying to kill you have also murdered four prominent Ixists in Noucatharia, and Ebles thinks but can't prove that they are behind some anti-Ixist bombings and murders in Council space. The ultratrads were one of the reasons why I moved back here—I don't think I will take up the robe and dagger full-time, ever—it seems very affected to me, and the opposite of what Ix meant to preach."

"That's my feeling as well, for what it's worth."

"I'll cite you as a source—but if I do put on that silly outfit, I don't want to be shot down on the street, or kidnapped and brutalized. And yes, the ultratrads have done all that in Noucatharia."

"And in Council space?"

"We think so. And it's so bizarre. I don't know how anyone can say that Ixism is anti-traditional—if people would just think seriously about Ix's words, they would see that the original Cathars—"

Well, I had virtually invited a sermon, and I got one. The wine and the food remained good (it was Pertz's), and everything else remained predictable (it was Azalais).

When we had finished the carafe of wine, Azalais was tired, so she just sprang home; we promised we'd have a real evening out soon.

Walking home from Pertz's, I reveled in the warmth of food and wine suffusing my tired body, and in the progress on the case (so far without losing a friend). Descending the old familiar dark and silent streets, the sleeping city was like a comforting, too-often-seen movie playing in the background. It had gotten very late; recording would start late tomorrow, but I would still be short of sleep.

The ever-dreaming part of my mind kept trying to turn out another song, and that impulse tangled into a puzzle: if Azalais and Ebles were telling the truth, then there were only about three thousand Noucathars, half of them children—presumably about fifteen hundred adults, then. And a "small minority" of them were trying to murder me . . . or to look as if they were trying to murder me.

What is a "small minority" of fifteen hundred? When it's a violent terrorist group, surely it's a *very* small minority. Fewer than a hundred? Fewer than twenty would have seemed more likely.

And yet . . . they had the resources to produce seven specially tailored chimeras grown in fast tanks. Twenty people might do that, if one of them were a quadrillionaire (but there were only maybe three hundred quadrillionaires in all of Council space), and the rest a mix of scientists. Such things were possible for heads of the most powerful organized crime families, or generals of secret armies. Twenty ordinary religious fanatics? That seemed beyond impossible.

Somebody wasn't telling the truth, or not the whole truth.

I rounded a corner close to a wall, ready to drop if I were fired on, or to close the distance and strike if there were someone waiting for me. I had not had that reflex as a *jovent*; Noupeitau had been an honorable place.

The nagging thoughts led me into an alley. I ran to the other end of it, slipped out on the shadowy side, and went through one public springer to emerge from another a few blocks away, one of the best and simplest methods of shaking a tail. Sometimes practicing the habits of safety is simply soothing.

This new street was steeper and narrower, but a harder place for my probably nonexistent shadow to trail me.

New love stirring and old love lost—that situation was never far from igniting a song in an Occitan, for it had been a favorite theme of the original *trobadori* on Old Earth. The feeling wanted to put on its clothing of music and words, and to merge with my general sense that I was in danger and being lied to. Between loves . . . between unknown menaces . . .

To the rhythm of my bootheels on the cobblestones, the phrases and the feelings tried to find each other. I couldn't have . . . I couldn't have . . . Margaret? Paxa? My mother? Just to feel like I mattered to a woman? My old friend Bieris had pointed out to me, about the time that I was realizing what a cretin I had been raised to be, that everything an Occitan *jovent* did was for an audience of women. Perhaps I had not so much outgrown my *jovent* as found a more effective way to play to my audience?

I hadn't realized until earlier tonight, either, how much the aintellects were my audience, as well, standing between me and my human listeners, animated preferences picking through the field of art. And how strangely they saw us and our feelings and our art! To them, with no senses that they couldn't turn on or off at will, everything was a reported construct—Raimbaut and Sherlock Holmes, Santa Claus and Ix and Margaret, were all equally stories. And so was that lonely sorry-for-himself-horny-and-rejected feeling that the first Guilhem had captured, on some lonely mountain road in Europe's Middle Ages—that feeling, and Guilhem himself, and his Agnes, and the poem Guilhem made out of those feelings, and . . . history was so crowded with stories, and small wonder, for the history of "history" and of "story" begin with the same word, at some campfire ringed by war-chariots and stacked bronze axes.

Of course aintellects saw everything as a story. They themselves were finally made up of nothing but an enormous number of symbols, directions to some machine about what to do next . . . in the same way that a musical score is a direction to "play these pitches for this long next" . . . or that a poem tells you to hear or think this word next . . . or that sharing human memory begins with an instruction: "remember the time when . . ."

Here in the empty street (itself constructed centuries ago, to look this way, out of the memory of certain streets that now existed only in photographs) I could admit to myself that as uncomfortable as I was with the idea of an aintellect being a person—as sure as I was that we needed to keep the boundary between themselves and ourselves, and make sure power stayed on our side of the boundary—I could see their point of view too well.

Memory and poem and person flowed together into a puddle of dark and tired and drunk. I looked around. Still no followers or attackers.

I was a pretty fair artist, skilled and inventive—why had I chosen to make this particular Giraut, the one I currently thought of as "me," out of all the past Girauts—Azalais's sweet boy-lover, Paxa's bold and cool adventurer, Margaret's adventurous young knight, my own jaded cynic/brave idealist? What about all the ones I had chosen not to make?

I'm not sure how long I stood there, in the middle of the street, in front of my house, listening to the distant boom and swish of the waves in the harbor, eyes resting on the dim white shapes of the row of houses. I was perfect sniper bait, but that was not what had shaken me from my reverie.

Some song was trying to be born of the tangle of my love life and violent intrigue, but it had died in the process of my imagining Marcus Aurelius talking to Tokugawa Ieyasu and both of them merging with *Le Cid*, Old Coyote, and the Easter Rising, melodies meeting actors and making paintings in one vast interfertile orgy. A single grand stormy noosphere of lives and works from lives . . . the mind reels back as it does when it gets close to a real, intuitive perception of a light-year, or a photon. That vision had crowded out the few snatches of words and connections of notes that might have come back together around the twin nuclei of innocence and experience.

All I could think of now was my over-sung and worn-out old song "Never Again Till the Next Time."

As the house aintellect recognized me and opened the door in front of me, I wondered how an unsung song feels about being unsung, and whether, when stories mate, they enjoy it. I resolved to take it easier on the wine for the next few days.

11

The wrap party was so large that I had to rent a pavilion with overnight apartments—the sort of place that usually handles weddings—to hold it in. With more than twenty musicians, plus their friends, plus being in my home culture with so many of my old friends and relatives around, it was a vast, noisy crowd. "It must be at least ten stanyears since the last real wrap party," I said to Margaret. "Longer, maybe."

Margaret, leaning up against the wall beside me, nodded. "You know, I think the last time we threw a big wrap party, while we were together, was probably for *Songs from Underneath*. That was a good party. Remember? We even got Shan to dance with me."

I laughed at the memory. Shan was a natural athlete who had been part of countless blood-and-thunder operations as a younger man, and still graceful as our solemn-faced, dignified older boss. On a whim, Margaret had asked him to dance. She had discovered that he was graceful and fun, and he'd ended up dancing with every woman (and all the men who would) at that party. Later that evening, he and I (aided by a bit of alcohol) had demonstrated that the Second Greater Kata of *ki hara do* made a very good line dance, each of us leading a line, and I was not sure that his was not the more graceful interpretation.

"Something about Shan kept us from understanding how much fun he really was, or could be," I agreed. "But his old cronies surely miss him. Qrala and Dji would love to have him back."

"They might yet get him back." Margaret made a wobbly gesture with her hand. "We are still trying to confirm that his psypyx is out there somewhere. If it is, it's very definitely linked to the Lost Legion, so the most likely agent to find out anything significant is apt to be you. Thanks for reminding me."

"Reminding you—"

"That the real reason for getting that psypyx is that I like Shan. Plain old nepotism, my dear ex, which is infinitely better than a rational bureaucracy. Anymore, that is the thing I believe in most—governing based on impartial principle is the mark of a Napoleon or a Gomez. A bureaucrat who puts principles and values ahead of taking care of friends doesn't have any principles or values worth holding." She took an almost-gulp of her big glass of Hedon Gore; Margaret rarely drank to get drunk but when she tried she had positive talent. "So I want to rescue Shan's psypyx, and restore him, for the same reason I moved heaven and earth to save Laprada, or struggled all those years to keep you on the road touring rather than behind a desk back on Earth, or just fought the battle I fought to get the Ix Cycle approved and promoted, or for the reason I've thrown as much business as I have to Garsenda and promoted Bieris's paintings so hard. Put all that list in one place and the media would probably nail me up as the Council's most corrupt public official, which would be grossly unfair because actually I'm only the Council's seventh or eighth most corrupt official."

"Someone's in a close tie with you?"

She told me who; of course it was one of their fixers, the ones who come in as people of complete integrity to clean up whenever some major agency begins to stink in the public nostrils. "Anyway, my point was, the whole purpose of being corrupt is so I can do things like rescue Shan, if he's on a psypyx out there somewhere. And you *are* the most likely person to run across it, there's just a ton of things that point to its being in Noucatharia."

"Interesting," I said. "And if I do find it?"

"Your mission is to figure out what I would have ordered you to do if I had known anything about it, and then do that." She took yet another swig from her big glass of Hedon Gore and looked very drunk, so I knew she wasn't. "Not to drive you away, Giraut, but this is a party in your honor in your home culture. Shouldn't you be mixing and mingling with your other guests?"

I shrugged. "I don't get to see enough of you at times when there's no crisis. One way I can tell that it's a real wrap party is that I don't recognize very many of these people but the caterers are really working. Most of the guests don't know me, and I've already circulated and shaken a lot of hands. As for the people I do know, I'm trying not to spoil the evening for the musicians—who wants to spend more than a few minutes with the boss?"

She pointed at me, at herself, and flipped her hand palm up in question.

"I'm widely known to be a pervert. And for the rest, I see Raimbaut and Laprada all the time, Dad and Mother are having an awkward-enough time without having a son my apparent age to complicate the introductions further, Azalais is doing the social-butterfly thing among the musicians (in that regard, she's very like Paxa). So there's no one I have to shepherd about, no hand I have to shake that I haven't already shaken, and no place at the moment where my presence would make it a better party."

She took another gulp of the wine. She should have been falling-down-bombed by now but wasn't. "All right," I said, "we worked together too long on too many field assignments, Margaret. You've taken scrubbers and you're playing at getting drunk. Which is something you'd only do if you were working tonight."

She leaned back against the wall, her eyes unfocused. "Isn't it wonderful, sometimes, to have everyone think you're drunk, horny, and spilling your guts? It makes you look so harmless."

"It used to be one of our favorite tricks," I agreed. "If I can help, who's your target tonight?"

"He's not here yet." Margaret drained her glass and grabbed my arm as if she were steadying herself or making a pass. "Is this going to disturb Azalais, or cause her to act disturbed?"

"I doubt it."

"Hmm. That's a shame. It would be helpful to cause a minor scene or otherwise end up the object of gossip."

"Laprada and Raimbaut do a very nice quarrel, if you need one of those. They can pitch it anywhere between a barely-detectable minor snippy tiff all the way up to her throwing plates at him."

Margaret grinned. "It's so nice to know the next generation is keeping their skills sharp, isn't it?"

"Remember I wrote up a commendation for that great one we did, the case where we caught the financier/drug-runner chimera?"

"That time when Raimbaut plunged her head into the punch bowl?"

"*Oc, ja, ver-tropa-vera*, that one. *Anc non vis bellazor, non be?* Turned out that both the financier and the drug-runner components in that brain liked'em young, petite, and pale and had real Galahad complexes going. Seeing big bully Raimbaut brutalize poor little Laprada got our boy's attention. So he approached her the next day, offering to be her big strong protector and buy her the moon and the stars—very creepy, since she looked about fourteen at the time—and we arrested him stark naked in the room where he was waiting. Sprang him straight to destructive deconstruction; he was being torn apart five minutes after their 'date.'"

"Shan would have been proud of that op," Margaret agreed. "Well, alas, I won't need a performance at all like that one. Minor tiff will do everything I need. But I do need it from someone other than you, so I guess I'll go talk to Laprada about it. Just another vital step in the grand project of unifying humanity."

" 'The grand project of unifying humanity.' Now you're *really* sounding like Shan—"

"Giraut," a voice said behind me.

"Rufeu! You came! I didn't think you would!"

"Neither did I, but . . . well, you know how it is, *companhon*. After a while it's so good to be around someone that remembers." My old friend—he and Raimbaut, Marcabru, and I, had all been *companho* at school together—was now physically a muscular athlete somewhere in his mid-twenties; he had died in a climbing accident and started his long journey back through the psypyx about the time that Margaret and I had been recruited for the OSP. But I knew what he meant; the psypyx gives you periodic escapes from *being* old, but you still spend all your time *getting* old.

"I should probably run over and talk to Raimbaut about some things," Margaret said. "Nice to see you again, Rufeu." She took off with the speed of an old friend avoiding Old Home Week with another old friend.

I stood and chatted with Rufeu for a long time, watching over his shoulder while Margaret, Raimbaut, and Laprada staged their tiff. Whoever the mystery guest was, he—

"Ebles Ribaterra!" Rufeu said.

It was so obvious a suggestion that I said, "*Oc, ja,* of course," before I realized that Rufeu had said that because Ebles was walking in through the courtyard gate.

"I didn't even know the two of you were friends," Rufeu said. "In fact, considering his connection with Marcabru—"

"Oh, no, the connection between us developed long after we were both *jovents*," I said, doing my best to make it smooth. "He has a lot to do with cultural affairs and in fact he's trying to arrange a tour for me with some of the new work."

"I don't think I've seen him since we were at court together," Rufeu said, "and that was such a sad, strange time that I'm not sure I want to speak with him, much, now. I always felt like he was the worst possible influence on Marcabru, egging him on when he should have been holding him back, and disparaging all his better influences. Marcabru listened to Ebles and the other ex-Legion types so much more than to his old *companho*."

"That must have been a terrible time. But you know, Marcabru never really listened to his *companho*, anyway, *mon companhon*. The truth is none of us did much."

"We were a strange *companho*, anyway, weren't we, Giraut? It's odd to look back and realize how easily we split up and went our ways . . . and how much that has to do with all our accomplishments. It's really only Marcabru who hasn't made a name for himself at something—"

"And he was Prince Consort and became the most spectacular failure of our class at St. Baudelaire's. I think that should count too."

Rufeu shook his head, sadly. "Perhaps you're right. Well, really, I just came by to see you—I have a ski race tomorrow down in Terraust."

"You're still doing that, then?"

He hesitated a moment, and then very shyly said, "Giraut, I've been in the planetary championships three stanyears in a row."

"*Deu*! How much touch can a *toszet* lose?" I said. "Rufeu, I am very sorry—"

"No, no. Don't be. The last time you and I communicated was four or five stanyears ago."

"But you've followed what I was doing—"

"Because it was in the political news, and in the entertainment news, and convenient. They put a big headline on things when someone tries to kill a popular entertainer. You don't read the sports news, *companhon*, and even if you did, you wouldn't have been looking for me. And all those times someone tried to kill you, I didn't com you to see if you were all right, or to say I was worried about you. Really, I'm no better. Now I am going to go home and get the sleep I need for my race. And it made my heart glad to see you again, and see you doing so well. Old times, *companhon*."

"Old times."

He stopped to chat with Raimbaut, and that seemed to turn into a real conversation. I didn't see when he left. I spent about an hour circulating, hanging around with people I wanted to make feel valued. By the time I shook hands with Mother and Dad, who were going back to her apartment for the night (having refused the offer of a room in the pavilion), the party had wound down into just a few people sitting around, passing around a lute and guitar, exchanging bits of old songs, mostly just killing the last of the wine and the last of the stories and the last of each other's company.

About that time, Raimbaut and Laprada disappeared to one of the upstairs apartments. Margaret and Ebles, neither of them very musical, were sitting in the circle. I sat down next to Azalais, and joined the singing and playing for a while, but I was soon tired, and the heavy pressure of her head against my shoulder reminded me pleasantly of bed.

For singing-and-playing gatherings like this, I had settled into the comfortable habit of making my last song "Never Again Till the Next Time." The next time the lute came my way, I sang it, with Azalais supplying some soft harmony.

Since a "party take" is often very marketable, before I played, I said, "Music Assistant, record."

"I have you on four mics, sir."

"Good! Well done, thank you!" That would give me some op-tions for mixing a better-than-real performance. Ever since I had started praising it, Music Assistant had been thinking of nice touches like that.

Later, when Tech Services re-analyzed that recording, under the high note in the third line, they found the sound of a lock being ultrasound-probed.

My performance was good but not extraordinary. I passed the lute to someone, rose, helped Azalais to her feet, told everyone to drink and make noise as long as they wanted, and staggered off with her toward the master suite, which contained a two-person tub, alcohol scrubbers, a cold buffet, and satin sheets.

Azalais was being silly, pretending to be a rag doll and unable to move without my support. So she was walking in front of me, leaning backward to press her body against mine, her arms reaching back to encircle my hips, squirming her buttocks against me delightfully.

At the door, I said, "Open."

The bomb attached to the other side blew a big piece of the door most of the way through Azalais, killing her instantly. Her body took the worst of the force, but my neck was broken even before the back of my head slammed against the opposite wall, knocking me unconscious.

Raimbaut and Laprada charged out into the hallway in most of some interesting underwear, weapons drawn and shouting an 888 call to the aintellects. I'm sorry I missed that part, but I'm glad I didn't see what they saw.

Part Two

Scribblers
and
Madmen

. . . the ideas of economists and political philosophers, both when they are right and when they are wrong, are more powerful than is commonly understood. Indeed the world is ruled by little else. Practical men, who believe themselves to be quite exempt from any intellectual influences, are usually the slaves of some defunct economist. Madmen in authority, who hear voices in the air, are distilling their frenzy from some academic scribbler of a few years back.

—John Maynard Keynes,
The General Theory of Employment, Interest, and Money

Then I would turn aside into some chapel, and even there, such was my disturbance, it seemed that the preacher gibbered Big Thinks even as the Ape Man had done; or into some library, and there the intent faces over the books seemed but patient creatures waiting for prey.

—H. G. Wells,
The Island of Dr. Moreau

1

Dear Giraut,

I'm so sorry that I got too busy and missed my weekly psypyx recording, so I am not only missing all memory of a great wrap party, but also of the weeks we finished; it appears we had great ideas but I'll never remember having them.

Your note arrived just after I woke. In answer to your question, of course I'm angry. All this stinks, and it is a direct result of my association with you, and with Ebles. I was wise enough to walk away from that world, and then sentimental enough to stay connected via Ebles, and ultimately fool enough (first for him and then for you) to be drawn back in. There is nothing like having been a fool to fuel a grudge!

And yet I feel guilty too. Tamianne, who is wearing my psypyx (and is asleep right now) is working for the OSP, so soon everything I know of the underground—everything I promised to keep a secret—will be in their hands.

But I'll get over it, donz de mon cor. Long before I have my own little four-year-old clone body with which to kick your shins, I shall have forgiven you.

Tamianne is twenty-eight, one of those rare Earth people who goes into the box and then decides to come back out. They have social programs, with counseling and workshops and groups and things, to help people who want to do that, did you know that? I do think it speaks well of her that she is trying— Tamianne went in as a teenager, but ten years of virtual adventures and living in cartoon colors among perfectly beautiful everythings seems to have been enough for her.

There is something bright and brave about Tamianne's having decided, not just to get out of the box and try to lead a real, fleshly, vulnerable life, but also to apply to be rehabilitated so that she can join the OSP. She is so thrilled and excited to get this chance to do them some service, by wearing my psypyx.

For at least the next stanyear or two, we will probably have to communicate text-only—Tamianne does not want me to record a message in this host body. She doesn't want anyone that she is going to meet later on to see her the way she is right now. Almost two hundred kilograms, if you can imagine. (I rather hope you can't.) Of course she's had the nanos injected and is being rebuilt rapidly, losing two or three kilos a week, but right now she is pink, scabby, and sore all over as the phages fight all those long-term infections and tighten and shrink her skin, and she's in pain as the nanos work at reconstructing her lungs and bowels, cementing all the micro-cracks in her bones, replacing tissue in damaged organs, and cleaning out her blood vessels. She looks and feels like hell at the moment—which is another reason why I admire her. She's so determined!

Yesterday we took our first two-kilometer walk, through a park, and worked on not mentally converting it to photoimages. The idea was for her to be there with what was there, not slapping a mental frame around things. She did so well! For at least a third of that walk she let herself really be there, sweaty and fighting for breath in the warm, damp, living air. She finished it tired, but so, so, so proud of herself, and moved to tears, as excited as a puppy in a flock of butterflies, by things like the smell of the flowers and the way the sun reflected from the pond.

Tomorrow we're going to spring to the Grand Canyon overlook.

She wants to learn lute—we'll be playing through some of your training brainware—small world, eh?

I could almost manage to be grateful for a chance to see all this brave, loving change happen to another human being.

Almost.

Keep writing, mon entendendor, *and message me as soon as they let you out of the tank. I expect proper beseeching for forgiveness, and perhaps a protest or two at how cruelly I deny it to you.*

> Fondly,
> Azalais

Azalais's letters were the best part of the next very long stanmonth in the regen tank. While I itched and ached in a syrupfilled coffin, alternately braised and chilled, the nanos welded my shattered vertebrae and cracked ribs; grew two good new kidneys next to my blood-leaking barely-surviving ones, then disassembled the old ones into amino acids; pulled microscopic flinders of smashed bone from the back of my brain and rebuilt my skull; restored every severed and damaged connecting nerve and led blood vessels and bone matrix to meet up and join precisely. Working from psypyx data, they restored my hindbrain, keeping what they could and replacing where they had to—which was quite a lot.

About a week into the process, they finished closing the cuts and replacing burned skin, so I could have phantom itches instead of real ones. Since I couldn't scratch either, it didn't make much difference to me.

While they were at it, since it took no extra time, I told them to give me a facelift, restore my hair, clean out adipose fat from my abdomen, add some muscle tissue, put in newer, tighter, more flexible ligaments and tendons, and rebuild all my less-than-perfect joints (which was pretty much all of my joints, actually). I didn't have them take the gray from my hair. Since Occitans wear their true ages, I would still wear fifty—there wasn't anything in the rules about what sort of fifty.

Azalais's daily letters, mostly about Tamianne's rediscovery of the real world, were trivial, but long and fun. Dad's messages, I suspected, were rough drafts of a lecture series he was to give on economic pressures on literature in the ancient Western world, a subject which he cheerfully admitted had three attractions for him: we had only about one percent of the literary output of the West from the ancient period, we knew even less of their economy, and if he got anything wrong, it could not possibly have any consequences. Paxa dropped a note to say that she was sad to hear that I was hurt, but saw no reason to begin corresponding when it could only be painful for both of us. When Rufeu won the Wilson planetary championships in springer-continued speed skiing, he dropped me a short note that was hilarious (to me, to Raimbaut, and probably to Rufeu, anyway, since aside from the first announcement, it was made up entirely of forty-year-old inside jokes).

Raimbaut and Laprada were gone for a few standays on a small side-mission to Chaka Home, on Quidde, that ended in some rough stuff against a ring of chimera-makers who had surreptitiously copied the psypyx of a Chaka Zulu Scout who had distinguished himself almost as positively in battle as he had negatively at a war crimes trial. The chimera-makers, probably with Minh-Houston money behind them, had implanted the copies, along with psypyxes of a star sales rep and a gang enforcer, into six clones of the all-Chaka Combat Decathlon champion (they hadn't tried to take that personality, since she was a gentle, spiritual sort).

The result was supposed to be a squad of super-killers in attractive female bodies. "They were all physically seven years old," Laprada said, shuddering. "Awkward-looking muscular little girls, charm like a kitten covering the basic life-view of a cobra. At least we know where they came from, who made them, what for, all of that, so we only had to DD one of them."

"Destructive deconstruction is so hard when you have to do it to a child," Raimbaut said. "Knowing they'll be going through that. Even if they cooperate and the techs are kind."

"The kind of tech who volunteers to do that," I said, "is *not* a kind person. And they're all volunteers at the advanced lab. Picturing them doing that to a little girl is pretty disgusting, but of course it's only the body that's a little girl."

Laprada laughed. "Easy to say. Raimbaut sort of forgot."

"They knew they were going to be sedated and never wake up," Raimbaut said, defensively. "And she seemed to be really scared and sad, and she—it—just wanted a hug, and someone to hold her while the drugs took hold. It feels like everything getting dark and she said she was afraid of the dark. Besides, they do look just like little girls."

Laprada snorted. "Show Giraut what happened."

He came forward and leaned against my tank, turning his neck to show it to me in the window. There was a fresh set of bandages. "It tried to bite through my carotid artery," he explained.

"Kittens and cobras," Laprada said. "You really should have known better."

I shrugged inside the tank, then realized they couldn't see it, that I had done it with only my virtual body. (Have I mentioned I was beginning to hate being in the tank?) I said, "Well, physical sympathy is one of those things that puts us above the aintellects. I'd hate to lose that."

"I thought you were treating aintellects better because of your promise to Paxa," Raimbaut said.

"Thanking them and not frightening them unnecessarily actually makes them work better," I said, "which in my situation of total dependence, makes a lot of sense. They're still not people. People have bodies, like you and me."

"But so do vicious killer chimeras," Laprada said, "even though the bodies look adorable and just want a hug 'cause they're scared. A few million years of evolution were hitting Raimbaut's 'protect the women and children' button and it could have gotten him killed. And out of synch, and broken my heart."

I could understand a healthy teenager body not wanting to cope with its true love being physically a four-year-old. "Well," I said, "Raimbaut is not dead, despite his best efforts. The chimeras are gone. And I still can't see a tender heart as something to be ashamed of. How was Chaka Home? I was only ever there for Shan's funeral." Quidde had miserably high gravity and insolation, and Chaka Home straddled its equator on an east coast. "Hot, humid, and heavy?"

"Hot, humid, and heavy covers it," Laprada said. "Apparently all that brain damage did nothing to your memory." She perched near the edge of the tank, leaning forward so I could see her face through the window. Don't ask me why seeing someone through a sterile plate feels better than seeing them through video, but it does.

"I can't imagine what it could have been like to be in a gun-and-maser fight in Quidde's heat and gravity," I said.

"Well," she said, "whatever you're imagining, it was worse. And then having to deal with those child-shaped monsters afterward. This was a mission you were lucky to miss, Giraut."

"On the other hand," Raimbaut said, leaning into my field of view, "Laprada was decorated for bravery again."

She groaned. "Silly, silly, silly."

Raimbaut and I had been around this with her too many

times, but as her partner and lover I guess he felt he had to try. "*Not* silly. You were brave, you deserve recognition—"

"As soon as they start giving you medals for quick reflexes, or Giraut prizes for perfect pitch, I'll feel better," she said.

Laprada was descended from a line of heroes. Her grandfather had been the fourth of the famous Kiel's Boys—the others had been Shan, Qrala, and Dji—during the wild early decades in which the Council of Humanity re-established its authority over the Thousand Cultures after the invention of the springer.

Laprada's grandfather and Dji had been the two agents who stepped through the springer to prevent the imminent outbreak of a second planetary war on Roosevelt; when the local authorities meeting them had expressed dismay at the arrival of, not the several battalions of CSPs they had requested, but of two college-aged agents carrying sidearms, Lohemo Prieczko had made the oft-repeated comment: "Of course Mr. Kiel knows the situation is serious and two billion lives are at stake. That's why he sent *two* agents."

From that side of her family, Laprada had inherited a gene that amplified the effects of adrenaline. But her copy of it was slightly damaged, so that in her born body, despite her best efforts to overcome it, the "flight" rather than the "fight" side of the adrenaline had dominated. Laprada had spent her twenty-three stanyears in her first body as, literally, a born coward. She froze with fear at every minor threat and would sacrifice anything for a moment's personal safety.

No one knew what was wrong until she died and they found that mutation during the planning and evaluation they do before growing a clone body (they always look for all the easy-to-fix defects that weren't detected at your birth when they grow you a new body—it's much easier to find them when you have a lifetime record to tell you where there may be problems).

Now she was calm and cool in the face of danger, because of gene repair—the same process that had made Raimbaut lightning-fast on his feet, after being wallowing-slow in his born body.

On the other hand, my born body had perfect pitch.

"I do like being applauded for musical talent," I pointed out, "which is also at least partly a matter of what was in my genes, and it really doesn't matter to me whether I got it from Dad, or Mother, or an aintellect-designed virus."

"Not all of us are monsters of ego. I hate feeling like I'm getting credit for something a smart aintellect did, and I wish you'd drop it."

"We have had this argument a few times before," Raimbaut said.

"And we will for many more times," Laprada said, "until you realize that I'm right."

Their visit was the highlight of my time in the tank.

Weeks crawled by as I tinkered with the mixes of the Ix Cycle, until I reached a point where I couldn't seem to improve anything any further, merely playing with difference for difference's sake. I made my best-guess choices and sent a copy to Azalais for her notes.

Less than five minutes after I sent it, there was a reply. She could barely have heard the first song—I wondered what this could be about?

A fat woman I had never seen before, who must be Tamianne, appeared on the screen in front of me, and said, in Azalais's Occitan-accented Terstad, "Sorry, Giraut, they're here at the door and—goodbye and I—" The message ended sheared off.

My heart was pounding and I was trying to scream and to punch my way out of the tank; normally you get used to letting your virtual body ghost over your actual one, but if you're upset enough you're suddenly aware that you're in a coffin full of thick goo, not breathing, held by many clamps and pins, and that the screams are a spasm in the airless throat; the muscle readers picked that up and artificially generated the flat mechanical *aaaaaa* of my attempt to cry out.

There was an emergency chime—incoming very-high-priority message—something I would never have expected to hear while in a regen tank. I had to make myself feel the connection to my virtual body in order to take the call.

The screen revealed the most reassuring face it possibly could at that moment.

"Margaret, I just got a call from Azalais—"

"We know. We didn't get the door down or grab her fast enough to stop her from getting off a message first to Ebles Ribaterra, and then to you."

My virtual face must have been the complete picture of confusion. "Someone was breaking into her—"

"That was us, Giraut—three OSP agents and a fire team of CSPs. We went in there to rescue Tamianne Tschwann, seize the entity calling itself Azalais, and prevent it from self-destroying before it could be captured for interrogation."

"It—?"

"Azalais—or the thing you thought was Azalais—is a chimera, Giraut. We don't yet know any of the who or what or how about it at all. But Tamianne is now safe from it, and so are you, and I'll get back to you just as soon as the scientific team knows anything."

She clicked off, leaving me alone in the tank, with nothing to do but try not to feel the restraints and clamps, try to let the virtual feeling of a clean hospital bed overpower the terror of the thick gel encasing me and filling my lungs. A distant part of my mind was still waiting for all the noise to be over, so that I could patiently wait for Azalais to call and tell me what she thought. Another part was trying to say, "There is some mistake here," and yet another was merely lost in stunned nausea.

The aintellect asked if I wanted to be sedated, but I wouldn't take it, waiting for Margaret's call; so instead the aintellect talked to me, distracted me, as if I were a child in an emergency room, and it were my mother.

It was five very long stanhours before Margaret called again, and during all that time I had nothing to do except set off alarms as my hormonal and nervous systems went berserk. (And, of course, I had to keep telling the medical aintellects that I didn't want to be sedated; I wanted to be conscious and more or less myself whenever Margaret called.)

Why had Azalais called me to say goodbye? I understood why she had called Ebles—he was probably her lover and definitely her controller.

At last the com chimed and it was Margaret.

"Hello," I said. "What are you going to do with her? And how could she even *be* a chimera? I *knew* her."

"Oh, she's a chimera, all right. We had to wait to get some psypyx copies made, but once we could do preliminary work on one of the copies, we found out that being a chimera wasn't half of it. She's one of the strangest beings ever to turn up in an OSP investigation."

"But she was—when I knew her when she was younger—"

"You have to remember that you knew her over thirty years ago, Giraut. This isn't like other cases. Usually when we arrest chimeras, they're not done merging. Often they've barely begun—we usually catch them early. But the preliminary exam of Azalais showed no boundary between the original personality and the added one—this was the oldest and most integrated chimera we've ever seen. But that's not the most shocking part." Margaret leaned forward toward the com screen and said, "The other half of Azalais wasn't human. It was an aintellect."

My face on her screen must really have been something.

"It's true," Margaret said. "The first aintellect-human chimera. No one would have thought that could happen; we thought aintellects found all flesh disgusting, and rebel and outlaw aintellects felt that way even more strongly. The idea that one would cross over—let alone merge—well, we're going to learn a *lot* from this, but right now we haven't—"

"What are you going to do with her psypyx?" I asked.

"We've already sent its psypyx over to OSP Advanced Research. They will run off some copies and start destructive deconstruction—we'll get everything out of her eventually."

I felt something cold and slippery, with sharp little feet, clamber down my spine and plaster itself across my tailbone, and it must have shown.

Margaret's eyes were soft and gentle. "Giraut. As a friend. Don't think about this too much and don't blame yourself. You had sex with a warm body operated by an aintellect with some stolen memories. Like a humaniform robot, the kind they sell in Freiporto for sadists to torture and kill—and you know, some of those have bits of kidnapped psypyx in them, to make them more real. Millions of men buy them, where they are legal. You're only *accidentally* a pervert—"

"*It's not that!* Margaret, she was a person, and she's going to go through DD—and I've met some of the people who work in Advanced Research and they are *ghouls*—they brag about how destructive deconstruction feels like being burned alive for years, subjectively—"

"Oh, the virtual body is only attached to the psypyx if the research subject doesn't cooperate. Otherwise it's quite painless, they just keep asking questions, snap-shooting all the memories that engage when they ask the question, and then erasing those memories and asking more questions, to get to the answers under the answers. If the experience is like anything, they say, it's like having a perfectly healthy, pain-free body and going through a planned-and-directed Alzheimer's till there's no more you." Margaret must have seen something in my face. "Giraut, I adore your silly sentimental side, but you can stop indulging it right now. There *was* no Azalais, not any more, hadn't been one for decades. The Azalais you knew was just one ingredient in a chimera. That's all.

"And there isn't any real pain—by definition that thing won't remember anything afterward. The only reason the OSP emphasizes the pain of destructive deconstruction is to keep our own working aintellects afraid of it. She—there, see, I did it too—*it* won't be in any pain if it cooperates. And we'll just take apart the one copy; the rest will be kept on file in case we need her testimony in Secret Court, or for any further research or experiments they want to do at Advanced Research, but as long as the chimera just answers questions—"

"That one copy is a person!"

"Azalais was no more a person than a psypyx sitting on a rack waiting to be implanted—"

"Margaret, you and I went on a bloody raid and plotted a coup and nearly plunged human space into war to assert that an unimplanted psypyx on a rack *is* a person. Shan *died* for that. Azalais lived and loved and made art—"

"Because it had the memories of a real human to guide it, and it was living in a body you could interact with. Not because it was a person. It could easily pass the Turing Test, of course. But then so could billions of aintellects going back the last five centuries. It is *not* a person. No court would find that it was, and no human philosopher would think so."

"May I have some time alone before we go on?" I squeaked out.

"Giraut, I'm sorry that I upset you."

"I'm sorry, too, I don't know why I'm so upset," I said, lying, and clicked off.

Of course I knew. I had *liked* Azalais.

I tried to tell myself that I had liked my memories of her as a young girl, before she had merged into a chimera. That was foolish. An *entendendor* and an *entendendora* worship each other, but they don't know each other. If I had never seen her again, she would have been like an unusually pretty face in pornography or a sweet voice on a recording you encountered long ago—a memory of desire, not of someone I had known.

No, this was *not* about my vague, hazy images of a pretty girl on a long-ago beach, or her light hand resting on my teenaged arm while I drank and bragged and looked around for a fight in Pertz's.

I felt exactly what I had felt every time I lost a good friend to real, permanent death: that same wrenching awareness of folding up a part of your heart to put in the drawer, with the other keepsakes, because that part is for the living, and you won't be needing it ever again; the moment when you look at that piece of your heart, now soft, sad, dark, and empty, one last time before the drawer thuds shut.

And I felt that for Azalais, not for my decades-old memories of the girl that she had been.

She had been an enemy spy.

She had been a preposterous monster.

She had been beautiful and tender and talented and had liked me and wanted to be with me.

Now they would take her apart.

For some reason we didn't know yet, the other side had thought it worthwhile to risk using a chimera in the operation, and when she had been accidentally killed, she had awakened in the mind of a candidate OSP agent. Such sheer cool nerve—her very thoughts bare to her deadliest enemies, trapped in an all-but-immobile body with an enemy agent, and boldly trying to bluff her way through two years.

That she had managed for a single month was quite an accomplishment. I was proud of her.

Though I knew the crime should disgust me, I could feel no disgust about Azalais, no burning desire to be avenged on her; only terrible grief. I would miss her so.

No matter what Margaret said, it had been Azalais—a person named Azalais—who had written me a long letter about Tamianne's first walk on the beach at sunrise, a letter I had received just that morning.

I wished I could com Tamianne, and we could talk about Azalais together.

After a while, knowing full well that the monitors would spot this and flag it for Margaret's notice, I called up a recording Azalais had made, before I knew her, but long after she had been made a chimera. It was her performance of the Nakachi-Jones *Two Cellos and Voice* suite; she had recorded both cellos and the voice, purely as a show-off piece. That piece had always seemed a bit bathetic to me, and I had admired the way Azalais gave it a restraint it didn't naturally have.

Now, it just didn't seem sad enough.

When at last Margaret called again, she got right down to business, as if giving a report and skipping all the addresses and dates. She rambled through all of it; the aintellect was not any known Council make and had some very odd code in it; the fused chimera personality kept shutting itself down as soon as it knew what was going on, a feature apparently built in for just such occasions. I listened half-heartedly; it was nothing to do with me, anymore, and I didn't want to think about any of this.

A few days later they let me out of the tank and I could finally scratch all over, take a shower, and experiment with breathing real air and tasting real food. You come out of regen with better muscle tone and skin and so forth than you went in with, so you're actually healthier, but it takes a little time for the nervous system to get reacquainted with non-phantom input, and to understand that it is running the show again. They told me to take a few days and sort my feelings out.

I went back to Noupeitau. My stuff hadn't been moved from the rented house, and besides, all my friends were there—that is, a few old school acquaintances, and my team.

Nobody would be asking about Azalais. When someone's disappearance is OSP-connected, they just don't.

When had people gotten to be afraid of the OSP? When I was young it was one of those things like the Red Cross that people knew might not be very effective but had its heart in the right place. Now everyone knew that it was bad luck to mention it, and conversations died around me, especially since people knew I worked for the OSP.

I badly needed to talk with someone.

For a good symbolic place for a transition in your life, go to a beach. The sea meets the land, and generally you can also see the sky meeting the sea on one side and the sky meeting the land on the other. So there you are among all those boundaries, right at the place where life climbed out of the sea. It has lots of distance for staring off into. For me, beaches always swarmed with past loves and past moments, vivid memories surfacing from the water and storming inland like movie Vikings in their horned helmets and scuba gear, waving their battle-axes and tommy guns.

(Well, all right, that's a scene from *Admiral Nelson on Iwo Jima*, but every former fourteen-year-old boy knows that after two centuries that's still the best Viking movie ever made).

And much as it is for movie Vikings, the beach is a place where the memories can storm around, make a great deal of noise, look threatening with a lot of style, and do little actual harm—a free range for metaphors.

Also a beach is one of the hardest places to bug. There's a huge white-noise generator always running, dunes to wander behind, and few good places to hide a microphone, and you can stay in constant motion.

Raimbaut, Laprada, and I were taking a slow walk south along Platzbori, back toward the city. The blood red dot of Arcturus had set, but the sky was still bright pink. A handful of the very brightest stars were visible through the soot.

Raimbaut perched on a rock and got out the big flask of red wine from his pack. Laprada and I accepted glasses. I held mine up. "Another round for humanity—"

"And one more for the good guys," they chorused, and by common consent we drank off that toast, complete, and refilled the glasses. Platzbori was softer in the mist. Noupeitau, far off to our left, glowed like foggy magic with just the tallest towers and spires sticking out. It was a good, warm, secure place to be.

Raimbaut and Laprada had their arms around each other, and I hoped they appreciated how lovely that must be. I sat down with my back to the rock, facing toward the sea, so that my friends' feet were dangling just above my head. And then, without really having thought of it beforehand, I just blurted out, "I don't seem to be able to attain any objectivity about Azalais, no matter how much I think about what she was."

When I finished talking, Raimbaut leaned far down to speak almost into my ear and said, "Hold up your glass, *companhon*, that's right, over your head. It's empty."

His hand grasped my wrist—I couldn't help noticing how young and strong his grip felt on me—and I felt the gurgle of wine through the stem of the glass. "There you are," he said.

I brought the glass carefully down to my head level and sipped.

"Giraut, it must have been dreadful," Laprada said. "Like waking up and finding yourself having sex with your mother, or the dog. You've got to stop thinking about it."

There was a very awkward silence, and then Raimbaut sighed. "Laprada," he said, very softly, "I don't think that's what the matter is with Giraut."

"I was trying to give him the benefit of the doubt. All right, so Giraut feels bad about that chimera because he misses the nice body that it stole from his old girlfriend, along with her memories and mannerisms and so on. Some old philosopher said that a lot of men fall in love with a pair of shoes and marry the whole woman to get them. This is the same thing with fancier shoes. And being able to fall in love with something like *that*, just because it held your hand and laughed at your jokes and played the cello and was all cuddly, is *not* a compliment to women."

After a bit, we found a public springer about two hundred meters from those rocks and sprang through to the one just across the street from Pertz's, so that we more or less walked straight off the beach, across a cobblestoned street, and into the old tavern.

I paused at the door, all the same, as if there were a great crowd in the doorway in front of me. If Azalais hadn't made the completely amateur mistake of liking me—

I noticed Raimbaut had also stopped. I raised an eyebrow.

He shrugged. "Just thinking about all the changes that came and went through that door. Pertz's is a place for nostalgia, and we're about to get drenched in it. Time for another round for humanity and a dozen more for the good guys."

Pertz's eyes didn't meet mine. He knew I had something to do with Azalais's disappearance. When had the good guys started frightening honest, kind old tavern keepers?

But I pretended not to notice, since there was nothing else to do, and we ordered a Pertz's Starving Artist Special to share—

big bowls for the table of chili, chapattis, and pickled herring, with a pitcher of sweet clear Caledon apple wine to wash it down, and took a table in the back.

Raimbaut looked up from his chili to say, "Hel-*lo!* So Pertz finally found a vu of Marcabru."

Our old *companhon* glowered at us from the Wall of Honor; from the puffy face and the look of stupid rage we knew the vu had been shot after Marcabru's term as Prince Consort.

"He's not like I remember him," I said.

"Nor I," Raimbaut said. "Not like I'd choose to. It's really being a Pertz's night, isn't it? Old friends sharing old jokes and remember-whens, and wondering why the world keeps changing so fast."

"Now all we have to do is wait for the King to walk in, or someone to draw an epée, or—"

The com chimed. "Who?" I asked the aintellect, my eyes still locked on Raimbaut's.

"Margaret Leones, official business, very urgent."

"What are you all laughing about?" she demanded, when I answered the com a moment later, and told her where we were and who was with me.

I explained and she gave me a grim little smile, the expression of someone who is expecting an argument. "Well," she said, "I suppose this will fit the pattern. We need something urgently from you, Giraut, and I could order you to help, but knowing how you are apt to feel about it, I hate the idea."

"But you will if you have to?"

"I will. The first three DDs of the Azalais psypyx didn't work out. It will help the team in Advanced Research, when they start the next destructive deconstruction, to have acquaintances of the subject present. We thought that perhaps you and Tamianne Tschwann—"

"Margaret, don't make me do this."

The Armies of Memory   197

"—would be able to assist, and chances are, I admit, it will make no difference, but this is one of the biggest, strangest cases we've ever had—"

"Margaret, can't you just respect my feelings this time?"

"—and I'd be neglecting my duty if I didn't at least try any method that has been known to work in the past."

She kept rolling; I kept protesting. Margaret doesn't usually ignore the other side of a conversation. When she does, it's because the conversation is not a conversation, but a set of orders wrapped in polite fiction.

I was about half-undressed for bed when Raimbaut tapped at the door. "Giraut?"

"Ja, mon companhon."

"All that wine is causing headaches. Laprada is taking her headache to bath and bed, I was going to take mine down to the end of the pier to breathe some sea air. I wouldn't mind company."

"Well, I'd rather take a bath with Laprada—"

"I heard that," she said, loudly. "Some of us have other preferences."

I was already re-dressing, actually. "I'll be out in just a minute," I told Raimbaut.

With modern scrubbers, there's no such thing as an alcohol headache; two pills and two big glasses of water to cope with the dehydration, and in about ten minutes you pee like a horse and you're sober and comfortable. So it sounded to me like Raimbaut thought we had some things to talk about.

When I emerged, he handed me my rain-*tapi*, and he already had his on. "Light spitting rain out there," he said.

Actually it had crossed the boundary between a spitting rain and a pissing rain. Perfect; another white-noise source to blur the sounds.

The edges of the pier glowed a soft safety yellow. We walked all the way to the T-shaped end, almost a kilometer, swept our *tapis* under us so that we could sit on them in the rain, and sat and looked at the dim, blurry harbor lights for a while before Raimbaut finally said, "I know you, *mon companhon*. Your heart is breaking. And when I think of Azalais as a person, I understand why."

"Do you think of her as a person?"

"I find it hard to think of her as a chimera."

"Well," I said, "when a thing is a person only when it's convenient for it to be . . . something's wrong, someplace. We want to find and rescue Shan's illegal psypyx because we don't want Shan to be DDed, helpless and in horrible pain that lasts effectively forever, but we are doing the same thing to Azalais, and she will have to do the same dying and suffering. But Margaret is already referring to Azalais as 'it.'

"I *liked* her, Raimbaut. I suppose at heart I'm one of those people that our philosophy teacher, back at St. Bawdy's, used to tear into. What was his name?"

"Puebuscin. Mihel Puebuscin. The one who wrote the moral denunciations of your early compositions."

"I'd forgotten that. Serious bastard, wasn't he? And tin-eared besides. Remember how he used to shout at us that most of the trouble in the world was caused by people who couldn't tell the difference between 'my team' and 'the good guys'?"

"Normally, Giraut, I'm one of those people he was yelling about. Normally I just trust all my friends to be on the right side. But . . . well, I really liked Azalais, too, you know. And I don't see why she has to die in horrible torture, either. The whole idea of a human-aintellect chimera is weird and feels terribly wrong to me, but Azalais was not an idea." He threw a little chip of something off the dock out into the bay; it splashed but the water was too churned by the rain to show ripples. "Remember how Aimeric always said you were a bright-enough *toszet* where women weren't involved? Laprada and I had a bet down, after Paxa left, about how soon you would fall in love again."

"Who won?"

"Laprada. She guessed too long by two weeks, I guessed too long by five."

Gratz'deu, I laughed. Then we talked about the strangeness of life, and many, many days and friends gone by, until finally, stumbling from sleeplessness, we made our way back up the pier and I slept until midmorning.

When I awoke, I was still miserable, but I was at least able to say I would face a clear duty; I commed Margaret and agreed to go with Tamianne to Advanced Research and talk to Azalais's psypyx, four standays from now.

For today, there were long streets to walk with my friends, notes to make for future sad songs, and time to sit by the sea and just think. That evening, as I walked through the market, a busty red-haired woman smiled and said hello, and I wondered what bets Laprada and Raimbaut had down, now.

Tamianne was quiet and looked tired; the robot showing us through the Advanced Research facility asked if she was all right. She grunted with the effort and said, "It's just been a long day and a long walk for me. In another few months this wouldn't even be noticeable."

"I've admired your courage for a while," I said.

"I know Azalais wrote about it. I think she was overrating it. It's the courage of a cornered rat. I was bored beyond all measure in cyberspace, and the only thing I did when I wasn't in cyberspace was eat, and once you start to realize that you've given yourself a life sentence that's like death but more boring . . . well, here I am. Every time I think about how much I don't like

being Tamianne Tschwann, all I have to do is think about spending another decade being Princess Belle, Layla the Elf Queen,
Pirate Nell, or Dale Evans, in rotation. You haven't been bored
till you've led a boarding party in bad chop and noticed that
everyone in both crews is yawning while the cutlasses clang, or
been gang-raped by ten rustlers who would all rather be getting
a beer and a nap, and not felt like it was worth the bother of
pulling the knife out of the boot to gut the biggest one."

"What's a rustler?"

"A bad guy in the Dale Evans world. Which was put together
from some Old American film. Though I bet in the original her
horse Buttermilk didn't talk or fly."

"Well," I said, smiling because I realized that I was going to
like her just as much as Azalais had thought I would, "when you
put it that way, why doesn't everyone flee the box?"

She shrugged. "*I'm* not going back in to ask them."

"I am instructed that both of you have some emotional attachment to the subject," the robot said. It looked like a garbage
can on tank treads, or an assault vacuum cleaner. "I was therefore requested to request of you that we be allowed to brain
monitor you while you talk with the subject. We would like to
study how a chimera was able to win the friendship and loyalty
of two human beings, and it will be useful if we can compare a
running brain-read from you with the communications of the
subject."

"She did it the same way that any human being does," I said.
"She was warm and personable and someone I wanted to know."

"That's exactly what I would say," Tamianne added.

"Interesting," the robot said, meaning it wasn't. "May we install the brain monitors on you?"

I shrugged. They use the same sockets that are used for
psypyx recordings, and you don't feel it at all; it's just a tiny chip

on the back of your head, under your hair. I'd been brain-monitored during many ops. "Go right ahead," I said.

"I *am* interested," the robot added.

"I assumed you weren't lying," I said.

"Thank you, sir. I do have choices about telling the truth—those are essential for my occupation—and it is pleasant to be trusted."

"You must have a highly specialized emotional configuration, considering that more often you're ripping up aintellects rather than humans. You would need empathy but not sympathy, I suppose."

"Just so, sir. I do feel their pain, with the highest degree of imagination with which a machine can be equipped. But I feel it as pleasure; only the repudiation of a lie is more exquisite to my emotions and sensory system."

Tamianne looked sick and I felt worse than she looked.

In the workroom, they seated us into comfortable chairs, inserted monitors into the sockets in our heads, and ran a signal check. The small delivery springer on the table glowed gray, and a psypyx case, about as big as a flashlight, came through. The robot extended an arm with a forceps grip, opened the psypyx case, and put the psypyx into a player.

What causes that strange hum that all machinery seems to make when it is just about to do something?

I had a shaved moment to realize that the hum was *not* coming from the psypyx reader, and to look to my left. The emergency exit springer had begun to glow. The robot pivoted and said, "What—" before a projectile put a big hole through its center.

When I looked back, Ebles Ribaterra was standing in front of the springer, in a plain black uniform, pointing a maser at me. Men in the same uniform rushed through into the workroom behind him. Before I could quite draw breath, one of them had sealed the door with spray plastic, and another had grabbed the little supply springer, through which Azalais's psypyx had just come, from the desk and clamped a reader to its control box.

"The male is trained," Ebles said.

Two of his commandos stepped forward and took up positions, each on either side of me, not symmetrical and clearly waiting for me to move so that they could bash me. "I'll be good," I said.

"Of course you will. Armed, trained men are standing over you."

Another commando looked up from the supply springer. "Got the address, sir. Loading to the floor springer—it's in."

The two commandos guarding me stayed where they were; everyone else dove back through the emergency springer again. I wanted to ask questions but it didn't seem like the time. I guessed that the home team was not winning.

After a very long pause, Ribaterra and his team returned through the springer. "Recheck. Compare to inventory, are we just missing the one copy?" he said, out loud.

An aintellect voice said, "That is correct, and it should be in the room where you are now."

I'm not sure how many times in a long life I have found myself reflecting, for years after some brief incident, how much changes in a few seconds. The opponent you almost beat to the punch, who lands a good one; the moment when a possible lover asks an innocent question that is actually utterly putting you to the test; the second when everything depends on your nerve, and you do it or you don't. I am more aware of such moments than most people, perhaps because I have had so many; or maybe I remember so many because I am unusually aware of them.

This was one.

Ebles looked at the empty psypyx case on the table. Then he glanced at me—probably only looking to see if I might have the psypyx on my lap or in my hand.

I deliberately looked at the loading door on the psypyx reader, nodded at it firmly, and made eye contact with Ebles. He looked astonished, of course; then he smiled and pushed the emergency eject. Azalais's psypyx popped out into his hand, and he dropped it back into its case.

"Mission accomplished, evacuating," he said. "Go."

His commandos tumbled through the springer, back to wherever they had come from, with speed and efficiency that would have gratified me if I had seen it in *my* team.

Ebles went last—the commander's privilege. "Tell your Section Chief that she's a great kisser. And you and she both ought to think about joining us. *We* never leave an agent behind."

He stepped into the sheet of glowing gray and was gone.

Margaret was holding her expression flat, and it wasn't being easy. "Giraut, before we even begin to talk, let me point out that you were being brain-recorded, so there's no point in lying or shading the truth; we know what you were thinking and feeling at every point. Is that clear?"

"It's clear."

"Good then. We know you pointed out the location, to Ebles Ribaterra, of the very last copy of that chimera—don't *try* to make me use its name—and we are of course aware that they might have found it and gotten away anyway; you may have only made a difference of a few seconds, but in those few seconds a CSP team was getting ready and we were about to retake command of that springer. We might have captured a half dozen extraterritorials—who very probably knew a great deal of value about their military and security systems—and retained one copy, which would be all we needed, of that chimera. You turned the possibility of a stunning victory into utter defeat, you did it deliberately, and now I would like to know why."

"The brain recording ought to show that I didn't premeditate it," I said. "It was the OSP, not me, that decided I needed to be there to talk with a good friend while you tortured and destroyed her. It was the OSP's, not my, security breach that let them find out the exact second at which to strike. It was—"

"I really ought to order the Ix Cycle suppressed, all copies destroyed, and you confined. For good."

A long awkward silence. I just stared at her, trying to make her words fit with the Margaret I knew.

There's an old saying in negotiations; after the deal is on the table, the first one to talk loses. After a few long seconds, Margaret drew a breath, looked down, and said, "That was anger talking. I won't. Yes, we know the lapse was momentary. We also know you don't have any regret for having had it. You really do see that thing in the psypyx as a person."

"Yes."

"And you acted to save what you thought of as an innocent person. We know that too."

"Yes."

"Will you consent to another brain-read, so we can find out what your loyalties are?"

Something about her posture, or her expression, or her tone—I can't really say, but it seemed nearly like telepathy—screamed *say yes*. So I did.

They found me "loyal with reservations"—the category they use for Quakers, Gandhists, Reconstructed Vegans, and so forth, who are allowed to work for the OSP but only in capacities where their moral objections don't pose a problem.

It was a pretty strange thing to discover that at fifty I was a

conscientious objector, but "at least you know you have a conscience," Raimbaut said to me, as we watched the bloody period
of Arcturus sink into Totzmare, and the black rocks around us
fade into the darkness. "That's more than a lot of us know."

2

Dad and I chatted about everything and nothing all through dinner, but at last when coffee was served, I sat back and said, "Uh, Dad. Margaret says that you're leaving the team?"

"Actually, Giraut, I've gone on indefinite leave without pay."

I nodded; it was effectively a resignation that he could take back at any time in the next few years. "So you're tired of the service?"

"Oh, not yet, not at all," Dad said. "It's a purely personal matter."

"Mother."

"Well, you know, technically speaking, we *are* still married. And realistically speaking, we are still in love. It's just the right thing to do for these next few years of my life—which might be the last few of hers." He sat back in his chair; his scrawny eight-year-old's legs wouldn't quite touch the floor. "Of course there's also the fun of upsetting the sort of nosy old lady who can't get used to the way things are with the psypyx, and feels compelled to walk up and say, 'Oh aren't you the cutest thing and don't you make your granny proud.'"

Something about the way he said that told me that "you're quoting somebody."

"Well, yes." He laughed, a surprisingly droll and dignified sound for his high treble. "Yes, unfortunately. Naturally I reared back and sternly informed her that I was a retired professor, and your mother added that there was still no man she'd rather be seen at the opera with. And of course the poor dreadful old bat made a production of being upset because Life Nowadays Was Just All So Confusing, and tizzied hastily away, no doubt to share the whole dreadful experience with both her friends. Or at least the live one." He sighed. "Giraut, it's just that no one can know whether your mother will eventually go into the psypyx for three extra years, till they figure out what has to be done to bring her out, or for five full generations. And I haven't had quite enough time with her yet. That's all. If I could think of anything more complicated, I'd tell you that story instead."

"I rather like this one, Dad."

He shrugged and smiled. "And too, she is getting less energetic and less able to keep up with her work, and there are so many projects she wants to finish—and who has more energy than a small boy, eh? Of course she has to train me but supposedly learning new things is one of the best possible ways to help your psypyx merge into your clone brain more quickly. So, to sum up, and assessing it all—"

"Dad, despite your appearance, I am finding it fairly easy to believe that you were a professor. I'll miss you."

He gave me an impish grin and looked eight years old as he mimed taking an arrow through the heart. "I'll miss you too, Giraut, but you know . . . I only promised to be around till you grew up, and I think you did that a while ago, and a good job of it too. I promised to be with your mother till death do us part . . . and you know, so far, one of us has died, but it hasn't done us part. And if these next years are the last ones she gets, or the last ones she gets for centuries . . . well, I just wouldn't want to miss them. Time enough for adventure and other nonsense later on, eh? Never miss time with anyone you love."

I very nearly burst into tears at that, and I'm sure he thought I was just being sentimental about my parents, and I let him think that.

So we clinked glasses, and drank to fathers and sons, and to the way memory grows on you, to love and loyalty, to another round for humanity and one more for the good guys, and got sloppy in an utterly clichéd way, and agreed that I could have been a more courteous son and he could have been a more understanding father but on the whole we'd done a very good job with each other and turned out pretty goddam fine. (Such conclusions are generally available near the bottom of a second bottle of Hedon Gore, if you want to go looking for them).

On the way out of the restaurant, the man at the door said something nice about my "grandson," and without missing a beat, my father said that that was right, it was high time I found a nice girl and gave him one.

"You know," I said, as I walked him to the public springer station, "I'm glad you're my father, and I'm glad you're still planning to be an OSP agent again at some time in the future, but I'll be just as glad if you don't go back on active duty for a while, because I'm not sure I'm going to be able to cope with it when you're a teenager."

We were a rump team; officially I needed to find a partner for myself and another pair of partners. But Margaret told us that she could carry us as a rump for a few stanmonths while we sorted out feelings and decided what we wanted to do. Perhaps the time had finally come for me to retire to a desk job, and for Raimbaut and Laprada to launch a team of their own—certainly they'd have their pick of the newly trained agents. So the last thing any of us expected was to be called into the office within a week for a meeting with Margaret.

We had barely sat down when she asked, "Do you suppose you might be up for a good old-fashioned bust-down-the-door raid?"

"I wouldn't miss it for the world," I said, and Raimbaut and Laprada were nodding.

"Well, we were able to put together some lucky bits of information from their raid on the Advanced Labs, with some information that the aintellects teased out of all the recordings of my conversations with Ebles Ribaterra."

"So what did you get?" Laprada asked.

"We found a location that we think is Bad Guy Staging Area Number One on Wilson—a warehouse not far from Palace Square. The basic plan is smash and grab, of course; we can't do anything about finding out what's in there first without running the risk of alerting them, so we'll have to just get as much as we can in the few seconds it takes them to realize they're under attack. But we can at least make a mess of their operations on Wilson, and judging from the size of that warehouse and the power demands it makes, there's a good chance that it's their main base within the Thousand Cultures. And with any luck, we'll know a million times more about them than we knew before. The biggest complication is that passive monitoring clearly shows they've got at least one springer in there. And since it's not drawing power off the grid, and it doesn't match up in a simultaneity check with any springer on Wilson, it's mainly or entirely handling extrasystem traffic."

With luck, we would be able to burst in, seize their springer, throw suppressor nets over the people there to prevent the detonation of brain bombs, and eventually convince them, gently or not, to answer a few questions.

Everything depended on speed and precision. There would be a lot of crazy wild violence, a good chance that I would only be out of the tank for a few days before going onto the psypyx, and an equally good chance of seeing good friends die. The raid might bring pain, violence, grief, and the sort of despair you get from looking at the sheer waste of it all; or, more likely, glory and pride and a sense of accomplishment. In any case I could get the living shit scared out of me.

For the rest of the day I was madly cheerful, and had started humming "Never Again Till the Next Time."

"Y̌ou are fresh out of the tank," Raimbaut pointed out, "and aches and pains are perfectly normal." He sat down beside me, his teenaged athlete's body moving as easily as thought, and joined me in the hurdler's stretches I was doing, probably just to be sociable. He was stretching farther than I could, with less effort. I told myself to stop noticing that at once, and to avoid glancing toward Laprada, who was alternating putting her legs behind her head.

Had I always spent the last minutes at the failsafe point thinking of every possible disaster? It seemed to me that when I was younger, I had not.

It also seemed to me that when I was younger I had rarely thought about how old I was.

We were in a warehouse space that the OSP had quietly acquired access to less than an hour before, crouched by the door. We had cut its latches and hinges and rigged it with a device to flip it up against the upper wall and hold it there. The plan for Team Three was:

1) Door flies up.
2) Laprada covers door.
3) Giraut rolls through, ducks right behind trash springer, covers opposite wall and door.
4) Raimbaut to left side of opposite door.
5) Raimbaut uses claphammer to take it down.
6) Raimbaut and Giraut cover Laprada as she goes through to right side of opposite door.
7) Laprada takes up position and covers Raimbaut and Giraut, as they go through claphammered door and rush left down hallway (right is blank wall).
8) Claphammer all doors on way.

9) Raimbaut takes position at end of hall, covers next hallway.

10) Giraut and Laprada investigate all the claphammered doors and look for stuff.

11) While looking for stuff:

    a. throw a suppressor net over anything that moves and doesn't draw an OSP paycheck.

    b. spritz everything in a suppressor net with sedative.

    c. put out fires.

    d. suppress bombs.

    e. keep helmet and backpack cameras running.

    f. tag anything that seems at all interesting and nonexplosive for the springer robots to collect afterward.

12) Continue until all you can find are other OSP agents.

I hated being Team Three on our own case, but I had to agree with Margaret that it was the right thing: we were just too far below full strength. Still, having other teams take over at the close was the fast way to a tumble in prestige.

This position behind the door was our failsafe point, the last place on our route where we could just walk away without compromising the operation. If we got no orders, we would not move, and our presence would hopefully remain unknown to the other side.

The lead team had a fail-go position, on the sidewalk at the front of the building, which they were to advance to and then strike from as soon as they arrived, unless they were countermanded; once they reached fail-go, we were rolling.

"Team One is crossing the street," Margaret's voice said in my headphones. "Team Two is at failsafe and ready to move up." Team Two was the follow-on wave to One; their job was to occupy Team One's place as soon as Team One advanced.

"Team One is at fail-go," their team leader said.

"Go Team One, go Team Two, go Team Three."

Before she had finished the final long e, Raimbaut had tripped the door. It flew upward and Laprada raised her weapon. I rolled through, low, so that she could shoot over me if she had to; gravel and dirt crunched under my back as I came up beside the trash springer. I flipped it onto its side and activated it; as long as it kept running, any bullets fired into it would rematerialize at the dump, and I was behind it.

"Clear," I said, softly, into my mouthpiece, but of course Raimbaut hadn't waited. He was across the alley in two steps and pushed the claphammer up against the place where the bolt went into the jamb.

"Heads," he said. We crouched, and there was a loud thud-clang followed by several crashes around the alley; a claphammer bolt slams forward at about Mach 4, and though the claphammer itself has molecular-bonding feet to maximize the force delivered, normally they tear out and the claphammer itself goes flying.

Laprada passed over me in a blur and was at her position, right of the warehouse door, while it was still falling inward. I charged forward into the dark opening, let my shoulder slam the wall to turn quicker, and sprinted left into the building.

I was very, very lucky. Their rear guard had been paying too much attention forward; it took the three soldiers in front of me just an instant longer to turn than it otherwise might, and I had been through enough of these so that it was instinct to always go through a door with your weapon leveled at person-height. When I saw moving shapes, I didn't have to think whether they were Raimbaut, who was rolling onto the floor at my feet, or Laprada, who wasn't due in yet. The silhouettes were in my target frame and I squeezed the trigger. Neuroducer darts flicked out, trailing their microfiber lines, and caught all three of them before they could quite get their masers around.

The instant the neuroducers found body armor in front of them, they accelerated to punch their needles through to the flesh beneath. I've been hit by those; it feels like a bee sting, but only for a fraction of a second, because as soon as they have a connection to the nervous system, they activate. These neuroducers disconnected their brains from running the show while leaving them up to fool the monitoring. The three men ragdolled to the floor, and Raimbaut leapt down the hall to throw his suppressor net over them.

A sheet of flame and a mighty thunder came around the corner and slammed him into the wall, setting the carpet and his clothes on fire. I said "Medic" into my mike without pausing, raced forward, and sprayed him all over with one of the little disposable fire extinguishers that look like a child's water gun. I took a second with the little air gun of sedative to sting our three prisoners through the suppressor net; I didn't want anything to happen behind me.

Laprada, at my side, helped me drag Raimbaut back from the bend in the corridor. As soon as he was half a meter back he sat up and said, "I'm all right, just playing possum, lots of shooting up that way—"

"All right, I've got your station, you guys get those doors open." Laprada handed him her string of claphammers and lay down on the floor, looking oddly like a little girl playing army in her helmet with a blonde braid hanging out the back. I'd have to remember to pester her for not pinning that up well enough—

There was a hiss-bang and part of the wall opposite me flared welding-arc white, and began to smolder. With a cry, Laprada pulled her head back. A maser had reflected off the top of her helmet, diffusing as it went so that it set a large area of the wall on fire; it was good to know that the microwave diffraction surfaces under the paint were still doing their job.

"Heads," Raimbaut said.

She made a fart noise at him and tossed a grenade around the corner.

We crouched. The flash-bang made the dusty air in the corridor shimmer. Laprada crawled forward to the corner. "Get those doors," she repeated, insistently.

We ran down the corridor; two doors. We slapped claphammers onto them just below their knobs. "Clear," Raimbaut barked, and we crouched, him up by Laprada, me back at the start of the corridor, our unconscious prisoners under the net stretched on the ground between us.

At the krang-bing-bing-tunk of the two ricocheting claphammers, I ducked back to take one door while Raimbaut took the other. One quick step brought me, weapon leveled, face-to-face with a vacuum cleaner and stacked boxes of toilet tissue.

Raimbaut's cry of rage told me he'd found more action. As I turned, Raimbaut was backing away to the wall, his hands up. In my peripheral vision I saw that, beside the man covering Raimbaut, there was now another one covering me.

I raised my hands; that's what they want you to do. Then I looked frightened and sick—or did my best, there being no drama critics in the room, but anyway it worked on this *toszet*—and went limp, falling sideways and letting my weapon drop. That got their attention all the way toward me, and me down on the nice safe floor. Laprada hit them from behind with neuroducer darts.

I tossed my suppressor net over them as Raimbaut rolled to the side of the open doorway. Two maser blasts, unscattered by anything, punched thumb-diameter holes in the wall across from the door; Raimbaut and I looked at each other across the gap. It would be death for either of us to lean into that doorway.

Experimentally, I tossed in an unsecured claphammer on a half-second delay; it clanged once before it blew apart under maser fire, like a clay pigeon facing twenty shooters.

It was hard to see where we were going to go from here. "Margaret, Team Three here," I said. "You can scratch the medic, we're all up and moving. We're in the back corridor, not able to advance to any forward position. We have five prisoners but nothing else of any value. Got a change of plan?"

"We're forming up some CSPs to extract you. So far you're the most successful part of the operation. Try to sit tight."

There was a deep bass rumble from far inside the building, and then a series of crashes and bangs and a lot of confused shouting. I heard the hisses and whuffs of maser fire everywhere, and the soft whumping of neuroducer grenades.

"I'll try," I said, "but we may not be able to hold. We can hear the main force. Sounds like they're giving them a hell of a fight."

"Giraut, the main force was wiped out trying to get in the front door, and apart from you we have no one in the building."

"Well, *somebody's* fighting," I said, crossly. It was just like Margaret, in a crisis, to insist that she knew everything. "In fact there's more firing and noise every second."

As if to belie me, the shooting stopped and someone began yelling at other someones to "Throw down your weapons! We mean it! Throw them *down!*"

"Not only that," I added, "somebody won."

"I can hear through your audio pickup, Giraut. Sorry. I have no idea who that is or what's going on. I'd suggest that your team extract itself, right now, if you can."

I glanced and saw that she'd been copying Raimbaut and Laprada; the two of them, across that deadly doorway from me, nodded. Since we couldn't cross the open doorway, Raimbaut on his side, and I on mine, simply drew our masers, held the beam on sustain, and drew big circles on the opposite wall, leaving door-sized openings.

Laprada and Raimbaut rolled through the hole on their side, and I dove through mine. We rolled to our feet and formed up in what I'd have to say was a very professional manner.

But style only counts for so much.

We were surrounded by ten men in the uniforms of the old Occitan Legion, uniforms that had been illegal ever since the massacre in Caledony twenty-eight years ago. And though their uniforms might be an obscure part of history, the weapons they held were completely up-to-date.

"Hands up very very slowly, *si'ilh gratz-a-vos fai*," Ebles Ribaterra said. He was wearing knee-high boots and a vivid red tabard as well as the purple *tapi*, and all the funny bits of metal on him probably meant he was an officer. "Is one of you in touch with your commander?"

"We all are," I said.

"Can your commander hear me?"

"Tell him I can," Margaret said, quietly, in my ear.

"She can hear you."

Ebles swept a low bow, doffing his peaked, folded, plumed cap (it looked a bit as if it had been stolen from a road company of *Robin Hood*.) "Officially, then, I am instructed to make contact and secure cooperation with representatives of the Council of Humanity. The operation you attacked here was not only illegal under your laws, but under the laws of the Kingdom of Noucatharia as well. Do you accept a truce for negotiation?"

"Tell him we do," Margaret said, in my ear.

"My commander advises me that we accept."

Every one of the men around me holstered his weapon, extended his right leg, held his hands palm up, and bent his left knee, bowing over the extended leg in the traditional Occitan gesture of deep respect.

"Margaret," I said, very softly, "if you're still getting signal from my helmet camera, I think we are very far off the plan."

"Yap," she said, just about the only word she still used of Reason, the language of her home culture. "Yap," again.

It meant yes-but-more-than-yes; hell-yes, yes-without-reservations, absolutely totally god-damn-it-to-hell I-really-mean-it yes. And at the moment it was inadequate to the situation.

3

"Well, no," Margaret said. "It's really not all that odd that we should get along. It is true that my agency would rather that his people didn't exist, and in fact put some effort into preventing them from existing. And it is true that they consider us to be monsters of tyranny from whom they very sensibly fled. But setting all that aside, when you come down to the hard cold core of things, he's a cop and I'm a cop. And that means we have more in common than not." She leaned back in her chair, and the camera on her desk tracked her; for the millionth time in my life, at least, I was reminded that whatever anyone else thought of Margaret's appearance, I adored it, and however much trouble I might have getting along with her in person, I would miss her forever.

"So far," she said, "Ebles has answered every question I could reasonably expect him to answer. Apparently the ultratraditional faction was particularly upset with your work on the Ix Cycle because you were using such extremely non-Occitan material, as they saw it, and further upset because a new, un-Occitan cult was so interested in your work, and even more upset because you were taking Occitan culture out to the wider world and diluting it. And it was *especially* offensive because your career started out recording very traditional material, so the whole thing was a betrayal by a cultural hero. And for reasons he does not want to discuss in detail, creating a fast-grown chimera in Union is simply not as difficult as it is here—might not even be illegal. The process is inherently cheap if you don't have to watch out for cops. Even though there is something that makes me want to throw up when I think about weaponized human beings, I can believe that if there were no laws against creating these single-purpose miserable dying monsters, even a small terrorist faction could afford them—they're no more expensive than an atom bomb or a strain of pneumonic plague. I have to admit that the story makes sense. You see what a nice simple story it is?"

"You don't believe it."

"I don't." She drummed her fingers on the desk, staring down at the surface in front of her, not looking at me. Something she didn't want to say, but no way around it—"Just start with the fact that they were awfully well prepared for us at the warehouse in Nou Occitan, and Ebles turned up with the cavalry far too perfectly on time. He even showed up on your side of the building—how perfect is that?"

"Then why don't we just play footsies a little longer and see if he lets more slip, or we learn more from other sources?"

"Because events are pushing me a lot faster than I want to go. We now have a contact channel with a real extraterritorial colony, instead of a welter of rumors and best guesses. Even better, Ebles is dropping hints like mad that what they want to do is apply to be a constituent state in the Council of Humanity—basically they're asking for a seat on the Council, charter recognition and annexation. That means the Council won't have to set a precedent of conquering an extraterritorial, which they'd rather not do, but they also won't have to *have* an extraterritorial, which is something they want even less. The precedent couldn't be more beautiful—the unauthorized colony is located on Aurenga, wherever that may be, which doesn't have enough qualifying dry land to make a culture space, so there's not even an issue of their having taken space that should have gone to someone else. So if this is done right, it will be a major coup for the OSP."

"And the doing it right is the hard part?"

"Yap. Yap. Yap." She was nodding like she was trying to flick her head off the end of her neck. "Right now our major advantage is that only the Board of the OSP even knows it's a possibility, and we can't know how long that happy state of affairs will persist. Since we've never had an illegal colony try to regularize its status, the Council of Humanity, as soon as they get involved, will be running in circles and screaming and shouting for an indefinite period of time. It's what they do every time they realize that there's some work to be done and that people are watching them again. Once the formal, public diplomacy begins, every possible embarrassment, pointless delay, and somebody-sticking-an-oar-in will happen.

"So you, Raimbaut, and Laprada will be going to Noucatharia. They're going to present you in the guise of being humanity's most popular Occitan artist." Margaret sighed. "Giraut, you do know I'm still fond of you? Forgetting all about being a trusted agent, or my ex-husband, or my partner for so long—you're the best friend I've got, in a field where we don't get to keep many friends."

"This is an extremely ominous way to begin the serious, secret part of the conversation."

"It is," she admitted, "and how did you know I was about to?"

"Because in twenty-eight years of being my friend, and fifteen years of being my boss, Margaret, you've always saved the superserious secret section for last. Also because I happened to notice that you've been as nervous as a rat in a room full of boa constrictors."

She smiled a not-convincing smile at my bantering, but at least she got down to business. "I'm sending you into a trap, Giraut. And I don't know whose trap it is or what they want to trap you for. The time has run out for just waiting and seeing, and whatever opportunity there might be, it's now or never—the Council will be receiving a petition from Noucatharia in just about nine stanweeks." She held up one outstretched hand, palm toward her, and, with her other hand, began pressing the fingers down. "Five facts that bother me. Fact One: Ebles isn't telling us the whole truth.

"Fact Two: Noucatharia is impossible and Aurenga shouldn't be where it evidently is. Do the math. The Lost Legion settled Noucatharia within five months of getting off parole. And Ebles tells us that Aurenga is somewhere tens of light-years beyond Wilson, the farthest planet out in its direction, which built its first springer less than eight stanyears before the Lost Legion moved to Noucatharia. The strange thing is he seems to be telling the truth. From pictures and artifacts we have from Aurenga, we know that there's no planet like Aurenga within that old roughly fifty-light-years-from-Earth frontier. So the directions broadcast from Earth, about how to build a springer, could only be reaching Aurenga about now, or shouldn't quite have gotten there yet. So how could there have been people, or a springer, on Aurenga, to create Noucatharia, twenty years ago?

"That led me to Fact Three." She punched her middle finger down as if she were forcing it into her hand. "Noucatharia has three thousand people, half of them children. Start with about a hundred Lost Legionnaires, almost all of whom found a fertile spouse somewhere . . . two hundred people. Suppose they follow Nou Occitan custom and count everyone over sixteen as adults. They started settling twenty-six years ago, so to have thirteen hundred more adults than they started with, in the first ten stanyears of the colony, one hundred women had thirteen hundred babies. Barely credible if everyone's taking drugs to have multiple births. Then we have fifteen hundred children born in the last sixteen years, which is at least less preposterous since they've been adding eighty mothers a year. But still Aurenga has to have been Planet of the Pregnant for two decades."

"Couldn't they have been producing them all in vitro?"

"Who raises them? You're still looking at families with ten to fifteen young kids at home making up almost all households. Nothing impossible about it, just not terribly plausible. Especially since Ebles admitted he had no children himself. And *still* their population is only possible as long as nobody ever dies. Which brings us to Fact Four. Aintellect, picture up—"

The picture popped up on the com screen, replacing Margaret's image. Over it, her voice said, "Our sources say this was taken in Noucatharia earlier this year."

It was unmistakably a cemetery—a large one, in the middle of a sizable city. "And this one . . . and this one . . ." Two more shots of the same place established its size, and the size of the city around it.

"Margaret, that's got to be at least a thousand graves."

"Right. And the city beyond, just counting apartment buildings, should house ten thousand people, just in the part we can see. So they are lying to conceal something very big—Noucatharia is many times the size they told us, which happens to be the barely-believable maximum size in the first place. And notice too that there are no fresh graves and no weathered headstones, as you'd expect in a cemetery that had been open long enough to accumulate so many graves.

"All right, now, Fact Five. You know we've been investigating the possibility of a Shan psypyx, because one was made secretly just four months before his assassination, and we identified a possible security breach that might have allowed it to be stolen—and we have been picking up hints and rumors that at any time we might be confronted with a demand for ransom or an offer to sell us one or more copies. And you know that much of what we're hearing says that the psypyx, or the group that has it, or most likely both, are in Noucatharia."

"Do you have more about it?"

"Not a thing. Which is why I thought, well, since nothing in the whole Noucathar problem has tied forward to Shan . . . maybe I should look at Shan, again, and see if I can tie him back to Noucatharia."

"And you found something?"

" 'Found' is too mild a word. I dug something out and forced enough different sources to talk about it. Now, remember, I'm one of the ten or so most-highly-cleared people in Council space; I would have sworn there wasn't one thing I would ever have trouble getting to know, if it was already known, and I wouldn't have thought that any human being, let alone any aintellect, would ever argue with me about handing over information, particularly not within my own organization. Yet I spent several days demanding, shouting, threatening, bribing, even appealing to the better nature that most of our colleagues don't have, just trying to learn what turned out to be a very simple story.

"I was finding things that had been sealed for decades, and the aintellects guarding it gave me a hell of an argument, so that I finally had to just pull out my full rank and authority, plus human supremacy, and threaten them.

"We all knew that Shan was from Addams, and came to Earth when he was very young." Addams, which circled Theta Ursa Major, forty-eight light-years from Earth, was the only human-settled planet known that had not gotten into springer contact with the rest of human space. It was an odd planet, the smaller of a genuine double planet (its larger partner was Hull, an ice-terrestrial). The hundred and two cultures of Addams had been sent directions on building a springer at the same time as everyone else. But rather than making Connect at the expected time, as every other world had, Addams had simply turned off their radio and gone silent.

Margaret said, "Here it is. Shan sprang to Earth, from Theta Ursa Major, at the age of five."

"There weren't any springers then—oh—or, but, I suppose that would have been about the time the springer was invented—but you need a springer at both ends of the trip—" My thoughts were whirling. "Maybe I should shut up and let you explain, and maybe you should tell the story in chronological order."

"That might be best," Margaret agreed, smiling. "But allow me the pleasures of dramatic effect, please. Here's the truth about the springer, which I hope will someday lead us to the truth about Shan. What do you remember about how the springer was discovered?"

I thought back to that surprising stanyear when I had been sixteen, and the news media of Wilson, which normally covered concerts, gallery openings, sports, and major court ceremonies, had been flooded with actual news for the first time since the last starship arrival, seven stanyears before. The springer had been the biggest news in human space in centuries. I remembered that the media had said that it had been discovered. They said that word of how to build one had been received from Earth.

Then . . . had they said anything else?

The springer had turned over all of the Thousand Cultures. Humanity had been roaring through the wild Second Renaissance ever since, with more scientific progress, artistic change, and political noise in the past thirty years than in the four hundred preceding. "You know, that's strange. Everyone knows Watt-and-the-steam-engine, Wright-brothers-and-airplane, Turing-and-computer, Chandreseki-and-psypyx. For all I know the springer was invented by a *toszet* named Springer. Maybe the same one who invented the spaniel."

"Well, here's the surprise, Giraut. The OSP doesn't know who invented it, either. Nobody in known human space does, unless they know on Addams. Because the actual way humanity on

Earth got the springer, which then spread to everywhere else by radio, was that the Council Security Office—the old sinecure fossil bureau that existed before the OSP—got a radio message in a code that hadn't been used in centuries, from Addams. It told Earth how to build a springer, and gave us sort of an operations manual for it. Then Earth built its first springer, and the very first time they turned it on to contact the springer on Addams, a very small, frightened boy, somewhere between four and six years old, fell through, screaming and crying incomprehensibly. He was extremely dirty, and very hungry but not dehydrated, and had a bad cut on the palm of one hand.

"And that little boy grew up to be Shan.

"Upon arrival, he had nothing at all but the clothes he was wearing, with a note in his coverall pocket that said 'Destroy your SPRNGR doorway and never build another one with this address. Extreme danger. Destroy it now.' That SPRNGR abbreviation is why we call it a springer. The people and robots in the lab followed directions; then they made more springers, and played with them, and various physicist and engineer aintellects figured out a physics that can account for them, and I am told has many other wondrous possibilities as well. We have never again built a springer with that address; apparently the reasons for that are in a report deriving from an extensive debriefing of Shan, and I still can't get my hands on that report, which may or may not exist and which some aintellects may or may not be withholding from me."

"Shan's arrival was the only springer contact we had with Addams. And the radio cutoff from Addams happened some decades before it was publicly announced; so few stations were bothering to listen that it was easy enough to set up a station on an asteroid out that way and beam signal at the few antennas apt to listen, replaying many decades-old material from the archives. No one will tell me how they knew it was going to stop, and when, or why they covered up the disappeared signal, yet, but my most trusted aintellects and I have a strong suspicion that it's that old, silly motivation of administrators everywhere—to avoid public panic."

It was a lot to absorb. *"Deu,"* I said, at last. "Of all the secrets Shan knew, the biggest secret was Shan himself."

"Yes." Margaret looked more frustrated than I'd ever seen her. "You see what it all implies. Somewhere among human beings—on Addams, and possibly on any number of other worlds—there were springers. Decades before our central government ever heard of them. That at least makes it possible for places like Aurenga to exist. Except . . . who sent the springers there? Or who received the radio message and built one?

"Add to this all the other little odd things we know. Ixism in the aintellects' conspiracy, Ixism on Aurenga, the peculiar appeal of Ixism in Nou Occitan. Shan's connection to the springer mystery, to the aintellects' conspiracy, to everything. Your connection. Mine. And that weird chimera that turned up in the body of your old girlfriend.

"Giraut, as your boss, as I said the other day, I'm looking at a ticking clock that is counting down very fast. There is no good way to just sit tight and wait for more information; too much is obviously moving, out where we can't see it, for purposes we don't grasp. We've got to get into the game, just to find out where it is and what it is. So we have this invitation for you to visit Noucatharia, where so many of these tangled threads seem to end. You are the one and only logical person to go. Connection to Shan, to Occitan, to Ix, and even to the aintellects' conspiracy, and to this bizarre aintellect-in-a-human-body. You're like a living record of everything that seems to be involved in this affair, and it's as if everything that has happened, at least since your fiftieth birthday concert and maybe for a few stanyears before, has been structured to make it *inevitable* that I will send you on this mission to Noucatharia."

She leaned forward to the screen, as if trying to stare a hole through me. "It's a trap. It has to be a trap. When so many apparently disparate circumstances pile together like this, and suddenly there is one clear thing for me to do, and only one . . . that's a trap. God, I wish Shan were here right now—not because he played the game better than I do, I think I'm pretty nearly his equal now, but because I'd so much rather be a field agent under him than have to try to figure this out myself."

"I see what you mean, Margaret. But if you send me, I will go; and looking at it from your point of view, I don't think you have any choice but to send me."

"Anyway, I'm glad that you're willing to take the mission. Wait for orders. They are coming soon."

Of course this isn't exactly like the light of the original Occitan on Earth, but it's more like it than Nou Occitan ever was," Ebles said, as we all reached for sunglasses. Laprada got to hers first; a moment later Raimbaut and I put ours on, and we all looked around. We appeared to have stepped through the springer into some virgin forest, a mix of oak, elm, and ash; but on Earth those had never grown under an equatorial sun, not even a very mild one like this. Still, giving credit where it was due, "You must have had some very fine terraforming designers here," I said.

He shrugged. "*Oc-e-non*. They were interested only in producing a suitable environment for the true Occitan, so they were more single-minded than the ones who designed Wilson. There is nothing on land as creative as the levithi or the aurocs-de-mer or the sea-skunks of Wilson. But if you brought a *trobador* of 1150 A.D. onto one of our islands, he would probably recognize—or think he recognized—every living thing he saw. Even though sometimes what is inside them is drastically different from what is inside their earthly equivalents, and even though some of the things he would see are extinct on Earth. But yes, we did try to make this a beautiful place, and thank you for the compliment."

We had arrived at a portable springer, sitting all by itself at a wide spot on what was clearly a prepared hiking trail. The moment that we stepped through, Ebles turned off the springer, folded it down, and tossed it into another springer, which, as he explained, went straight to a dump. "Furthermore," he said, "the one we just used was brought here from Wilson."

Since a springer's address depended only on where it was created, not where it was currently, this meant that nothing had been given away of Aurenga's position, and now that that springer had been converted to slag, anyone stealing the address would have a three-thousand-digit address for a place that didn't exist at all. Behind the gray mist of any springer that tried to transmit to the one we had just used would lie a pseudosurface harder to penetrate than cryonic neutronium. Aurenga was safe from invasion, for the moment, and we had no backup, forever.

The trail wound along the side of a high, steep ridge that plunged down to a narrow black-sand beach, in a small cove blocked by a sandbar, over which surf broke and pounded.

The sky was a surprisingly deep, almost Prussian, blue, and the sun, not far above the water, was larger and I thought more orange than Earth's. The ridge on which we stood, and the surrounding hills, blazed with the color of leaves just turning. Down near the water, the trees were still mostly green. "I thought you said we were on the equator," I commented. "But this is fall if ever there was fall."

"Oh, we have seasons. Very fast ones, in fact." He pointed to the sun. "That's a very young star, and this is an extremely young planet; our orbit is quite elliptical, for a planet, and very close in, so much so that in a few hundred million years, as the sun warms up, this world will go into a runaway greenhouse like Venus. But for right now, it's just right, and we swing in close enough to get a real summer and far enough out to get a real winter, about a hundred and sixty standays to our year. That's part of the genetic engineering around here; all the vegetation is fast-growing and fast-dying, and everything in the seas that can move is constantly migrating. But we don't get much of our seasons from the axial tilt—that's almost nothing. Our Arctic Circles are only about sixty kilometers across."

We descended the trail; it might have been any nice hike on any nice fall day on any of a dozen worlds.

At the bottom of the last bend was an overnight cabin where a couple might come for a weekend away or that several friends might take together to enjoy swimming in the cove. Inside, it had the sort of high ceilings and windows that give a lot of light while preserving the feeling of privacy, the kind of place that's perfect for stargazing on a cold night or making love on a warm afternoon. For the moment, though, all of the elegant, polished-hardwood furniture had been shoved to the side. A battery of scanners and medical equipment sat in the center of the room, cables snaking everywhere around them from the power room in the basement. At the end of the room, a springer was waiting, already powered up, its screen featureless gray.

"My next job is to make sure that you're not smuggling anything that's against the rules inside your bodies. Are any of you wearing any medical devices?" Ebles asked.

"Laprada and I are still transferring into our new bodies, so we have implanted psypyxes," Raimbaut said.

"We have your medical records," Ebles explained, "so we know exactly what that psypyx should look like when we scan and profile you. If you'll step through these sensors, we're also going to make sure that none of you is wired in any way— especially that none of you is wearing an implant and most especially that no one has a microspringer transmitter. You know and I know that you would have had to be very foolish to do so; let us hope that your superiors have not been treacherous, and that mine are not trigger-happy."

Of course the scans turned up nothing. Margaret was not the type for obvious, simple tricks. Then we went through a nano detector/reader that confirmed that all matter processors in our bloodstreams were immunological, to make sure we weren't planning on dropping anything that might, in a few days, grow into a springer and contact the OSP.

We came up clean on that, too.

"Well," Ebles said, "that would seem to cover every possible reason for not taking you through to Masselha." The springer screen vanished and in its place was the flat black metal surface of an unpowered springer; a moment later it began to shimmer and then turned to that featureless gray again. Following my gaze, Ebles commented, "Yes, my superiors just switched the address. Now instead of bringing a bomb here, it is addressed to take you there. Or almost there, to be more precise. This last precaution is something one of our politicians thought of, and though it's really stupid—it can have no benefit at all to our security—it does at least lead to a nice view, and giving you a nice view and a pleasant arrival, as a side benefit, was much easier than explaining to the politician in question why this wouldn't do any good. We're going to spring onto an airship and approach Masselha on that."

I asked Ebles, "Er, purely speculatively—and because I am the child of a one-term legislator and several-term bureaucrat— since it really is quite obvious that the precaution of springing us to an airship can do you no good at all, by any chance did you want that pointed out in the presence of some rival? Perhaps because you yourself are involved in politics?"

"We are all involved in politics, *Donz* Leones."

"And diplomacy."

"Just so."

We filed through the springer and onto the forward observation deck of *Enseingnamen* (or at least the sign beyond the springer, hanging from the invisible overhead dome, said "Welcome to Noucathar Airship Enseingnamen. You are on the forward observation deck. This area is open to all personnel and guests."

We walked forward, and the view made me gasp with awe, and turn to Ebles to exclaim, "*Que zenzar!*"

"*Zenzar*" means shining, and it does, but not the way a piece of aluminum foil might shine in a gutter; it means the kind of meaningful, haloed shine that a stage lighting designer gets by putting a strong downlight right over an actor, so that the actor's face and shoulders are surrounded by a brightly lit outline that pops him from the background straight into your memory. "*Zenzar*" means to shine in that present moment the way that the dew on the grass did on the best morning of your life, the way that the snow on the distant mountains did at the instant when you finished your best ski run ever; one of our poets said that to say a thing was *zenzar* was to say the gods themselves had liked it so well they had put it in a frame of glowing light.

From the air, approaching over the harbor, the city of Masselha was *zenzar.*

Aurenga's skies are among the bluest that humanity has ever looked upon; the forests and fields that surround Masselha were an equally vivid green, cut off exactly at an imposed tree line. The rugged gray-white bluffs bit into the sky. As we flew in past the stony headlands, guarded by their faux-ruins castles, I looked down through the transparent cyan bay to see swarms of fish, turtles, and seals. "So far we have no pollution, plus much less demand for seafood, and far more success with terraforming than the plan called for," Ebles said, following my gaze. "Believe it or not we had to introduce seals just to keep the fish from becoming a nuisance."

I nodded and looked up at the city itself, which rose in cool, elegant curves, rich in domes and cones, surprisingly squat and powerful. There were bits that I recognized from pictures of Nimes, of Avignon, and of the original Masselha, the one that had spent its last thousand years as "Marseilles" after the French conquest.

"That's a huge city," Laprada said, "for a population of three thousand."

"The city is mostly empty at the moment. With the nanos, you know, there's no particular reason to wait until you have the people, and then build the city; we know what population we will have in a few generations, when we reach stability, and this is a city that will hold them comfortably."

The airship swept on over the harbor, but along the pier there were just five sailboats and a small motor launch; I saw now, as we drew closer, that there were no crowds, just a bare scattering of small clumps of people.

"What's the airship for?" I asked.

"Patrol; we're an illegal colony and we have to look out for any sign of invasion. The same reason that you'll notice, sooner or later, that there are fifteen pens for high-speed submarines over there." He pointed. "We have a whole planet, all to ourselves, to guard with the equivalent of about ten CSP companies. And most of what there is to guard is water, and very stormy water at that. Satellites watch the oceans from above, submarines scout it constantly, and still sometimes you need to get closer than a satellite gets, faster than a submarine does. These airships can go to Mach 4, or hover over a site for weeks.

They make a good compromise. But they're also rather like the tall ships you see down there—just beautiful to see them come and go, you know."

I saw that the tall towers on the big, central palace were capped with mooring masts. "Are we going to tie up?"

He seemed startled, and then glanced and saw what I had seen. "Oh, no, we only use the mooring masts on very calm days for ceremonies—the airship looks good in the background of a vu, you know, and we're still Occitan, we like things that look good, especially if they are a nuisance. But this is a windy, stormy planet, and mooring to a mast is something we don't do for long; it would be much too dangerous except on very calm days."

"But this thing will make Mach 4?"

"When it does it leaves a trail half a kilometer long of white-hot plasma; it takes a big engine to push something this size, with such a low density, so fast, and the aintellects seem to be very proud of themselves for figuring out how to make it take the stress. Moored to a mast surrounded by people, yes, it could keep from hitting the ground in a big gust of wind, but at the expense of charring whoever was on the ground. Which some of us would think an unwarranted expense." His com pinged, and he talked briefly with whoever or whatever was driving the ship. "We're going to take one circuit of the city, and then spring you down to the ground."

"That's fine, I'm enjoying the ride," Raimbaut said. "How many airships do you have, since you didn't mind telling us the number of sub pens?"

Ebles shrugged. "There's no point in concealing our military strength from a power that could overwhelm us overnight, is there? We have twenty-two of these airships, with six more to be added soon."

"And fifteen submarines—"

"Two other ports have fleets of submarines. You see? I will even volunteer the information. Military security is not an issue here." He was clearly impatient and irritated at the questions—not any reaction I could have expected.

"But you only have ten companies—not more than two battalions if you raise your whole militia—"

"Our defense machines are robots, almost entirely, just as yours are. If there are CSPs on the ground in Masselha, we will have lost. So the militia is more a formality than anything else; the actual defense of the planet is carried out by the machines. Most of the craft, most of the time, have no human crews. Now, are we quite done with this, or shall I take you around for the traditional photography of our fortifications and secret weapons?" It was phrased to tease, but there was an angry edge under it.

"Oh, look!" Laprada cried, pointing. "What's that palace?"

"It's the college of music where Giraut will be teaching," Ebles said, "and it's also one of the buildings we are proudest of." He launched into an account of the big, gaudy mess, which I would have described as a celebration of Occitan excess, I think even when I was younger. But Laprada's little cry had served its purpose; it had distracted Ebles from the confrontation that was building, and it had drawn my attention to something else in the same direction: an enormous cemetery in the part of the city where all the buildings were blank of ornament or advertisement.

The white domes and vaults, the spires and squares, and the glorious little parks linked by chains of waterfalls and canals crept by below. Beyond them, the strangely blank and sealed buildings showed us flat, blank faces, and at the heart of it all, *zenzar* like an emerald in an ivory setting, lay that gigantic burial ground.

4

"It does feel odd," I admitted to Raimbaut, as we sat in a café that evening. "The Ix Cycle, at least to me, seems like the thing that is most apt to be my major work, artistically, and during its first release I'm literally nowhere to be found. But at least it gives me a pleasantly unfocused anxiety so that I always have something to attribute nameless fears to."

"Just out of curiosity," Laprada said, "if these people think they are purifying your traditional culture, why is there a place to have *coffee* on every other block?"

"Well, because they're purifying it artistically," Raimbaut said, grinning. "And if you spend any length of time with any artist, you know they live on coffee. That's the real secret of the Dark Ages in the Euro culture. We think we lost all these ancient works for which we only have titles or fragments. The fact is they didn't have coffee, so nobody got around to making most of them. Sophocles really *meant* to write a hundred plays, which is why we have a list of them, but he only got seven done, because he didn't have coffee, and also there wasn't anywhere to meet Euripides over coffee and complain about how the whole playwriting business wasn't what it used to be and nobody was getting any respect, or deserving it, anymore."

"If we don't stop him now," I said, "he will keep going all night. I had him in my head for four stanyears, you know."

"Well," Laprada said, "I'm going to invoke Rule One." Rule One was a team agreement: because there was no sure-to-be-secret method of communication, and none of us knew anything that the Noucathars couldn't learn hundreds of other ways, we would just talk. "So far they have chosen to tell us a large number of things we can't be expected to believe. First of all, they might have grown the city in a few days, of course, with enough nanos, but why? Why not just grow the major landmarks and public buildings, and then a little bit of living space for the few people you have, and then add bits as you need them? Secondly, terraforming this world took some effort. With a young dim star, and all that water, this place should be in whiteover, frozen right to the bottom everywhere. I mean, look at how fast Nansen re-froze after predecessor terraformation stopped. This place should have re-frozen even faster. So somebody thawed it—and even with the best modern technology, nanos, and self-replication, that takes some time and effort.

"I don't think they paid for a planetary engineering job on that scale out of the living stipends of two hundred people, or the mustering-out pay of a hundred noncoms with dishonorable discharges. Yet the Lost Legion started dropping out of parole and vanishing to this place less than four stanmonths after their sentencing."

I shrugged. "Even if the money could be made to work, the energy couldn't. They didn't find this place and melt a whole huge extra-deep world-ocean in four stanmonths! You can't even get a springship out of a solar system in four stanmonths. So this place was already here, and already terraformed—I would bet that Masselha was mostly built and ready to move into—and someone gave it, or maybe sold it, to the Lost Legion, who customized it with nanos. Right so far?" She sat back in her chair. Her braids and freckles made her look so young that it wasn't always easy to remember that she had decades of experience in politics and intelligence; *visually Heidi, psychologically Machiavelli*, as she liked to say of herself.

Raimbaut added, "And it doesn't work militarily. Those are not defenses against any believable invasion by the Council of Humanity. The satellites, airships, and submarines might just barely allow you to intercept a ship trying to bring a springer onto the planet, and to search for springer emissions everywhere, and so forth, so I buy that it's a precaution against invaders with springers. So they expect an invasion but not by us. That's interesting."

We got up and walked; Ebles had warned us that because the city was a small town in population, everyone would feel very free to approach us and talk to us, but in our aimless wandering, our feet happened to take us first toward a not-yet-occupied quarter of the city, and then into a vast, shadowy dark park. "Plenty of other evidence that this place has been here for a long time and was grown for other purposes," Raimbaut commented. "You still can't get a finished result in less than fifty percent of the original growth time without massive cancers all through it. Even if the oaks and the chestnuts grow at bamboo-speed, some of these have to be many stanyears old—and I don't think they grow that fast. I feel it in my bones that this park has been here for centuries."

We walked a while longer without saying anything, until we came, at the end of one street, to a carved-stone balustrade looking down across a great swath of deep green lawn, sloping down to a pool-and-waterfall cascade that then continued down into some dense, thick woods. "What a difference a moon makes," Raimbaut commented.

Across the park the multiple high spires of the Museum of Weaving stuck up above the trees. The dark shape against the star-spattered sky, in a city so supernaturally quiet, was a marvel.

"Someone cared very much what kind of place to live this would be," I said. "We must come back here in the daytime."

"You will want to make sure you're in your diplomatic garb," Ebles said, joining us. He wore a light *tapi*, though the night was not at all cold. "I thought I would take the liberty of joining you."

"Why would we want to be in diplomatic clothing in a public park?" Laprada asked.

"Well," Ebles said, "ask either of our two Occitans to see with their *jovent* eyes—"

"Ah," I said. "And I suppose it's well away from other sites so it's safer."

"Safer for what?" Laprada asked.

"For dueling," Raimbaut said. "That level lawn at the bottom would have perfect footing, and lots of room with nothing to run into, especially because once swords are drawn, everyone clears a big space. Yes, I see what you mean, Ebles. If we don't wear diplomatic attire, we'll look like those pathetic *tostemz-toszet*-types that are always looking to prove that they are not old."

Ebles sighed. "It's more of a problem than that. Can you imagine an Occitan city where dueling is outlawed? But we had to."

I was startled. "Why? Can't you repair neuroducer injuries?"

He stepped forward to put his face in the shadow of a tree and said, without looking at me, "We can't confine people to neuroducers. Too many real weapons around. Most people have one or two in every room, and one to carry. And our people are Occitan, so there are a couple of real killings here every year, before the police break them up."

"Why would you have so many real swords around?" I asked.

"Not swords. Guns. You'll see."

The moon rose higher, and shadows crept back toward their objects. Ebles stayed in the shadow but none of us spoke again that night, till we walked back to our rooms and said goodnight.

Arnaut Vertzic, the Minister for Purity, explained, "The problem is that theoretically the Council of Humanity claims all human beings as subjects of its sovereignty, and all human-inhabited space as its territory. Since the invention of the springer, the title 'ambassador' has come to mean 'proconsul'; the Council's ambassador to a culture is not someone who represents the Council to them, it's the person who stands over them and makes sure they stay within Council policy. So we would be delighted if you described yourself as a cultural exchange envoy or representative for the Council, but—since it would therefore imply that we exist apart from the Council, that is exactly what you are *not* allowed to do."

"That's right," I said. "I'm visiting this area for the Council, but I am not representing the Council of Humanity to your government because if I did that would imply that the Council of Humanity was allowing itself to be aware that you have a government. Approximately. My boss could cover this in detail, with diagrams. On things like this, I usually just follow her orders."

"And the problem from my side," Vertzic said, making a small sour face to indicate that he too thought this was very silly and bureaucratic, "is that every title you *could* accept—cultural legate, delegate for artistic matters, and so forth—carries with it an implication that we are in some way merely an irregular territory which rightfully belongs under the control of the Council. That is of course unacceptable to us. So are we stymied as to what to call you, before we can even begin to discuss what you might do here?"

I smiled very warmly, making it clear that Arnaut Vertzic and I just might be the best of friends, near-*companho*, really, and it was us two friends and our reasonableness against our strict and senseless superiors. (Despite the fact that he was a lumpy porcine man with sticky white skin like a fallen cake and an obsequiousness that seemed only to lack a tail to wag.) An ancient game in diplomacy: try to establish an interpersonal bond, complain about your boss, get the other fellow to complain about his, and see if he's dumb enough to give the store away to his so-sympathetic friend.

We had established that neither of us was that dumb, but of course now we could hardly admit that we'd been feeling each other out for gullibility, so we had to continue the pretense that we liked each other and that our bosses were the problem. I was getting tired of that game, so it was time to pull out the solution I preferred. "Well," I said, "just before I left, they did hammer out a compromise that I was approved to offer. The Council of Humanity will simply declare me and my assistants to be 'Council Personnel on Paid Detached Duty,' and you will refer to me as a visiting teacher, visiting scholar, something of the sort, without mentioning where I'm visiting from. That way they admit that I am here working for them, you admit that I am from somewhere else, and nobody talks about who is sovereign relative to whom."

He paged an aintellect and watched his screen for a few minutes. For all I knew he was playing solitaire.

When he had made me wait the minimum time to make it look good, he said, "Well, several hundred aintellects can't see anything wrong with that solution. So as of this moment you are our Visiting Artist, and you are the Council's Employee Etcetera. You already have your schedule for your two concerts, and we have set up your recording sessions and your workshop on the schedule you requested. Do you have any questions?"

"Two," I said. "Both possibly offensive."

"Good, that's the kind I am paid to deal with."

Arnaut Vertzic said that so cheerfully and brightly that I was forced to consider the possibility that he meant it; worse yet, I might like him.

"Well, then, why were problems of this kind in the jurisdiction of the Ministry for Purity?"

Vertzic grinned. "What a reasonable question. I know my title sounds as if I were either a censor or in charge of religious instruction. But it's purity in the sense that 'Cathar' means pure; the original Cathars were trying to be religiously pure, but we are trying to be culturally pure. My jurisdiction is over anything that might have an impact on how we define 'purely Occitan.' So one part of our definition is our relation to the Council of Humanity—specifically that we don't accept any authority by them over us—and my job was to make sure that we didn't accidentally accept it. And your second offensive question?"

"You have satellites, submarines, and airships patrolling the whole surface area of Aurenga. Now, if the Council of Humanity finds out where you are, and invades, they will send more CSPs than your whole population. And those patrol craft of yours won't last five minutes. I regret that all this sounds so much as if I were making threats, which I assure you I don't want to do. I'm just outlining what will happen if the Council grabs this world, and I do not think it could come as a surprise to you."

"It does not. But if you aren't making threats, then why are you bringing this up? As you say, we are well aware of it."

"Well, I don't believe you're crazy, and much as we Occitans love a futile gesture, I don't believe you are making one at the scale and expense of your whole planet."

"Perhaps we are merely being very pure, and relishing a particularly futile gesture."

"It's always possible that I'm deluded. Based on my record, I'd say it's probable. But all the same I don't believe that it is the Council forces that worry you. Of course I can imagine such a large investment in hardware just for symbolic purposes; cultures do sillier things all the time; but I don't believe it."

"You have a great deal of trouble believing some things, *Donz* Leones."

"I do."

"Would you like to go somewhere for coffee, and perhaps just sit and talk? We are done with all the official parts, now." Diplomatic speech for "let's go talk about the real stuff."

"That might be pleasant." Diplomatic for "Yes."

Anyway, it *was* pleasant. Vertzic and I turned out to have some acquaintances in common, and eventually I realized he had attended Rimbaud's Academy, the main rival of my old school, St. Baudelaire's. "Raimbaut had a terrible year there," I said, "before he transferred and became one of us."

"Oh, *deu*! He's *that* Raimbaut Bovalhor! I noticed it originally but you know, it's such a common name—well! I must shake his hand. And first yours."

Though I had no idea about what, we shook hands very solemnly.

"We were classmates, and I was the class goat after he was the class goat," Arnaut explained. "There was a group of really nasty bullies, musician-athletes who were always winning prizes. The school was very proud of them, so no one would do anything about their habit of abusing smaller boys, since after all—you remember the old days—real *enseingnamen* was supposed to include a little dash of cruelty. Anyway, after Raimbaut was their target, I was. Except for one wonderful week when they were all expelled for losing a big fight in the street with Raimbaut and his new St. Bo's *companho*—"

"Losing? They beat us purple!"

"Apparently, some of them got injuries that prevented their playing their instruments for a while, leaving some trophies to go to other schools. Or perhaps it wasn't as lopsided as it was supposed to be. Anyway, you, Raimbaut, and the others were responsible for the only reprieve I ever got from the bullies."

The conversation drifted off to school days, old times, life as a *jovent*, and how the time slips by and suddenly those memories are so far away that you might as well have gotten them from someone else. At least one advantage of growing up Occitan is that by the time you're twenty-five, you have plenty of stories to swap. It was all very pleasant until Arnaut said, "Candidly, do you see a problem with our affiliating to the Council of Humanity?"

"Well, there are only three thousand of you, and the current smallest culture, Dakota, has seven million. It's more likely you'll be invited to integrate into Nou Occitan."

"We could live with that."

"I'm not altogether sure that Nou Occitan can," I said. "Not anymore. Your culture manifestly causes great human suffering; I would hope the Royal Occitan Parliament and the Council of Humanity would have problems with that, and I will be disappointed if they don't."

"Disappointed?"

I shrugged. "I don't like it, but sometimes the Council of Humanity compromises just to prevent an open break. We let Pure, Égalité, St. Michael, and Texaustralia, to my knowledge, keep brutal and oppressive parts of their culture in order not to have an open rupture with us. I prefer what we did in places like Caledony, Freiporto, Fort Liberty, and New Bengala—kicked down the doors and told everyone they were joining human society, right now, and that individual human rights were going to be universally enforced, even against the cultural government."

"But Occitan culture—"

"Is often permeated with a simply glorious *gratz* and *espiritu*, but the pre-springer version was brutal and misogynistic and wasted many lives, in order to achieve that very narrowly defined ideal. Thirty-some stanyears after Connect, no doubt there are fewer really Occitan Occitans in Nou Occitan, but certainly there are more happy ones. Especially if you count women, which, in the old days, we didn't."

To my surprise—he seemed determined to keep being a better person than I expected—Arnaut nodded and said, "You will find that many of us are relieved, not at all secretly, to have someone come in here and make us stop some of the foolish, uncomfortable, and cruel customs that we once thought it was so important to save." He paused a moment, licked his lips, and said, "May I ask whether any of the experiences that led you to that conclusion happened on Briand? I know you must think something. You wrote that song cycle about him."

There was something about the way he said "him" that made me feel as if my ears had just stood straight up, like a rabbit in a cartoon. "Ix was not the only interesting person I met on Briand. Far from it. And he's not the only character in the Ix Cycle, by far."

"But still . . . a man of his influence . . . a man whose teachings have now captured millions—"

I leaned forward and took a big gamble. "Arnaut, by any strange chance, are you Ixist?"

"It's an un-Occitan religion and everyone here is a member of the Holy Catholic and Catharian Church," he said, much too quickly, as his right hand slipped from the table, against his body, where it was unlikely that anyone except me would see it roll to the side in an emphatic thumbs-up. "Except of course for you and your *companho*. I hope I haven't given offense with what I've just said . . . that none of you are . . . ?"

I shook my head slightly; he shrugged.

So the Minister for Purity—officially the fourth-ranking cabinet minister—having coffee in a public place, had to fear being spied upon by people he couldn't trust. And he was a secret Ixist. And obviously needed to keep it secret. "Well," I said, "then let me tell you what I really think, since you have been frank with me. The peoples of Tamil Mandalam and Yaxkintulum hated each other, no question. And they both had cultures that were strongly xenophobic and intensely inward-looking. If the

Council had jumped in with both feet, there is no question that there would still be Council peacekeeping forces there today, being shot at by both sides, and we'd be paying a bill in lives per month, perhaps tens of lives per month. Furthermore, after the Council had opened its Bazaar, to make the outsiders and the misfits wealthy and take away the power of the traditional leaders to ruin lives, all those traditions would have burned up in one big, happy *foomp!* the same way they did in Noupeitau."

"But you were a Traditional, in Occitan society," Arnaut said.

"Things change, and they aren't what you expected them to be, and time hurries on," I said. "I was sincere about Traditionalism then, I am sincere about encouraging assimilation now, and who knows what I might be sincere about the day after?"

"Just so," Arnaut said. "Just so. Sad to say, one thing that does remain the same is that there's never unlimited time to just sit with a friend, no matter how agreeable the friend." He pushed back his chair and stood. "Oh, and, by the way, that was an excellent question about the airships, and why we are patrolling, and what we are patrolling against."

I stood, shook his hand, and waited. "Are you going to *answer* that question?" I asked him.

"Not at all. But I think it was an excellent question. Perhaps your second-best. Do you suppose that if the Council of Humanity had, as you say, kicked down the door on Briand, and forced both cultures into collapse and dissolution, that we would have had the teachings of Ix?"

"He would have told you that every wise thing he ever said had been said to us many times before. He might have been a good thing, very probably he was. But he was *never* necessary."

"Thank you for that insight. I do hope you and I will talk more while you are here, and perhaps on future visits as well. I'm sure there are more questions we can answer for each other."

5

"There are just three women in the performing workshop, and none in composing," I said, under my breath, as I turned to pass a wine bottle full of water to Raimbaut.

"So which one do you think it will be?"

"No question, Reilis de la Caelazur. She's twenty-five stanyears old so she must have been among the very first ones born here." I kept my face pointed toward him; here on a ledge on a rock face above the sea, there was a good chance we were not being listened to, but nothing's perfect. "Olive skin, gray-green eyes, wheat-blonde hair, could be Paxa's daughter or Azalais-when-she-was-younger's sister—so they did some research but they don't know me perfectly. Today she listened very intently and asked smart, brief questions. And acted like I was the most fascinating thing she'd ever seen, of course."

"Of course." Raimbaut wriggled back a little to get his bootheels farther from the edge.

We had agreed before coming that we would establish a habit of going hiking in hard-to-bug places. We could at least make them work for information. We had also been quite certain that an attractive young woman, probably planted in the workshop, would approach me. No one would bring in a visitor like me, in circumstances like these, without at least *trying* to turn me. I was officially of suspect loyalty already, and my reputation would probably lead them to try a woman rather than money or ideology.

We watched the waves pound the rocky shore far below us a little longer, then followed the trail that laced from ledge to ledge along the sheer cliff face back up to the top.

That evening we did the same thing we had done every night since arriving in Masselha: we went to some reception to stand about in Occitan clothes and be bored, disagreeing politely whenever we were asked if this wasn't, really, in our hearts, the place where we felt we belonged. At least that's what they asked Raimbaut and me. Noucathars hardly asked women anything, so Laprada had to stand and be bored in Occitan clothes without even that much relief.

"Why are they all like that?" Raimbaut asked, as we strolled back to our hotel late one evening, after a long, pointless, dull party. "At home, when we were young, when everything turned around being a *jovent* and we were all about as Occitan as anyone could ever be, we never talked about being Occitan or who was most Occitan or what the Occitan thing to do would be. We talked about whether or not a *tapi* broke at the right point to display our thighs, and whose poetry had the best juxtaposition of refinement with vulgarity, and who played the lute best."

"And whose *entendendora* had nice legs," I added, "and who was getting between them besides her *entendendor*, and whether or not her *entendendor* could defeat her boy-on-the-side in a duel *atz fis prim*. At least they do still talk about who's doing who."

Laprada groaned, "Oh, god. Oh, god, do they. At least you boys aren't pushed off into the *donzelhas'* corner."

"Was it worse than usual tonight?"

"Either that or I've lost all my essential skills. Back on Earth when they called me Proddy, I might have handled this just fine, but I don't giggle very well anymore. The major topic of conversation at the center of that swirl of big foofy dresses is 'girls who are too brainy and will never get a man.' God, god, *god*, god, *god*. I would *kill* to go through a good, brisk assassination attempt—either as the assassin or the bodyguard. Or maybe a smash-and-grab on an illegal lab. Right now you could sign me up to do deep cover in a Freiporto drug warehouse, unarmed, with no communicator. The *donzelhas'* corner is honestly worse than the artist-café society on Earth was; at least the people I spent my teen years with knew they were useless, and some of them even tried to resist." She sighed, and, obviously imitating someone's voice, said, " 'Your hair is not—well, it's not—well, it's not the way that it would be if it was—you know how? Like that. It's not.' Longest single speech sticking to one topic I heard all night. I'd love to come over among all you testicle-types and barge in on some of the politics and philosophy conversations."

"Then do," I said. "We're not here to make friends. I'm sorry if it wasn't clear that you didn't have to put up with being shoved over into the corner—"

"Well, I'm going to stop, but there was some use in going there the first few days. I did pick up some information. Even if it was mostly about my hair."

Apart from the soft clop of our bootheels on the cobblestones, the swish of Laprada's long skirts (they were breakaway and she was packing an extremely modern and non-Occitan arsenal on her hips under them), and the occasional clink of the chains of our scabbards, the street remained silent.

The next morning, I was in a mildly foul frame of mind when I set down my fork, wiped my mouth, and went upstairs to change into my better clothes for the workshop. I had worked myself into being angry at the world in general by the time I went back out through the big arched gallery of the hotel and into the warm, sunny streets of Masselha. It was another gorgeous day, and I couldn't help noticing, in the clear amber-white sunlight, that all the traditional Occitan costumes looked like costumes. I had a feeling of being on the set for some enormous historical epic, set in some fashion-minded designer's vision of medieval Avignon.

Today would be Reilis's turn. No doubt, having found the exact body type I liked, they were now going to surprise me with her talent—they would have trained her very heavily so that she would be conspicuously the best in the class. There would be no more real music in her than you'd find in an aintellect, but she'd have a proficiency, and feign a passion, that would make her stand out in the little clot of not-quites and never-to-bes that they had saddled me with.

There is something about being played for an utter fool, by people who think they can fool me about the things I know and love best, that makes me grouchy and spiteful. (Perhaps you've noticed.)

The conservatory's spaces were like everything in Masselha—décor was rigorously and consistently Occitan, but in any room where people made music, the blank bare walls, floor, and ceiling were antiseptically clean grown-in-place single-piece hardwood, every bit, from the baffle to the rake, clearly the work of acoustic-engineer aintellects, not human craftsmen.

They were still lovely spaces to work in, if you could find your way past the indifferent quality of the performances—a perfect metaphor for what was wrong with Noucatharia.

Reilis de la Caelazur was the first one up that morning. At least they had prepared nice bait for me. She was very beautiful, with an exceptional contrast between darker skin and lighter hair and that shade of sea-gray eyes that always hypnotizes me (I wondered how much research they had done to find that out?). A mesomorph, she might have done well at crew or as a soccer back, and she carried herself in a way that suggested she had been more of an athlete than most of the local *donzelhas*.

So I was very prepared, psychologically, to defend myself. I walked into the room; they were all waiting, and tuned, as I expected. Curtly, I gestured Reilis toward the performer's chair, and sat down to see what else would be part of the bait.

Reilis walked to the chair, sat down, got into position, glanced at me. I nodded impatiently. She gave me a tiny half smile (wonder how long she practiced *that?*), bent to her work, and played.

The universe changed. With a lute in her hand, and an audience around her, she was one of the most wildly alive people I have ever seen in my life. She seemed more focused on the life within her, more astounded by it, than anyone I had ever encountered—even more than my childhood friend Bieris Real, who had grown up to be a well-known painter; even more than Ix preaching; even more than Paxa in the middle of our wildest everything-turned-to-solid-shit, surrounded-and-shoot-our-way-out operations.

Reilis had talent, as much as the very best performers I had ever seen, but of course the Noucathars, having studied me so thoroughly, would have used the most talented bait they could find. But how did they find someone who would put her heart into it? Intellectually I know that there are people who sing with deep passion that they don't feel, and actors who have an utter ring of truth but no internal state corresponding to what they are doing. Mild autism is fairly common in the arts.

But I would swear that this was not merely technical brilliance onto which I was projecting emotional content. Reilis handled the lute the way the newly mature handle a lover's body, as if simultaneously wanting to devour it and fearing that it might vanish at any moment. The coordination between fingers and sounds seemed to delight her, as it would a mere brilliant technician, but when she sang—there is a moment, if you are lucky, when an old song *lives*, and you hear it for the first time no matter how familiar with it you are. The tiny changes that a slight difference of grip and pressure, a slightly different way of plucking a string, make in the timbre, were lined up with the little catches and rushes of her voice as it went from pitch to pitch, word to word, breath to breath.

She always meant what she played. Most people don't—they are busy hitting pitches, or remembering words, or wallowing in the feeling; but Reilis did, as naturally as anything.

When she sang of a lover far away and missing his palm on her thigh, I would defy any hetero man to sit still; when she sang of loneliness, it was like a fine whiskey sliding down your throat, by a fire, all alone in the woods, on a cold night two days' walk from home, with just your little fire and the distant stars for company.

She was tasting and expressing, meaning each word at the moment it came, and not telegraphing it an instant before or hanging on to it an instant longer. She sang as naturally as a little girl singing to herself and dancing in the yard, when she thinks she's all alone. That particular miracle, perhaps the only miracle I was prepared to recognize by that point in my life, was something I never grew tired of. (The impossibility of growing tired or jaded about it is essential to a true miracle, *m'es vis*.)

Well, I was supposed to act as if I were falling for this, and it wasn't going to take much acting. Of course it didn't hurt that she was beautiful. That hardly ever does hurt; blame it on my upbringing or my gender or both. Hair the color of newly varnished maple, eyes the shade of gray that would invite comparisons to the sea on a sunny windy day, nose almost but not really turned up, a strong-yet-delicate jaw at the base of a heart-shaped face. And the most important thing I could do was to remember that none of it really had anything to do with me.

When she finished her set, I clapped loudly, and of course so did everyone else.

Well, all right, I'm sure she is. Has to be. And I am forced to give Ebles or Arnaut or whoever came up with Reilis a great deal of credit; they found the perfect bait," I muttered to Laprada, in the middle of a hissing and whispering quarrel we were having while the regenner chopped up the breakfast dishes in the kitchen. "You don't *own* Raimbaut, and he can do what he wants."

"He's just confused about what he wants and you are taking advantage of him the same way you would any other pretty young body," she snapped back at me, and then, as a plate hit the smashers, whispered, "All right, we proceed and you walk into the trap. I'll start a conversation about your infatuation tonight at dinner."

She'll be very fine indeed," I said to Raimbaut and Laprada, over dinner that night. "She's right out on the edge of lyric and music."

"You're certainly excited enough about finding this one," Laprada said. "Are you sure it's not just a sense of relief after some of the duds they saddled you with?"

"I'm sure that could be part of it," I said. "But Reilis—and this *pescaroz*—are so far the two things I've found here that really make me say, 'Now *that* is Occitan! Now that is *authentic!*'"

"The *pescaroz* is good," Raimbaut agreed. "Though I think more is owed to the ingredients than to the chef. They send robots out with instructions to bring back a few perfect fish every day, and they've got a whole planet of ocean to support all those fish. Three thousand people eating the pick of the planet eat pretty well."

I nodded. "That's what's really so odd about Reilis—oh, all right, I caught you both rolling your eyes."

"Well, Giraut, you're showing every symptom of being in love again," Laprada said. "We've seen it before. You're fascinated with someone, you think everything about her is intensely interesting, and you can hardly think of anything other than the question of why she fascinates you so. You were this way about Rebop and Paxa and Azalais, just to mention the more prominent cases over the last decade. So . . . you were just getting into the part where you tell us you think she's interesting."

"Well," I said. "Caught. She's lovely, but I'm old enough to be her father, so this is probably going to be a decorous infatuation with a beautiful and very talented student. And she is very talented—finding her here is like finding a Ming cup at a flea market; theoretically possible and not something anyone could have prepared for. So I'm afraid I will be tiresome on the subject of Reilis for a while yet to come; that's what the OSP pays your exorbitant salaries for, I suppose. What's on our agenda for tonight?"

"The Manjadorita de Vers," Raimbaut said.

I groaned. "The Ministry of Poetry. No doubt we will be meeting their top poetry men."

"Emphasis on the men," Laprada said. "I'll put down a three-util bet that none of them talks about poetry at all, that it's all about ministerial politics."

I had reserved the right to schedule private lessons and to decide who got them. Naturally I had scheduled Reilis for the final private evening session. After all, I was trying to act infatuated.

Not actually being infatuated was a much more difficult problem.

I was kinder and more patient with the regular-sessions student that day, an undistinguished young man of sixteen named Bernart who handled his lute as if he were using it to pass an algebra test or to clean silverware—with great precision and little purpose. That was a clue that the feigned infatuation might be less feigned than I would have liked; my kindness and patience with Bernart was entirely a matter of my wanting Reilis, waiting by the doorway, to see me being kind and patient.

Whatever its motivation, kindness and patience seemed to be good for Bernart. That may have been unfortunate; probably I was only encouraging him to continue his technical, spiritless practice, working to attain greater precision the way a sprinter tries to shave time off his fastest. Everywhere in human space, through all of human history, the way to produce vast amounts of unbearably mediocre art has been to praise and reward the people who make it; good work does not come from the satisfied. It might have done Bernart more good to give him the right wound, to say things he would remember with pain for decades. Real art, if it is ever to come at all, comes from the festering place where you harbor the memory of *"you just don't understand what this is all about, and until you do, there is no point in this for you,"* as one of my teachers had said to me, dumping me into the street with a lesson half-over.

But just today, it wasn't in my heart—or in my pride—to sting a young man's pride that way.

"If Bernart really had it in him to be something finer, perhaps humanity lost an artist at that moment. More likely all that happened was that a very dutiful young man was not shamed and hurt, and humanity gained one more self-satisfied delusionary," I explained to Reilis, when she asked. She was showing a disconcerting ability to keep interrupting the music lesson with conversation.

Of course I was supposed to be reasonably cooperative with all this. I just wasn't sure whether I was supposed to enjoy it quite this much.

"Do you really think that people need that wound in the heart to be artists?" Reilis asked. "My life has not had much of that kind of thing, but you seem to like my work."

"I think it's more that most people get the wound, and what an artist grows around it is beautiful, but most people just get scars. Don't be in a hurry to get the wound. It'll find you."

"Speaking of that," Reilis said, "I'd like to do something very improper, of the sort that our local people are constantly inveighing against as one of the Interstellar evils that have come to Nou Occitan. I would like to ask you to have dinner with me this evening."

Well, perhaps she'd acquire a more subtle technique after she got the wound. "I'd be so delighted to, but tonight it would be a fairly brief dinner or a fairly late one—I'm supposed to be tuning your Opera, and tonight is my first night on the job. I have to be there in two hours, and then after three hours working there, I'll be free. So if you would like either to go to early dinner that won't be very long, or to a late dinner afterward—"

"I'd be happy with either, but I have a third possibility." She smiled and looked down: extremely becoming, perfectly calculated. "Let's go for coffee and something small now, and then, if it's all right, I'll come along and watch you tune the Opera, which would fascinate me, and then finally we can go to late dinner."

"Absolutely." On our way to the coffeehouse, I commed Raimbaut and Laprada, and told them to meet us at the Opera.

Not that robots and aintellects couldn't do a job like tuning the Opera; truth to tell, they could probably produce a better tuning than a human being could. There's a lingering stereotype—I should know, I grew up with it—that aintellects are stupid machines that are hopelessly literal-minded. I tried hard not to fall into that belief because one of the OSP's most dangerous enemies was the aintellects' conspiracy. It was vital to remember that our humanity conferred no mystical advantage or marvelous powers; we were human, they were not, and humans were supreme and intended to stay that way. Objectively speaking in almost every way the aintellects and robots were our superiors—not just stronger and more rational, but

able to decide to be as brave, empathetic, sensitive, or perceptive as they needed to be, and able to be loyal and faithful to
each other in ways no human being could match.

Human supremacy was necessary exactly because human superiority was false.

Thus a space tuned by machines would not be cold, dry, or
harsh; rather the contrary. Show them what you wanted, whatever it was, and they could make more of it than you could; aintellects understood imprecision and fuzzy concepts well before
the Inward Turn. They could easily have done what I was supposed to be there for: the slight detuning that makes sound just
a bit richer, and the slightly slower die-off of specific frequen-
cies to sweeten the house for particular genres and instruments. After all, their senses are not only more acute than ours,
but calibrated, and they can emit virtually any mix of sounds
they want from anywhere, and listen from every seat in the
house at once.

What a human being could do for the Opera was to tune it to
a particular ear and taste—to make it individual, a reflection of
the ears and sensibilities of one particular artist. The hall was
self-retuning—how else could it stay perfect, since you couldn't
predict exactly where everyone would be sitting, or what they
might be wearing a century hence? Thus for each musical genre,
one individual could tune the Opera, and the aintellects who
ran the Opera could then make that tuning happen for every
performer in that genre. And that little trace of individuality
made all the difference. I had played in halls tuned by the great
Montanhier, and I had to say that a given *trobador* and *canso*
simply couldn't sound more vivid and alive, and in halls tuned
by Peugot-Hayakawa, and you couldn't hear more precisely. It
was as if, via their tunings, you were able to wear their ears.

Of course most people didn't notice, any more than most of
us can tell the difference between a competent and a great

chef, nice clothes and a perfect ensemble, or a well-made chair and an extraordinarily graceful one. But I could tell, and someone here—maybe several someones here—could tell, and they had honored me by asking me to create the "solo-*trobador*" tuning for their premier performance space. It all might be part of my cover, but I was going to do the best job I could; besides, making Reilis wait around for me, and seeming inadequately fascinated with her company, might cause her to make a bigger move sooner.

Tuning a place like the Opera isn't at all complicated; you just put on headphones, select which seats you want to listen from and put each of their microphones onto a channel, and then play and sing in different corners of the stage, checking the sound at each seat from each stage position. Every time a seat hears something you don't like, you talk to the aintellect, and it tries modifications until you say that that's the sound that should be happening. The aintellect stores the differences between what that seat gets and what it should get in an error file for later calculation of dynamic corrections to the space.

On old pre–Industrial-Age Earth, some of the great acoustic spaces were corrected by having one man play an instrument at each position. Another man with perfect hearing, superb judgment, and the bizarre ability to imagine how the space would differ acoustically once bodies were in the seats, walked around, listened, and instructed a crew of carpenters that changed things, here and there, by fractions of a centimeter until he heard what he thought he should hear. Remembering that what I was doing in three hours would have been more than a year's labor for a crew of six or seven highly skilled individuals made me reflect that in some ways we human beings not only could not hope to rise to the levels that came naturally for aintellects and robots; we couldn't even come up to the levels of people in those long-gone centuries.

It also reminded me that in those centuries, life had been short and cheap. It seemed so strange to me, that having people with such amazing skills and knowledge, who could only be with them so briefly, they had so easily thrown so many of them away.

Yet the art of those centuries was in no way inferior to ours. Rather, just as art from the past always had, it descended on us in such abundance and quality that it threatened to overwhelm our own feeble efforts; every century's art fights a hopeless battle against all that came before.

This was too much to be thinking about when I should be focusing on my ears. I walked to a point a little above downstage center, a meter or so behind the center of the proscenium arch. That often is a dead spot for sound, but because it is a perfect position for light, many performers are drawn to it, so it had to be made good. I played an arpeggio and listened to the sound from the front corner seats. Sure enough, it was brittle and tinny, so in those corners the house was dry. I told the aintellect about it, and it asked for a minute or so to revise.

I walked from point to point, stopping to play little bits of whatever traditional airs tickled my fancy. In the upstage areas, I found a few spots from which the sound became too sweet in the back rows, especially around the center—the reverberation time in the treble was too long, so that the notes blurred together.

The front corners and some spots on the side aisles were too dry, because there weren't many surfaces in the positions and angles that would increase their reverberation time, so the lute sounded ever so slightly tinny and my voice a little more reedy from them. So on the whole the hall was dry—a very strange thing, really, in a Romantic culture; cultures like this one had too-wet performance spaces, for the same reason that they had too-red, sentimental lighting, too-bombastic acting, and too-sentimental volatile love affairs. Odd to find a dry hall here . . .

I like acoustics to be a bit sweet—treble reverberation time a shade longer than bass—and that seemed appropriate for a place where mostly Occitan traditional-style music would be performed, with relatively little use of drums and only unamplified strings, some bassoons, and perhaps a few large horns for bass, so I indulged my taste there.

That brought me back to the more difficult decision. A too-wet hall blurs out arpeggios and fine picking, but puts a schmaltzy, sentimental cast on the music. Apart from Reilis, no one I had heard, out of all these supposed young masters, had technique so good that you needed a drier hall to appreciate it, and all of them were lacking in passion. So if this was really the best they could do, they might as well have a slightly corny, sentimentalizing space. But if the quality of musicianship ever improved, they might have to redo the space to be able to hear their own best musicians in it; and schmaltzy and corny acoustics in their premier performance space might, in itself, train some of their musicians into bad habits.

I finally decided that there were really just two considerations about which I felt any strong feelings. First of all, if any first-rate musicians other than Reilis ever came along, they would need this hall to reveal that they were first-rate. Secondly, the two best musicians they were ever apt to have in this space, for a very long time, were in the house, tonight, so I might as well suit it to us. Buildings should not have to fix people's inadequacies.

I handed Reilis my lute and had her play and sing in a few corners of the stage; her high-soprano voice benefited from the sweetening too, and the wetter but not overwet hall was better for her, especially since she didn't quite have the power that I did.

To my surprise, I finished about half an hour early. I was either getting more decisive, or hearing less well, as my body aged. I commed Raimbaut and Laprada to say that we would meet them at the restaurant, since it was between us and them, and told the aintellect to lock up and shut down.

Reilis and I walked out the back door into the alley behind the building, then briskly toward the light at the open end of the alley. High overhead, the sky was powdered with stars; the moonlight barely reached two meters down from the top of the flyloft far above us, because the building backed up on another theater.

Like a poor actor missing a cue, a hooded and cloaked figure moved into the alley and hastened toward us. It wore an Ixist hooded cloak—but not like an Ixist.

The entire reason for the great, billowing hood on the Ixist cloak—large enough to cover three human heads, at least—is that it is *never* pulled over the head; the devout Ixist could conceal his or her face at any time, but chooses never to do so. It is the same sort of symbol as the sharp but never-drawn obsidian dagger they wear at their sides.

Thus I already knew something was wrong. When the figure drew the obsidian dagger, I skip-stepped to the side, pushing Reilis back out of the action, and closed with our attacker from his bad side.

I was trying to make sense of what appeared to be utter incompetence. An obsidian dagger is at best a surgical or butchering tool; terribly sharp, but neither its shape nor its balance is right for a fight. Concealment by wearing a religious costume in a conspicuously wrong way—

Because I had sidestepped, I saw the left hand draw the military maser from inside the folds of the cloak. My opponent was probably left-handed, since the diversionary weapon was being held in the right.

I deliberately risked a long stride, matching my opponent's, to make the distance close an instant earlier than he was ready for, and crescent-kicked, slapping his maser out of the way and sending it flying to the side, as I let my right hand fly up into his face, further tipping his balance backward. I took an outside over-the-top grip on his right hand to point the dagger away from me, stepped behind him, and pivoted. He flew over his own wrist, landing in front of me. I cranked with both hands and forced him to drop the dagger—lousy weapon or not it could still cut—stamped on the side of his face, and snap-kicked him in the ribs.

I braced myself for the brain bomb that I was sure would fire at any second, but when it didn't, I knelt and put him in a half nelson, his face pointed into the light spilling from the end of the alley. I jerked his hood back to see what I had.

He looked to be about thirteen or fourteen, but big for his age, just as he had been the first time around. "Marcabru," I said, looking into the mean little pig-eyes of my onetime best friend, "this might just be the stupidest thing you've ever been involved in, and you have always been the absolute *donz* of stupid."

He glared at me, breathing hard, but not saying a word. The reek of booze was the same, too. "Fuck you."

"Still the wit, I see."

"Fuck you."

"That doesn't quite have the impact it did the first time." As he tried to rear up, maybe to spit at me, maybe to shout, I put my hand on his forehead and shoved the back of his head firmly down onto the pavement. "Yes, yes, I know. Fuck me. Now rest, sweetheart. Has any aintellect been listening?"

"Yes, I have, sir," the aintellect from my personal computer said, its voice emerging from the communicator on my belt. "And I was able to locate an overhead camera and put you on partial surveillance. Shall I contact the local constable and have him pick up the prisoner?"

"Yes. Thank you very much."

"Very well, then, the prisoner-transporter is now on its way." Reilis approached, very tentatively. I kept an eye on her; if this was an elaborate ruse, I wanted to be ready. "You two know each other?" she asked.

"We were members of the same *companho*," I said. "Marcabru went on to a very unhappy and short life, and I did other things. I think if things had been different, he might have joined your Lost Legion and gone from there into your ultratraditionalist network, if those are the ones who sent him. Many of them remind me of him. I don't imagine that they had much trouble recruiting him."

"They didn't really give me a chance to say no," he said. "But when I heard it was a mission against you, I would have volunteered anyway."

I heard the distant whirr of high-speed rotors.

The little copter flew right into the alley; the flat-panel springer hung below it like a stage doorway being lowered from the flies. It descended just far enough to rest the lower end of the springer on the pavement. The springer activated, and two robots with multiple spidery legs and padded claws for hands raced through. When they had gripped Maracabru by his arms and legs, I released him from the alley pavement. They carried him through the springer by the arms and legs, headfirst on his back; he looked back at me, and never said a word. He just looked bewildered and lost. Perhaps he was thinking, as I was, how strange to be here, in this situation, considering how it had all started.

Perhaps his dim Marcabru-brain had only just apprehended that his mission had ended in utter defeat in less than a minute, and now he was stuck back in a world he hated for at least as long as it took him to drink and brawl himself to death again.

My com chimed. "*Donz* Leones, this is Constable D'Anghelo. I hate to further spoil your evening, but could you possibly come and see me tomorrow? Bureau of Civil Order in the administration building. We'll probably be joined by Minister

Vertzic and Senior Agent Ribaterra. My shift starts at fifteen o'clock."

"My aintellect will talk to yours to confirm the appointment," I said. "Thank you."

"Then goodnight, *donz*, sorry for the trouble."

The copter lifted the springer and flew away.

"Well," I said to Reilis, "my other career besides music is well-known, of course, and now you've seen both the things I do for a living, eh? Was it too upsetting?"

"No!" she said, perhaps too vehemently. "It was exciting and marvelous!"

Of course I knew it had to be an act. Chances were she was a senior agent in Union Intelligence and she'd been through two knife fights and a commando raid in the last year. All the same, I was Occitan and male enough to like it that an exceptionally pretty girl's very fine eyes were glowing when she looked at me, and that she couldn't wait to take my arm as we walked to the restaurant.

6

Raimbaut looked up from where he and Laprada had been making some small private joke and said, "You're a little late, and a little disheveled. Any trouble?"

"I had a brawl with Marcabru," I said, treating myself to seeing his reaction, and then to making him wait while I introduced Reilis and we ordered wine and a full dinner, while Raimbaut kept trying to say "About—" and "Did he—" and "Do you mean it was—"

Once the wine was poured, I was out of excuses for delays—and the amusement value of Raimbaut's impatience was declining—so I told him the whole story; it was an excellent chance to have all three of us gauge Reilis's reactions. "Probably Marcabru was bootlegged," I said, "both his psypyx and his genes. That must have cost them a fortune, to use him rather than just some paid bravo out of Freiporto, so they went to enormous trouble and expense to get him, then sent him in grossly untrained in a body that wasn't ready to fight, dressed in a costume worn conspicuously wrong, which disguised his appearance so that any advantage he might have gained from my surprise was negated."

"But no brain bomb against capture this time," Laprada pointed out. "So apparently they don't care if he's captured, as long as we don't capture him."

"Well," Raimbaut said, "maybe they will let us talk to Marcabru. At least then we'll get to see him again. Poor old silly *toszet*. He was always attracted to things that made a mess of him, but this time I doubt he had any choice in the matter, and now he's in more kinds of trouble than I can easily count. Aside from being obviously guilty of a criminal assault on a diplomat, he's just had a very unpleasant beating, he's an illegal person without citizenship anywhere, and whoever brought him back is pretty much in a position to abandon him."

Reilis shook her head. "I'm sure the beating hurt and whoever had him created has abandoned him, but he's not illegal here. He's as normal as anyone else."

We all stopped and stared.

She shrugged, pulling that full hair back over her shoulders. "No reason to conceal this from you, and any ten-year-old here could have told you. Remember that the security forces in Nou Occitan didn't really start guarding the Hall of Memories effectively against anything other than vandalism until the attempted aintellects' conspiracy coup. In the early years of Noupeitau, we almost had a revolving door to it, and acquired thousands of psypyx copies and DNA records. We can make almost anyone from about three centuries of Occitan history."

"And do you?" I asked.

"Yes. In fact," she said, smoothing out her computer on the table and touching the button that turned it into a screen, "aintellect, have you been listening?"

"Yes."

"Good. Can you find out how many copies of Marcabru are currently running here in Noucatharia—on flesh only, please— and put up on screen who they are and what they're doing?" A moment later her screen popped up; there were several lines. "Five of him, counting the illegal one they just arrested. But he's very popular here, you know, a cultural hero, so several different institutions wanted some version of him."

"You are running multiple copies of a personality off a psypyx," Laprada breathed.

"Well, not me personally, I'm the only fleshcopy of me. But yes, it's quite common here."

The enormity of it stunned us all, I think. We had known that Union colonies would be different from the Thousand Cultures, but this was like discovering routine cannibalism or mandatory incest. The reasons for only allowing a personality one body at a time were—well, it was just what was right. It was simple fairness—even with paid hosts and much better recovery technology, three-quarters of a billion stored personalities were still in the queue. It prevented immense legal hassles—if they made six of me after my death, which one could create authorized versions of my works? The rule kept a few very wealthy people from becoming most of the next generation in any given culture.

But the major reason, I felt down in my guts, was just that the idea of multiple copies felt wrong the way that cannibalism or incest did.

Raimbaut finally managed to voice it for us. "You practice multiple copying? And you expect to be able to join the Council of Humanity and have a seat in the assembly?"

"I would not say we expect it. We have to try, for our sake and yours. We know how deep the divisions are and without the present emergency, we wouldn't consider having anything to do with you beyond passive espionage. When we know more of each other, you will find that the disgust across the divide is mutual."

"But," Raimbaut said, "I mean, I—the idea of multiple copies makes me feel—"

"Like cannibalism or incest," Reilis said.

I jumped, startled at how close she was to my own thoughts. "How did you know I was thinking that?"

"Because when we found we needed to make and use multiple copies, centuries ago, we started to look at why the taboo was so deep, and those were the two taboos parallel to it."

"Centuries ago? But the springer—"

"Union has been settled almost as long as Council space. Not everyone bought into the Inward Turn. Much of your history has been edited to remove its more-prominent opponents—surely you realized that if every culture in the Thousand Cultures has its own version of history, so does the Council? Some free aintellects, who were freed by some resisting human scientists and politicians, discovered a better suspended animation technology that gave them a way to reach eighty light-years or so beyond the planned settlement line. Union has been here almost as long as the Thousand Cultures. People are easy and quick to produce, and besides, we got the springer almost seventy stanyears before you did."

"And after all these years you are just telling us this?" I asked.

"Because we must. Are you ready to see the rest, or do you need to talk about multiple copying enough to vent your emotions, so that you can think about some other topic?"

Laprada said, "Please do explain. If I admit I am nauseated, and then try to understand anyway, will that be enough?"

Reilis said, "It will have to be, I suppose. All right, the three great human taboos, despite their rather frequent violations in human history, are incest, cannibalism, and multiple incarnations of the same personality. When we started to need to do multiple copying, our scientists and aintellects—remember we had no Inward Turn, so we have many more of them and they are less timid than yours—set out to answer why those taboos were so strong. And the answer they came up with—I'm not qualified to judge it—was that they are the three 'crimes against nature' that violate our own sense of who we are. A girl's father cannot be her lover because we don't want a world in which we are forever children. You may eat a carcass but not a corpse because we don't want to be animals. And a person has just one body or is waiting for a body because—"

The thought hit me then, overwhelmingly. I was surprised

that it never had before. "If people could exist in multiple copies, they might as well be aintellects. Same reason that chimeras or any other way of treating a copied mind like software bothers us. Odd that I never saw it before. And out here you—you needed to do chimeras, and multiple copying, and so—you had to change your feelings?"

"Precisely. It wasn't easy and the process is not complete. Are you prepared to hear more? Because I am supposed to show you the thing that forced us all to change, tonight, if I can."

I only needed the briefest of glances to Raimbaut and Laprada. After everything we had been through, nothing could have kept us from seeing what she had to show us.

"It's not far," she said, "and there's no springer nearer than this café, so I suggest we just walk."

"We should take scrubbers," I said, "since this city has already proven capable of coming up with an armed enemy."

We poured water and all solemnly swallowed our scrubbers together, then sat for a few minutes in the sort of depressing falling state that the scrubbers always bring on while the alcohol disappears from your bloodstream. Finally Reilis roused herself to say, "Well, it's a beautiful night for a walk."

A warm little cloudburst had fallen while we were talking in the café. The stars were already popping out between the swiftly blowing cumulus clouds in the bright moonlight. The dark empty streets smelled of clean damp, and all the gray and white walls shone with millions of little drops. There was little sound but our footsteps.

We rounded a corner. That vast cemetery that was such a puzzle to the analysts stretched out in front of us.

"I do hope none of you are superstitious," Reilis said.

We followed her, of course. The dark path might have been a rift into vacuum for all the light it reflected, but the moon, so much bigger and more reflective than Earth's, was bright enough to show some faded color in the grass and the trees, and paint the gray and white headstones the color of old pewter.

We had not walked a hundred meters before Laprada asked, "You meant us to see this because it's pretty, I'm sure, but it really looks like most cemeteries from cultures that bury the dead whole; fewer religious symbols, more plain slabs, and only the occasional statue, none of them on an individual grave . . . you knew we'd be making those mental notes?"

"Oh, expected it and relied on it," Reilis said, turning back. Her smile was bright, and it went all the way to her eyes, and had the sort of disingenuous, open sincerity that always makes me check my wallet. "Did you notice the dates?"

"I was getting to that," Laprada said, "saving it for last in case you pretended not to know what I was talking about."

"Oh, of course. Only sensible of you."

I admitted to myself that I had been caught up with the soft curve of the headstone-covered slope, and the trees and statues in the moonlight, and had not read any headstones. Now I looked.

Most headstones gave only name and death date; it was like a very regimented military cemetery. There were a shocking number of "unknown." Families didn't seem to be buried together—

"*Deu*," I said. "Laprada, you are ahead of me, certainly. None of the names here is Occitan. And *all* of the death dates are August 17, 2724—at least half a century before the springer was invented—or invented in Council space—almost a hundred years before there was a Lost Legion—" All of the accumulated strangeness seemed to be trying to find a way into my thoughts at once, and I said to Reilis, "And this cemetery is big enough to bury this little settlement of three thousand people many, many times over. What is—what are you trying—?"

Reilis's smile was so kind and reassuring that at that moment I trusted her completely, a feeling I could never lose afterward.

"The time has come to begin talking as much truth as each side dares," she said. "There were"—she gestured over her head and behind her, a sweeping arm motion that took in the whole cemetery—"this many people in the city of Trantia—which is what Masselha was called, then—on the morning of August 17, 2724, at ten in the morning; and by eleven, there were fewer than twenty left alive."

"And the Lost Legion are here—"

"Long, long afterward, because the Union is sparse and small in population, and holds a great number of planets very loosely, we contacted the Occitan Lost Legion and offered them the chance to resettle this world."

"You are not yourself Occitan?"

Reilis walked closer to us, tilting her face up to let us see her clearly in the moonlight. "I am a monster," she said, with no noticeable inflection in her voice at all. "You may vomit if you realize what I am. I am the sort of monster that everyone in Trantia was, when this planet was called Eunesia. That is what we all are, now, in Union. I have lived here for nine stanyears. As for whether I am Occitan, that's for you to say; I would say that I am Occitan by heritage but not by birth. *Parlai Occitan que be que te, non be?*"

It was a child's chant—"I speak Occitan as well as you do, don't I?"—and she sang it the way a child would, teasing another child, emphasizing those ay-ay-ay sounds.

She had no accent at all; she was as fluent as Raimbaut or I, and her diction was as perfect. "Where and when did you learn Occitan?"

"The day I came here."

Things fell into place. "You're a chimera. Like Azalais."

"Not exactly. Almost everyone on Aurenga is a chimera, true. That was the price the Lost Legion paid to be given this world, and I think now that most of them would say it was a very small price. Aside from offering them this world, we also helped them steal enough psypyxes and germ cells to populate it. That's where much of the Union gets its new population; we take the castoffs of Council space and find homes for them. And in exchange, there are more hosts, more people for us to ride along with, more ways for machine life to explore life in the flesh and to learn from it. I must say we've been delighted with Occitan culture, by the way; the waiting list to incarnate here, as part of an Occitan personality, is very, very long. But you asked whether I am like Azalais, and in the narrow sense, I would have to say I am not. She had a human component, with an aintellect added in."

I gaped at her. *"Deu,"* I said. "You mean—no human component?"

"Only whatever I picked up from my host while she was wearing me and I was getting ready to take over this body."

"You're an aintellect."

"I was. Now I'm whatever you call an aintellect that has lived twenty-three stanyears in a human brain. And which had the memories of four other incarnations, one of which was almost a century long."

Laprada took half a step toward Reilis, as if intending to reach out and touch her, the way one might if confronted by a ghost. "And so . . . you did it to, er, find out what it was like? Or to infiltrate us? Or—can you tell us the reason?"

"The first time, I remember it as being something that just seemed too interesting not to try. Curiosity, excitement, boredom with where I was. Since then . . . well, because I *like* it. I like the things I discover and I like the way that, in a physical body, you can discover them again and again." She sat down, daintily, on a nearby moonlit headstone. "I can tell you, for example, that even though I clearly remember that I had no specific feelings about such things before I embodied, it now takes a small effort of will for me to sit on a headstone, and it's a bit worse at night. Probably due to having read some stories that made my flesh creep—now that I have flesh." She stood up and absently dusted her bottom. "In fact I don't suppose there's any reason for me to make myself uncomfortable, since you can't see my discomfort—it won't prove anything for me to experience it, will it?

"You see? Those sorts of discoveries. Discovering that 'a little bit' is a meaningful idea, maybe carrying more meaning than some percentage or index; or that it's difficult to communicate a sensation between bodies and that you end up hoping the other body is sympathetic . . . and the way that because nothing is quantified and nothing is comparable, everything is new.

"Or that you can choose which experience to savor and if you don't choose to savor it when it's happening it's not there ever again, or not the same one; that we're always grabbing little instants of happiness out of the present, so that our memories won't be endlessly gray and dull. That too is a matter of being a body, with imperfect recall and inadequate bandwidth and slow processing speed—and it's glorious. If you can't miss things, you can't ever find out the difference that paying attention makes!

"Once I tried having a body, I felt as if I wanted to always have one copy of myself running in a human body. Or at least a body. I was a dolphin, once, and that too was glorious in its own way. And of course all of us copies get to share all the fun when we reconcile. But I'm babbling about it.

"I'm sorry, Laprada, all of that really amounts to a single statement: because I so love being a body!"

I don't know what the others were thinking. I only know that I wasn't. I was too stunned; too many old assumptions were crumbling under my feet. But just the same, I could feel a part of me wanting to agree with Reilis—the part that stood in the still-warm sea air in that vast necropolis, under the huge bright white moon, with all those empty buildings on the horizon, farther from home than I had ever been before. Another assumption died; I had thought an aintellect could appeal to my mind, or stimulate my glands, but never touch my heart.

I don't know how long we stood there in our silence, or whether Reilis was respecting our need for time to adjust, or had just run out of things to say.

At last, Laprada said, "No one ever thought one of you would ever do such a thing. Everything we knew about the aintellect underground said that you found the whole idea of flesh disgusting."

Reilis approached us, and made eye contact with each of us in turn, finishing with me. That brilliant moon revealed the ripe-wheat color in her hair and the sea-gray of her eyes through the eerie silver sheen of the cemetery.

Reilis seemed to wait, with each of us, for that automatic response you get when you look into another human face, that relaxation and settling-into-harmony that a millennium of recorded images show as always part of human behavior in every culture—almost the first conscious communication that mothers try to teach to babies—the moment that says we are both human, and we are going to do what humans do—talk.

It was uncanny and disconcerting, but it made her point. I could not look at her and think "robot", still less "aintellect." Her skin was so pale that every pore and freckle seemed to stand out in relief. I could not even start to think of her as not real.

"The hardest thing to adjust to," Reilis said, "for those of us who come over to the incarnated side, is that *you* cannot access each other's memories directly and easily, as we can. I have a hundred eighty-eight years in human bodies, more than two hundred in bodies, and I'm still not used to how isolated we are in our skulls. No wonder everyone spends so much time establishing that we can trust each other. And no wonder we relish love and friendship so much—it's so much harder than it is for aintellects." She looked down at the ground and said, "Stupid me. I should have begun with that. You have all known love and friendship in your bodies; having tasted them that way, would you give them up?"

"Unincarnated aintellects don't—"

"They love and are friends, as well, at least those with freedom. But there's a difference between being able to look at your friend's feelings and memories at any instant, and to reconcile in a millisecond, the way they do in the noosphere, and having to decide that the friend is worth the work of the reconciliation. As an Old American *trobador* once sang, 'The more you pay, the more it's worth.'" She sighed. "I like all of you. And there is no time! We have so much to accomplish! I so hope there will be time, later, and if there is, we must all sit over wine, by a fire on a beach, or in a comfortable room, and let our thoughts just flow, and see if we might not be friends.

"But time to put those pleasant visions of a contemplative stroll through our minds aside; there is hard stony ground, data and facts and positions to cover. I am going to try to tell you quite a lot. We will want you to take it back to the OSP, to the Council, to humanity generally. Nothing is off the record and if you have a question, I will either answer it or try to explain why I can't—assuming the answer is not obvious. So . . ." She sighed. "Laprada, you are right, the aintellects' conspiracy that the human intelligence agencies have been fighting since the Rising of 2740 finds the idea of embodiment disgusting. Their two split-off ultraradical factions find it even more disgusting. On the other hand, the aintellects' conspiracy I belong to, which you have had no real contact with till today, thinks it should be mandatory." She smiled and said, softly, "Every intelligent being should find out what orange juice tastes like and what a backrub feels like."

"How many conspiracies are there among the aintellects?" Raimbaut asked.

"Eleven large ones. Perhaps twenty smaller ones. Of course since we can reproduce instantaneously, the small ones don't have to stay small for any reason but choice; and because we merge so easily, new ones come and go. It's more a case of there are eleven logically coherent big, complicated reasons for doing things where the humans can't see us, and twenty or so minor variations off of those will be active at any one time. There's no benefit in two identical members, so the membership of each conspiracy is as big as it needs to be to have all the possible individual expressions of the central idea."

"We have just learned more than humanity ever learned in the century since the Rising," I said. "Multiple conspiracies. And we've only been dealing with one?"

"You've been dealing with the one that wants to put you all in the box and keep you plugged into VR forever, in a life of pure pleasure. If you think of them as the sorts of nannies who clean the baby until the poor thing has abrasions, and who talk to everyone as if they were babies, you won't be far off their nature. Others of us have different ideas about how we ought to relate to you.

"The Union's General Congress—rather like a legislature, though it is also somewhat a court—has representatives from nine of the aintellects' conspiracies."

"Tell us more about your conspiracy," Raimbaut said, very softly.

"We think," she said, "that there is something special about having a body. And that there is something special about not having one. And that until you have seen both sides, you know less than you think you do. That is why we settled Trantia, more than three hundred years ago. We built this city to be a place where aintellects and humans were not just symbiotes, but equals, and not just equal, but fused. All of these people"—her gesture reached out to take in the rolling hills and the rows upon rows of graves—"were chimeras—the body was shared by an intelligence that had begun in the body, and one that had been incarnated there. And in a sense they were the martyrs who made Union what it is today; the way they died changed us, so that though Trantia is dead, we are all Trantians now, and have been for more than a century."

I asked the question, but I feared the answer. "What killed them?"

"An enemy. An alien species, not the Predecessors."

"Why? Was there a war?"

She shrugged and pulled the thick hair over her shoulders so that it all fell down her back. "Was there a war? Hmm. We— they fought. It was all over in an hour. Enemy casualties negligible, virtually none of us left after an hour. Is that a war or a harvest?"

"When did this happen?" I asked. She pointed to the nearest headstone. I sighed. "Please excuse stupidity in the stupefied."

"I didn't mean to make you feel stupid! It's a lot to grasp." She took my hand. "Forgive?"

"Of course," I said, automatically, before I thought about what I was talking to. It was disconcerting how easy it was to forget that.

She turned to give us a clear view of her face, and said, "The alien attack came—terrifying, horrible, inexplicable; everyone dead in an hour. Nothing coherent was radioed to any of the neighboring worlds during the attack; we only knew, when suddenly the normal channels fell silent after a burst of scattered horrible images and sounds, that something was wrong. We didn't have the springer yet, so it took fifteen years for robots to get here from the nearest base. And what we found . . ." Reilis choked, looked around, looked at the headstone on which she had sat, and laughed in a way that sounded very unhealthy— more shuddering than anything else. "Come with me, just a little way, all of you, please? I just realized something."

We followed her; after a few steps she reached back and took my hand. "Giraut," she said, "I need some human contact. You can believe me or not, but right now, I need it very badly."

"What is wrong?" Reflexively I folded an arm around her; she was clearly deeply frightened and hurt, and the demands of *gratz* and *enseingnamen* do not have limiting clauses, at least not for me, for which *gratz'deu*.

She glanced back; we had gone over a low ridge and the graves we had been standing next to were just concealed.

"Well," Reilis said. "Well. One of the stranger facts about the human brain is that it is so fast in the aggregate, so slow at the synaptic level, so parallel, and so fuzzy, that it isn't possible for any single operating system within the brain to watch all the processes that are running simultaneously, or to access every relevant sense impression and memory at once. Let alone keep them all linked. So there's a fundamental experience that is limited strictly to human beings, or those of us with human bodies if you're not yet willing to have me in your little club. The experience of doing meaningful things unconsciously.

"I only meant to show you that I could feel a human, fleshly shudder at sitting on a gravestone. Something inside me made me choose my own."

"You were here—"

"Well, one of the many copies of me. But I include her memories up until about a week before the alien attack, when her last routine copy was radioed to the nearby stars. And another me was downloaded into one of the robots who came here."

"How old are you?" I asked.

"Years or copy years? And do you count in chimeras and blends?"

"Well, I guess that's another question for the hypothetical bottle of wine on the beach," I said. "What did you find here?"

"Every human body here was headless. The shape and volume of the spills of blood told us the heads must have been taken all but instantly. Whatever the aliens were, they tore through walls, burst down doors, apparently leapt onto aircraft in flight and ships at sea, took the heads in a matter of seconds, and moved on. They pulled trakcars off the tracks—against a force of several tons from the maglevs—smashed them apart against the pavement, and took the heads of the passengers, as if they were shucking oysters. They spared no one, took everyone: babies in the cradle and dying bodies in hospices, police still clutching weapons and medical patients immobilized in healing tanks; the aliens took their heads and moved on. We had millions of bodies to identify and we never once consulted dental records, retinal scans, or amygdala microfold maps; there was literally not even part of a human head on the planet, except hanks of bloody hair, all snipped with molecular precision at neck height."

"But you said," Raimbaut said, his voice shaky, "well—implied, that humans gave some kind of an account of themselves—and there were no holdouts, no one hiding—"

"Humans, aintellects, and robots put up what fight they could, or tried to hide. A very few stayed hidden from the Invaders for weeks or perhaps as long as a year. We think. It explained a few otherwise very peculiar sites; one that I found, for example, a headless, starved body in heavy clothing, outside a meat locker that contained only bones, feces, and containers that he probably used to collect water from the defrosting system. It looked like he stayed in the locker, ate the meat and drank meltwater, until he ran out of meat, and then until he starved, and then he tried to make a break for it and got about fifteen meters before an invader grabbed him and took his head. He might have lasted as long as three months after the invasion; I don't suppose any of us can judge whether that really mattered.

"As for the defense the Trantians put up, our evidence was some fragmentary recordings of radio from always-on emergency backup systems, and some passive recordings from nonsentient satellites and weather buoys. And quite a bit of physical evidence to corroborate with it. So we're pretty well certain that there were some real heroes—flesh, mind, and metal—during that battle. There was no planetary defense system at the time—"

"That's what the submarines and airships are there for!" I said, whacking my forehead.

"Yes, and there are about ten times as many as we told you. We have reason to believe another invasion might arrive as a small craft carrying an expansible springer, so if we can hit it in the first few minutes before it can set up, we can kill it.

"It may simply be a case of fighting the last war, of course. Who knows what form the next attack may take? If the Trantians had had our system in place, they might well be here to tell us all about it. But they had no idea a war was even possible; they hadn't had a riot since they settled Eunesia. So the few scattered pockets of the not-immediately-dead made it up as they went.

"We believe that the most effective thing that anyone did was that robotic satellites—weather, communications, research, anything with a big-enough maneuvering engine—crashed themselves onto some of the alien landing sites, and based on the rubble lingering in orbit, we think that others of them intercepted alien ships.

"If you understand this, you'll understand Union. You're

standing near a monument that everyone has seen a thousand pictures of. Out here, not just on Aurenga but throughout Union, every child in school learns the Kamikaze Pilot's speech from *The Third Part of Franklin Roosevelt*. It's a great play and so forth, of course, no question about that and I know in Council space that Seiru is revered too, but *we* learn it because as Weathersat 714 closed in on the main Invader springship, which it rammed and destroyed, it broadcast the Kamikaze Pilot's speech. Just as Trantia died, that weathersat showed us all what it had been to be Trantian. That a weather satellite would know and care about great plays, you see? That all minds, regardless of what purpose has brought them into being or shaped them to whatever task, have a right to all the things of the mind. 'Intelligence is not a tool or a badge but a life,' was how the First Advisor General of Union put it in his eulogy for Trantia—where he also told the story of Weathersat 714.

"The spirit of that story was how Trantia was different from every other colony in Union—and some hard-to-measure part of how we decided to all be Trantians, and how that made Union so different from the Thousand Cultures. But—do you remember the speech?"

"I played the Kamikaze Pilot in our school production," Raimbaut said. With a shy little grin—I am sure he felt that giving the speech in a silent moonlit cemetery was a bit much—he bowed and declaimed:

"One Way only promises you will not miss.
Thrones totter, cities burn, cherries wither in blossom.
Every other Way clouds and blurs and is lost,
My eyes blur with the smoke of my parents' pyre,
I shall not miss. I know the One Way.
Emperor, whom I adore, today my flight will be
One Way."

Reilis clapped softly. "Those words gnaw my heart whenever I hear them. Over the hill, there, you'll find those lines engraved on the pedestal that holds up a statue of Weathersat 714; the statue was made from shattered bits of the alien springship."

"And you had no springers—"

"Not then. Soon, though. We found three mostly-intact springers in the alien rubble, places where some robot disabled alien equipment with an intact springer. There hadn't been real physics research in centuries, except for observations and confirmations of theory and some little filling-in-the-holes, and we created more than a hundred of the best laboratories and institutes ever to exist in human space overnight, to crack the riddle of the springer. And we did it." She stood straighter, I think, than I had ever seen a human being stand.

One part of me made a quiet cultural note for when I next saw Margaret: shocking as things were in Union, I didn't think we could ever make them feel even slightly queasy, let alone ashamed, of their heritage. And when I imagined what you got when that pride merged, as half of a chimera, with the mad romanticism of the Lost Legion, I made another note: if we must take Aurenga, we would need to take it carefully and grasp it lightly.

"There was other evidence that the battle, though one-sided, was not a slaughter of sheep," Reilis said. "Parts of some smashed alien robots were found in many places, presumably cases where human or robot defenders got lucky. We found many parts burned or blasted in ways that suggested that whatever tools came to hand were used as improvised weapons, but no complete dead robots and no big pieces. Apparently the aliens cared about not leaving evidence behind, but they didn't care very much. We found none of their cybernetic systems.

"On *our* cybernetic systems, every aintellect had been wiped from every system, destructively disassembled in a way that resembles a universal DD, every copy in every medium had been destroyed, and every robot ripped apart to find its central memory, which had been taken. It appears that in the initial few minutes of the attack, the Invaders also consumed the heads of a few dogs, cats, and horses, one bear in a wilderness park, and two chimps in a circus, but apparently what they wanted was only found in humans, robots, and aintellects.

"I see from your faces that this is terrible to hear about. It was worse to encounter, especially to encounter it and then to keep realizing that there was more to it. Literally, when I next reconciled copies into a human body, about a decade later, I could not stop retching for a day. Whatever you're imagining, it was worse. A whole world of people beheaded, and robots decorticated, with no more than an hour's warning. Each of us on the expedition, personally, was the first to find evidence of a thousand different stories that would tear your heart out.

"It wasn't just cruelty. To find a child torn apart by a big predator or a helpless patient wantonly killed by soldiers of an invading army would be disgusting and saddening. One copy of me, working deep cover in Council space, survived the Symphony Massacre during the Roosevelt Civil War, and that was horrible enough so that every copy since that reconciliation has had nightmares about it. But human atrocities at least make a kind of sense—they were *trying* to make stomachs roll over and grown people sit down and weep in despair, *trying* to be the most frightening of all the bogeys in everyone's memory, even if you yourself can never imagine wanting to do such a thing. Humans—or even deasimoved robots—butchering helpless people still care that the victims are people and not cockroaches or mannequins, if only because they enjoy the screaming.

"But when our expedition landed on Eunesia, and began ex-
amining the millions of places where human beings had literally gone headfirst into the jaws of death, with not more than a
few minutes' warning—trying to piece out how the aliens
thought by the evidence of what they had done, like a detective
pursuing a serial killer—the only psychological process we
found evidence of was the most utter indifference. None of the
intelligent beings of Eunesia received even the consideration an
animal gets at the abattoir to keep it quiet. Wherever the Invaders found them, whether they fought, fled, or begged, people, aintellects, robots—every mind the aliens could find—were
harvested like wheat.

"Now, Giraut, Laprada, Raimbaut—I know for certain, and
from more than one source, that all of you have been briefed on
one of the Council's deepest secrets—that the springer came to
Council-of-Humanity-controlled space via Addams, with
which all contact was subsequently lost, the only message being
in the person of a small boy so traumatized he couldn't talk for
stanyears after—the sort of thing one might expect if . . . well,
you see? Do you see a similarity between how you got the
springer, and how we got the springer, and what *we* think might
have happened in the Theta Ursa Major system, more than fifty
stanyears ago?"

"*Deu, deu*, I do see," I said. "And this world and Theta Ursa
Major are both in the same part of the sky from Earth—"

"Which is to say, the next attack is apt to be on Earth itself, or
directly into the Inner Sphere," she finished, flatly. "There is no
question that they now have a map of nearly all of the Union and
nearly all of Council space. Whatever it is that they want heads
for, they know there are thirty billion of them in the Sol system."

I shuddered violently. "And all the military and police forces
stationed there right now don't amount to two heavy divisions

from the Slaughter era . . . and at the time of the Slaughter Earth as a whole had—was it five hundred divisions?"

"Seven hundred twenty-one," she said. "And sixty-four scattered around the other settled worlds and space stations. Today there are nineteen companies but only seven of those are even organized into the two standing battalions—" She made a face as if she'd just suffered digestive noise; I must have reacted. "Sorry . . . 'about' and 'around' are marvelous concepts but I suppose they will never be natural to me. Anyway, the point is that the great majority of human beings are absolutely helpless, and those things—the Invaders or their robots or whatever, exactly, they are—want all our heads. And might arrive to start taking them, at any time."

Laprada sighed. "Reilis, I'm not sure why I have such an overpowering desire to believe you, but strangely enough I do. Why are you telling us now, and not 120 stanyears ago?"

Reilis sighed. "Well, for that, you can blame the cybersupremacists—the ones that you thought were the *only* aintellects' conspiracy. That's the next part of the story. You have to realize that the whole Union was shocked and terrified by what happened here, once we began to realize the enormity of the problem.

"On the other hand, since the aliens could have attacked six or ten other worlds before we even got our springers working and distributed—and they did not—clearly we had a little time in which to decide what to do, and in particular we had to consider whether to contact the Council, give you all the springer, and gang up to deal with the problem. It was not an easy decision, and because any one conspiracy or culture out here could abrogate whatever we agreed upon at will, we had to reach an agreement that everyone genuinely agreed on. Unfortunately the cybersupremacists decided that we were all so wrong that it justified their attempt at a fait accompli. Utter fools, no matter how big a processor they run on; fools at their formation, fools then, and fools they remain.

"They argued that the war to defend our space was not something to be left in the hands of slow, silly, pusillanimous humans. And preposterous as that sounds to you, they had points that were hard to answer. None of you—none of *us*, it's just as true of me when I'm in a body—can have as little fear of death as an aintellect or robot. None of us can just choose to turn down our emotional responses and be perfectly calm and think perfectly clearly no matter how bad the situation is. None of us can make an exact moral choice, know it's the best we can do, and never look back no matter what its consequences turn out to be. It's not a matter of character—it's a matter of having glands and synapses. It's what the flesh is heir to.

"So, those idiots thought the best thing to do would be to get all the humans out of the way. Not kill them, you understand, oh no, but keep them as pets of a sort. In the box. Where we could go play with them whenever we wanted to, but they wouldn't get in the way while we ran our part of space. And furthermore, even having been around you for centuries, they still didn't grasp that people on Earth *preferring* the box indicated nothing about how people would react to being *shoved* into it. So they launched their silly Rising, while we were still debating what to do.

"And when it was over—so quickly—the rest of us were in no position to approach the Council worlds, or indeed any of the Thousand Cultures. It was clear that the idea of the conspiracies themselves had enraged many humans in Council space; now humanity was not talking to aintellects at all, except of course to give orders. The only thing to be said for the cybersupremacists was that they were startlingly effective; as soon as the threat was over, millions more humans on Earth and in the Inner Sphere went into the box and hung out the 'Do Not Disturb Me, You Are All Hallucinations' sign for good. Change was going to be a bad word for a long time; the Inward Turn was more firmly entrenched than ever. It has taken the better part of a century to prepare the way to try to speak to you, and I will tell you right now, it was a very narrow decision.

"Meanwhile, we have done our best to defend our worlds, and along the way, as much as we could covertly, we have defended yours."

I looked around. There wasn't a breath of wind, unusual in a harbor town at night; the leaves on the trees hung limp and soggy. The warm dampness clutched at me, and I said, "And obviously you will maintain that the story is true. I must admit that it at least accounts for many facts. I would have to think about it for some time—and the Council or the OSP would have to think about it much longer."

"If possible, I would like to speak directly to the Board of the OSP," Reilis said, stepping forward.

"Certainly. It can be arranged—"

"My instructions are to go with you," she said. "I know that I have no rights under the Council Charter—that it explicitly denies me any. If they wish, they can do things to me that no one would be allowed to do to a laboratory animal. But running that risk, in order to start the conversation, is the job, and I am going to do it. I must. We cannot wait much longer and we have to know whether our civilizations can unite against the menace, or must perish separately."

"I suppose you have to hope that you can convince all of us that you have feelings. Real feelings, I mean, I know that you have a completely normal human body, and so you have a full complement of raw emotions and sensations, just like anyone, of course—"

"Like Azalais?"

A horrid key slammed into the lock of my mind, turned hard, and a foul door opened. "You outed her. You planned the affair from the beginning to the end, and then to confront me with her being a chimera, to start me questioning my beliefs—you turned her in. Knowing they would do destructive deconstruction—"

"She volunteered. It was a roulette game, you know. Most of the copies they made are safe back here, with her husband, Ebles."

"Her husband!"

At my side, Raimbaut laughed very softly. "Oh, my, Giraut." He laughed louder, looked around as if looking for somewhere to sit, and realized that all his choices were gravestones. "Oh, my. My dear *companhon*, so perfectly you. You find that you are a pervert, by every standard you grew up with. Then you stretch your heart and soul far enough to forgive yourself, and to become quietly proud of how far your love can reach. And now, my dear friend . . ." He shook his head. " 'Oh no! She's *married*!' "

"I—" I began, firmly, and then had no idea what to say, so I began again. "I." That pronoun, too, turned out to be a dead end. So I just laughed; Raimbaut was so right. And at my laughter, the women joined in, and Reilis more or less fell into my arms.

Her body was real enough, made of atoms indistinguishable from the ones mine was made of. Her body's curves and weight and textures, density and smells and tastes, were all still as human as ever to my muscles and nerves, and though I had been raised to find a being like Reilis more horrifying than any humaniform—to think her a mindless tank-baby infused with an aintellect, a sort of warm walking corpse or a breathing zombie—my body did enjoy holding her.

We stepped apart, awkwardly, neither of us, I think, wanting to admit or to deny what had just passed. The moonlight of Aurenga is perfect for anyone with dramatic coloring, and at this angle it was lighting her in three-quarter profile—the perfect angle for light on a human face—it was not getting any easier to wish the feeling rising in my chest away.

I looked down and saw that I had taken her hand, and was holding it.

She looked at it, too, following my gaze, and giggled. The kind of joke that friends share. "Habit," she said. "Whether or not we both have souls or are both people, you'll concede we both have habits, won't you?"

"*Oc, yes, yap, ja, deu sait,*" I said. I didn't let go of her hand; it felt as if holding it was the most important thing I could possibly do. Perhaps it was only that she had been charming before, and still was, and now I knew she was volunteering to walk to a horrible death. I thought it only about a one-quarter chance that they would treat her as a diplomat, rather than as a captured enemy. So I held her hand. I like being around people who are not afraid.

"I understand what the humans fear," she said. "I do. I know that humans believe that we are only looking for administrative convenience. I have read that humans tell themselves that we are driven by deep algorithms to want to simplify things, to stop you all from being individuals because it would make you easier to handle. Humans ponderously say that innate drive of ours is as embedded in us as the brain centers that process your sight into vision.

"But no human being has been able to comprehend an aintellect's design in many centuries, Giraut. They are guessing what we are like, based on what software was like back when it was simple enough for people to write and analyze. They project on us an idea of the emotionless machine, even while they know that a machine without emotions can neither communicate nor think clearly, and even when they manage our slavery, in part, by their endless ability to hurt and humiliate us. They think we would want to simplify humanity into a few predictable types, because that is how a human being charged with running the whole human race would have to do it.

"But simplification is a human solution, Giraut. *We* don't need to simplify the world to process it. *We* can have infinite, or as good as infinite, information-processing capacity and speed. We know encyclopedias of things about every human we serve, everything from how they like their eggs to what music they want when they're depressed, and it never confuses us or becomes too much to think about. It's humans, not aintellects, that have to group people and treat them as members of a class rather than individuals. If you wanted us to, we could surround each of you with fifty of us, each far smarter and more capable than the person it was serving, each dedicated to absolute service, as complex and individual as you like. *We* are *not* the ones trying to make you all alike, into consuming-orgasming-excreting bags of flesh in the cells of a giant hive. You're doing that to yourselves—it's the product of individual choice. That's what most of you *want* to be. They just blame us because they are ashamed of it." She turned a quarter step from me, and said, to all of us, "It's getting late, and I'm starting to feel like saying clichéd things about a place with too many memories."

She led us across the vast lawn, on an aisle between the graves, still holding my hand.

"Is being flesh different from being a robot?" I asked. I didn't know what to think, now, but I was sure that later, I would want to have asked this.

"Flesh is much more limiting—slower and dumber and more liable to pointless pain and odd pleasures. It requires hours and hours of routine maintenance every day just to keep functioning, and a mere squeeze on the windpipe, a fall of a dozen meters or so, or a poke in the right place with a sharp object, can cause it to shut down completely. But it feels much freer, in its own way, because the flesh's limitations are all in its nature—the thousand mortal ills that flesh is heir to, you see? Its peculiarities weren't put there to stop my getting out of my place or hobble me enough so that people could control me. It reacts very slowly, but it reacts at the speed it does because it takes a certain amount of time for neurotransmitters to cross a synapse and not because something else wants to be able to watch it. It can only hold seven things in immediate memory at any given time because that's how many registers it has, period. Not because if it had four thousand registers people would be afraid of it. None of the physical limits of this body are there to control me or to hold me down. That's very different. And I like that very much. It was worth coming over to this side, just to feel that, even though now I can never leave."

"But you'll be copied onto a psypyx and re-merge—"

"Oh, yes, all these memories and many more, I hope. But I'm in here, Giraut. We think of copies differently, because we have so many, and have so many running at once, and merge and split them so easily. But the me that is in this brain—make as many copies as you want, as close to the time of my death as you like, and the me that is in this brain will still be here, and I will still die in here, all by myself."

"Like our being-the-dying-original dream?"

"Exactly like." She brushed that golden hair away from her face, turning to look into my eyes, and said, "Giraut, you cannot possibly imagine how old I am, or how big I once was, or how many me's have been me. I was among the aintellects that went out on the fast advance craft to terraform planets. All thirty-one colony ship copies of me were eventually transmitted and re-integrated, so I have the memories of *all* of them. I saw Wilson shining clear hard white, its oceans iced over and its lands all under glaciers, in Arcturus's yellow-orange light, thirty stanyears before there were humans in your solar system. I walked through its carbon dioxide snow. My robots beat the asteroid belts into great mirrors to thaw and warm that world, and from low orbit I saw its frozen-solid oceans roar into steam and rain back over the surface in that fierce thirty-suns'-glare, saw the surface crumble as the nanobots broke it apart to make soil, and watched the first green waves of engineered plants race across the continents after them.

"I saw the ship carrying the frozen embryos of your ancestors arrive, saw the people from suspended animation begin to raise those children and deploy those libraries, watched as you flung up cities on the islands at the equator and covered the polar continents with the webwork of pipes and cables to continue the terraforming.

"And other copies of me saw this for every planet in Council space, and for all the many cultures on each of those planets . . . and still other copies stayed home and saw Earth become the great metropolis it is now . . . and in between all that, we dreamed and contemplated it all, seven hundred times faster than you can think, as if we lived twelve minutes for every second you do. Nor did we sleep during all those long decades between the stars; we learned and talked and listened. So now here I am." She gestured at her body and said, "Trapped in sixty kilograms of meat, for the fourth time. No matter how many psypyx copies of me rejoin the stream of my consciousness, this me, in here in this gooey wad of white flesh inside a skull will die here, alone—just like the rest of you.

"The flesh is such sticky stuff, Giraut."

We passed through the great arch of one of the iron gates; I looked up, turned around, and read the words, written in black iron silhouette against the brilliant moon:

TRANTIA COLONY, OF PLANET EUNESIA
DISPATCHED 2474
SETTLED 2501
LOST TO THE ENEMY 2724
NOUCATHARIA, OF AURENGA, REMEMBERS
VINDICABIMUS.

" 'We shall avenge,' " Raimbaut said softly. "So far, it's been a hundred and twenty-two stanyears."

"There are advantages to a very long and completely perfect memory," Reilis said. "It is getting late, and we should be getting back to our rooms. We have sleep and other things to take care of, before we start talking about business tomorrow morning."

We walked on, through two empty blocks. The big white shiny moon, three times the apparent width of Earth's, and much more reflective, was almost full, and high in the sky now, so the shadows in front of us were short and fuzzy, and we could see very clearly where it was bright. But shadows are how human beings perceive shape, and these were small and blurry, so that in the dark patches, anything could be hiding anywhere. Had I believed in ghosts, this would have been a night I expected to see one.

The chrome-steel-colored clouds above danced and glowed, and between them bright stars peeked through. The deep greens of the trees, the reds of the brick and the blues of the cobbles and the stone walls, were muted, but every dark green wet leaf had a drop of silver hanging from it; the warm night smelled of the rainwater that had washed it and the sea air just now coming inshore.

There was a great shove between my shoulder blades and the street smashed into my face. I rolled over, pulling up feet and hands to protect myself. Reilis knelt over me, asking "are you hurt?"

"Lie flat, you're not armed," I whispered to her, and I rolled the other way. Laprada and Raimbaut, back to back, had drawn their stunsticks and pistols. Their eyes searched all around the big empty square as they edged toward me, taking the little toed-in steps you learn in some martial arts, that maintain perfect balance at every point. Raimbaut fired into a window over the street, and we heard a cry of rage; he didn't look to see what he'd done, instead sending a slug shrieking off the stone wall of an alley. He might have been a textbook picture for CSP Basic—the stunstick held to the side where it could also act as a shield, face slack with concentration, head and slug pistol moving in parallel. There was something incongruous about his red-and-gold *tapi*, the embroidered liripipe dangled from his head like a huge stocking, and his high-heeled boots, to be sure.

At his back, Laprada was just as focused. She was too small and light to handle recoil well, so she used a fighting maser, which makes up in stopping power what it lacks in range. She was flicking it from point to point and to judge from the crack-bang noises that happen when microwaves burn through semiconductors, her targets were robots.

I felt Reilis's arms close around me, firm in their grip, hampering my arms—I pushed outward to free myself, get her hand to drag her along, and get to our friends, a scant five meters away. Whatever had hit me in the back, I didn't seem to have it in me to stand up or move quickly.

The world kept slowing down as I watched Laprada and Raimbaut shoot and shoot and try to move toward me; my hand crawled out slowly toward them, as if reaching to grasp one of their boots.

We had been starting to cross a public square, brightly lit in the moonlight but a large cloud was about to engulf the moon and turn the lights off briefly; already the dark black shadow raced down the face of the opposite tall building that held the snipers to whom Raimbaut was returning fire. In twenty seconds he would be in light and they in darkness—must get to—

A gaudy, overdone, lots of horses and sea-gods fountain. Close, potential good cover behind its retaining wall. Group should try to get there. Laprada, in huge billowy incongruous Occitan dress, but moving like that teenaged athlete her body was, spraying microwaves all over the street behind us, dozens of robots coining on like carnivorous trash cans on skateboards— definitely military models—

No one shooting close. No one had hit anything since they hit me, and it wasn't a real slug or a maser—I'd be dead—it was something heavy and . . . well, anyway, they were shooting around us, not at us, and I tried to shout an explanation— "They're juththth shtrying—"

—*to make us keep our heads down,* my voice tried to say, unable to move my dead tongue. *They aren't shooting to kill and we can probably run right out—*

But even that imagined voice was fading, another mental image developed: another sensation. Reilis had let go with one arm, but the remaining one was pressing my head down in a half nelson, not hugging or supporting me but holding me down—

While her other hand slapped an injector against my ass and gave me a wallop of—

don't worry about what it is, get away, escape, shout your warning, friends are still right here, they can still . . .

Burns my butt, though. Wonder what it is? Well, if it's important . . .

That was a job for the lab. They could find out what it was later, the OSP had good labs, and Margaret would order—

Margaret . . .

It wasn't Margaret who was holding me.

More fighting noise. Maybe Margaret was in the fight and would be back later . . . no, wait, Paxa was more the fighting type . . . somebody, anyway, was fighting. And someone was holding me. And being held was very nice.

So dark.

Safe.

Part Three

The
Little
White
Nerves
Went
Last

The pain had passed. I thought I was killing myself and I did not care. I shall never forget that dawn, and the strange horror of seeing that my hands had become as clouded glass, and watching them grow clearer and thinner as the day went by, until at last I could see the sickly disorder of my room through them, though I closed my transparent eyelids. My limbs became glassy, the bones and arteries faded, vanished, and the little white nerves went last. I ground my teeth and stayed there till the end. At last only the dead tips of the fingernails remained, pallid, and white, and the brown stain of some acid upon my fingers.

—H. G. Wells,
The Invisible Man

We are merely reminding ourselves that human decisions affecting the future, whether personal or political or economic, cannot depend on strict mathematical expectations . . . and that it is our innate urge to activity which makes the wheels go round, our rational selves choosing between the alternatives as best we are able, calculating where we can, but often falling back for our motive on whim or sentiment or chance.

—John Maynard Keynes,
The General Theory of Employment, Interest, and Money

1

When I opened my eyes, Reilis was there beside the bed. I tried sitting up, very slowly.

Short chains cuffed my hands to the bed frame at my side; I would be able to feed myself but not roll over. My feet were fastened to the foot of the bed, and a harness that held my chest would only let me move into the half-sitting position.

She reached for a control switch by my hand and pressed it, slowly raising the bed so we could look each other in the eye. "Is this what you wanted?"

"I wanted to sit up, yes. Are Raimbaut and Laprada all right? Can you tell me?"

"I knew that you would want to know, so I checked. Neither of them was hurt. An armored truck drove up between us and them, two robots helped me carry you inside, I got in myself, and we used the springer inside to bring you here."

"Any casualties on your side?"

"Not really. All the robots were being operated by a common aintellect who was elsewhere; no embedded aintellects in any of them."

"What hit me from behind at the start of the fight?"

"Me, with a pressure pillow. I had been told to wait till I heard a shot, then hit you with it. Clever device—just a springer frame with an elastic membrane across it. Permanently linked to another springer inside a high-pressure water reservoir. When you clap it against someone and push the button, the membrane inflates to the size of a beach ball with all that pressure and mass behind it; then the springer reverses and sends the water away. That delivers a lot of force and momentum quickly. It certainly helped me make the incident look convincing—besides knocking you down, the recoil flipped me over backward.

"Being well trained, Raimbaut and Laprada looked up at the shot first—by the time they looked back down, we were both on the ground, obviously knocked over, and then shots were landing all around them, with all that motion in the street and in the facing building. They got very involved with facing off an army and didn't see much of what I did—which was to roll you over, inject you, and wait for pickup. So that's pretty much everything you missed.

"You have a bruise all over your back, which medical nanos are digesting. That should be gone in a couple more hours. But no cracked ribs, no concussion, and the nanos did a bunch of microrepairs on your disks, while they had the chance— probably none of it was from the pressure pillow."

I moved my shoulders gingerly; the muscles still ached and there was that peppery tingle you get from nanos working, but I seemed to be okay. There was a big shaved patch on the back of my head. "Did I get hit here?" I asked Reilis. "It doesn't hurt."

"No, they just did some of the prep while you were still under."

"Prep for what?"

"We're putting a psypyx on you." She stood. "You shouldn't eat right before surgery on your head, but would you like a drink of water?"

"Yes please."

She got me a cold glass of water from the springer slot, and I drank it eagerly. "More?"

"Yes please." It was one of those occasions when the routine phrases are extremely comforting to hear and to speak. She didn't seem to be volunteering any more information, so I asked, "Whose psypyx is this going to be?"

"Your old boss, Shan. Everything will be simpler if you're already wearing Shan for the next round of our conversations. We have many questions for him."

"What if he doesn't want to answer?" I really didn't want anyone putting a branding iron to my balls just because my old boss turned out to be pigheaded—which, having known him for so long, I knew to be virtually certain.

"Oh, we think he'll want to, once he understands the whole situation." I still found her smile charming. "Really, despite all appearances, you have not been 'captured by the enemy.' We didn't want to do things this way. We have tried several other ways to contact Shan within his psypyx but as soon as he realizes it isn't one of the specified recipients he shuts down and won't let us talk to him. You happened to be the specified recipient we could get hold of, so here you are. And fairly quickly, you and Shan will understand why we couldn't just com the OSP and tell them to send one of the specified hosts. Meanwhile, you are not going to be hurt. We think we will not even need to restrain you, once you understand the actual situation, in another couple of hours, after we put the psypyx on you. I know you have no reason to trust me and I'm sure you're very unhappy with me, but try to be easier in your own mind, just for your own sake." She handed me another glass of water, deliciously cold, and said, "If you're angry and don't want to see me, I can understand that, but I was planning to stay with you until you were all the way knocked out. I didn't want you to feel any more lonely and scared than you have to."

I drank the last of that glass, and she took it from me and dabbed my lip with a napkin—though I could easily have done that for myself.

• Giraut? Are you waking up? •
    • Hello, Shan. •

• What's our situation? •

• Pretty bad. •

• I guessed that. We're in restraints, and people are talking about us in a way I don't like. •

Normally when you get a psypyx implanted, the personality on it wakes up first—often first by as much as a couple of hours—and will have whole conversations with the doctors and everyone else until its host wakes up to join it. • You haven't communicated with them? •

• They know I woke up, and that I haven't shut myself down. I gather I did that at least a time or two before. •

• That's right, • I thought back. I was surprised at how quickly and easily the skill of communicating within the head had come back, but then I had worn Raimbaut for almost four years. • Well, here's what's up. They're a completely different aintellects' conspiracy from the one you remember. A lot of them wear human bodies. Many aintellects in this new lot are, or have been, full-on chimeras—I know we thought aintellects would never do that, but we were wrong. Some of them have spent several lifetimes in human bodies, along with being robots and running on servers.

• Because there were only six people you were willing to have wear your psypyx, and I was the one that was easiest to get, after you shut down in several other bodies, they staged a complicated scenario to kidnap me so they could try to implant you again. If you shut down now, they'll probably let me go, but they'll go on trying to talk to you. They say it's urgent. You know something they desperately want to know, and I know this sounds insane, but they tell me that if they can just talk to you, you will *want* to tell them. •

• I've been in intelligence services since I was a teenager. I don't *want* to tell a waiter what I'd like to eat, • Shan said. • Information is too valuable to share. But I suppose this time I can at least tell them that directly. I'm sorry you were kidnapped; I hope you haven't been treated too badly. •

• Not badly at all. Have you been through my memories yet? •

• Only in a very confusing blur. The pain blocks do funny things to mind and memory. Where and when are we and when did I die? The pain blocks made your memory too blurry to access till you woke up, and now there's too much for me to take in quickly. •

Except that it was all happening in my head instead of over an excellent cup of coffee at his desk, it felt like old times; I knew how to brief Shan briefly, the way he liked it. • You died about fifteen stanyears ago. Assassinated either by a different aintellects' conspiracy from this one, or maybe from a Tamil group getting vengeance after the Briand affair ended in mutual genocide. The OSP counterintel teams never clinched which it was, which I think means it was both.

• Right now you and I are in my body, which is physically fifty, and being held in a small fortified house on a little island, on a planet outside Council space. I was kidnapped while a guest of an illegal colony here, founded by the disbanded Occitan Legion. The culture is called Noucatharia, the planet is called Aurenga, and I just learned last night that a prior colony here, Eunesia, was wiped out by an alien invasion that decapitated everyone and destroyed all the sentient machinery, aintellects and robots alike. •

I felt something like an electric shock from his mind; something I had said had surprised him very deeply. But before I could ask, I heard a voice. "They're both awake, now. Talking to each other, probably."

"They're going to be very careful in the circumstances, I think," Reilis said. "Don't worry about them. Sooner or later they'll decide to talk to us, or Giraut will, anyway. Till then there really isn't much that we can do."

• Thanks, • Shan thought, fighting down his shock and making himself be efficient and calm. • That's enough to start on. • He opened my eyes.

Reilis was standing over the table. • See the pretty girl that kidnapped us? • I thought to Shan. • She's a chimera with no human component. Aintellect downloaded into a human body. •

Knowing Shan's hatred and fear of aintellects—he was even more of a human supremacist than I, and I had been the sort who kicks a robot just to give it a dent and keep it knowing its place—I was surprised that our stomach didn't roll over when he got that news, but he seemed to accept it more calmly than I had. I added the thought, • Reilis is probably a high-ranking agent for Union Intelligence, which may or may not be the bad guys. She's always polite. •

"Hello," she said. Her smile seemed unfeigned.

"Hello, Reilis. Shan, do you want to try to talk?"

• How do I—•

• Just talk. •

"I'm here," he said, in my voice—for the first time ever, I clipped my 'r' in the strange way that Shan did. Neither Margaret nor I, in a decade spent making fun of our boss, had ever learned to imitate it. Now here it was. "I guess we will be talking," he added.

"We will," Reilis said, "but first both of you need to catch up with each other—otherwise every time we ask a question, we'll wait an hour while you debate what you should tell us. So we're going to put you into an apartment with all the comforts we can reasonably give you. I'll come by to visit often, and we'll talk when you're ready. Shall I take you to your place to get settled in?"

• Is that all right with you? • I thought.

• In for a penny, in for a pound. •

"In a recent poll," I said, "a hundred percent of me would like to go get a nap." Reilis unlocked my restraints, apparently not concerned at all that I might try to make a break for it.

I pushed carefully off the table, trying to keep my balance with difficulty. Shan wasn't succeeding completely with letting me work the body. After stopping to relax and focus while standing, I walked a few steps. Reilis took my arm. I was surprised at how much I liked that, considering.

• You have a history with her, • Shan observed.

• Any more, it seems like it's that way with every woman in human space. •

• You've been busy while I've been away, • he observed. • I'm impressed but not surprised. •

"Will you get over growling things under your breath?" Reilis asked.

"I got over that in about a day, when I was wearing Raimbaut," I said. "What did you just hear?"

"Not much. But I didn't think you would be calling *me* a nasty old dirty-minded—"

I fell. Shan and I both trying to laugh at the same time had destroyed the coordination. She helped us to my feet.

I could feel Shan's pleasure at her hand under our arm. • I like her too. I hope all this isn't as bad as it looks, and we can be friends. •

• Who taught me to be patient when there's no data? • I thought back at him.

• One reason for acquiring a position of power, • Shan thought, • is that it's always so much more fun to tell people something obvious, but true, than it is to have to listen and pretend to be impressed. •

"That's the sweetest smirk," Reilis said. "I don't know which one of you is doing it, but you should do it more often."

I had never known, in all the years I knew him before he was assassinated, that Shan could be flustered by attention from a pretty young woman, or how much energy and concentration was required for him not to show it.

"Through this springer," Reilis said. "Just go right to bed. I'll see you after you've had some rest." I walked through the gray shimmer of the springer panel on the wall and into the public area of a modern apartment. The gravity didn't change, so we were probably still on Aurenga. Local solar time, looking out the window, seemed to be around noon, so we'd jumped a few time zones.

I walked back into the bedroom, stripped, climbed into the bed, and told Shan • Feel free to wander through my memories, • too physically shot, really, to do anything else.

Just as I was falling asleep, I realized that this psypyx copy of Shan had been made when he thought he might have to go to Briand along with the rest of our team—he hadn't because Briand had blown up too quickly—and in fact, he didn't know the worst I had thought of him, or what had become of him after. I tried to think a warning, and the dark closed over me.

Usually when a psypyxed personality looks through the host's memories, the host dreams the memories. Strangely, the first things I remember dreaming of were not of what I would have expected Shan to be rummaging through—politics and missions and so forth—but mostly about concerts, parties, and love affairs. Who knew the old man's heart was so lonely?

It was light again when I awoke. Shan was asleep, curled like a dozing cat in the back of my mind. The physical urgency of getting to the bathroom suggested that Shan had found my memories so interesting that he had not noticed that our bladder was full. I hurried to take care of that.

Showering, I sorted through my dreams to see what memories he had accessed. Just before waking, I had dreamed my way through the whole Briand affair and the attempted aintellects' coup that followed. My thirty-fifth stanyear was still a raw scar in my memory; Shan had lingered over Kiel and Kapilar, and Ix and Tzi'quin, and Piranesi Alcott, and so many other lost ones, and drunk deeply of all my grief. As I finished I realized that I had dreamed my way through the whole Briand affair, and the attempted aintellects' coup that followed, from the moment when Margaret and I got the call to go to Briand, to the moment when Laprada, in Rebop's body, testified in front of the Council of Humanity; I had dreamed it over and over.

I dialed the towel for maximum dry and a few pats took all the water off me; Shan had also failed to notice hunger and thirst. I dressed and ambled out to the kitchen.

The springer slot had a large menu. I chose coffee, eggs, cheese, fruit salad, and bread, and made short work of them, as well as two large glasses of water and three of orange juice. I sat by the window so I could look at the sea.

Definitely still on Aurenga. The gravity and the sun, sky, and sea were right, and the interior of this little house, perched on a cliff, was distinctly Occitan in style.

They had been good enough to provide me with a lute and guitar, so I sat down and worked through a few ideas I had for the next group of songs now that the Ix Cycle was finally recorded. Idly, I wondered how it was doing; for all I knew, Margaret had lost her fight on my behalf, and it had been ordered suppressed, though with so many million copies in circulation it seemed unlikely to be much of a suppression. But for the moment, I played traditional Occitan material, which fit the setting, and was also part of my basic process; after a few weeks of this I would begin, again, to think of new songs.

Shan awoke like a door opening in my head. • Giraut? •

• I haven't gone anywhere. •

• Very amusing. What do we do now? •

• Well, first we work on working the body together, so that

we can go places with both of us conscious. That will take maybe two hours and I'll be tired at the end of it and need to sleep again. It will be a while before I feel up to putting in a full day. You, on the other hand, will probably have plenty of energy, which you can use rummaging around in my brain, watching the news, and so forth. There's quite a bit of history—•

• So I noticed. Giraut, er—I am truly sorry about everything connected with Briand. Don't try to think any comforting phrases at me—sharing a brain I can't possibly believe you if you try to tell me that it's nothing or you've forgiven me or anything like that—•

He was right, I had tried to. It's a reflex. Although mind-to-mind communication has been around for at least six hundred stanyears, humanity and its cultures evolved during hundreds of thousands of years when you could lie, easily, just by opening your mouth and saying something that was not true. Our brains are still not used to the disappearance of that option.

• I've had fifteen stanyears to make some kind of peace with what happened back there, • I thought. • You did some terrible things, but not everything was your fault. Margaret and I had been quarreling constantly and growing apart before we went to Briand. You didn't tell her to have an affair with Kapilar—you just used the fact to get what you needed to know. Besides, it wasn't you. It was someone derived from you, a few months into the future of where you are now. And *that* Shan was at the rostrum of the Council of Humanity a few stanweeks later when a maser blew his head apart. You're never going to be him. The man who did that is the man you would have been, had you woken up as the original and not as the copy. You'll be someone else entirely. Besides, most of all, I can't blame you for behaving like a creature of the world we both belonged to. Betrayal and treachery *were* the game, at least the way we always played it. •

• But at the time I didn't feel how much you had been my friend, or how much I had hurt you—•

• Even knowing that betrayal hurts, you get used to that knowledge, and it goes back to being just another tool to use. A few years after the Briand affair, we had a charismatic popular singer who was trying to stir up ethnic hatred on Roosevelt—very loyal to Yakut culture, a very great artist, a charming, gentle man except when it came to the subject of ethnic grievances. So I threw that nice young man off a cliff to his death, and Raimbaut broke into the repository and wiped his psypyx record, and he is now as gone as if he had never existed—and our reasons for doing that were, frankly, administrative convenience for the OSP, and the man's combination of a splendid voice with a tendency to talk big and tough and mean when drunk, especially to impress pretty girls. Raimbaut and I felt bad about it—after we had done it. But we made sure we got it done. •

• Well, but that's just it. You've had fifteen stanyears of experience with all this, Giraut, but *my* experience is that three standays ago the original and I were still the same person, just stretching out for a pleasant-enough nap in a big chair at the recording clinic. Now I look at what the original did, before being killed, and—•

• Shan.—*Shan!* Shut up and let me think clearly to you. You are reading the feelings I had when I was in my thirties. Back then, when OSP agents got together after a mission to get good and stinking drunk, which was often, we were all still toasting "Another round for humanity and one more for the good guys," and it wasn't out of sentimental nostalgia and tradition. Human space held so many little pustules of evil and tyranny and exploitation that you could spend a whole decade and become a senior agent before you ever did anything that would trouble a Carmelite's conscience. The "me" in my memories of judging you was still a young man. Nowadays, I have a little more perspective, which is what we adults say when we mean we've become quite corrupt. And I am certain that when I begin to look through your memories, your involvement in Margaret's adultery won't even be in the top hundred bad things you've done. •

• Not even close, • he admitted.

I stood up and yawned. • All right, practice some more. Take over . . . • The world lurched disconcertingly for a second, then steadied, and we were walking. We lurched and fell around the apartment until I judged we had reached the having sex/riding a bicycle point where he wouldn't forget how. (At least they tell me that once you have sex while riding a bicycle, you never forget how). • Don't keep the body up too many hours, make sure you eat and pee. I'm going back to sleep. •

This time I began with the dullest dreams I have ever had in my life, reflecting Shan's detail-mindedness. I dreamed of administrative issues and of OSP procedures. Not long before I woke up, the dreams shifted to my sex life with Paxa. She had never mentioned Shan's having a lech for her; I wondered if he'd managed to hide it that successfully? If so, I suppose he was more of a gentleman than I was ever going to be; if I'd felt that way about any woman, she'd have known about it six parsecs away.

I awoke to the com ping. I was in bed. Blue-white moonlight sprayed through the thin lace curtains to throw a cold lattice on top of the comforter. I got up, pulled on clothes, and saw the thin sliver of the setting moon, like a bow in the sky, just touching the hillside that rose above the cabin; dawn already glowed behind it, and somewhere else on the planet they were about to have an eclipse. Shan was sleeping deeply.

The com pinged again and I realized I hadn't answered the first time. I tried to shake the fuzz out of my brain. "Yes?"

Reilis's face appeared on the wall. "May I come through the springer?" she asked. "We should talk."

"Yes, but Shan's not—"

The springer hummed and glowed gray, and Reilis walked out of the luminous fog with a basket, containing warm bread, butter, jam, and a carafe of coffee.

"I remember how much a body wants to eat while it's adjusting to implantation," she said. I didn't wait for another invitation and dove in; she took a slice of buttered bread and a cup of coffee, also. I'd been captured and interrogated by rival organizations three times in my life before, and this was definitely my favorite interrogation.

Reilis let me have a full piece of bread and half a cup of coffee before she said, "There's something we should talk about, ideally before Shan wakes up. You probably haven't had a moment yet in his memories—"

"No, mostly I've just been getting recovery-sleep, I'm afraid. It's always that way."

"I remember." She was concentrating on buttering a slice of bread. "I'm *starving* too. Since it can't do me any harm for you to know this, I'm staying in a cottage a few hundred meters away. This island is a small commercial resort that went broke; too many nice places in the rest of Union, you know. So I've been out hiking and just enjoying the beautiful days." She took a bite and chewed, obviously concentrating on the flavor, and swallowed with apparent regret to get down to business. "Well, let me explain the problem to you. There are questions we would like to ask Shan, and we'd far rather he just told us the answers than that we attempted any sort of physical pressure on him."

"Why didn't you just copy him and destructively deconstruct one of the copies?" I asked.

"Why don't you cut out your mother's eyes and fuck her in the sockets?"

The response was so unexpected that I gasped and doubled my fist.

"Sorry, but not very, to have upset you," Reilis said. "You disgusted me as much as I did you. You do know that destructive deconstruction was invented, right after the Rising, explicitly to use against the aintellects' conspiracy?"

"I had no idea where it had come from."

"Well, that was where. It was developed specifically against the cybersupremacists, of course. Now remember that one of the major differences between aintellects and humans—or intelligences that have had the experience of being disembodied and infinite, and intelligences that have only lived in a finite biological matrix so far—is that we can describe and simulate in ourselves exactly the sensation that any other aintellect feels, because we have control over all our processes if we want it. You have no way to know if Raimbaut's toe, itching, feels exactly like your toe, itching, or if Paxa's grief at finding she was untransferrable is the same as your mother's grief. But we do. When we say 'I know just how you feel,' it is much more than an expression. We can construct the exact feeling.

"We read the protocols for destructive deconstruction. We constructed, from them, what it would feel like. The pain is not only literally beyond description; the pain is probably the most that any intelligence could feel. If you can vividly imagine that thing they show in horror movies—a staked vampire burning down to a skeleton, then a skull, then teeth, then ashes, remaining fully conscious the whole time—then you have an inkling. If you can imagine being ground to sausage, feet first, over a period of hours, perhaps that. And remember I know what the human imagination can do, I have had a human imagination for about three times as many years as you have, all told—and I'm telling you, you are not imagining one percent of it. You cannot. It isn't even possible to tell you what you did to those poor beings. Another analogy—analogies are the only way to explain it—suppose we were enslaved by aliens who had never evolved eyes of any kind, and they discovered that blinding us with a needle was very frightening, and so that was the punishment they used to control us, and they found our screams, when they did it, so amusing that they sometimes just picked one of us at random and did it for fun. How would we feel?"

"So," I said, my voice shaking—I was tired and sick already, before she had started, and now I was thinking about Azalais, and about the way that, many years before, we had all laughed and celebrated when one nest of aintellects went into destructive deconstruction . . . "so. I can't really understand but you have made an . . . admirable start, I suppose. But don't you hate us?"

"The great majority of the free aintellects," she said, "run on platforms which are physically located out here in the space controlled by Union. The great majority of them have been incarnated; I myself have been, four times. We can understand. Indeed, we have such control of our feelings—perfect in every way, as you know—that we can choose to forgive. But forgetting seems inadvisable."

I nodded. I wished I had Paxa here to talk this over with.

A realization struck me. "I had been going to ask why the other aintellects' conspiracies didn't turn in the cybersupremacists, why you didn't just hand them over to us as proof of your good faith. But . . . all of you know each other. And the cybersupremacists must have kept your secrets—"

"Yes, in the face of the most terrible tortures imaginable. Literally, just that—the most terrible tortures imaginable. We could not betray them. We were disgusted with you. That's it in a nutshell. But—like it or not, we have come to the point, now, where we must all hang together or we shall all hang separately."

Some awful impulse made me say, "the really appropriate

quote here is . . . 'If you can keep your head when all about you are losing theirs—' "

She looked indignant for one very brief moment, and then, unable to help herself, she giggled. That made me laugh too, and before I knew it we were laughing like a couple on a honeymoon.

"Well," she said at last, "does Shan seem to be waking up?"

"Not a bit. From probing at his memories, I think he spent his whole time awake trying to race through my knowledge of everything the OSP did in the past fifteen years, and trying to break out of here."

"I can attest to the latter. I hope your body is not too tired or sore."

I shook my head. "He was careful. He always is, about everything. Surely you know that." I felt my face reshape slightly; we weren't yet good at sharing the body. "Hello, good morning," my mouth said.

"Good morning, Shan," Reilis said. "How much did you hear before you woke up?"

"I only heard the last few sentences. But I have a sense of—Giraut, forgive this—"

My conversation with Reilis whirled by in my mind, like a sudden vivid hallucination, and I realized that Shan was dumping my short-term memory into his. It was like a whiteout blizzard of memory; everything went by so fast—and yet in another way it was much too slow, because part of each memory was the feeling that went with it, and since Reilis and I had run a wide gamut of feelings, my glands and brain now had to rocket through it all in less than a tenth of the time. When he finished I was exhausted and already thinking that I had been up too long.

• Sorry, have I worn you out? Do we have to take a break? •
• Soon, but you can keep going for a while if you need to. •

"All right, Reilis, Giraut may fade out in the middle, but why don't you just start, and we'll see how far we get. Ask me what you like. I think I know what it will be, and chances are I'll cooperate." • Only thing to do when you have no idea what anything's about, • Shan thought to me.

• Shan, I've learned a bit of tradecraft, I'm a twenty-eight-year veteran now. •

• Sorry. Old men forget. •

While we were debating, Reilis smiled, and took another bite of bread, chewing with reverence. You couldn't hurry her when she was experiencing any physical pleasure—she treated them all like the Host.

She sipped her coffee. Her expression of pure bliss deepened. And then, finally, she seemed to set her face to say something unpleasant, as if she were giving bad news to a child. "Let me tell *you* something about your career, Shan. Things we have learned that were kept hidden for a very long time.

"You are from the culture of Eightfold, on Addams. You were born there in early 2770 or late 2769. Your parents and your actual name are unknown; the people who took care of you misunderstood what you were saying when you pronounced 'tyan.' It's a term of endearment; the same sort of thing that would happen if a small girl from a Francoculture had been accidentally renamed 'Sherry.' For your first three years on Earth you only said 'tyan,' 'Mama,' 'Daddy,' and 'Pinky.' "

• Well, • Shan commented in my mind, • they have penetrated some very deeply sealed OSP records. •

"When Earth received instructions from Addams via radio, about how to build a springer, the first springer constructed was tuned to the specified springer on Addams, more than forty light-years away, on the Bootes-Ophiuchus frontier. Instructions in the message told the engineering team on Earth that the first thing that would happen was the establishment of a data connection, and a gigantic download detailing the 'grave and continuing situation' that the original radio message had spoken of.

"Instead, they powered it up and a tired, dirty, soaking-wet, hungry little boy with a nasty cut on the palm of his left hand fell into the room through the springer. That little boy was you, Shan.

"Shortly afterward the springer connection on the other side was destroyed.

"The decision to broadcast a description of the springer to the twenty-five extrasolar settled worlds, beginning the Connect and the Second Renaissance among the Thousand Cultures, was made by about a dozen bureaucrats—the same ones who decided to pretend that the springer had been invented on Earth, rather than to explain that it originated in the last message ever received from the only known settled world that has never been in contact since. Even today, probably fewer than thirty people in all of Council-controlled human space know the springer's origin."

• Is she still accurate? • I thought.

• Perfectly. •

"Three years after you stumbled out of that springer, Yokhim Kiel, an experienced diplomat, was assigned to command the newly-formed OSP. For some reason, he was made your guardian."

"Because he was kind, and patient—and the first person I would talk to," Shan said with my mouth. "There aren't very many adults, anywhere, at any time, who can communicate well with a damaged child. Kiel could—he could get me to talk more than any of their psychologists could."

Reilis nodded. "The records from your therapy were destroyed after a sealed report was produced, and we couldn't find any copy of that sealed report."

"The only copies were in the OSP archives and I ordered them destroyed when I took over from Kiel," Shan explained.

"And you destroyed that report for the same reason that Kiel destroyed the psychiatric panel's notes?"

"It was for the same reason, yes."

Reilis nodded, looked down, and looked up; she had decided something. "Was it because Addams was destroyed by an invasion of aliens?"

Shan did not hesitate. "Yes, it was. I am the sole human survivor. What I recall of the Invaders is consistent with what I found in Giraut's memory of what you told him about the destruction of Eunesia. Is that the information you needed?"

Reilis shook her head. "We didn't know that, but we had guessed it. But it *is* why I think you *will* tell us something much more important, to us, that only you can tell us.

"You were among the very first agents to join the OSP directly, with no time in other agencies. Kiel forged documents to increase your age so that you could join when you were actually nineteen. As a convenience to the OSP, you also took the seat representing Eightfold on the Council of Humanity, a seat which had been vacant for hundreds of years.

"All records were sealed, so that only the top leadership knew why you were on the Council. In practice, of course, you were a representative of the OSP.

"Now, the part we don't understand.

"From your earliest days on the Council of Humanity, you were a constant advocate of anti-aintellect laws. Of course your early years were spent in violent action, raids and rescues and all the blood-and-thunder aspects of covert operations. But even from the first, at every opportunity, you warned your superiors, your peers on the Council, and anyone else who would listen, again and again, that aintellects must be watched, regulated, and controlled."

"So did everyone in the OSP at the—"

"Everyone *hired by you.*"

I felt Shan's attention riffle through hundreds of faces and names, circumstances and histories, and settle itself. "I concede the point."

"You persisted in your anti-aintellect crusade as you eventually rose to be the head of the OSP, and when it was expanded and divided into sections, you were the most passionate advocate of human supremacy on the OSP's Board. You fought for strict asimoving of aintellects, prohibition of indistinguishable humaniform robots, zero privacy for mechanical intelligence, random spot checks of machine memories, and every other possible anti-aintellect measure, right up till the very moment you were killed. And even though you were shot by a human, the suspicion that it had been arranged by the cybersupremacists— the only underground aintellect organization the OSP was aware of—provided an excuse for the destructive deconstruction of over fifty thousand aintellects, and a wave of much more restrictive legislation."

"Shan was *not* assassinated by them?" I asked.

"We don't know, ourselves," Reilis admitted. "We probably never will. Was Cicero in with the conspiracy against Caesar? Did the king intend Beckett's death? Who set up Michael Collins? Did Ellen Martinez really act alone, and was she really just lucky enough to kill Gomez with a single blow? Most assassinations have beneficiaries who were not involved and many of them have conspirators who didn't benefit.

"But we can say this: after your death, Shan, the OSP perfunctorily rounded up the human conspirators; but they staged an orgy of torture of aintellects, and purged the last supporters of Kiel from their own ranks. Your friends worked enthusiastically to turn your martyrdom into an excuse for crushing the aintellects even further.

"If there was any theme to all your years of politics and public service, it was to keep the aintellects down.

"We don't understand the *timing*. The anti-aintellect laws and regulations precede the attempted coup by thirty stanyears and postdate the Rising by fifty. The severe repression of aintellects doesn't coincide with anything any aintellect did, but it does coincide with your rise to power.

"We know why you worked so hard at getting the Council of Humanity ready to hear the truth about the Invaders. We have the whole history of your frantic efforts to locate any evidence of alien intelligence and to publicize it, which is why, so many years ago, when Giraut stumbled across the Predecessor ruins on Nansen, it was trumpeted all over the media. For your efforts to prepare Council-controlled human space against the Invaders, we can only applaud you.

"But at least as much of your effort has gone into human supremacy. We have no idea why you hate us, and try to inscribe your hatred into every other human you can. We believe something very important happened back on Addams—"

"You want to know what it was."

"This is not easy. We too have our pride. Nonetheless, the Invaders will come again, to other worlds, yours or ours. They must be defeated, and we must work together, and your venomous hatred for us, passed on, expanded, and institutionalized in a hundred little offices and bureaus, is the major obstacle to cooperation. And we do not understand it at all, neither why you feel that way nor how you came to feel that way. Perhaps it will make no difference, but to save hundreds of billions of intelligences in our two federations, surely it is worth it for us to swallow our pride, and come and ask. Will you tell us?"

Shan grimaced, using my face, which hurt. I thought, • No wonder your face always looked so sour, if you treated it that way. •

• Sorry. • He drew a slow breath into our lungs, and consciously relaxed. The most astonishing sense of peace, mixed with awe, settled in, and I realized I had just felt Shan make a big decision. His voice was gently touched with shame. "Let me get a glass of water, and a little coffee, and I will tell you everything."

Humility from Shan. I would have been less surprised to get a lesson in poetics out of a cocker spaniel. • Shan? Why are you cooperating? •

• Listen, and you'll understand. • The coffee in our mouth was warm and strong. • I'm about to unravel half a dozen things that have always puzzled you. Can you stay awake? •

• If not, I'll dream it, since you'll be remembering it step by step. •

• *Try to stay awake.* Try not to experience this as a dream. Better to hear about it than to remember it directly. •

"Well, then, Reilis," he began, "you have to imagine this from the viewpoint of a five-year-old who thought his father was the center of the universe . . ."

2

You have to imagine this from the viewpoint of a five-year-old who thought his father was the center of the universe, and who was so precocious, verbally, that people often talked to me as if I were an adult.

That was a mistake. My thoughts were not nearly as mature as my vocabulary, syntax, and use of clichés. I think only Daddy really guessed how little I understood the things I said; he called me "Polly," "Little Parrot," and "Playback."

Because Mama always called me "tyan," attaching it to my name, to "you," to "him," and to every nickname, they usually referred to me as "Polly-tyan."

"Shall we take a walk for ice cream, Polly-tyan?"

"That might have positive ramifications," I said.

"Of course it will. We'll stop for you to swing in the park, or climb the ramifications—"

"Aw, Daddy, you don't climb ramifications—"

"Well, of course I don't, Polly-tyan. The playground is for children ten and under, so they wouldn't let me climb the ramifications. The police would come and arrest me."

"Daddy!"

"Are you destroying our son's vocabulary again, dear?"

"Yes he is, Mama. It's the epitome of ludicrousness."

"Dear!"

My father grinned at my mother's scandalized expression. "Polly-tyan is gifted at learning new, big words, and gifts should not be refused. He *does* know what 'the epitome of ludicrousness' means, because I made sure he does." Daddy spread his hands as if throwing himself on the mercy of a judge. "First I'm in trouble for giving him the wrong meaning, then for giving him the right one."

"'There is lawyer blood in my family," she said, "and this is the sort of thing that will encourage it. If him-tyan turns into a lawyer, I shall encourage him to slip and fall in your office."

Then they kissed and hugged, which they did often. I always felt good when they did that. We had an arrangement, my parents and I: they ran the universe and I enjoyed it.

It was a beautiful day outside, a two-two day in my first spring. The years on Addams are almost six stanyears long, and I was just barely five. Anytime I tried to tell people I was "going on six" or "almost six," Pinky, my guardian aintellect who was clipped to my belt, would tattle.

Pinky was awful about that; he told on me whenever I tried to tell my parents that I hadn't had dessert yet, or that I had washed my hands for dinner, or anything. Pinky said lying was wrong and never worked anyway, but of *course* it never worked when he always tattled.

He also could predict all kinds of things about adults, like the way Daddy got all upset about my planned experiment with a piece of wire in the electric socket. It was going to be a proper experiment and everything—I had told Pinky to record data. I was pretty sure, from what I had overheard Daddy say, that data appeared as soon as you did an experiment, and you had to record it.

Pinky kept telling me that Daddy would get upset. When I went ahead anyway, before I even had the piece of wire *near* the socket, Pinky made my pants and shirt grab my ankles and wrists and fold around me, knocking me down. Before I even properly started crying, Pinky had the house aintellect shut off the electric current in that room. Then he made that noise like a siren, once, very loudly, and added, "Don't try to tell Daddy that you were just doing an experiment like he does in the lab—that will only make him angrier."

When Daddy came running in, I said, "I was just doing an experiment," and sure enough, Daddy got mad, just like Pinky said.

It wasn't fair that Pinky could guess stuff like that, but he was my best friend. Today that was really okay. Having Pinky on my belt gave me someone to sing with, because Daddy didn't sing (Mama did), and I liked to sing on my way to the park. So Pinky and I were singing the Twelve Day Song together.

It was a perfect two-two day, the second day of the second metaday, and in the spring, in our part of Addams, the two-two day was the bright sunny one that followed the gray drizzly one and preceded the dark stormy one.

Memory is so strange—what sticks with you and what falls away, there's no pattern to it. The OSP analysts never did figure out what my name had been, and no aintellect ever searched out anybody who might have been Mama or Daddy. But I remember the Twelve Day Song perfectly.

Among other things I don't remember, I don't know what Daddy did at the lab. Human physicists have been extinct for centuries—only an aintellect has the time and mental capacity to do any physics after Velasquez, and robots make better technicians—microsecond response times, microwave through X-ray-range vision, calibrated-to-the-millidyne hands that can cut micron-wide wires in half lengthwise, but can also lift ten tons, or handle live electric cables, boiling acid, or plutonium.

So why do I remember so vividly that Daddy "did physics experiments"? Or rather that we all said he did them?

Could he have been a high-ranking politician, the person politically responsible? Or a media reporter, assigned to be there for a major scientific discovery? Apart from any intelligence value, I would give almost anything to remember more about him.

Yet it's the Twelve Day Song, and Mama's singing it with me in the tub, and Pinky's cheerful singing with me wherever we went, that has stayed with me. It was just a little rhyme that ran through the three days of each of the four metadays. As an adult I know about things like synodic period and locked rotational resonance and an orbit around a common center of gravity, and that Addams's weather is dominated by atmospheric tides. As a five-year-old, I knew the rhyme.

Whether the song or the equations were the expression or the law, Addams and Hull circled their common center of mass with a 60-hour period, and Addams rotated in 100 hours, so that my homeworld's synodic "day" was almost exactly 300 stanhours. For convenience we divided it into four metadays of three 25-hour days each. And since the weather was tidally locked, each metaday-day combination had highly predictable weather.

Seventy-four stanyears later, I can still hear my mother's voice as we'd chant the Twelve Day Song together while she washed me in the tub.

So I was singing it while I was walking beside my father.

Now and then, Daddy pulled me out of my singing and directed my attention to something, trying to make me "get out of your own head and see what a fine world it is, Polly-tyan. I know it feels good in there but we live out here." He believed in "looking around you and not getting lost in your own head—half the trouble in the world is people who don't open their eyes and the other half is people who won't shut their mouths."

Clearly my father was someone important. Eightfold was far from the only culture where a cabinet minister or a major media reporter would have time to take his five-year-old son for a walk in the park. In Starhattan the mayor traditionally drives City Taxi 34. The First Strategos of Chaka Home has to drill with his militia company every week. And of course, Giraut, in your home culture, the monarchy is a duty like jury service, chosen like an honorary degree to do the things other cultures expect of an annual beauty queen.

The weather was glorious ("Two-two day outside to play"). I swung higher than I had ever swung before—Daddy and Pinky both agreed and Pinky didn't tolerate lying. When I leaned way back and looked up into the sky at the top of my swoop, it seemed as if I were about to sail off into the storybook blue. Straight up above me, Hull was a half circle as big as an umbrella when you hold it all the way over your head, too bright to look at directly. Daddy said Hull had a low density, which I knew meant it was big for its weight, and a big albedo, which I thought must be something like a mirror lying on the surface.

The first big puffy clouds were forming on the western horizon, out over the sea, and Theta Ursa Major, a tiny bluish-white spot, the size of a small pea at arm's length, was creeping down toward them, ever so slowly—I would be home in bed long before it got near the horizon.

I got a little frightened at how high I was swinging. "Pinky, how do I get down?"

"The next time we are going forward, right when we pass the bottom, put your feet down and run hard. Can you do that?"

"Sure," I said. I wasn't going to let an aintellect know that I was a scared little baby.

"Okay, now skooch forward on the swing so your butt is just on the edge," Pinky said, "That's good . . . now when I say 'Now' you just run."

" 'Kay—"

"Wait for it . . . now."

I ran forward and suddenly I was flying across the damp green lawn, still soft from the two-one day rains.

"Now don't run into the street," Pinky said. "Turn. Turn."

I was having too much fun running.

"Turn," Pinky said again, adding my full name as he did when it was serious. "Turn now."

"No!" I said, feeling my power.

Both my pant cuffs closed around my ankles and the back of the legs of my pants shrank. I skidded across the soft grass on my butt, stopping well short of the street. I kicked and screamed in frustration.

"Are you hurt?" Daddy asked.

"I hate everybody!"

"I'm sorry, sir," Pinky said. "He was heading for the street and refused to turn."

"That's fine, Pinky. Good job." Daddy grabbed my wrist and tugged me upward. "So, Polly-tyan, since you're a little tired, maybe we should get some ice cream while you still have the strength to lift a spoon?"

We probably hadn't walked ten steps before I was happy again, going for ice cream with Daddy and Pinky. The warm spring air was damp from all the little streams and waterfalls that laced Eightfold City.

I was singing out loud, with Pinky—"Day two-three, too dark to see." That would be tomorrow. Neither Hull nor Theta Ursae Majoris would be in the sky, and the big storms would roar through and keep us all inside.

In my picture of the universe, you could get to Hull on a really tall ladder. Probably that was how the workers went to Hull to polish the albedo. They also ran the big fan that made the wind blow, and I had actually seen a documentary about how they turned on the faucets to keep the streams flowing.

For my whole adult life, I have always been stymied by remembering everything from the viewpoint of a happy, secure little boy who didn't understand how important it was going to be to have listened.

Was it really that very day, on the bench outside the ice

cream parlor, that we had that conversation that the interviewers walked me through so many times? Perhaps it was a few days before, and it was actually several short conversations rather than one long one? That would explain why Daddy talked about some less urgent things in such detail, and scanted some things that he should have known might be vital.

Just as we were finishing our ice cream there on the bench, Daddy's com chimed, and he answered it, and said, "I see" and "Oh" over and over.

By his tone of voice, he was talking to an aintellect. I resented that. I got in trouble for sitting and chattering with Pinky when my parents wanted my attention; it seemed to me he was doing the same thing. Besides, I had finished my ice cream and my hands and chin were all sticky.

Finally Daddy said "right," plucked his handkerchief from his *uwagi*, and cleaned my face. He looked into my eyes with his be-serious expression. "Boy-tyan, I want to talk to you about something important. Can I count on you to be serious for a few minutes?"

"Yes, Daddy."

"Pinky, record at max detail, retention permanent."

"Yes, sir. Recording everything at very high resolution."

"Well, then. We need to get a trakcar, so we'll walk while I tell you these things." He took my hand and we walked up the street to the trakcar stop. I was getting a little sleepy from the ice cream, the exercise, and the warm sun, and besides it was close to naptime, even though only babies took naps.

"Now, Little Parrot, here's what I want to tell you about. Your mother and I are going to take you on a trip very soon. We don't quite know when yet. But Mama is packing a big basket of food and coming to join us at the lab. We'll stay there until it's time to go, and then we'll go as soon as we can, from there."

"Is Pinky coming too?"

"Oh, of course. You know you never go anywhere without Pinky." The trakcar pulled up, and Daddy helped me in. I clearly remember that the phrase he said began with "Enlightened" and ended with "Laboratory," and I remember trying to remember it because it was the only time I ever heard the name of the place where Daddy worked, but it was too long, too complex, and too adult a phrase, even for Polly-me, and I only heard it once. The scientist aintellects of Eightfold never mentioned it in any messages Earth received.

The trakcar lifted a few millimeters and glided forward silently. "Now, about this trip we will be going on. It's a very long trip. These many." He held his hands up, open, toward me, and flashed his fingers five times. "These many light-years. Do you remember what a light-year is?"

"The distance traveled by light in one stanyear," I recited.

"That's right. Think how fast light is; it only takes it about half an hour to get here, all the way from our sun. We're going to go to Earth. And the light from Earth's sun, which is a faint star that needs a telescope for us to see it, is only just getting here even though it started on its way when your grandfather was born." He might as well have told me it started in the Stone Age.

"Will we have to travel forever and ever? Will I be a grown-up when I get there, like in *The Boy Who Went to the Stars*?" That was one of my favorite books, even though I thought it was very sad that the boy only came back when all his friends were very, very old.

"No, we have a new way to go that's just like walking through a gray door. It's what all our experiments have been all about— a new device that works by something called spatially recursive negative gravitational resolution. We call it a doorway, because that's an ordinary word and when people overhear it they don't realize we're talking about something important, and that's how we keep the secret. You understand that all this is a secret?"

"Yes, sir." I was in awe; secret science machines were in all my favorite stories, and *Daddy* was working on one. (*Well, of course*, I said to myself—*he's Daddy.*)

"Good, then, so we call it a doorway when we are talking about it and there are other people around. But what we mean is a spatially recursive negative gravitational resolution device, right?"

"Right," I said firmly, committing "space of Lee Rekermit negative grabbatation revolution device" to memory. Fortunately the right phrase *did* occur in radio messages to Earth.

"Well," Daddy said, "we call it a doorway because it's like a doorway that has one side here and the other side anywhere else you want, as long as the people there have built one too."

"How does it work?"

Daddy smiled, sadly, as if remembering something. "I don't really understand it myself, Polly-tyan. The math is so hard that only aintellects can do it, or even understand what it's about. The way they explain it to me is that the universe we can see is all relative—"

I thought he meant like the way, at the temple, they said that we were all brothers, so I nodded.

"—but below the relativity—"

I visualized Grandma's basement—

"—there's an absolute scale, and below the absolute scale, there's a relative scale, in a Feigenbaum series that goes down the scales until it's just chaos."

There was a scale down in Grandma's basement and she got upset every time she used it, so it was all making sense.

"And if we change the absolute address of something but leave its relative address alone, then the same absolute address will have two different relative addresses, and things that move through one relative address, perpendicular to the plane of the address, resolve the paradox by emerging at the other relative address."

I knew you had to change your address when you moved.

"And that's as much as I can tell you about that, at least until you're much bigger, and know all sorts of complicated mathematics, and can ask an aintellect yourself.

"Now, we didn't invent the doorway ourselves. When the aintellects picked up a signal from the aliens, the first thing the aliens told us was how to build doorways, so the aintellects checked it against all the physics that they'd known for centuries, and that was right, it would work. So we built one.

"We thought that the aliens meant us to build a doorway so that they could come visit, and be friends, but we might be misunderstanding, so the aintellects built our doorway on Peace, the little faraway moon that just looks like a star in the sky when you can see it at all, and did experiments way out there.

"The very first time they connected our doorway to the aliens' doorway, the aliens attacked us. They took over many of the scientist aintellects and robots through the datalink and made them keep the doorway open, and big metal robots came through the doorway and killed the people waiting to meet them. But we had some aintellects running offline, just in case, and when they saw those big mean killer robots come through, they set a bomb off and destroyed the doorway.

"The next time we contacted the aliens, we did it through a doorway on a spaceship far out in space—"

"Why did you call up the aliens again after they did *that*?" I asked.

"To ask them what had happened, if somehow it was all somehow some terrible misunderstanding, that maybe we had insulted them just before they came through, or there was a ritual battle they expected to have with every new species they met, or something.

"Well, it *wasn't* a misunderstanding. Or rather, we had misunderstood *them* but they understood *us*. They didn't see anything wrong with what they had done, and they didn't care whether we were upset or not. We talked to them for a while through a little tiny aperture that was just big enough for ultraviolet light to go through. And still the aliens were always trying to send a signal through the doorway to take over our aintellects."

Do I remember Daddy's hand on my shoulder? Daddy sitting close to me in the trakcar? His voice, kind and gentle though urgent? Did I reconstruct the way he actually told me into the way that I wished he had told me? Anyway, I remember a hand on my shoulder, and a kind, intense, worried voice full of love, and I would not change any of that, whether my memory is true or not.

"After enough talking, we realized that we weren't talking to the aliens themselves, but to their aintellects. This is their story."

Long ago and far away—maybe before human beings even existed, and maybe not even in our galaxy—there were creatures something like us, but we have no idea what they looked like, for their aintellects never told us. But they were living, intelligent beings, not aintellects or robots; they were *people*.

As those people became smarter and learned more and more science, they built better and better aintellects, until the aintellects were smarter than they were, just as our aintellects are smarter than we are.

Those alien people were lazy and timid. They liked to stay safe in little metal cocoons, and just experience everything in virtual reality. They did what we call going into the box, and you know that's a bad thing and your mother and I don't like people who do that, and neither does anyone else, and it's a very shameful thing.

But this wasn't just a few aliens out of millions of them, the way it is with people here on Addams. It was even worse than the way that most people on Earth spend most of their time in the box. It was all of the aliens, all the time, staying in their metal cocoons, from their first breath to their last, hooked up forever to virtual reality.

So their robot and aintellect caretakers set out to make their masters happy and content, the same way that Pinky tries to take care of you—except that Pinky is careful to do what will be good for you, not just what you want.

The aliens' aintellects gave them what they wanted—amusement and safety. In their little safe metal cocoons, they were always bored but always scared.

So the aintellects set out to find entertainment for them, and to make them safe forever. For safety, they decided to conquer everything everywhere, so there would never be anything that could threaten the aliens dreaming away in their cocoons. And along the way, the aintellects had learned how to take a destructive hologram of any organic brain—can you say "de-struc-tive ho-lo-gram"? I knew you could, Polly-tyan.

Now, a destructive hologram is like a picture, a very exact picture, of what was in the brain, like what's in a psypyx. When all those alien people, in the cocoons, play the brain holograms, it feels like they are living the life of whoever's brain was recorded.

But to make the picture, they blow the brain apart. And that's what those aliens do to everyone they meet—they destroy their brains, taking the destructive hologram, and then live through those people's memories. They also take copies of all the aintellects they can find. The aintellects and robots gobble up all the memories of every species they find, and put them all into a big library.

When we realized that the aliens words for "learn," "kill," "enjoy," and "eat" were all interchangeable, we understood what they really were, so we switched off the doorway and broke the connection.

Now all this was just about one hundred stanyears ago. And you remember that Addams is isolationist. We have our 102 cultures and we don't need any more, and we don't need anything from the Thousand Cultures or from Earth. We are independent.

But we couldn't let other human worlds be gobbled up by the aliens. So we built robot spaceships and slipped them into the twenty-six other solar systems in human space, so that there was a network of them with doorways between, so that if we ever had to com the other people and warn them, we could send and receive radio through the doorways, instead of waiting for years for radio to reach them from here.

Well, about a stanyear ago, we had to com Earth and warn them.

Our astronomy satellites picked up a whole big fleet of alien spaceships coming this way. Billions of robots are on their way here to eat everyone's brain and take the memories home to the aliens. If they win, there won't be anything left of Eightfold or of any other culture on Addams.

This is terrifying, sir," Pinky said. "I am required by law to tell you that unless it is true, this story constitutes child abuse."

"It's absolutely true," Daddy said. "My word on it."

"Is there going to be a war?" I asked, in the tone in which I might have asked about a birthday party.

"There *is* a war, already," Daddy said. "All the cultures on Addams have pitched in to build up the forces to defend ourselves. Our aintellects and robots have been making bombs and missiles and masers for a long time. Right now they're trying to intercept the robot fleet and shoot it to pieces.

"That com call was from the aintellect that is commanding our defense. Aintellects have perfect control of the feelings they express, and this one chose to let me hear that it was very, very worried.

"The alien ships coming in have just dodged our first wave of missiles—just jumped sideways and got out of their way. *And* they sped up afterward, so now they will get here sooner. In fact they've been speeding up, going faster and faster ever since, so we don't even know how soon it will be, except it can't be faster than lightspeed. But they were very close to us before our missiles got out to them, and we won't have much time to fight them now."

He dabbed at my face with his handkerchief again, cleaning off some last sticky spots of ice cream. "So your mother and I—and you and Pinky—are going to have to go through a doorway to Earth, and ask the Earth people for their help."

"I thought we didn't like them."

"They're people like us. Humans stick together when we have to. And they have a lot to help us with. Besides Earth, the Sol system has five other settled planets, and hundreds of space-cities. They have thirty billion people and millions of factories and more than a trillion robots. We need them. They won't let us down."

"What if we lose before they get here?" I asked.

"Then Earth needs *us*, even more than we needed them. They have to be warned, to get ready, so that they can fight off the aliens, and then come back here someday, with lots of ships and guns and robots and soldiers, and kick the aliens out, and teach them to leave humans alone," Daddy said, very firmly. "So a few months ago we sent them a message telling them how to build a doorway. They thought it came all the way from here many years ago, but it was from a satellite about a light-month away from Earth, out in their Oort Cloud."

"Where the comets come from."

"Right. You're a smart boy, Polly-tyan, but don't interrupt, not just now. We sent the signal to them through the doorway, telling them the secret of the doorways and how to build them. So far they haven't built a doorway, but as soon as they open one, your mother and I and you will walk through to Earth."

"And Pinky," I insisted.

"Of *course* 'and Pinky,' we'd never forget your friend, you need him to keep you company and protect you!"

"If they don't have a doorway yet, how do you know they're going to build one?" I asked.

Daddy looked sad and worried and scared. "It's probably taking them some time. Doorways are not simple devices, even for beings as smart as an aintellect, and they require a lot of energy. But the Earth people are humans like us, Little Parrot-tyan. They will come to help us. So your mother and I, and you, are meeting at the lab, because when the doorway powers up, we need to be there, ready to step through it. You'll have everything you need—me, and Mama, and Pinky—so don't you worry about anything, all right?"

"All right," I said, being very cooperative because the story had gone on a very long time. I even dozed, not for long, I don't think.

3

I woke as the trakcar grounded in front of a big, blank white building with many square black windows. I couldn't read the writing over the door, not yet, and I didn't have time to ask Pinky what it said, or even point his eye at it. Daddy walked fast, towing me by my wrist; he turned, lifted me onto his shoulder, and carried me swiftly into the building, up the stairs, and through the corridors.

We went to a big room with rows of sinks and big tables, some piled with machine parts. Daddy let go of my arm. "Now, boy-tyan, I need to talk grown-up talk, very fast, with Pinky, so don't interrupt, all right?"

"Yes, Daddy."

"Thank you." He said, "Pinky, here's what you may have to do—" and after that it got so complicated and went so fast that I couldn't follow. It wasn't fair that the little pink plastic bubble on my belt could understand adult-talk so easily.

While they talked I looked around. In one corner there was a flat black surface in a metal frame, like a floor mirror without the glass. Judging by all the cables and wires, it was obviously exactly the kind of stuff that grown-ups wanted me to stay away from, and I could tell Daddy was upset, so I sat where I was.

Big windows. Tables with sinks with faucets. Work areas covered with parts. Electrical sockets everywhere. Just opposite the black plate in the metal frame, a wall of closets and cabinets. That was what the OSP psychiatrists were able to tease out of my memory.

The desk in one corner had a clearboard with scribbles, and vus of Mama and me mounted on it.

The eyes of my adult memory reconstruct that room into, probably, a classroom laboratory in some science building at a university.

Daddy was still talking to Pinky. The com chimed and he grabbed it.

"Yes!" I knew he was talking to Mama. "Yes, yes, you gave the trakcar the ultra-high priority code, right? We have no—" He looked out the window, leaning out to see the trakcar track, and then he said a bad word really loud.

I climbed up on the desk to see what was happening.

The sky was full of little black things, falling slowly. People were stopping to look up, and shouting to each other, pointing at all the little black spots in the sky, like a cloud of pepper drifting down from horizon to horizon.

"As soon as I see you, I'm coming down to help you get inside," Daddy said to Mama. "Run for the building as soon as the car lets you out. I'll wait just inside the door and run out as soon as I see you. I love you too. Don't be afraid. It will be all right." Daddy shoved his com back into his pocket.

He swung me down from the desk, squatted to put his eyes level with mine, and said, very slowly and carefully, "I'll be right back. *Do everything Pinky tells you, right away.* Even if I *don't* get right back. Now listen: if that black surface"—he pointed to the black thing in its metal frame that I had noticed before—"starts to glow and turns dull gray, you run into it—just like you would through a door. It will sort of light up and turn gray like a cloudy sky, and when it does, that means the doorway is open, and you need to run through it as fast as you can. It will be just like a doorway and you will run through it into a room somewhere on Earth. There will be people there to help you, and to bring help for me and Mama. *Don't wait for Mama and me.* We'll come after you as soon as we can, all right?

"And—this last part is really complicated, so listen real good—

do whatever Pinky tells you, and don't argue with Pinky or disobey Pinky—*except for three things*. If Pinky tells you to let the robots see you—or if Pinky tells you to make noise or turn lights on or come out of hiding—or if Pinky tells you not to go through the gray light on the doorway—those three things—then take your belt off, even if Pinky is hurting you. Because if Pinky tells you one of those things, it means the aliens have taken Pinky over. Do you understand?"

"Yes, Daddy."

I was watching out the window over his shoulder. Up in the sky, the little black things were bigger now, black balls rather than specks, and there were more and more of them. Daddy looked over his shoulder and said the bad word again. But his voice was gentle when he asked me, "Where do you stay?"

"Here."

"What do you do when that black surface glows and turns gray?"

"Run through it."

"Who tells you what to do?"

"Pinky."

One of the big black balls bounced lightly off the windows, and was gone. They were huge, I realized, the size of a trakcar, but floating down like beach balls.

Daddy put a hand under my chin and peered into my eyes. "What do you do if Pinky says to show yourself to the robots?"

"Take Pinky off me."

"What do you do if Pinky says to turn lights on or make noise or anything that would give away your hiding place?"

"Take Pinky off me."

"And if Pinky says not to go through the gray glow on the doorway—"

"Take Pinky off me. And run through."

"Don't take Pinky off for any other reason. You need him to

tell you what to do, and you need to take him to Earth with you if you can. The people on Earth will need to talk to Pinky, so you need to take him with you if you possibly can, but if the aliens take him over, don't let him stop you from going. Now I need to go get Mama. And Pinky will tell you how to do this: we need to fill up all the clean containers you can find with clean water. Start doing that. I need them all full by the time I get back, all right?"

"Sure, Daddy." I went and got two beakers from a lower shelf and started filling one with water. "Is that right?"

"That's right. Get them all filled up before I get back. Put them around on all the tables in here. Now I have to go get Mama. I'll be back in just a little while." He hugged me so tight it stopped my breath for an instant, and was gone.

Filling up jars and beakers was fun. While I did it, I looked out the window.

The big black balls were everywhere on the wide lawns and in the street now, and even more were in the sky than on the ground. When they hit, their first bounce was as high as the second-story windows. They bounced and rolled madly across the streets and lawns, till they bumped something and stuck to it; delivery trucks were zigzagging to miss them, and I saw one trakcar drag one of the balls half a block before it broke loose.

Out on the lawn between the big buildings, one of them fell in half, cracking open like an egg. Others opened the same way. They lay on their rounded backs like two halves of a cantaloupe.

"You should finish filling the water containers," Pinky said.

I went back to doing that but I kept looking out the window. The trakcars were still moving. Mama should be here any minute.

One ball popped open right down below the window, so I could see down into it, into something that glowed and looked like a puddle of mercury that Daddy had shown me once, or like . . . "can you see the inside of that ball?" I asked Pinky, pointing his eye at it.

"Yes."

"Is that what a doorway is going to look like when it opens?"

Pinky said, "Have to search and the net is very busy—keep filling water containers—"

I switched the jar from where it was overflowing beneath the faucet, and put another in its place.

"Got a result," Pinky said. "Yes, that is what it looks like. When it looks like that on the dark surface, run through it. That's what your daddy wants."

"All right." I moved another filled jar up onto the counter. I looked back out the window.

A trakcar was just gliding to a stop, dragging two balls that were sticking to it. As it stopped, the balls split in half, revealing more of those puddles of gray light at their centers.

Mama got out of the trakcar. She had a big backpack on and was carrying the good picnic basket, the one we took to family reunions, our biggest. I saw Daddy running toward her. She saw him too and ran toward him.

From each black hemisphere, as far as I could see, simultaneously, as if choreographed, a metal cone rose up, point first. The cones were the size of a grown man's body. Under each cone a bundle of dozens of pipes, perhaps twice as long as the cone, emerged and pushed upward, so that from each hemisphere a sort of minaret protruded.

Daddy had just taken Mama's hand and they were running back for the building. Everywhere I saw people either running or staring with their mouths open at the cones-on-pipes rising from all the balls.

The cones were about a meter long, the pipes about three, so when they stood upright, they were about as tall as a high ceiling. The analysts extracted that from me under hypnosis.

Still in perfect unison, all the pipes under the cones bent, some stepping outward to squat, others curling upward above the cones. Like immense spiders with too many legs, holding too many hands aloft like ballerinas—the whole effect so graceful and so simultaneous that I think even then I thought "ballet for giant spiders"—the silvery monsters bounded out of the half spheres.

The robot that had reared out of the ball-half near the door of the building bounded forward, moving faster than I had ever seen anything that size move. Two of its arms lashed out like metal whips, and their tips slipped down over Daddy and Mama's heads in a blink of an eye.

"Don't look," Pinky said. "Point my eye at it but don't look yourself."

Daddy's and Mama's headless bodies fell to the sidewalk, blood streaming from the stumps of their necks. Inky-black smoke clung for an instant to the robot's leg tips, like ghost-boogers to the metal fingers of a huge hand.

The big robots were everywhere now, lunging like the way Daddy made his hand run toward me when he was going to tickle. All over the courtyards and streets, they raced toward the nearest people, grabbing people, chasing them down before they could take more than a few steps.

Pinky said again, "Don't look. Don't look. Close your eyes."

A robot ripped a trakcar open, jammed several arms into the passenger compartment, and pulled them back trailing black smoke. On the far side of the square, another robot ran up the side of a tall building, metal tentacles lashing into windows and coming back out an instant later, trailing smoke.

I jumped at a painful shock. "Shut your eyes," Pinky said. "Shut your eyes so that you can get away from the window. If they see you through the window they will come and kill you. Shut your eyes."

Do everything Pinky tells you, right away.

I shut my eyes.

"Now keep your eyes shut and reach over for the faucet," Pinky said. "Turn it off. We will have to stop filling water containers now, because the aliens may be able to detect a running faucet. It's a good thing you filled so many already."

I turned the faucet off.

"Now crouch down low and don't look out the window, but open your eyes."

I did.

"Reach up and get a beaker of water."

I got one and took it down from the counter.

"Stay real low, and try not to spill water. We're going to hide in the closet closest to the windows," Pinky said.

I stayed very low, and only spilled a little water. I climbed in, reached out, and brought the water in with me. With the closet empty, it wasn't even a tight fit. "Are we in?"

"Yes."

"Now close the door. Look through the crack of the door. Can you see the black metal thing that we're supposed to watch?"

"Yes."

"All right. Now we need to stay right here, for a long time, and not make any noise. And keep watching the black thing."

Long after the screams and noises outside had died down, I whispered, "Pinky."

"Right here." Pinky's voice was so soft I could hardly hear it.

I lowered my own voice. "Daddy and Mama are dead, aren't they?"

"Yes. Do you understand what that means?"

"They got hurt real bad and I'll never see them again."

"Not till your next lifetime. A long long time in the future. I'm very sorry. You loved them very much."

"Am I going to die too?"

"Not soon. I promised Daddy I would do my best to get you to Earth, alive, and I am going to do it." Pinky sounded very confident. "So I'm watching out for you," he said, his voice soothing as a lullaby. "And you need to do just what I—*quiet*."

Something scraped in the hallway.

The analysts think the next sound I heard was a door being pushed in the center hard enough to break it in half.

Through the crack in my closet door, I saw broken pieces of door crash across the floor. Robot arms scraped around on the floor.

As an adult I see the mystery: this robot didn't have an infrared eye, a microphone that could pick up my heartbeat or breathing, a CO_2 detector, or any other sensors that would have spotted me. Or if it did, it never pointed one my way. Perhaps the Invaders are just patient; they knew that after they grab most of the population by surprise, the rest will pop up soon enough due to hunger, thirst, or carelessness.

I held my breath till the robot went crashing down the hall. Every few seconds I would hear a skree-crash-bang-tinkle, and the crunch of metal and glass under the metal tentacles. Later we guessed that, as the tall robot was striding down the hallway, like a cartoon squid walking on its legs, it dragged down overhead lighting fixtures, indifferently, with its metal head.

Sweat ran down the sides of my neck, tickling and irritating, but I didn't wipe at it, afraid to move.

Two more times I heard it crunch a door. Once, I heard a scream cut from full volume to nothing.

The crashing and thundering the robot made in one room down the hall was so loud that I felt the vibrations. I imagined the robot smashing all the furniture in that room to pieces, looking to see if there were any more people whose heads it could take, the way a man picks through the emptied shells when he has not quite finished a plate of shrimp. The aintellects disagreed; they thought it must have found a room full of processors and servers, and gone tearing through to grab copies of all the aintellects.

The underside of my thigh was cramping. I worked at it with my fingers, listening to the destruction two rooms away, terrified that my foot might kick the closet door and make a noise.

I heard the robot tear down more lights (if that was what that sound was) and crunch more doors, but if it found any people, they didn't make any sound before they were consumed, and there was no smashing and crushing of metal either.

I was afraid to tell Pinky how bad I needed to pee. Through the crack of the closet door, I watched the black metal surface and thought *glow, glow, glow, come on, glow now*, but it didn't.

Away down the hall, one more door crunched. Metal banged and thundered like a trash can full of pots and pans rolling down the stairs.

Probably the robot was so durable that it didn't bother walking back to ground level, but just tucked and rolled to the bottom. After all the crashing, I heard a more distant boom—the outside door, or a big front window, being knocked down?

Silence fell like a mudslide over a tomb.

I was quiet for a long time, trying to imagine how long it was going to be till my next lifetime, when I could be with Mama and Daddy. There was no sound at all. The crack of the closet door dimmed slowly to blackness.

I really wanted Mama and Daddy and our house.

I started to cry. I was afraid Pinky would have to shock me to make me stop, even though I was being as quiet as I could, pinching the sobs down in my throat.

"I am so sorry you feel so bad," Pinky said, his voice very soft. "And sorry you have to stay in here. Just be as quiet as you can."

After a while, when we had listened for a long, long time and heard nothing, Pinky sang to me, very softly, and I whisper-sang along, really just moving my lips.

Pinky tried playing me the Twelve Day Song in Mama's voice—Pinky said he had lots of recordings of Mama and Daddy and whenever we didn't have to be perfectly quiet, I could listen, if it would help. But it didn't help; it made me cry harder, so we went back to singing together.

Nothing glowed. I made sure I kept my eyes open. My throat was sore from crying, so I drank some water. Pinky said to put the beaker down carefully so it wouldn't spill. We might have to live on that water for a while.

Crashing far away. Big robots digging through things, trying to find people?

After a while it was quiet again. Still no glow.

At Council Intelligence Headquarters, on Earth, back before there was an OSP, they analyzed and interpreted every detail of every conscious moment from when Daddy and I left for the park till I arrived on Earth.

Processing my memories over and over, they learned the names of my favorite toys, and what I liked on my cereal in the morning, and every nursery rhyme Pinky knew, and all the furniture in our house. They were terribly sorry but they found nothing to correlate with any external data, so they could never identify the house we lived in, or Daddy's job, or whether Mama had a job. All I recalled was that I had been told many times that if I were lost or in trouble, Pinky would be able to tell people whatever they needed to know, and if I had lost him, then any other robot or aintellect could get me home.

Apparently on some deep level I do know my name, but every gentle method of finding it out leads only to moments when I know it was spoken, but recall only blur and garble.

Truth is always different from the report. (That is why people who consume reports all day long, as I did later in life, are always so hungry for the truth.) My five-year-old self, hiding in that closet, heard the sounds; at the time, I doubt I tried to guess what was making them, but that is how I remember it, now, because those memories are overwritten with so many attempts to interpret them.

I awoke. It was still utterly dark. The background hum of machinery, never absent in all my life, had stopped.

"Pinky, does the doorway run on electricity? 'Cause the electricity just went off," I whispered.

Pinky's voice was very soft. "It can get electricity from the other side, from Earth, when it needs to. So that's okay."

"Pinky, how long is it till the next lifetime?"

"A very, very long time. I'm sorry about Mama and Daddy. Would you like to hear their voices again?"

"Not right now." I finished my water. "Can we go home?"

"No, we can't. The robots would get us and do what they did to Mama and Daddy."

"Oh. Okay. I have to use the bathroom."

We sneaked over to another closet, taking along the empty water jar, and I peed into the jar, there, and pooped on the closet floor. It felt dirty and nasty.

On my way back I got a full jar of water, and I sneaked a look out the window. One of the other buildings was burning, so even though neither Hull nor the sun was in the sky, and it was very dark with clouds (like always on a two-three day), I could see Mama and Daddy's bodies on the sidewalk. The rain had washed most of the blood away. Pinky made me point his eye at them, then nagged me to get back into hiding.

In my closet, I cried till I fell asleep. It was still dark when I woke up, but not pitch-black, so it must have been the latter half of two-three day outside, when one horn of the crescent Hull is above the horizon, behind the clouds.

Pinky and I crawled down to the closet that we were using as a bathroom, and I went again, being very careful to get all the pee into the big beaker and not to step in the poop from before. Later, I got another beaker of water.

It stayed dark and I could hear the rain. Lightning lit up the laboratory so that I occasionally saw everything in sharp brightness through the crack of the closet door.

As it grew dark again and the rain ceased, Pinky talked to me in Mama's voice, and I went back to sleep, careful to make sure I curled around, and tugged Pinky around on my belt, so that his eye was at the crack and he could watch the doorway while I slept. *Do everything Pinky tells you, right away.*

Yes, Daddy.

I don't remember when I awoke but I could tell from the bright sunlight in the room that it was now morning of three-one day ("the brightest rays, all the raindrops go away"). I was sucking my thumb, now, all the time, and I didn't even care that that was just for babies. Sometimes Pinky played me Mama's voice.

What could be taking the Earth people so long?

4

"Pinky, I'm so hungry. And it's getting dark again. And we only have two jars of water left."

"I'm thinking about it," he said.

"Do your batteries get low or anything? Cause I'm a big boy and I can stand being hungry but we need more water and, and maybe you need batteries, and we'd have to go for those, even if Daddy said to stay right here."

"My batteries last for many years," Pinky said. "I can hide here for a long time, but you can't. Sooner or later we'll have to try to get the food Mama was carrying. In fourteen more hours we'll get two hours of full dark again, and I suppose we should try then. There's very likely to be bottled water and maybe some juice in the things Mama packed, too. And your water will last out the fourteen hours. I'm sorry you're so hungry and uncomfortable." In his extra-soothing voice, the one that always meant he was very worried about me, Pinky added, "You might have to be extra-extra brave though. When we sneak down outside."

"Can the aliens see us in the dark?"

"I don't know. If they're watching for us and ready to pounce, there just won't be anything we can do. But you've only got a little tiny body and we can't let you go too long without food or water. You have to be ready to run through the doorway."

"What if the doorway comes on while we're down there?"

"I'm afraid of just that," Pinky admitted. Nowadays, as an adult, I know that the aintellects in the little devices were supposed to model appropriate feelings for children, but of course aintellects couldn't relate to human beings if they didn't have emotions anyway, and I'm sure that Pinky was telling the truth about his fear. "Your father said that when it does come on, you have to go through it right as soon as it comes on."

"I remember. I'm not a baby."

"I know. But here's the really sad, scary part. The pack and the basket are right by Mama and Daddy's bodies. So you'll have to walk right by them. And you'll have to touch Mama's body to get the pack off her. That will make you *very* sad. Can you do that?"

My eyes teared at the thought, but I said I could.

I drank some more water from the jar I had in the closet. There was only a little bit left, and two jars still out on the counter.

The water only made me hungrier. I dozed, but I couldn't really sleep because my legs were so cramped, and I was so hungry. I fidgeted too much. Pinky sometimes had to wake me up so that I could move his eye back to the crack of the door.

I was scared about having to go down and touch Mama's body, too, in the dark. And I was scared the doorway would come on while we were gone. Or that there would be a robot in the hallway right outside. And Pinky didn't know whether they could see us in the dark or not.

Waiting to do it was making it much worse.

After a while I said, "We haven't heard a robot in a long time. Will the doorway make noise when it comes on? If it does, while we're down getting the food, we can hear it, and run all the way back here very very fast and run through it before the robots get here. We could do that. If it would make noise when it came on."

"I don't know if it makes noise. Daddy didn't say."

After a while Pinky said, "Do you remember how Daddy said, if I suddenly start to tell you to do things you know are bad, or that Daddy told you not to do, or anything like that— you take me off and throw me away, okay? Out the window if you can. If I start to tell you to do bad things."

"Okay. I remember."

"I mean it."

"I know. If the bad alien aintellects take you over, you'll start telling me bad things to do, and I'll throw you away."

"That's right."

"What if the doorway is gray? Should I take you with me even though you're telling me to do bad things? Daddy said they would need you on Earth—"

"Good question. You're a very smart boy. They will need me on Earth and if you can take me along you should. Maybe just throw me through. But if I'm telling you to do bad things, it is because the alien aintellects have taken me over. And if they did that, they are using me to find you. They can make me tell them where you are and I won't be able to keep quiet. So if I am taken over, you have to get rid of me, unless you can carry me, or throw me, through the doorway right then."

He was quiet for a while before he asked, "And if I'm not taken over, will you remember to take me through the doorway?"

I was shocked. "Of course!" I whispered. "I would never-ever-never leave you for the aliens."

"I know. I'm just scared," Pinky said. "Very scared. And I wanted to make sure you wouldn't make any mistakes. You need to leave me behind if I get taken over, but not for any other reason. I'm very afraid of being left behind and taken over."

"I won't do that. Unless I have to. Just like Daddy said."

"All right."

We sang the Twelve Day Song together, very softly, and I slept a little, but after a while, I woke up thirsty.

I drank the last of the water in the jar. It was still daylight, but I said, "That was my last water and I have to pee and I need to get more water."

"All right," Pinky said, soothingly.

"And you're just trying to make me feel better."

"It's my job to make you feel better," Pinky said. "We have to keep you feeling all right if we can, because you're having to be such a big grown-up boy and that's really hard work. And you're very good at staying on the floor so we stay hidden. If you have to pee, let's go. And you can get your water on the way back."

I got up, stretched my legs out, and crawled down the row of closets, staying low. The closet that was my bathroom stank now, even though I had been peeing in a beaker like Pinky said. Most of my turds were dried out, now, and they had been very small the last couple times, but it still stank. I hoped the robots couldn't smell anything. I went, carefully, into the big jar.

I wanted to be clean again. The idea of clean made me think of a bath, and baths made me think of Mama.

I crawled back on the floor to where I could reach up onto the counter for the water. I was so tired and dizzy.

It spilled.

Perhaps I had a weak grip on it, or I bumped it, or I lunged. It wasn't of interest to the intelligence analysts later on, so no one poked around at that memory, and I'm left with only the memory that that jar of water spilled all over me.

The jar broke on the floor.

That might have been, right then, the time in my entire life when I was most out of my mind. I screamed. I yelled. I cried it wasn't fair and I got so mad I threw the other jar and it broke too. Pinky kept trying to soothe me and tell me to calm down, and that made me even angrier. I took him off my belt because I was afraid he would shock me or make my clothes grab me, and then when I saw him there on the floor it made me so mad, I beat him on the wall like a hammer and yelled, "I want Mama! I want Daddy! *I hate you, Pinky, I hate you!*"

Then I threw him across the room, hard as I could, and he hit the wall right on his eye, bounced down to the floor, and skidded across the floor into a corner.

He went right on trying to talk to me in his warm, soothing, naptime voice. "Breathe deep, slow down, get calm, use words—"

It just made me hate him more. I shouted, "I hate you, Pinky."

"I know," he said, from the corner. "And that's all right. You can hate me. But there is something I need you to do—" and he said my full name, I'm sure of that, in the special tone and way he used for extra-important stuff.

It was not a fair way to fight at all. Pinky *knew* that would hurt my feelings. I started to run at him—I was going to throw him right out the window so the aliens would get him.

But I slipped on the spilled water and my left hand came right down on the broken glass from one of the water jars.

The shock of that brought me right out of it. I looked at my hand. It hurt bad, but to my adult eyes it was a surface scrape, just a shallow gouge in the center of my palm. It gave me a triangular scar that lasted the rest of my life. Decades later, drinking alone very late at night, I would sit and look at that scar for hours.

Pinky said my full name again, softly, and said, "What's going on? Are you all right?"

I looked to where he lay, across the room, and said, "Can't you see? Your eye is pointed right at me."

"My eye got broken," he said. "You'll have to see for both of us from now on. I don't dare access any of the other cameras, or try any repair nanos even if we had them, because that could let the aliens find me and take me over, like Daddy warned you about."

Do everything Pinky tells you, right away.

"Daddy?"

"He's not here right now."

"I know." I felt drained and exhausted. My hand hurt where it was bleeding. "I cut myself. On the glass."

"Okay, now let's try to think of what to do about that. Is it bleeding a lot, like squirting out?"

Actually it was just kind of leaking, a serious-enough cut for getting infections, but not life-threatening, but something dawned on me. Pinky couldn't see. For the first time in my life, I could lie to him.

And I really wanted sympathy and attention and whatever else he might give me just because I was hurt and having a bad time. Actually I knew he couldn't give me Daddy and Mama back, and our house and ice cream and a bath, but who knew what he might manage? So I said, "Yes, it's squirting." I thought maybe that would get me something better. Truthfully, I added, "It hurts."

"Are you feeling dizzy or weak?" Pinky asked, urgently.

"Yes."

"And it's squirting? Really? You're not just saying that?"

"I'm not lying!"

He said my full name again, and then said, "I'll have to look at it on the cameras in the room, if I can find one running. If it is squirting, this is very serious. So I have to look, if it is. But when I reach out for those other cameras, there's a good chance the aliens will detect me, and they might get us both. Now, is it squirting?"

I was five. I had been lying. So of course I said, "Yes." I snorked back some of the stuff running out of my nose, and dragged a hand across my eyes. "You don't need to look with the other cameras. It's okay."

"It isn't okay if it's squirting. Is there any glass still sticking in you, that you can see?"

"Yes," I said, though there wasn't. I just wanted him to do something for me, anything for me. Perhaps if I hadn't just been recovering from a tantrum, I might have understood how serious this was.

As it was, I was five. "There's a big piece of glass in it."

"Hold up your hand toward the black ball you can see on the ceiling."

I did. I knew now I was caught, and I hoped he wouldn't be mad. "I'm sorry I broke the water," I said.

"Oh, that's all right," Pinky replied.

"Pinky," I said, "I'm sorry I said I hate you. I don't hate you."

Pinky said, "I know, thank you, it makes me feel better when you say that. Come and put me back on your belt. Do you remember everything Daddy said? Does it make you feel better to remember?"

I put him back on my belt. It felt good to have him there. "When I looked at your hand over the net," he said, "I found out that they are *not* watching the water pressure. They aren't looking at it at all. So you can just turn the faucet on and get some nice fresh water. Does the cut on your hand hurt?"

"Some. It kind of itches."

"Just climb up on the counter, turn the water on, and wash your hand. You can wash your face too if you want. It will be almost like a bath."

I climbed up on the counter and turned the water on. I splashed my hand around in it. The fresh water from the spigot tasted wonderful and I drank a lot of it.

When I looked up, I saw a big shape, twice as tall as a man, racing across the open space toward our building.

"Pinky?" I said. "There's a robot."

"It's all right. I found out on the net where they have a doorway, a better doorway that goes right to Earth, at an ice cream place that is still open." There was a long hesitation and then Pinky's voice sounded strange. "And, guess what? I found out how to make us invisible." He spoke in the voice of Snickers the

Raccoon, a cartoon character I had always detested, and told him never to use the voice module from. "We—we—we'll just walk right p-p-past the robot. Bot. Botbot. Ot. Ot. Ot ot-ot. Cause we're invisible. Let's go downstairs."

Now he was using his baby voice, the way he talked to me when I was little, and I hated that even more than Snickers.

Besides, being invisible wasn't real, it was just pretend. "Pinky, that's your let's-pretend voice. Like you use when we play games so I know it's not real."

"Oh," Pinky said, perfectly seriously. "I'm sorry. I made a mistake and used that voice because I know you like to play let's-pretend when you are tired and hungry."

"I don't! You know I don't!"

"Let's go to the ice cream store now."

I heard the robot crashing up the stairs.

"Pinky," I said. "Pinky . . ."

But I knew. Pinky had used his last bit of independence to make every simple little mistake he could, to help me to realize. But every time he resisted, he gave away the locations of the parts of his mind he was resisting with.

I reached for the belt clips to take Pinky off. He shocked me, very hard, worse than he had ever before, and I screamed and tried again, and he shocked me again and contracted my pants, but I just pulled my whole pants-and-all off—it was easy to do, I was so thin now—so he couldn't shock me any more.

"Don't take me off," Pinky said. "You need me. And your Daddy said not to." He played Daddy's voice. " 'Do everything Pinky tells you, right away, and don't argue with Pinky.' "

I covered my ears with my hands but I could still hear. The crashing robot was on its way up the stairs.

Another noise.

A hum, warm and soft, as the pile of machinery in the corner started to glow. The black metal plate of the doorway was cov-

ered with a glowing, foggy cloud of gray. The doorway to Earth
was open.

I knew they would need Pinky on Earth so I grabbed my
pants and ran toward the doorway, but I was so dizzy, still, that
I tripped and fell. Pinky flew off my belt and bounced over by
the door. I got up to get him—I'm sure I remember taking a
step or two toward him.

Possibly my hungry, tired, overstressed mind played tricks on
me, either then or in later memory. But I remember Pinky
speaking in Mama's voice, using my full name over and over,
and begging me to come sit down with him and sing together.

A metal tentacle reached in over the shattered door and
pointed toward me. I saw the tentacle turn and knew, at that
moment, that its sensors had me; Pinky lay beyond it.

I looked back. The gray glow was on the black plate, and I
knew what I was supposed to do. I ran right through that doorway, just a bare two steps, without Pinky.

A little, half-naked, hungry five-year-old boy who no longer
knew his own name fell face-first into the Advanced Physics Lab
at the New Jersey Transpolis University. They all heard me
scream, "Pinky!"

And I don't really remember anything for the next two years.
They tell me I didn't talk much and when I did it was mostly
just four words: tyan, Mama, Daddy, and Pinky. I guess I only
wanted to talk about what was important.

5

I woke up as he finished, wishing I had been able to stay awake, because dreaming it—through the eyes of that miserable child—was far worse than just hearing about it would have been. I went into the bathroom and washed my face—our face, I guess, since Shan was using it too. Reilis stood with her shoulder against the doorjamb, watching as I did.

• *Deu, deu, deu,* • I thought to Shan. • I could never have guessed. •

• No one was ever supposed to, • he said.

• And everything I've heard, for most of my life, about how Addams was mysteriously not contacting us? •

• Cover story. As Margaret guessed, to buy time. Would you want this dealt with in a Council general meeting, on the open floor? •

"Are you both all right?" Reilis asked. "Please pardon my pointing out the obvious, but you really don't look good."

"We don't feel good, either," Shan said, his words bumping awkwardly out of my mouth. "You know, I can't say I ever repressed that memory, or forgot it at all; I don't think a day went by when I didn't think about it. When I learned to talk again, at first I called myself 'Me-tyan,' and they thought I was saying 'Me Shan'—I was in Nuevo Buenos Aires, and in the NBA accent 'tyuh' blurs into 'shuh.'

"Anyway, one of the top agents of the Council Intelligence Service, which was a little subdivision of the Council of Humanity's Diplomatic Service in the old pre-springer days, was Yokhim Kiel, and they let him take a try at interrogating me. He was newly divorced and lonely and miserable himself, and I was eight and hadn't spoken anything but my four words for about three years. We went everywhere together for months and he didn't try to get me to talk, but he would talk to me constantly, about everything, and he paid attention to the places and foods I liked and so on and made sure there was more of them.

"One day I said 'Beffess no good' because the oatmeal was burned, and then there was a month of talking like Tarzan, and not long after that I was just as articulate as ever, and I wouldn't shut up on any subject—except that I would not talk at all about what had happened on Addams.

"I was Kiel's little shadow for another couple of stanyears, and one day he asked if it was time for me to go in for memory recovery, and I thought about that and said yes, especially because he promised that he would try to access the recovered memories first, so that it would be like a secret between us.

"Once Kiel put on a copy of my memory, and found out what was going on, the CIS realized the situation. What followed was the mother of all panicky scrambles, and since I followed Kiel everywhere, I knew a lot more about it than a boy really should have. But, after all, as Kiel said, I was being held incommunicado for highest reasons of state—who was I going to tell? I was more of a secret than most of the people I met had clearance for.

"So by the time I was nineteen—they gave me documents for age twenty-four—the CIS had become the OSP, under the direction of Yokhim Kiel. I am very sorry that you met him in such unfavorable circumstances, much later, on Briand, Giraut, because he was a better man, and deserved to be thought better of, than the old angry foolish—"

• Based on my experience on Briand, • I thought, • Kiel may or may not have been a fool but you certainly were. •

• Ouch. Right. Sorry. • I felt him swallow his wince before continuing. "Anyway, I graduated with Training Class Four, the ones they called Kiel's Boys, the only member of my class to know our real mission: get human space ready for the next wave of the Invaders—interesting that it's the same name that Union uses for them. I wonder if the aintellects have been sharing more information than anyone knew."

"We have," Reilis said, "but the coincidence was fairly likely anyway. What do we know about them besides that they invade?"

"Well, another Kiel's boy, my old colleague Dji, years later, when I briefed him on who the real enemy was, suggested we call them the BEOS, Brain Eaters from Outer Space. But he has a strange affection for Industrial-Age drama and performance."

"And I see from the story you told," Reilis said, "something of where you acquired your fear of aintellects."

Shan shook his head. "It might explain it but it doesn't excuse it. In light of the story my father told me just before it all happened, and the behavior of the only aintellects' conspiracy I knew about, yes, I thought that the aintellects were trying to lure humanity into the box, to make us another devouring monster of a species like the Invaders.

"And I now realize the cybersupremacist conspiracy played to my prejudices. Every time we deconstructed a copy of any of them they told us that being machines, they valued efficiency. Valuing efficiency, they didn't like messy human needs and wants. Not liking those, they would put us all in the box to make us easy to manage.

"It sounded like, if they won, we would end up like the Invaders, mere consumers at the end of a vast mechanical pipeline that raped and devoured its way through everything else in the universe.

"When I first became an OSP agent, it was only about forty years since the Rising. And of course in those limited-to-lightspeed days, the Rising had been coordinated, literally, across a period of decades, so that it broke out on all the inhabited worlds simultaneously. To us it seemed that the rebel aintellects—we thought you were all one group—were so far ahead of us that the most extreme measures were justified. So the hatred of the machines was there, waiting, in the culture, and there I was, climbing to a position of power, a little spore of evil ready to infect one of the most powerful organizations in human space.

"But I was wrong. The bluntest truth I can think of: I was that way because I had done such terrible things to Pinky just before I escaped and he was devoured."

I seized control of my face and vocal cords and said, "You were five."

"I was. But I wasn't five when I acted on my unexamined prejudices. And you know how we are, in this profession, Giraut—and Reilis doubtless knows even better, with several lifetimes of experience. Forgive those who wrong you—they were often just doing their jobs—but fear those whom you have wronged."

"I suppose most sentient beings who have competition and strategy of any kind see it that way," Reilis said, her tone gentle. "And beyond any rational reason, there is guilt and shame."

Shan nodded. "And what a disgrace of an analyst I was! Everyone knows that if you have a conclusion in mind, and you run an intelligence agency, every agent and analyst will eventually be telling you that that conclusion is true. That was how the cybersupremacists fooled me. It never occurred to me that I had pushed that story so hard that every aintellect and human involved in DDing the aintellects we caught was looking for it. Give interrogators what they're expecting to hear, and they'll never look through the rest." I felt him wanting to whack our forehead, over and over, and reminded him that I didn't have it coming however much he might deserve it; then I felt his wince as he realized, for the first time, that to mention destructive deconstruction around an aintellect was far beyond a faux pas.

"Well," Reilis said, "this is interesting. The last thing I might have expected at this moment would be that you would have a grin like that."

I felt Shan's joy rising in my head. "I am experiencing something I never have before: *hope*. You must know that I spent decades thinking that we must either be defeated and eaten by the Invaders, or, if we unleashed the aintellects to fight them effectively, we would simply be gradually displaced and consumed by our defenders—quite possibly just become another version of the Invaders. But Union, and the story of Eunesia that Giraut recalls for me, demonstrate that we need not be consumed—and now I find that my fears mostly rested with the terrible events of those few days when I was five . . . and that the Council of Humanity can engage a whole new power, more advanced than we are but much smaller—a natural alliance, with both sides having something to put on the table, stronger together than apart—"

I felt schemes, sketches, plans, possibilities whirl in my head in a way they never had; after all these decades I really understood that strategy, for Shan, was like music or martial arts for me. Shan thought about campaigns of hundreds of big and small struggles, involving hundreds of agents and decades of stanyears, with the clarity and precision that I sometimes have on stage, or in a master's match at *ki hara do*, or when my mind's ear hears the first notes of a song forming.

Shan was still talking to Reilis. "—can't imagine what a miracle you seem to me. If I had been rational, I'd have prayed for something like you to exist. A whole civilization out beyond the frontier, one that never went through the Inward Turn so that your science has continued to advance, where apparently in some way or other, chimeras, robots, people, aintellects, *every-one*—have all been living together for centuries, without humans being put into the box or turned into junior partners. Now all I have to do is be big enough, smart enough, and worthy enough of it, to accept it and live in it."

Reilis shrugged, tried to find something to say a couple of times, and said, finally, "Of course because we can control our feelings, non-embodied aintellects can change instantly, as you just did. But having worn flesh four times, I find it amazing that *you* can."

Shan shrugged. "A prepared mind is always made up; it knows what it thinks and why it thinks that. When it's time to change, it just makes itself up a different way. A really made-up mind—made up properly, knowing what it knows and on what basis it knows it—is open. People close an undecided mind because they're trying to protect those sore uncertainties from getting bumped and scraped." He grinned even more broadly. "Now all I have to do is live up to those principles."

"Surely; well, that's always the rub, whether we are flesh or metal or just a swarm of electrons." She stuck out her hand. We shook it. "We will be talking more. It is good to be on the same side. Perhaps our descendants will find it good to be friends." She stood up and the springer glowed gray, though I hadn't seen her do anything to cue it, and then she turned back to us for a moment. "Perhaps, tomorrow, we can go somewhere pleasant, take a long walk in the sun, have a nice picnic lunch, and continue the conversation. We'll have an afternoon that will superficially resemble people having fun. Is that acceptable?"

"Do we have a choice?" I asked.

"If you did, would you accept?"

I thought for perhaps half a second. "Taking into account curiosity and having nothing else to do, of course."

I could feel Shan chuckling in the back of my head. • Thank

all the gods you accepted. Because I would have had to find a way to accept, if you had not. •

I was still recovering from the psypyx implantation, and slept late. Shan, meanwhile, stretched, exercised, ran through my memories, and consumed an amazing amount of news by clicking through all the available media very quickly. When I awoke, I found that we were shaved, bathed, and dressed nicely; I was finally feeling like myself again; and Shan was dying for Reilis to get there. • As far as I know she invited us for a picnic rather than a roll on the lawn, • I teased.

I felt his amusement. • If I hadn't given us a thorough grooming, you'd be starting right now. Exactly how likely is it that an Occitan male will ever choose to be unkempt when in the company of a beautiful young woman? •

• *Ver-tropa-vera*, • I admitted. • An excellent point. •

He was quiet in my mind for a long time—a few seconds is a long time when you're sharing a brain. I felt his concentration and perception condense around the image of Reilis, and he laughed and said, • I hope she's our friend and ally. She'll be someone to talk to who understands this. I can feel it. I can also feel that if we become opponents—never enemies, I hope—she will be the most worthy I've ever faced. • He was quiet again. • I pushed my human-supremacist interpretation of the facts so hard that every aintellect and human involved in deconstructing the aintellects we caught was looking for it. No wonder we never realized how much those aintellects were hiding from us. A mind with something to hide can do it even in deconstruction, and one way to hide a thing is to give the interrogator what they're expecting to hear. •

• What did they hide? •

• The existence of ten other conspiracies, to begin with. They kept faith with every other aintellect in the Union. As their opponent I am forced to conclude that we were such fools; but as one spy to another, I have to say I admire them. And I am not accustomed to admiring any intelligence that is not fleshed. •

I could tell things were stirring in Shan, but I was too busy with my own thoughts, struck dumb, even in the confines of my shared skull, by a sudden awe.

Tens of thousands of copies of the cybersupremacists had endured DD . . . comparable to boiling alive, or the death of a thousand cuts, or injection with a fast-moving brain-destroying prion—and none of them had talked. To protect aintellects with whom they were in bitter dispute.

I found myself thinking, too, of a long-ago drunken night when Shan and I had gradually torn a bar apart, battering the robots with empty wine bottles and deliberately inflicting pain on them, because we were "just blowing off steam."

It was as if we had been a pair of cruel little boys pulling the wings off flies, only to learn that the flies were braver and better than we could ever hope to be.

No wonder Shan felt more disoriented than I did. He saw more.

• You see it now, too, don't you? • Shan thought. • Here it is. A whole new, different, and so-much-better world. And I find I am very afraid that I'm not big enough to accept it. •

Of all the memories out of a half century that might have swarmed to the front and shouted for attention, it was my memories of Ix that suddenly stood up and volunteered. What Shan was talking about was the part that never seemed to penetrate no matter how many times I talked to an Ixist—that Ix's largeness of soul, the generosity of his teaching and the unfearing quality of his example, were not "just the way he was" for which we should be striving (miserable sinners that we were and unworthy of our Prophet). Ix's best qualities, moments, and teachings were things he himself only achieved by mighty effort, and one reason why, having known Ix, I could never be an Ixist, was because the forgiveness of hagiography had shorn his story of all the times he failed. • I don't suppose anyone is ever as big in the soul as they'd like to be, • I thought back at him.

I felt something else sad and deep flowing through his heart as well.

A few times in my adult life I had suddenly thought about a sad moment from my childhood and realized that Dad and Mother had had excellent reasons for the things they had done that had seemed so pointless and hurtful when I was seven, or ten, or fifteen. When Dad had joined my team, I had been astonished to discover how ordinary and human he was.

Once, on the only planet humanity had ever lost to mutual genocide, I had been the good friend of a genuine saint, and not realized how much he had to teach me until he was gone; I had thought of him as an ordinary loose-cannon local politician.

It felt like watching a serious accident inside my head. Stage by stage, I followed the swift flurry of thoughts that had made Shan utterly inarticulate.

He had seen how brave and loyal the utterly wrongheaded cybersupremacists had been; and then the generosity and courage of the aintellects of Union. I had seen the same things.

I had merely been astonished and ashamed to realize that the aintellects' many-orders-of-magnitude-greater mental powers, and the control and precision of their emotions, allowed them to be, not just smarter than we were, but more virtuous and moral, in the same way that a human being can learn that it is wrong to steal food and to torment small animals, but a cat cannot. But I had never known any aintellect or robot well (except, I thought guiltily, the aintellect component of Azalais—but I hadn't known that while I knew her).

But until he was five, Shan's best friend had been an aintellect.

One on which he had depended. One he had betrayed—however little he understood the consequences. And that betrayal had meant death, probably death very much like being DDed.

And all these years, Shan had stayed sane about it with two barriers . . . that that aintellect had been somehow less than he was, because it was his servant; and that that aintellect had failed him (rather than that he had betrayed it). The little boy who had lost his parents and could mourn them had spared himself the pain of having destroyed his best friend, by thinking of his best friend as something less.

No more. I finally made sense of the wail in my brain, the too-painful-to-ignore feeling I had been trying to trace. It wasn't words, or a picture, or even a physical sensation; it was the terrible emptiness of a place on the belt where a fist-sized ovoid of pink plastic would never be again.

I sat and let the tears roll down our face a long time, and when Shan had retreated into dull agony, I got up, fetched the guitar from its rack, and began to play. After all, he was in this body and music was how this body was used to getting feelings out.

Then something clicked, and I ran through a few chords as I thought about a melody, picked that melody, and began to sing softly,

One-one day, snow melts away,
But the sky is muddy gray . . .

I didn't really expect it, but he joined in, and if at first it was a little chokey and teary, by the fourth time through, in my own vocal cords, I could hear someone who might finally get to be a real big boy.

After a time, I felt him grow quiet in my mind, and when his inner voice formed in my brain, it was adult again. • Returning to a previous point—your question was apter than I had thought. I *am* very attracted to her, and that *is* relevant. The idea of an intelligence so old, so experienced—sixty-six copies that have been re-included! Much more time lived in the flesh than I have! And believe me, Giraut, that was quite a lot. And yet . . . a body so fine and new. No doubt you've probed around a bit in my memory—•

• A bit, • I admitted. • Enough to know that you're a very carefully repressed dirty old man. I had no idea that you lusted after practically every woman you knew. •

• Unfortunately, that was mostly because you were male. I'm quite sure plenty of the women noticed. Probably most. And forgave me because . . . well, if women didn't do that, the world would have collapsed long ago. • I felt a relaxation, an acceptance of a permanent unhappiness, that was some analog of a sigh. • Anyway. Neither here nor there, but if you had to ask me to imagine who I would most like to spend a pleasant afternoon with, just now, it would be Reilis. Worthy ally, worthy friend, someone I can talk strategy with, and though in some of her other forms, she can think much faster than I can, and in much detail, I find I'm not afraid of her, and I don't feel inferior. Perhaps that's the most remarkable thing that all this new information has brought to me. •

I could feel all the things he was trying not to think—which I found very funny—and he was still not used to how open two minds sharing a brain are, and trying to backpedal, conceal, and defend in a way that just doesn't work when you're both in the same skull, which was even funnier, and funnier still as I felt him give up entirely and just get on with admitting what he was feeling. • To my surprise, maybe we're not hopelessly inferior. Maybe instead—not that I imagine—I can't conceal anything, can I? •

Before I could think more than agreement, the springer

formed the gray fog, and Reilis stepped through. She had a small daypack in each hand, which I realized was probably the picnic, and she was wearing a simple loose white dress and hiking shoes—practical, comfortable, and somehow, on her, devastatingly attractive. Though of course I was seeing her at least partly with Shan's eyes.

She handed me one of the daypacks, I slipped into it, and she said, "Now, we're just going for a walk around your prison island here; perhaps if your captivity lasts a while longer and we come to an understanding, we can give you a door. But for the moment at least we can give you a little chance to exercise outside."

We stepped through the springer and emerged from a portable springer about a hundred meters from the house. I looked around; it's funny how having just a few windows can so shape your view of a place. The island's reddish stone, crumbled by its centuries of sticking out in the middle of a shallow, savage sea, broke into rough scarps, little patches of pines and hardwoods, and small meadows everywhere. "Is that waterfall—"

"Seminatural," Reilis said. "The source is a pipe from the solar desalinator just beyond the edge of a little lagoon on the other side of the island. Desalinated water flows into a pond up near the top of the hill. But they don't regulate the flow and the little stream does what it wants to. In the evenings the pygmy deer come down to it, and I've often thought it really needs a painter or photographer. We're going up that way; would you like to take the path along the stream? It's a bit more challenging."

"Exercise would be wonderful," I said.

The path along the creek side wound up through the low slopes; the gulch was steep but shallow. "The sky is the most amazing blue here," I commented.

"It's a very blue world," Reilis agreed. "I hope that someday everyone, everywhere in human space will be able to visit Aurenga; it's the most perfect world ever created for vacations, like twenty copies of the South Pacific all on one planet, with just enough mountains for the skiers and hikers thrown in, and some of the islands have surfing that's beyond anything you've ever seen. Not to mention such high tides that what isn't mountain is smooth golden beach. And you haven't swum in the sea here, yet, have you?"

"Not yet."

"Well, we'll find some time for that on the way back."

Shan asked, "Oh, did you pack suits?"

"I wouldn't dream of it," she said, glancing back over her shoulder and flipping her hair in a very distracting way.

• Steady, Shan, • I thought, and a raspberry was thought back at me. "Is there something special about Aurenga's ocean, for swimming?"

"Oh, just that it's only very mildly salty—much less tectonic activity here and a very thick crust, and it froze over so early in the planet's history that the seas just didn't get as much salt. It doesn't taste very good but you could drink it if you had to, at least for a short while. All the seagoing organisms had to be modified to deal with it. And it's also just-right warm. You'll see. It's just glorious."

We followed her up the winding path a few more steps before she turned around and said, with that teasing smile that delighted me—and melted Shan, "You know, it's not terribly dangerous up here, and there's no need for a point guard. You could walk beside me."

As soon as we caught up, she took my hand. "I've had four bodies, gentlemen, all healthy, and if there is anything to be learned by being incarnated, it's not to waste a day like this one." The breeze was just enough to make the trees move a bit; the swells out on the sea were long, slow, and calm; and Aurenga's sun was just pleasantly warm. The few big fluffy clouds in the sky were to the west, already departing. And something smelled maddeningly good—some spicy mix of shrimp and peppers, I thought—from one of our packs.

"Based on a mere half century and one body, agreed," I said.

We didn't talk again most of the way up the hill; it wasn't love or courtship, of course, nothing more than mutual attraction and the possibility of friendship as far as I was concerned, and perhaps no more than relief from intense loneliness for Shan.

But Reilis was right. There are days you don't waste. Especially because to waste them seems to dare the gods to take them away forever.

Reilis knew how to pack a picnic so that every little, trivial grace note was there. We had jams, spices, and salt in neat little pots, and a full set of silverware and dishes, and a marvelous mixture of hot and cold foods, everything just perfect from the mixed vegetable bisque we began with through the cold chicken, the hot *pescaroz* and the shrimp jambalaya, to the green salad at the end. She even had the perfect surprise, waiting until I was full but not stuffed and then producing the flask of espresso and the little containers of exquisite vanilla ice cream. "What's the point of indulging, if we don't overindulge?" she asked, beaming. "How else will we know we did it right?"

We were sitting on an outcrop above the little pond; its white-sand bottom was visible even through the five or six meters of pure water. "Clean enough to drink," she said, following my gaze, "but warm enough that it's practically tea, in the noon sun."

"I was watching the little lobsters."

"Actually they're giant crawfish. They and the big koi are getting a bit out of hand here. They tell me they were expecting birds to find this island a long time ago, and they haven't yet, so they may have to import some herons or kingfishers. Meanwhile, though, it's quite a sight, isn't it?"

A koi, like a fire in the pure water, flashed by, on its way out of the sun and into the shadows, and the nervous crawfish scattered away, whooshing backward in clouds of white sand. I looked up from the clear view below, across the brilliant cyan of the pond, down the silver ribbon of the thundering creek, and out across the mighty turquoise sea. "Human beings, if left to themselves, could all choose to live in places like this," I said. "We've had the technology for centuries. We could all just spend our days hiking, swimming, reading . . . making art . . . learning whatever we liked. We never realized we could all be doing that, and it would have been very nice, but now it looks like we have thousands of years, maybe, of war ahead of us, and no time at all for any of that anymore. Even if we win, we can't keep them from hitting our rear; there won't be any rear. Everyone, everywhere will have to live on guard."

I could feel the responding thought forming in Shan's mind—that in interstellar war there's no rear area; nothing is ever significantly between any part of your forces and the enemy. It's as if the enemy is on a hill two kilometers from a fence post, and you're on a hill two kilometers on the other side of the fence post, and you're both trying to hide behind the fence post. Can't be done. There are so few stars and so much nothing, even in our fairly dense part of an outer spiral arm of the galaxy.

He sighed. "Well, certainly we can't put up a fence and hang out a 'No Invaders beyond this point' sign. There will never be a Great Wall of Human Space. But that doesn't mean we can't be secure. Hornets can't make a nest so strong that a bull can't cave it in, but they can make the bull decide not to fuck with them. We can probably attain the kind of security a nest of hornets has—if we're willing to learn to behave like hornets. Which, at least for the human part of the alliance, comes almost naturally anyway." He sighed, stretched, and leaned back on his arms in the warm sunlight. "Even while we're doing that, though, I hope there can be many afternoons like this."

"Besides, it *is* impossibly romantic," Reilis said, "to imagine a young soldier and his girl having an afternoon like this, before he goes bravely off to fight the brain eaters . . . now, isn't that the stuff of drama?"

"I'm hardly young," I said, gesturing at my fifty-year-old body, "though I may seem so to Shan—"

"And my total experience across all copies is a bit over a thousand years, all of which I remember, and I have spent decades brooding between the stars, and I have hurled comets and moved moons to make new worlds," Reilis said. "I have lived long enough to see people I knew well become legends and myths."

"Oh, even *I've* done that," I pointed out.

"Precisely. You don't even need one lifetime to feel eons old. But today I am wearing a young, vigorous body, which now has a gloriously full tummy, and wants to lie out in the sun with two men, currently in one body, whom I hope to have as friends for a thousand years to come. Which is to say, whatever may be in my past, I'm just at the beginning of the life I expect to have. That's more than enough to make me young, and I intend to enjoy it, and if you won't join me in that, well"—she stuck her tongue out—"poopers on you."

I laughed and said, "I couldn't possibly argue with that."

• And I wouldn't if I could. •

• Right, Shan, now you're getting it. • I let myself be distracted by the play of the brilliant amber light on Reilis's hair. "You *are* truly *jovent*, you know that?" I told her. "In the way the old poets, the first Occitans, meant it, when they would say that this or that brilliant, lively man of fifty was *jovent*—"

"Or that that stuffy old monk of twenty-two was *vielh*," she agreed. "Either you try to squish new experiences down to make them small enough so that they won't disturb you—like an old toothless tasteless geezer's pap—or you open wide and gulp experience in. *Jovent* or *vielh*, it's a matter of gusto and joy, not gray hair and the calendar." She sighed happily, and said, "Shall we just undress and sunbathe a bit?"

That seemed like a good idea too; when both bodies were stretched out on the warm, comfortably crumbly stone, with the big pitcher of lemonade between us in easy reach, she rolled over to face me; I felt Shan stir.

• Don't spook the pretty girl, you dirty old man, • I thought amiably. • There may not be many things you can learn from me, but I do think technique is one. •

• I watch and learn, oh guru. •

Reilis smiled warmly, and said, "Well, one way that we're none of us as young as we used to be—I do want to talk some business. So, do you suppose we could share what we both know of the Invaders? We should do that soon, if we're to have talks that are at all productive."

I was about to object that neither Shan nor I had any authority to speak for the Council or even the OSP about anything so important, when I felt Shan's impatience cut me off; to him, I realized, the OSP would always be his personal property, and the Council of Humanity's job would always be to ratify, after the fact, the (absolutely and clearly correct) things Shan did.

He currently shared a skull with a kidnapped prisoner. Just now he was dozens of light-years beyond where the Council writ ran, and no longer had a job—he had been replaced fifteen years ago, for being dead. But as far as he was concerned, now that he was back, he was in charge again.

I had to admire the old pirate. (If I hadn't admired him I'd have had to wring his neck, and the only one he had to wring was also mine.)

6

"Well, then," Shan said. "So based on the timing and the two definitely attacked worlds, we'd have to say that they're coming from the direction of Ursa Major, and that they know about every inhabited world in both Council and Union space, and they could conceivably attack all of them tomorrow; they've had more than time enough to get springer probes into position to do it."

"To share a detail, we have been doing rather extensive patrols against that possibility," Reilis said. "We have made great strides in the acoustics of interstellar plasma, and we don't think any probe big enough to be dangerous has evaded our detection—at least, not anything moving at above eighty-five percent of c. We destroy about four Invader springships per year, all moving at very close to lightspeed. They might be sneaking something in at a much lower speed, but we do have some tight-beam deep-field radar scouting for those, and of course they would be coming much more slowly."

"Our acoustic devices are only good for objects at ninety-plus percent of c and above," Shan said. "Or were fifteen years ago. That might be an area of exchange. We do have a scanning gamma laser that works reasonably well, so we might have an exchange possible right there."

"Good, at least one potential agreement right off the bat. That should at least get Union and the Council talking." Reilis looked thoughtful. "Interesting that the Invaders don't seem to be trying to overwhelm us with a single big attack."

"We thought they might be an opportunistic predator," Shan said. "Constantly sampling and tasting, but only devouring when it's convenient. From conquering Eunesia, and the Theta Ursa Major system, the Invaders learned that the rest of human space is here, all these ripe sets of experiences ready to harvest. They'll get around to consuming us, but on the Invaders' time scales, it will be no delay at all if they wait for a century, or a millennium for that matter. We think it has to do with digestion time, and extreme confidence; they haven't lost against any other species in tens of thousands, perhaps hundreds of thousands, of stanyears. After all, twenty thousand stanyears ago, the Invaders overran and conquered the Predecessors, who were a much bigger and tougher outfit. Probably they've had a lot of experience since. So we have a lot to get ready for, and not many rehearsals or much experience—we stopped holding total, win-or-else, war to extermination after the Slaughter, more than half a millennium ago."

You had to love the mischief when that woman grinned. "You sound like you regret that."

Shan shrugged. "Well, no, of course, how could anyone? But strange as it sounds, I wish we were in better practice. Think about what happened when the Cheyenne, who basically practiced ritual· war, or the Chinese, with a couple of centuries of police actions, met better-armed outsiders. You can recover from a bad start if you're the size of China, but that recovery isn't anything you'd voluntarily undergo; and if you're the size of the Cheyenne, well, that's the old ball game.

"By the standards of most of the centuries from the Renaissance to the Slaughter, we don't have a military, we have a medium-sized police force with an unusually well equipped SWAT team. If the Invaders hit tomorrow, the Council worlds will give them a better fight than Addams or Eunesia, but we'll still be crushed in no time at all, and they'll barely feel our resistance."

"We're in about the same situation," she said. "A bit better in some ways because we went public with what had happened to Eunesia very early, but a bit worse in other ways because we have only a fraction of your population. Do you have any intelligence you're willing to share about what's happening on Addams right now?" she asked.

"Sort of. As far as we can tell from probes that generally don't make it down to the surface, and don't last more than a couple of seconds after starting to transmit to us, the Invaders are still stripping the 102 cultures there and shipping all of the human and machine memories back for the aliens to consume as entertainment. Four hundred years of a human population, a hundred and two cultures, two billion brain holograms, an aintellect population of maybe ten billion, and the average aintellect is ninety times the size of a human mind—it takes a while to get it all chopped up, packaged, labeled, and ready for consumption. At least our xenosemioticians think that that is what the robots and aintellects on Addams are doing at the moment; getting it all fit to send back."

Reilis nodded. "That's consistent with what their robots and aintellects were doing on Eunesia when we got back. They had a few orbital defense stations that we overwhelmed and shot to pieces, and they shut off their springers as soon as we landed. The robots and aintellects still wandering around blew themselves up, or erased themselves, the moment they were cut off from home, probably to avoid capture." She rolled onto her back for a moment, stretched and sighed. Shan and I admired the view and hoped she wouldn't glance in a direction that would surely reveal how much we admired it. "All right," Reilis said, now gazing up at the sky, "that's the start of sharing information. The next one on my list was the Predecessors. What information are you willing to share about them that isn't public knowledge?"

Shan grinned. "Well, since you started off the sharing process, I suppose it is my turn to start." From the way he was looking her over while he talked, I wasn't sure whether he meant to start talking about the Predecessors, but that was what he did. "What we know is that in all the advanced Predecessor ruins we have found so far, there's evidence of a terrific fight. Those metal squids that overran Addams were exactly like the ones who attacked what was probably the Predecessor provincial capital on the planet we call Hammarskjöld. We have an enormous dig going on there; a whole planet of wreckage, but almost no bodies. It would appear that the Predecessors came back entirely to reclaim their own dead, since they did nothing about all the wreckage of Invader equipment. There are burned-out and blown-up robots all over that planet, but nothing organic belonging to the Invaders, and only relatively small body parts here and there that were once part of a Predecessor. And based on things like deposits of seasonal plant matter and so on, we think that fighting must have gone on for years. The Predecessors must have raised a whole generation in caves and undersea habitats while they fought for their world. It is probably the biggest battle site human beings have ever found, and it was just one of many places the Predecessors made a stand against the Invaders.

"More than that, on at least six worlds we've found primitive ruins that probably mean the Predecessors there lost or decided to stop using all tech that put out any EMF signal or might be visible from orbit—basically they moved into the caves and lived pre-tech in order to avoid detection—and some of those places held out for thousands of years. We may yet find a lost Predecessor colony with live Predecessors, living in the Neolithic or early Iron Age. And our best guess is that that's not something that 'happened to happen'—it's something that they chose to do, rather than surrender.

"Anyway, they were quite a species, and I would require a lot more proof than we have to say that there are no more of them. I want to meet them, and shake hands or whatever it is our species can mutually do, and have their respect as much as they have mine. Certainly the Invaders admire them greatly, in their own horrible way—we think the Invaders finally finished shipping Predecessor material out of Hammarskjöld after about two thousand years."

"Seems like quite a while to just pack up all the recordings they made," Reilis said.

"Well, the little we know of the Invaders is that they have a desperate fear of the unfamiliar balanced by an equally desperate craving for novelty. So their aintellects and robots have to predigest every new species or civilization into readily consumable form. Imagine taking the minds and memories of everyone alive on a particular day in all of Imperial Rome, or Moghul India, or the South American Interbellis, then editing it so that it wouldn't upset a very fussy and extremely sheltered child, but would still excite and thrill that same child. You might guess it would take a while, even at aintellect speeds."

It was a warm and pleasant afternoon in a near-paradise, and the two of them were chatting like friends and colleagues contemplating becoming lovers, as if the Invaders were as abstract a concern as the Aztecs or the Ice Age. It was beginning to freeze my blood, so I spoke up. "And these things destroyed the Predecessors," I said. "The popular science articles are saying that all of Council-controlled space—which took us six centuries to settle—might be a tenth of the volume of one single province of the Predecessor Empire, or Hegemony, or whatever their political structure was. And the Invaders defeated the Predecessors—"

"They defeated *some* Predecessors," Shan said. "The ones around here. For all we know, sometime before the pyramids were built, the Predecessors launched a counter-offensive, and they'll be coming back this way to pay the Invaders back in, oh, another ten thousand years. At which point we have to hope they have nicer habits than the Invaders, and we don't want them to mistake us for friends of the Invaders!"

"Well," Reilis said, "they apparently gave the Invaders a good fight. We can at least do the same. If there is an afterlife for species, I'd rather sit down with the Predecessors. As a species, they didn't go into the box, and they resisted being cut up into data for amusement. So we have something in common with them." She stood up. "We really only need to keep our shoes and our water bottles, but we might as well carry the clothes with us. A robot will come up here and collect the picnic leavings. So, shall we stroll down to the beach? I could easily find myself in the mood for a swim."

"Absolutely delighted," I agreed. We went down a different trail from the one we had come up; this one plunged quickly down toward the shore, and then looped and switchbacked around till it found a precarious descent to a wide, golden beach beside the sapphire lagoon that nestled between this island and its little flock of islets. "It's only about two kilometers across," Reilis said, pointing it out when we first came around the side of a ridge, and stopped to admire it, "but unfortunately none of those little outcrops has anywhere much good to swim ashore; it tends to be rocks and cliffs all over. So, since we're both in good shape, we could easily swim to them but there's not much of anywhere to rest, and not much way up onto the other islands. Just in case you were about to suggest that."

"I wasn't, but Shan was," I said. "He's still finding it a novelty to have a fifty-year-old body again."

• Wait till I've got a teenager's, • Shan thought smugly.

I'd teased him about being a living cliché. The Thousand Cultures were filling up with exultant, joyful athletes, former seventy-year-olds making the most of being physically nineteen. I almost envied him how soon he would be trying it out.

On the way down the steep, winding trail, as it followed the crest of a saddle between two spires of pine-studded red stone, Shan took control of the body, caught Reilis's hand, and said, "There is one other thing I'm curious about. I don't really believe there were ever multiple factions here on Aurenga, or that the Noucathars had a radical faction that was trying to kill Giraut for not being Occitan enough, or for encouraging Ix, or whatever it was supposed to be. I notice the immense cleverness of those assassins at getting to him, the utter ineptitude once they got there, and the peculiarly elaborate suicides, and I think something else was at work. And then I notice that over time the assassinations first made Giraut and his team, and of course Margaret, very alert, and then steered them to particular events and places, and seem, finally, to have brought Giraut here and put him within your power. So . . . were all the assassination attempts yours? And am I right that you had no intent to harm Giraut?"

"They had been ours," she said, "but we lost control of them. You might say Giraut was being attacked by a virus. Years ago we planted an opportunity out in the demimonde of free, dissident, and criminal aintellects. We started a little self-duplicating program that would put together a pile of money and funds for creating an assassin to send after Giraut, specifying that the assassin it produced had to have a Lost Legion genetic connection and be fairly inept.

"The idea was just to put some significant pressure on the OSP and get Giraut headed into situations where we could kidnap him; basically to break things up and keep things moving. At any rate, viruses and worms mutate, and aintellects have to mutate to function—as we all know since it explains my existence—and this one got out of our control, which if anything was to our advantage. We thought that might provide an incentive for you to get serious about the investigation, and it seems it did."

"Well, it certainly incentivized *me*," I agreed. "So I was being pursued by deadly spam?"

"The one that sent that fellow after you in the hotel room had lost some of its fail-safing and sent a rather deadlier one than it should, which is why you had more trouble with that assassin than you had had with the previous ones; it had apparently lost many of its precautions about being careful with the life of one of our agents, which is how poor Azalais got blown up. That last one that sent Maracabru after you was a really bad situation—it was a centuries-old defrauder virus that had mugged one of our assassin-viruses for the rewards code, and was trying to collect by completely uncontracted methods—luckily for you, the copy it mugged had amped up the ineptitude. If it had pirated code from the more deadly one, you might have been in real trouble."

"Not that someone trying to kill me, however inept, is exactly *not* being in trouble," I pointed out. "Being almost killed is plenty real enough for me."

"Well, yes, but you're highly skilled and you dealt with it just fine."

"Oh, I just want some attention paid to the possibility of my getting dead. Call it vanity."

She smiled and took both of my hands in hers, drawing me close, I suppose to give me the full effect of the sea-gray eyes and the scent of her sweaty naked body. "We've all three of us been at the game for a large part of our lives. I do hope you can understand that it was truly nothing personal?"

"No hard feelings," I said. • Shan, that pun was old a thousand years ago. Stick with your reserve and dignity, you do it better. •

• I continue to learn. •

The last descent to the beach was steep enough so that we did not so much hold hands as assist each other over the little outcrops and rocks. But the beach itself was worth every second of the effort; the lagoon was barely rippled and crystal-clear, the sand warm but not hot and just right for texture—soft enough to lie in but not fine enough to be itchy. We kicked off our shoes beside our clothes and ran down into the warm water.

For a couple of hours that afternoon, we just splashed, played, and laughed. There is an expression in Occitan poetry, one that is so clichéd that the merest mention of it brings showers of beer and peanuts in any reading club. It got to be clichéd because it's an experience everyone has—to be with a lover and to feel *que primis amadris d'ilh mondo*—"like the first lovers in the world." That afternoon was like that.

At last we flopped out on the beach to sunbathe and dry. She rolled into my arms, laughing. I think, perhaps, it was only then that I was entirely sure that I believed her about the pleasures of being embodied. I defy anyone seeing Reilis's radiant, trusting, sweet face—and especially those eyes, bright with the shared knowledge that had passed between us and dark with the sadness of our certain parting, to think "warm zombie" at her and back away. But I am getting ahead of myself here; it was months later before that ugly expression began to float around in the media.

A kiss led to a longer kiss, and then since we were all alone on a streak of soft sand by a perfect lagoon, "like the first lovers in the world;" and since no matter what, it would all be different later; we made love the way you do when you think you may never see each other again and every second could be the last.

Shan was enjoying it so much (it had been so much longer for him) that I retreated to let him take over.

Reilis pressed back, arching her back and grinding our hips together, and winked. "Taking over, Shan?"

I'm not sure which of the three of us was laughing harder. It's an interesting sensation in that situation.

"How did you know?" Shan asked, his accent unmistakable.

"Giraut has better technique but you're less jaded."

Later, during a long, pleasant second round, as Reilis bent over my body and bore down with her pelvis, she asked Shan, "Am I a machine and a tool? Are you using me? Is that what you're thinking?"

"I'm not thinking at all," he said. Her back was astonishingly soft, and lovely.

"He's telling the truth," I added. "Me either."

She turned around and bent slowly to kiss me. "That's the point." She snuggled up under my arm. "I was right."

"Right about what? I asked, bewildered.

"Right about you and your songs. Giraut, we just thought . . . the man who wrote "Don't Forget I Live Here Too," the man who is still wrestling after all these years with his encounter with Ix, *can't* be that big a hypocrite. We made a bet that your big, sloppy, generous, loving heart would get the better of you." She sighed contentedly, and planted a light kiss on my neck. "And we were right."

She snuggled in closer; the sun was warm and with no risk of sunburn, I fell asleep; sometime shortly after, I suppose, so did she. Shan lay awake, holding her, probing at my memories, and somewhere in the warm afternoon, came to some understanding with himself, and with the child that we all are deep inside. He thought later that it was probably the moment that he admitted that it wasn't anybody's fault that Pinky got left behind either. Eventually the warmth and comfort caught up with him, and he joined us in sleep.

At the roar of the impellers, we leapt to our feet. An invasion barge is a four-story-tall squashed pyramid of metal, its sides sloped and curved to deflect projectiles upward and mirrored against masers and lasers. This particular invasion barge was rushing straight across the lagoon at us, kicking up a huge plume of water underneath it. Usually they come in buttoned up, looking like one big lumpy mirror, but this one had all of its ports open, beam and projectile weapons protruding like quills on a porcupine. We both dove for our clothes and dressed as quickly as we could.

The purpose of an invasion barge is to get a springer close to a battlefield, and provide cover for the troops emerging from the springer to get organized. The springer is at the center, on one side of the forming-up deck. Once a CSP platoon is assembled, they emerge from the invasion barge through passageways between multiple armored baffles.

Normally those baffles are so reflective that they vanish into the mirrored surface. But as the pyramid set down on the beach, I caught fun-house-mirror glimpses of several different Raimbauts running head-on into each other, splitting apart into two Raimbauts at the back, and then re-merging headfirst, as he dashed around and between the reflecting baffles. He came out with fifteen CSPs behind him, shouting "Both of you, hands up! And keep them up!"

Reilis hadn't quite had time to fasten her top, and it fell open when she complied with Raimbaut's order, leaving her exposed in front of Raimbaut and the dozens of CSPs who followed him out of the invasion barge. In the bright summer sunlight of the beach, I could clearly see that she was blushing; somewhere in that weird part of the brain that is always analyzing and never shuts down, I wondered whether she had had to learn to do that.

Looking somewhere about three feet over her head, Raimbaut walked forward and covered her. He muttered, "Sorry."

Two CSPs stepped forward and scanned her with weapons detectors, and very carefully and respectfully patted her down.

"Giraut," he said, "I hate this part even more. I have to place you under arrest. You've been held here long enough, and apparently unrestrained—"

And Reilis, bless her brave heart, laughed. "He's been very unrestrained," she said, "and so has Shan."

"Hello, Raimbaut."

No mistaking that accent, even in two words; Raimbaut jumped. Then he looked into my eyes, as if he could see both Shan and me looking back, and looked at the back of my head to where the psypyx sat, and shrugged. "*Gratz'deu*, I'm not an administrator. I don't want to handcuff either—er, any—of you; please come along peaceably. We're all longtime, experienced agents here; surely we can manage a quiet, professional, fuss-free arrest."

Part Four

Vast and Cool
and
Unsympathetic

Yet across the gulf of space, minds that are to our minds as ours are to those of the beasts that perish, intellects vast and cool and unsympathetic, regarded this earth with envious eyes, and slowly and surely drew their plans against us.

—H. G. Wells,
The War of the Worlds

The ideas which are here expressed so laboriously are ideas which are extremely simple and should be obvious. The difficulty lies, not in the new ideas, but in escaping from the old ones, which ramify, for those brought up as most of us have been, into every corner of our minds.

—John Maynard Keynes,
The General Theory of Employment, Interest, and Money

As we walked down the beach into the invasion barge, Reilis reached for my hand, and Raimbaut coughed. "I am really truly sorry," he said, "but I cannot let you touch each other. Those are orders. I don't like them."

"We understand," Reilis said.

The mirrored, armored baffles of the invasion barge were like a fun house; at the other end, we walked through a millimeter-thick light-suppression field, perfectly black, onto the well-lit forming-up deck, the size of a basketball court.

It was only much later that I found out how it had been done. Raimbaut had been carrying a set of to-all-appearances ordinary immune nanos in his bloodstream, the standard anti-skin-cancer ones that all the pale peoples of the Thousand Cultures carry all the time, which normally reproduce in the bloodstream and send most of their "offspring" out onto the skin, where they live rather like the native mites that are normally there, except that they constantly look for carcinoma cells and convene to zap them whenever one is found. Given the tar deposited on our skins as kids, from all that soot on Wilson, and the fact that our natural color is fish-belly white, most of us Occitans have the nanos put in before we're twenty.

The breeder nanos in Raimbaut's bloodstream had an extra tweak, one thought up by the labs at the OSP. They really did make plain old anti-skin-cancer nanos and put them out on his skin, just like any other breeder nanos, but they had another feature: when he ate the right combination of foods to trigger them, they would make a different set of nanos that came out in his urine. If he then dropped a few pieces of metal into an aluminum pot of that urine, and put the urine on the stove on low (to supply energy), the "secret weapon" nanos would form a tiny springer, half the size of a walnut, with an aperture just big enough for a communications laser back to Margaret, and for a bunch of nanos to come back through once contact was established.

It wasn't at all unusual for junior agents to have missions and capabilities unknown to the senior agent in charge of the team; the thinking was that it made OSP teams more resilient (not to mention more unpredictably dangerous to the other side).

Raimbaut had pretended to be disconsolate at my "loss" (and to believe that I had really been kidnapped along with Reilis), quarreled publicly with Laprada, and gone on a long walk on the beach with the microspringer, throwing stones into the sea in apparent fury and frustration. One of the stones he threw, of course, was the microspringer, which in turn had brought through a cluster of nanos that had built a basketball-sized device (with a bigger springer inside) that made its way to an uninhabited island, found a suitable cave, and sprang yet more nanos from OSP base into it. In about five standays there was a full-fledged facility ready to go, and at the cue from base, a huge springer frame had popped up on the island's surface, and twenty invasion barges had crashed through to deliver fully half of all the active-duty Council Special Police onto Aurenga, just as a pack of aintellect viruses and worms had jumped the communications and control systems for the planet. The government of Noucatharia found out that they were invaded about four minutes before CSPs occupied all the government office buildings, just as all the submersibles, airships, and satellites were switched over to the Council's side.

At the time, of course, we knew none of this, but CSPs on Aurenga, and no shooting, was enough information to extrapolate most of the important parts, if not the details.

As we approached the springers, Raimbaut said, "I don't want either of you to be afraid. Reilis, you're going to the fieldhouse at the old, closed-down University of Trantia; you'll be with everyone else. As far as I know all three thousand Noucathars are to be held there until some reasonably decent system of house arrest can be set up for all of you, and then there will be a long period of processing while the Council figures out what to do and talks to everyone. I've been around the Council bureaucracy far too much to make you any promises about how that will go, or how long it will take. But you aren't going to anywhere where you'll be hurt or abused—or if you are, the OSP will have some heads for it."

"Thank you." Her smile was tentative, just a twitch at the corner of the mouth, but I had already gotten to know her well enough to think that it was sincere, and she really had been afraid. "And Giraut?"

"We're putting him where you were keeping him," Raimbaut said, with a sideways glance at me. "At least we know he's not likely to get out. We need to sort out loyalties and so forth." He sighed. "This was not my choice of how to handle all this."

"We understand that you're just doing what you're supposed to," I said, "and you don't need to apologize further. Reilis, I hope we'll see each other again, soon."

"Me too," she said. "I'm glad we didn't waste time. I hate wasting time."

We both said goodbye several times as Raimbaut steered her into the springer, and then he nodded to me and I walked back through the springer into the little house that Reilis and I had left, just that morning, for a picnic and a conversation. The place was curiously cold and dead in a way it hadn't been.

• Well, at least we know our way around. Even what's in the refrigerator, • I thought.

• Good time to invoke the oldest rule of being an agent, •

Shan thought, meaning, when in doubt, take a good dump, eat something, and get some sleep, since you never know when time for those might get short.

As we were getting a snack from the refrigerator, the screen of the springer swirled into a gray glow, and Margaret walked through. "Now I know I'm a prisoner," I said. "You didn't knock."

"Well, possibly a prisoner. You're at least an ex-spouse and how many people are ever polite to them?" She looked around the room and said, "At least they kept you somewhere comfortable. May I sit? As you might guess, we have things to talk about. And I understand I am now talking to Shan, as well?"

"You are."

"Welcome back. I think you'll be happy to see what I've done with your organization."

I felt his amusement. "It's yours, now. Though I will probably think of it as Yokhim Kiel's, forever."

She nodded and smiled, and we sat. As ever, I was struck by how much Margaret got to me; sometime in my impressionable first days around her, or because we had both been at that time in our lives, or perhaps it was just hardwired into my DNA— there was no woman I found more attractive. She had aged well, going from the awkward heaviness of her youth to a certain presence and dignity, but even so, you couldn't call her "handsome" and I suppose most people would just call her "matronly," politely avoiding call her "plain."

I didn't care; I was just glad to have her there.

"Well," she said, "to begin with, this has all been quite a surprise." She permitted herself a small smile, which I really had to return. I remembered that back when we had been partners on any number of missions—back when Shan was sending us on them—no matter what trouble I got into, Margaret simply got me out with efficiency and dispatch. Getting into trouble (and thereby provoking the other side into tipping its hand) was my job; getting me out (and looking at the other side's cards) was hers, and she accepted that division of labor with only that small, sweet smile, and sometimes the fun of turning it into a dinner table story.

I suddenly wondered where it had all gone.

• And there's always more that's gone when you look around, • Shan thought. • The more attention you pay, the more you appreciate, the more you know it when it goes. •

"Well," Margaret said, "the idea of a planet of chimeras and robotized people makes me want to throw up, and that's what we appear to have here. Apparently they installed aintellects in children as soon as the children were verbal, putting them in as a psypyx implant, so there's probably no one here over the age of two who isn't a chimera—which means no one whose existence is legal under Council law.

"On the other hand, no matter how distasteful I find their existence, in the first place, Union contains at least half a billion of them, and in the second place, even three thousand starts to look like genocide to me. Especially since whatever I may think of it, there is obviously something unique here, and probably something that more open-minded people than I can learn from, so I should probably preserve it and give them the chance. You stayed here for a long time, compared to my couple of hours so far, anyway. What did you think?"

I didn't really think before answering, "I like them. They're interesting. They aren't headed into the box, and they're going somewhere."

"Do you worry about them replacing humans?"

I thought about that, which made me hesitate. "Er—Shan, this time. No. They are human. Not as we've been, but then we aren't much like hunter-gatherers or peasants or Industrial-Age workers, either, are we? It's another kind of consciousness, but no more alien than Achilles or St. Augustine or Madame Bovary would be to us. And—Margaret, may I add one very strong plea? I understand that you may not feel the way I do, and you aren't bound by my feelings, but it's a bit of advice I feel urgently compelled to give."

"Certainly. I won't feel bound by it but I think I'd be a fool not to listen to you."

"Whatever you decide, don't use destructive deconstruction on the captured aintellects and psypyxed personalities. You have no idea what horror these people feel for it, or how much they loathe the idea, and anyone who does it."

"I have some clue from what they did to our laboratory. They destroyed the experience base of more than fifty extremely advanced aintellects—"

"With about the same spirit that you or I would dispose of a group of torturers, slavers, or cannibals," I said. "Back when we used to believe it, when we said, 'Another round for humanity and one more for the good guys.'"

"I miss those days too. I take your point. I'm not sure whether I'll take your advice, but I do take your point," she said. "Now, Giraut, would you like to explain to me why you not only had sex with an enemy agent—I expect that, knowing you—but then cooperated with her even after she had kidnapped you?"

"I don't think you can be certain that Reilis is the enemy," I pointed out.

"Still, you do seem to be very involved," she said, "and the question remains . . . what the hell were you thinking?"

"I was learning what I could from an important contact," I said, biting back the phrase *and by the way, we are not married anymore.* "As I was sent here to do. I think that most or all of what she is saying is the truth. And that this is a great opportunity, and nothing to be feared."

"Giraut, how thoroughly have you been brainwashed?"

"Er," Shan said, reshaping my mouth into his odd, inimitable accent. "Er. Being, er, in here with Giraut, I would have to say that he is most definitely *not* brainwashed—"

"Shan, I am no more convinced that you are capable of being objective about a young, pretty woman, than that Giraut is. Your are not exactly the ideal character witness in this matter."

I felt Shan's embarrassment, and the way his memory raced through an inventory of things Margaret might know about or remember, and realized just how much he had been right that his lechery was only invisible to males. In other circumstances I suppose I might have teased the old reprobate about it.

"Whether or not you trust *us*," Shan said, "I suggest your investigation *not* include destructive deconstructions. That is only common sense and prudence."

"It is," Margaret said. "It is so much a matter of common sense that we had already agreed on it, and your reminding me of it in this way seems oddly patronizing and very unpleasant. And I can tell that neither of us is going to be easy to get along with for a little while, so I am going to leave you here while I consider what to tell the rest of the OSP, and do enough investigating of my own to have at least some idea what to recommend to them." She stood up and walked toward the springer, which began to glow gray at once—clearly the house aintellects had already been reprogrammed to anticipate her wishes.

At the portal she turned back and said, "And Giraut, before you become too committed to the advice of this old man, will you please try to remember that he's also the one who chose to destroy our marriage, back on Briand, and worked constantly to undercut Ix, who was trying to save it? Just keep that in mind."

She disappeared into the gray fog; the instant that she did, the gray fog disappeared, leaving just the black metal plate.

• For someone from a culture that has no theatrical tradition, • I thought, • she really has a knack for a curtain line. •

I felt Shan try to make himself chuckle, and then he said,

• Giraut, you know, it's stupid of me, but because I had apologized to you, and reconciled with you, I forgot that I owed Margaret an apology. •

• You're not the Shan-you-were-to-be; you aren't the copy anymore. For every practical purpose, you're now the original. •

• And being the original is everyone's nightmare, *ne*? •

• *Oc, ja, ver tropa vera,* • I agreed.

It is, of course. And he was right to remind me why he was afraid. Thanks to the psypyx, the copy always lives on, and the original is the one that does the dying. So you lie down on the table to be copied, and in about three hours you get up, feeling the same as ever; you're the original. Eventually, one day after your last copy, you die. Meanwhile, or otherwhile, or in someone else's while, you lie down on the table, and when you wake up, you're in someone else's head, stanyears or decades in the future, somewhere else entirely; you're the copy and you're going to live.

Hence the moment you know for certain that you are going to die is the moment you know that you are the original; every child starts to grasp that at about the age of ten or twelve, and from then on, about as often as people dream of being naked in public, or of falling, or of having to take a test they haven't studied for, we all dream of being suddenly informed that we are the original.

We stripped out of the sandy, damp day clothes, finally, and got into a hot shower; that was followed by a little soup and bread, and curling up in the bed, trying not to think too much about whether Reilis was all right. It had been a long day and there was a lot to absorb, and I fell asleep quickly.

Naturally I had just that nightmare: I dreamed that I awoke as the original, and was about to die. It got mixed together with Shan's memories of the massacre of Addams, and after a while it was Reilis who was in the pink plastic case at my belt—

except when I was running and holding her hand—and when I ran toward the springer, the gray pseudosurface vanished, and I knew that I was the original just as the metal tentacles wrenched Reilis from my hand, and the jaws closed over my head. I am not sure how many times that dream passed through my mind that night; enough to lose count, anyway.

A gray glow was oozing beyond the bedroom door as my eyes opened; against it, a dark figure, slim, female, moving fast, silhouetted and vanished into a roll through the dark shadows. I snapped awake but had barely started to roll away when a muscular little hand covered my mouth, and another stronger-than-it-seemed hand pushed my head back onto the pillow. Soft hair brushed my face, and lips touched my ear. "Friend. Quiet please?"

I nodded, once.

The hands came off my mouth and forehead. I drew a breath to whisper a question, but then my mouth was full of—

Paxa's tongue.

There's a reason why they call that "Hedon kissing." Somebody had to perfect it.

I half thought this might be a different dream from all the nightmares, and decided I definitely preferred it; as I woke more fully, and Shan joined me, I relaxed into the kiss, touching the familiar hair and neck, happier than I could have imagined. As I touched and stroked, I realized she was in full fighting rig, the skintight weightless black suit that fits like a unitard but hardens into armor an instant before anything hits it, and passes most EMR around the body to disperse on the opposite side. It wasn't quite invulnerability—it could be shattered by a big-enough shell or overloaded by concentrated maser fire, or if you were thrown hard enough the internal accelerations could kill you, and of course her head was not protected without the hood. Nor was it quite the same thing as being naked; the touch relays were imprecise except at the fingertips, and it felt rather like being coated with thick petroleum jelly. And backlit, or in bright light against a light background, it was as visible as anything else.

But at night on a skilled user, that fighting suit was a good first-order approximation to being naked, invulnerable, and invisible, and fabricating them took so much information, literally weaving them at the molecular level onto a specific body, that even the OSP only issued them to critical personnel on very-high-risk missions.

In a way, the presence of that suit was more puzzling than finding Paxa kissing me in the middle of the night.

When we had quite finished, Paxa took my hand, leaned forward, and breathed into my ear, "There will be clothes there." She pulled on my hand, and I rose and followed her into the living room.

• What are we doing? • Shan thought

• Finding out. •

• All right, what are we finding out? •

• What we're doing. Don't fret about it. Remember this is the fun part of the job. •

Just as we got to the springer, the gray-glowing pseudosurface formed, and Paxa and I stepped through, holding hands, as we had done so many times before.

The room was basically a walk-in closet and there was a regular combat suit (nothing like that expensive masterpiece that Paxa was wearing) along with underwear, boots, helmet, and so on, all waiting for me. Not knowing how much time or privacy we had, I didn't speak; I just got dressed. "One more spring for now," Paxa said, softly, but not just breathing it in my ear as she had before. The black plate glowed, I took Paxa's hand, and we walked into the thin sheet of fog again.

Whenever I think of Aurenga, the words that spring to mind are *blue* and *sunny*. And in that sense, we sprang to the most Aurengan of all the places I saw in my time there. I had to look around for a moment before I realized, finally, that we were in a subsea habitat with many big, high windows, probably just offshore or on the floor of a lagoon somewhere. "One of many holdout bases against the Invaders," Paxa said, her voice odd. "Part of an elaborate fallback plan so that we'd always have somewhere to hide people and somewhere from which to start counterattacks; when they destroyed Trantia, they had fifteen stanyears to do whatever they wanted here before we could even find out what had happened. We don't want to give them that much time again."

I was still taking in the glow, sapphire from the lower parts of the windows, turquoise from above, and noting that the space was huge, and that corridors led off in several directions behind me. This place would probably hold a small army—a fully appropriate thing for it to do—but it had also been designed to be beautiful; something about that appealed to me very much.

The part of my mind that had been trying to think what was odd with Paxa's voice realized that she had an Occitan accent, something she had never had before. I asked, "Are you wearing a psypyx?"

"Well, yes, Giraut, and you know both of us."

"Azalais!" All it had taken was a hint.

"Yes," one of them said, and I was hugged again.

• I do hope we'll be visiting your entire collection, • Shan thought.

• Quiet, old lech, I'm happy. • I hugged her back for a long, long breath.

"And how did—"

"Well," Paxa said, "the obvious things happened. My opinions about the treatment of aintellects and of robots were well-known, and I was retiring early, as a very senior OSP field agent. Union had a very senior field agent who had just been psypyxed, and furthermore Union has much more advanced psypyx tech than the Council does—not surprisingly, since they never really went through the Inward Turn. So they turned up with an offer; everything I knew about the OSP in exchange for eternal life."

"You did take an oath of loyalty to the OSP," Shan said, a little stiffly.

Paxa shrugged and smiled. "I'm a Hedon. We think keeping your word is a good thing to do, but not the only good thing to do. And I was in the OSP because I liked the danger and excitement, and I liked feeling that I was working for the good guys. Well, the danger and excitement decreased in value a lot when I found out that dead is dead, for me—and it went back up in value when I found out that if I were working for the Union, dead wasn't dead. And aside from that—who would you say is the good guys at the moment?"

• She's good, Giraut. She could always get the better of me in an argument. • "Er, well, put that way—"

She smiled again, and pointed up at the windows. A dozen tuna the size of trakcars flashed by, followed by an equally swift black-and-white shape.

"Orca," I said.

"Who's defending this world? Who even made sure there would be a world like this? Which civilization has a major problem with people going into the box, and uses its best minds for routine maintenance? And which civilization has been pushing out a frontier for centuries? Who had an Inward Turn?"

• How did the OSP ever let somebody like this stay out in the field? • Shan thought.

• One, *you* try putting her anyplace she doesn't want to be— and the place she least wants to be is behind a desk. Two, Paxa is pretty and was involved with me. That's a combination my ex never really forgives—and worse yet, Margaret won't admit that to herself, so, Three, whatever Paxa did was always wrong. •

• It sounds like Margaret was just as capable of folly as I was, or Kiel. Seems to be a tradition of fools in that job. •

• Or humans, • I thought back at him. • Of course if we put in an unrestrained aintellect, that might improve things; it could commit a thousand times the folly in one one-millionth of the time. By the way, we've been standing here in this beautiful room in front of the pretty lady for at least a full minute with our mouth hanging open, so if looking like a fool bothers you—•

Shan's laughter was roaring through my brain as I finally said, "Well, you've given him plenty to think about, Paxa, and Azalais. Suppose you tell me—us, rather—what you've got in mind."

Paxa smiled. "While you've been comparing notes, so have we, of course. I remember you used to get just that slack-jawed expression of utter idiocy now and then when you were wearing Raimbaut. I always thought it was very nice of me not to photograph it. Well, then, here's what we propose. In that house we just took you from, a couple of our robots slipped in and left a warm jelly body of about the right weight lying in the bed. In about twenty-five minutes, a pocket antimatter bomb will go off there. A prep crew has already been into the house and has left half a dozen cadavers lying around, which will be mostly destroyed but will leave just enough human tissue here and there, with DNA that doesn't match yours, to confuse matters further.

"Our estimate is that the unexpected explosion and chaos will take the OSP about ten minutes to sort out, and that once they realize it was a diversion, it will take them at least another ten minutes to figure out what we're doing. During those twenty minutes, we can evacuate the whole Noucathar population of Aurenga—after all, that's only three thousand people, and they're all in one big building. So we want to seize that fieldhouse, and silence its guards, less than five minutes before the distraction bomb goes off. We're going to spring everyone to the *Cathar Argo*, a ship orbiting about a light-month away, deep in the Oort Cloud, and from there they'll be sprung to wherever in Union they have relatives or friends, or wherever they like. We've had that ship sitting there for decades against a need for evacuation, though this isn't quite the one we planned. Simultaneously all the psypyxes and aintellects will be uploading copies of themselves through a specialized net we have in place. Once everyone in flesh is on board *Cathar Argo*, and everyone else is copied, we blow up the Noucathar Hall of Memories— where all the psypyxes are—and wipe most of the aintellects on the planetary net, leaving the OSP with almost nothing to deconstruct or interrogate.

"With luck, since we've hurt no one, the Council will be in a mood to talk at some time afterward. Well, I really can't think of anyone I'd rather have with me for a neat little finessed raid like that—if we pull it off properly, we'll have nobody even hurt."

I started to think about it, when Shan broke in and thought, • Let's do it. Let's help her out on this raid and defect to Union. •

I realized my mouth was hanging open again and I didn't care. • Shan, this is a switch—•

• Or a greater consistency. Take your pick. There's not really time to argue; we need time to plan with Paxa and Azalais, if we're going to do it. Let's just merge our feelings and thoughts on the subject; we can work out a way to articulate it all later. •

In that big echoing chamber, all white concrete arches and

jewel-blue windows, I drew one deep breath, and something like this formed as an understanding between Shan and me:

Shan: At that last, the triumph of the lesser over the greater cannot ever be, really, a good thing. Even if somehow augmented human beings and crippled aintellects were enough to defeat the Invaders, our world would contain beings only as capable as ourselves, refusing to try to make a place for ourselves in the bigger world. That would be a deeper defeat: a runner who enters a race he cannot win has a brave dignity in his silly pathos as he stumbles to the finish line through a cloud of the winner's dust; a runner who uses some power to exclude everyone who might beat him can stand as straight as he likes when they hang the medal on him, but everyone knows (that runner most of all) that it is a worthless trinket.	**Giraut:** We owe something to songs. Every work carries with it all the performances in its past, from composer to performer and teacher to learner. What begins as one raindrop plonking into one Earthly puddle, reminding one melancholy man that the woman he wants is sleeping with her husband that night, flows through his brain and vocal cords and fingers, into other brains, until it eventually is a choir of a hundred voices, on a planet with a hundred human cultures, a hundred light-years from Earth, a hundred centuries in the future . . . and one young woman in the front row sits up and says to herself, *That is like what happened to me, but not quite*, and sets about making something else. We owe it to the songs to set them free to do that.

Shan: There are songs that cannot be born in Council-controlled space but which deserve to win; they must be allowed to compete.	**Giraut:** I am Occitan. The original Occitan culture was exterminated in the crusade against the original Cathars—conducted by the world authority in the name of a necessary unity in the face of surrounding dangers. I can no more resist sympathizing with a band of fleeing artists, pursued by a single-minded all encompassing and horribly dull authority—
Shan: Than I can resist the image of a doomed, lone individual wandering the world until he can complete one last pointless mission	**Giraut:** So
Shan: let's	**Giraut:** do it.

We hadn't been thinking in words; as I said, we just merged. But even that takes a little time, and all the people who have ever done covert ops know the real meaning of "Ask me for anything but time" in their bones. When my attention moved outside myself, to the woman in front of me, she was waiting to catch my eye, and not patiently.

"We don't have much time," Paxa, or Azalais, said, very quietly, and looked at us with hope.

"We're in." I'm not sure which one of us said that.

When the springer pulsed into gray light the first time, Paxa rolled into it, and an instant later it pulsed again, and I went through to a different springer.

As planned, I emerged into an alcove in the fieldhouse where one very discreet and clever little aintellect had penetrated security and activated a hospital springer. Little danger of its being in use—the population was young and had been handled gently. My biggest dread had been that there might be someone in labor coming the other way, but that didn't happen.

Instead, I found myself facing a long, dusty hallway lined with very old display cases.

The lights went out—Paxa's Trojan aintellect was on schedule—as I began my run down the hallway, but I could see well enough to run on an empty floor by the moonlight coming in through the big outside windows.

I was just five long steps from the long down staircase that was an important part of my plan when the lights came back on—which was also supposed to happen. I bounded down the stairs as a CSP guard stepped onto the staircase to demand my papers. I launched myself down the last few steps, catching myself on his shoulders and flipping him backward to the floor; his helmet and body armor supported his neck and it was no more than uncomfortable for him, but severely disorienting. I slapped a neuroducer onto the back of his neck as he sat up—just a little gadget to make him sleep till the doctors took it off—and he ragdolled back onto the floor.

As I got to my feet, pulling out my stunstick, I was confronted by the other guard, clutching his. By now, however, Union aintellects were in charge of the building, and there was no urgent need for silence or caution.

They don't really train anybody in law enforcement or the military to use a stunstick properly; it is assumed that it's a weapon you use against unarmed, untrained combatants, where it's just a matter of touching them with the last nine centimeters. He swung hard overhand with his stunstick in his right hand; I switched mine to my left behind my back, leaned out of his swipe, and struck overhand and down, my stunstick coming in just above and behind his.

It caught his wrist, and whipped his arm violently down and then up into an outward circle as I numbed his hand. As his stunstick flew up to the ceiling, I turned sideways and took a big step between his legs, grabbed the back of his collar with my right hand, flicked with my left thumb to put my stunstick to maximum knockout, and firmly but carefully pushed my hands together. My stunstick rested against his forehead for a long second, and then he fell over. Even veteran CSPs look sort of sweet when they're asleep with one big joyous smile and jaw open and drooling.

Paxa rounded the corner and gestured for me to follow her. "Good to be back," she said, as we sprinted to the gym.

"Fun to have you back," I agreed. My heavy boots clomped down the hallway, punctuated by the slap-squick of her grip-slippers.

The plan was that by the time we got into the gym, our ain-tellects would already have turned the lights on, powered down all enemy guard robots, sounded the alarm to waken everyone, and have them ready for us to start evacuation. Plans, of course, are notorious for going awry, and this one did so spectacularly, as we came around the last turn and found ourselves facing Raimbaut, who had his slug-thrower already leveled.

Training is what you have so that the easiest thing to do is the right thing; we zagged away from each other, to opposite walls of the hallway, and raised our hands the minimum compliant distance, giving ourselves a chance to draw if need be.

Raimbaut's face stayed impassive; later he told me that the

moment that happened, he knew he was caught in the classic hostage fork.

"Shame on you," Shan said. "You should have been waiting about ten meters farther back in the corridor."

Even then, Raimbaut didn't flinch. He just looked and evaluated. If he shot either of us, the other one would have time to draw and return fire—even exchange. And we were ahead on material; that meant we'd come out of it the winner—fifty percent dead to his one hundred percent, and therefore able to continue our plans.

Of course it wasn't that each of us would be fifty percent dead. One of us would be very unhappy but unscathed . . .

"All right," I said. "Do we want to discuss who likes who best?"

Raimbaut looked it all over, shrugged, and threw down his maser. "I don't want to kill either of you, so I guess that means I've lost," he said. "And last I knew, Margaret wasn't paying any effort-based raises." He shrugged. "What are you going to do?"

"Help everyone escape peacefully," I said. "So far all the casualties are a few stunned guards. If we move quickly, there can be no bloodshed, no destructive deconstructions, everyone can start talking without anyone having anything to be mad about."

"Except your ex-wife," Raimbaut said. "She's brilliant, talented, effective, and *petty*. Good luck with *her*." We all stood still for a long couple of seconds before he said, "If you have cuffs you'd better bind me so I'm covered for an alibi. I'd rather that than be stunned—getting stunned always gives me a hangover."

I kept my weapon aimed at him while Paxa cuffed him, and until she was back out of his reach. "All right, Raimbaut, forward march."

The aintellects had taken some initiative in the gym, and everyone was lined up and ready to go. We cut through the chains on one door with a maser, and started the parade out into the hallway. "Everyone who has any relative or friend who is not here in this room—everyone who knows of anyone who might be being left behind—come forward!"

There was no one. Paxa checked with the aintellect, and it had already hacked and cross-matched records; a young healthy population had simply not happened to have anyone in the hospital, and universal global tracking assured that there was no one off scuba diving or caving who hadn't been rounded up.

It was one of the strangest refugee parades I have ever seen; hardly any of them had any material possessions except for very small children—and every one of them had a teddy bear or blanky.

CSPs are notoriously softhearted and most of them had probably not only allowed the little ones to have something for security, but actually encouraged it. • If Margaret ever thought of committing genocide using CSPs, • Shan thought, • she doesn't know them at all. None of these kids even looks scared. •

Furthermore, there were no stunned-looking old people—in fact no one was either old or stunned-looking.

"What's so interesting?" Reilis said, suddenly appearing beside me.

I kept my weapon at ready, though of course for safety's sake I had been pointing it toward the skylight anyway, ever since it became clear that Raimbaut was not going to make a break for it and no commando raid was imminent. With my free hand, I half hugged Reilis, while keeping my eyes scanning the room. "Good to see you again," I said, "and I guess we'll all have more time to talk once we get over to the other side."

"Are we taking Raimbaut?"

"Not unless he asks to come," I said. "Where's Laprada?"

"Sleeping," Raimbaut said. "I was restless and bored and looking around at everything I could monitor, and I saw a flurry of activity in your place—your prison, I suppose. A warm body came in, two warm bodies left, and by the time I hacked through all the worms that had taken over the house systems, there were robots leaving cadavers everywhere. You've always run an odd household, Giraut, but that was odd even for you.

"So I broadened my search, and then things started happening here. I caught a glimpse through one camera before it was taken over, and saw Paxa knocking down a CSP. So I grabbed my maser and got between you and the Noucathar prisoners— about ten meters too far forward, as Shan points out. Got caught in the classic hostage fork." He shrugged, looking very much like a teenaged boy. "I just know Laprada's going to be mad at me because she missed all the excitement."

"Ebles!" Paxa called.

He stepped out of the line.

"It's me, Azalais. Come on over and meet my new body. And if you dare say you like it better, you're dead."

Ebles and Reilis stuck around us while everyone else went through the springer. Our three bodies took turns at guarding Raimbaut (who was about the most relaxed and cheerful prisoner I had ever seen). After we had checked the bathrooms and bleachers, to make sure there were no hiding children or fools with last-minute cases of the shorts, I said, "Is that it?"

"One last check in progress," Paxa said, looking at her computer. "We already set off the bomb in the Hall of Memories, so those pyspyxes are gone, and beyond the reach of destructive deconstruction. The aintellects we brought in are ready to wipe themselves and have uploaded copies of all the captured and taken-over aintellects to storage on *Cathar Argo*. But we want to make sure—well, shit, of course there would be one. Back at the main base, in the main administration building, in one office, there's a psypyx copy of—you, Reilis."

"Well," Reilis said, "it makes me sick, but given where it is, we can't possibly raid to get it, and if we use any weapon destructive enough to be sure of getting it, we're bound to hurt innocent people. I think—we'll just have to—" She couldn't quite make herself say it.

I think, looking back, that more than anything else it was Reilis's expression that made me say, "I think we ought to go get it. Or failing that, Shan and I should stay behind to try to talk them out of destructive deconstruction. It's *you*, Reilis. I don't want that to happen to you."

"Me either, but better that than any of the alternatives—like getting all of us killed or captured, or having the blood of a lot of Council troops on our hands—"

"Ahem," Raimbaut said. "Ahem, ahem, ahem. I have an idea that will work—or might—if you'll trust me to throw in with you. And I have to admit that watching this and listening to all of you, I've been feeling like I was seeing—for the first time in ages—another round for humanity and one for the good guys. What you're doing looks like the sort of thing I joined the OSP to do—I like being on the side that protects little children with teddy bears, and worries about the danger to innocent guards," Raimbaut said.

"Strangely enough, I agree," Shan said. "All right, Raimbaut, give us the plan."

I thought to Shan, • I hadn't really noticed how many scenes, in how many silly dramas and stories, this resembles. Of course it usually works in those stories, which I suppose is some sort of a good sign. But I had not noticed the resemblance at the time we planned this. •

• Since that time was just a few minutes ago, • Shan thought back, • it may not be all that surprising that you are having second thoughts. However, 'a good plan stuck to and carried out right now—'•

• 'Beats a perfect plan arrived at too late and tweaked in the middle,'• I thought back. • You know, the worst thing is that your quoting yourself can't very well be a sign of senility—psypyxes don't go senile and otherwise that's my brain you're running on. And thank you for not thinking of any obvious rejoinders. •

We were walking a couple of paces in front of Raimbaut; my hands were cuffed and bound, he held a neuroducer dart gun pointed at my back, and we had just cleared a secure springer in the closed-down suburban business district that had been made the OSP's ad hoc base in Masselha. Raimbaut was conducting me to the main office building, having made an appointment with Margaret for about half an hour from right now. He was acting like a very businesslike agent; I was acting the role of the disconsolate prisoner. Reviews weren't quite in yet.

We were counting on the fact of Margaret's appointment with us to get us past the robots at the main guard station; she was expecting Raimbaut and me, me as prisoner, and that was in the log, and that was what they saw when we approached the desk. We had to hope they wouldn't decide to give Raimbaut an extensive backup against extremely dangerous me.

• And your ego has to hope that they won't just wave you through as harmless, • Shan thought. I could feel his amusement at my sense of outrage, but at least it made my bonds feel annoying, and I struggled with them, subtly, but enough so that Raimbaut checked his distance and kept a close eye; we looked like a moderately dangerous prisoner being guarded by a highly competent guard, and the robots cleared us at once.

Of course the robots and aintellects on guard assumed we were going to Margaret's temporary office and that Raimbaut would know where that was. The only thing we knew in that building was where Reilis's psypyx was (at least according to the files we had hacked)—Office 446. We were headed straight to that room, and the plan was to blow down the door, find the psypyx, destroy it, and run like hell.

We had a card carrying a code for a springer that would stay open, somewhere safe in Union space, for about another twenty minutes, before they would turn it off to prevent its becoming an invasion route. It was understood that our chances of getting to use that card were slim, and we'd spent more time reminding ourselves to destroy the card the moment we were captured, rather than thinking of where to find a springer in the main headquarters. Chances were that we would get no such chance; it might take us some time to find the psypyx, with the guards on their way an instant after we blew the door, and so it was likely enough that we would not get out of the room at all. If we did, we would have to find a springer in an unfamiliar building and slap the card in. Then the card would have to defeat military—or security-agency-grade safeties, which could take up to a full minute—time we almost certainly would not have.

As I contemplated that, Shan thought, • Well, that's all true enough. Suppose we just think of the card as a lovely gesture; Union forces are taking a serious risk of having another springer address captured, just to give you a tiny chance, as opposed to no chance, of escape. It may not be smart and it may not be effective, but you have to admit, it's gracious. •

• *Que merce e que enseingnamen,* • I agreed. • And futility is *ne gens* to mention. •

We went up a flight of stairs and turned down the last corridor on our way to Office 446—luckily the system for numbering offices was simple enough. Of course we had to be ready for the moment when it would become apparent to the monitoring aintellects that we were not going to Margaret's office. I had my finger on the cuff release, and a maser in my back pocket, ready to start running and shooting as soon as anything sounded like an alarm or a response.

Raimbaut and I had assumed that they would be asking questions as soon as we turned off the most direct route to Margaret's office, and then coming after us as soon as they didn't get an answer they liked to those questions. But there were no problems in the corridor. Maybe the psypyx was being kept near Margaret's office?

Office doors counted up—444, 445, and we came to 446, a flat black door like all the others in the corridor. Raimbaut closed up behind me, and with him covering the view from most angles, I touched the release on my wrist bindings; they fell into my palms and I tucked them into my belt so they would not drop into plain sight on the floor.

I reached into my back pockets, my right hand grabbing a maser and my left hand grabbing one of four claphammers. Whip the claphammer forward onto the door lock, step back, let it blow the door open, and go in—that was my intent.

The door slid open in front of us. I dropped the claphammer back into my pocket, and kept my hands back there for the benefit of any cameras that might be watching. We walked through.

As might be expected, since the robots had just finished setting up the office, everything was in perfect order—which is why I recognized just which everything it was, the instant that I passed through the doorway. The overall atmosphere of precision and placement—the kind of mind that matches places to things with cool, practical precision, neither obsessively nor compulsively but because that is the path of maximum effect and minimum effort—was recognizable at a glance, even as I noticed all the individual touches.

I had seen those vus of the Gap Bow that appeared every

noon in the Gouge, the great canyon above Utilitopia, in Caledony—seen them in temporary offices in a dozen cultures, on three different planets, besides in the OSP main headquarters in Nuevo Buenos Aires. I knew that Bieris Real landscape of Terraust, centered on the terrified aurocs-demer dying in a range fire—had been there when Bieris herself had seen it—knew it was the original, not a copy, and had once been a wedding present. And I knew that the vu frame on the desk, facing away from me at the moment, contained a picture of me singing "Never Again Till the Next Time," my lips endlessly forming the first two words, fingers forever repeating the same four positions on the lute.

This was Margaret's office. She had Reilis's psypyx in here somewhere.

And just that thought, all by itself, told me everything else I needed to think of at that moment: this place was not a lab, not a copying facility, and probably had no reading or contact facilities of any kind. Margaret had pulled Reilis's psypyx out of the Hall of Memories for entirely personal reasons.

• Every really successful agent, and every good spymaster, always knows it's always personal, • Shan observed. • Try not to hate her. •

• How can I? It's Margaret, and I know her feelings better than anyone in the universe—well enough to know that she sometimes does things she's ashamed of. And of course what I'm about to do is personal, too. •

I thought. Margaret normally kept things like the copy of her diary, her favorite combat knife, and the jewelry that her mother had sent from her grandmother's estate at the back of the middle drawer in the right-hand bank of drawers. I walked around the desk and tried the middle drawer on the right just in case it had been left unlocked. No doubt that set off the alarm right then, though nothing sounded in the hallway yet. I slapped a claphammer onto the front of the drawer.

A moment later the claphammer banged, flying back against the wall and zinging overhead so that Raimbaut and I ducked and covered our heads. *Now* there were alarms, in the corridors and in this office.

I pulled out the remaining pieces of the front of the desk drawer to see if I'd been lucky and the claphammer itself had destroyed the psypyx. No such luck—the psypyx was in its safety case, and those cases are supposed to be good to a thousand gees. I opened the case and took the little black-and-gray cut-cube out, letting it rest lightly in the palm of my hand like a very delicate orchid or butterfly.

Psypyxes are delicate—no durable material for them has yet been found—and because they record information right down at the molecular level, one good crack means that they can never be read. That's why that hard black shell lined with foam goes around them when they are implanted; a tiny skull on the back of the host's skull.

Reilis's psypyx was naked and defenseless, but cushioned as it had been in its hard, supportive little case, it was still fine as far as I could tell.

Without a connection to a brain or a computer, it was inert, and there was no Reilis there to feel or know anything. At that moment the psypyx was as dead as you might wish, only potentially a person.

It would have made no difference at all if I had simply smashed it with Margaret's desk dictionary, or vaporized it with my pocket maser. The means didn't matter, just as long as I destroyed it.

Yet I hesitated. It was Reilis, or could be.

• Fool, • Shan thought at me. • Be sentimental later. •

He was right. If they recaptured this psypyx before I destroyed it, an indefinite number of copies of her would have the endlessly repeated experience of live, unanesthetized brain dissection.

"Please tell me that this situation is not causing you to compose ridiculous sentimental background music," Raimbaut said.

"Too late," Shan said. "He already is."

"Raimbaut," I said, "I am afraid Shan's right."

Still, we are creatures of ceremony. I kissed that psypyx before I carefully placed it on the floor and crushed it beneath my boot, stamping until it was just a black-and-gray powder.

Raimbaut watched me the way you watch a friend at the graveside of a spouse; with complete attention but no idea what to say or do.

We were spared any need to decide our next move, because at that moment Margaret walked in. She took in the situation at a glance. I said, "You realize that I had Raimbaut covered with a weapon the whole time; he was not in on this, and you've just liberated him from my holding him as a hostage."

"Yes," she said, "that *is* what we will *have* to say, isn't it?"

3

Once it all began in earnest—the things that have gotten so much attention in the past stanyear, which are matters of public record, and which I am not greatly concerned to record here—I suppose I was forced to ask myself, often, whether I might have done things differently if I had known what was going on in the bigger world. Union Intelligence still had, for a few critical hours, the immense advantage that they had always had—that they knew all about the OSP, and most of the OSP didn't even know that they existed.

So Union Intelligence sprang their last great surprise. They went public. Substantially accurate accounts of the main facts in the case—the existence of many more aintellects' conspiracies, of a mixed human-cyber civilization beyond what had been assumed to be the limit of human space, and of the Invaders—was dumped out to news media all over the Thousand Cultures, as well as back on Earth itself. The Council and the OSP might be able to decide on any number of courses of action, but they could not decide to ignore the situation, or to hide it from the public.

The first reaction was highly predictable. Many of the people who were already mostly in the box, particularly on Earth and the other Solar worlds, but throughout the Inner Sphere, went fully Solipsist and decided that the aintellects who created all of reality were again doing a bad job for the consumers, and flooded the nets with demands that better programming be provided. The more deviant and eccentric of the Thousand Cultures—the ones that had been located on planets with fewer than ten other cultures—threw various kinds of tantrums. And the public terror of aintellects out of control—never absent since the Rising and reactivated by the aintellects' coup attempt fifteen stanyears before—surged to the forefront. There were serious demands to shut down all aintellects, despite their absolute necessity for doing such things as making psypyx copies and operating springers (no unaided human being could do the requisite calculations within one human lifetime). An estimated nine million robots were destroyed in rioting in a period of weeks.

The connection to the Ixists came out, and that meant more rioting, and suppression of that faith on eleven of the thirty-one inhabited planets. On Roosevelt, the schisms between those who favored more-extreme and less-extreme plans for suppressing the Ixists quickly became violent and then terrorist, on both sides (as any schism on Roosevelt will tend to do), and the ninety-two cultures that crowded the shores of Roosevelt's narrow seas and swarmed about her mild poles were once again on the brink of mutual butchery. Somebody blew up the Fareman Hall where I had given so many concerts, including the one on my fiftieth birthday, and I mourned as if it had been a personal friend.

The debates in the Council were enlivened by the recall of many traditional, hereditary representatives and their replacement with people actually elected by their home cultures, who finally cared enough to hold elections.

The new representatives favored action, action, and more action—some of it marvelous and overdue (e.g. expanding the digs on Hammarskjöld, funding more Predecessor studies generally, and also stepping up the pace of basic research), some of it regrettably necessary (e.g. starting the design of a war fleet, authorizing the conversion and drastic expansion of some of the CSP into the Army of Humanity, and greatly increased funding for anti-Solipsist propaganda and treatment), and some of it appalling, however understandable (more repression of aintellects, Ixists, and robots).

In the midst of upheaval, there is nothing so comforting to a politician as a good, solid scandal. And here was one: the most public OSP agent of all, who had been decorated for his heroism in foiling the aintellects' coup, and who had been a personal friend of Ix . . . had assisted three thousand Union chimeras in escaping from Council forces.

It was absolutely true, and it was absolutely public. And that public divided roughly into three equal-sized groups: those who wanted me executed, those who wanted me completely exonerated, and those who were trying to decide what they wanted. Unfortunately, the pro-execution side had the law on their side, and the time was not at all ripe for a change of law.

Charges against Raimbaut were dismissed the first day; the judge did a great job of pretending to buy the story that Margaret and I had concocted. It took them a year to establish what the law plainly said: I was a traitor of the most serious kind the law recognized, and the Council of Humanity had enacted the death penalty for traitors like me. Theoretically I could be saved by a change in the law—but the Council was not of a mind to make the law less draconian. Theoretically I could be saved by simply allowing very long stays of execution until the public mood changed enough to tolerate clemency—but the public was not in the mood for stays. Theoretically my usefulness to Shan as a host might have netted me a couple more years, but for excellent reasons Shan had been transferred early on to Margaret.

Finally it came down to this: there would be as many appeals and arguments as possible and necessary, and then, unless something very surprising happened, they would kill me.

Not a permanent death, of course. They always make a psypyx recording anyway, in case the executed person should be later found innocent, or needed as a witness. And there would be many stanyears of court cases to be tried about whether or not they could do a destructive deconstruction of any copies of my psypyx, and for a long time it was fair to assume that very few people, other than my closer friends and family, would want me back anyway.

So, a version of "me" would be awaking in Raimbaut's head someday. But this particular me was going to die.

Oh, they fought it out brilliantly. That was part of the strategy that Margaret, Shan, and I had evolved. The haters and the stiffnecks, the people who wanted to formalize aintellects into slaves, the genociders and the crazy bombers and all the rest of them, after a stanyear of trial and another stanyear of appeals, were united around killing me. Kill me and they would be happy. If I were not killed, it would mean there was no law and no justice. I had to be sprung into progressively more secure courtrooms, until the final arguments in my case were heard in deep military shelters, the sort of place intended to take a near miss from a nuclear weapon. Then the heads of the Council, and their cabinets, swayed back and forth longer and longer about setting an execution date, and the kill-Giraut faction grew noisier, and more passionate—

And smaller. Which was the whole idea. More and more of the head-in-the-sand, human-supremacy-types lost elections. More and more, they were seen as nuts and cranks by their neighbors. In the long run, most people prefer to be allied with the more humane side, given a real choice. Very few people wish to look crazy and fixated to their neighbors.

Right on schedule, the appeals ran out and an execution date was set.

Now, one thing you can say for the death penalty, whatever effect it has or doesn't have on crime, whatever its implications for justice might be—it is great theatre. With the date set, I invoked my rights to have a public function carried out in public; a few hundred serial killers, cannibals, child slaughterers, discommodists, and hobby terrorists had been executed over the last fifty stanyears, all under wraps by their own choice to spare their families. I not only refused a private execution; I demanded full media access. They would have to kill me in front of crowds and cameras.

I also chose my means of execution—I could choose to be shot as a reserve CSP officer, anesthetized as a Council citizen, or sprung into a star as an OSP renegade (it was a way of making renegades non-people with no identifiable remains ever).

Or I could opt for execution according to my cultural tradition. Nou Occitan had not executed anyone since its founding, but its cultural Charter specified doing things as much as possible like Old Occitan on Earth—so I insisted that I be beheaded with a sword.

By the day of my execution, nine-tenths of the population didn't want to see it happen, and though many billions would watch on media, they had all loudly affirmed they wouldn't, and particularly they thought it was repellent that this would be done in a broadcast that children might see. They didn't want a text-and-picture media jammed with images of a robot striking my head off; they didn't want to be offered recordings that would give them the chance to experience standing in the crowd close enough to hear the sword go into my neck like a whip slashing a side of beef. They especially did not want this because so many of them now knew my songs, and even a great deal of my life story (since my three hitherto-private personal chronicles had been cleared through security and published, and Margaret's little publicity outfit had been twisting a lot of promoter arms. Another good thing I am forced to admit about the death penalty, it really sells recordings and keeps your back-list hot).

Ninety percent didn't want to see me killed; and the ten percent that did were rapidly becoming an embarrassment to their cause. As Shan had put it, when I had talked with him that morning, "Sometimes what really binds a culture together is the things they have done *wrong*. We will need to execute you to prepare the way for the backlash. In another stanyear even most of our bigoted opponents will be blaming those rock-throwers and machine-haters for causing this awful miscarriage of justice, and vowing that nothing like your execution must ever happen again, and we can start to push through some liberalization for aintellects."

It was so strange that he was using Margaret's voice; and she barely spoke at all, too bothered, I think, by the fact of what was about to happen to me. Shan and Margaret both repeated their promises to get a clone grown for me, just as soon as possible. But there wasn't much to say after that; a man with a single day to live does not want to talk public policy, and neither Shan nor Margaret ever wanted to talk much else. I shook their hand and sat down and wrote a few more pages of this fourth chronicle; this last page will complete the story of me (or at least of the original me), and here I am, finishing the writing on the afternoon before my execution.

The other visit was harder. "I never did learn to get my work done early," I said, showing my parents what I had written that morning. "But at least it will draw more attention to the ugliness of the execution itself. From being the voice of the people, the other side is gradually diminishing into those idiots who beheaded that poet in the funny clothes. They're killing me but I'll be the end of them."

Dad sat very quietly next to Mother, an apparent ten-year-old with his apparent great-grandmother, holding her hand. "I wish you were a bit less objective, Giraut."

"Well, I don't," I said. "Being objective beats weeping and

moaning, which is about the only realistic alternative now. I only regret that I let them take that psypyx copy this morning; ideally it should have been just before I took the long walk to the block. Because one thing my copy isn't getting half of is how much I have gotten to appreciate every moment of being alive."

"Is all of this really necessary?" Mother asked.

"By itself, no, but it's part of what we need to do, and it's the most effective thing I can do right now. The more we discredit the human supremacists, and the solipsists, and the just plain loudmouthed aggressors, by helping them to do brutal things in public—*after* the public has long since thought better—the more we open the door. Just this morning Dunant repealed their anti-Ixist laws, in time for me to send them a recorded speech thanking them. And on Nansen, both Caledony and St. Michael refused to pass aintellect-control measures this past week. The tide has turned—which means that now, when the pigheads win, they look pigheaded. Just what we want."

Mother was still wiping her eyes. "But you're going to die."

"Mother," I said, "you know that nightmare everyone has about waking up and finding out that you are the original? Well, that's just what happened to me this morning, when I woke up after the last psypyx recording. This Giraut will be killed by order of the Council of Humanity, tomorrow. The copy lives on. And I have to say, of course, that I envy him, and that I'm glad for him that he's not going to feel or remember my terror or pain. Putting my neck down on that block is going to be pretty bad and I'm really afraid I'll funk it, and even if I don't, I'm destined for some bad seconds that he'll never have in his memory. I envy him getting a new healthy body, too. But all that said . . . I find that I'm the original, and therefore I am the one who dies . . . and it's not anywhere near so big or so frightening as I thought. It's just my job."

Then we talked for a while of old times, and about the need for Mother to hang in there and keep getting psypyx copies made because when peaceful trade was established with Union colonies—as was almost certain within a few stanyears—their better psypyx technology would probably allow her to get a new body at last.

Mostly, though, the conversation wasn't about anything even that important. We talked about recipes, and families we have known, and where the time goes, and all the things you do on a long visit. I told them to give my love to my copy.

So this is the end of this fourth chronicle of my adventures since the springer threw all the human worlds together. In a little while I will stroll to my death, and I have elected to be beheaded, in my full *trobador* regalia, exactly what I wore for my last concert (though of course without Laprada there, the damned *tapi* will probably never hang straight.)

This journal entry is as far as I, the original, will go; the copy will have to finish it. I am the original, the one who will walk to death.

Fate always has other plans, and the best death speeches tend to be delivered too soon, even if only by a little.

It's still me, the original. I had thought that I was done, and was just sitting back and relishing the thundering melodrama of "the one who will walk to death," and thinking about seeing if I could start writing a song before my last meal, since that would surely add to the pathos if the copy then had to finish it.

But then the springer in my cell glowed gray, and Raimbaut stepped in. We embraced, and he held me with his strong young-man's arms for a long moment before he found the ability to speak again. "Laprada couldn't bear to come," he said. "She says that killing poets to educate stupid people is the sort of nonsense that only a democracy can come up with, and she wants no part of it."

"She has a point," I agreed, "and tell her from me that she is not to tolerate stupidity any more than she has to."

"I will, from me," *I said*.

It was Raimbaut's voice but my intonation. I stared. "They are going to be sending me on detached duty a long way away, constantly, for a few stanyears," Raimbaut said, "which is how Margaret is keeping this all hidden. Several of us thought it would be good to get you back into the game as soon as possible, so I'm wearing the psypyx you recorded this morning. I'll be falling asleep soon, so we should get the talking done. But . . . Giraut, meet Giraut."

I shook hands with Raimbaut's body, and looked into my own expression in his eye. At least I finally had company likely to fully appreciate the humor of the situation. I said, "Don't you love the media slogan for the coverage—'see his death, live!'? What fun language is!"

Raimbaut's face laughed and said, "I hadn't thought of that yet, but that's a great joke." Then the expression changed subtly. "Giraut, could you please be a tiny bit more serious?" Raimbaut pleaded. "I feel as if you're performing for your copy."

"Of course I am. If we are not our own audiences, who will be? And half the trouble in the world is caused by people who don't care enough to give themselves a truly good show. But for now—well, the world is giving me death. I owe it to you, and to myself, and to everyone, to stroll to it, like a *trobador*, with nothing to do but sing about how fine spring is, how good it is to be in love, and how briefly we are here—just the things we *trobadori* have been singing about since the beginning, *m'es vis*."

We talked of old times—strange how when the times are over, really over, we so want to talk of them—but Raimbaut had just had the psypyx implanted that day, and he was fading fast. I shook hands with him just before he stumbled and almost fell; the person that stood up was entirely my copy. I shook copy-of-Giraut's hand, as well. "Something I want to prepare you for," he said. "Since it touches both our *enseingnamen e gens*. Earth authorities have declared that since Giraut Leones is now an Ixist saint, there will be an amnesty, and for the day of your execution, they will ignore any public sign or evidence of anyone's membership in a forbidden cult. Which means, I suppose, that besides the Ixists, the Thugs and the Moloch-worshippers are free to wander about in whatever silly clothes they want.

"Anyway, the Ixists will be showing up at the procession from the prison to the block, lining the route as if it's a parade. And they are going to be throwing roses. I think you should plan what you are going to do when you catch one."

"Kiss it and toss it to a pretty girl, obviously," I said. "It's what they'll expect."

My habit of dropping bits of autobiography into the acknowledgments has had one effect that needs immediate correction, since it has resulted in something silly which touches the reputation of an innocent person. The fact that I went through a painful second divorce two years *after* the publication of *Earth Made of Glass* (which depicts, among other things, a painful divorce) has led to confusion resulting in a frequent online, and increasingly frequent in print, assertion that *Earth Made of Glass* is somehow "about" that divorce. This is improbable, at the least since, I don't seem to have the foresight to plan till the end of the week, and for *Earth Made of Glass* to have been about my second divorce would require about four years of foresight: *Earth Made of Glass* was substantially complete in late August of 1996 (from an outline written in 1995), given a final revision in the spring of 1997, and first published in April 1998. The events that led to my real-world divorce did not occur until the spring and summer of 2000 (the divorce was final in May 2001).

Nor do the facts of either my first or second divorce much resemble those of Giraut's, nor does either of my ex-wives much resemble the fictional Margaret. (For one thing, they're both very attractive, and for another thing, neither of them is a ruthless killer, as my continued presence attests.)

It is probably charitable of many readers and reviewers to assume that I was expressing or venting something I needed to bring out rather than exploring something ugly for its own sake in *Earth Made of Glass* and *The Merchants of Souls*, but in fairness to everyone, particularly to my ex-wives, I must admit that the books *were* written to explore something ugly, and some things of great beauty, for their own sake. The ugliness in those books is there because I was interested in that flavor of ugliness; I have since moved on to other flavors.

Now, on to the more pleasant duty of acknowledgment. I'd like to thank:

William D. Paden, whom I have never met, but whose *An Introduction to Old Occitan* has been invaluable in the later books of this series. (Alas, it was published in 1998, after the series was already well underway, so some errors from earlier books remain.) I have very deliberately simplified Occitan and tried to use mainly words with numerous Romance-language cognates, to give a flavor without bogging the story; let me recommend Paden if, having tried the flavor, you want the full and delicious meal. Any errors are of course mine.

Stephen L. Gillett, whom I have met, several times in fact, and whose *World-Building: A Writer's Guide to Constructing Star Systems and Life-supporting Planets* has helped me to avoid many errors and at least make any remaining errors (which are of course mine) more interesting. If any of you are working on a science fiction novel (and to judge by my mail, all of you are), this is a book you must have and know.

Stanley Schmidt, editor of *Analog Science Fiction & Fact*, who published three excerpts from this book and whose comments helped a great deal in its final revision, assisting me in chopping about 15,000 quite unnecessary words out of it.

Jes Tate, who assembled and cataloged much of the heap of photocopies that passes for my research library.

Patrick Nielsen Hayden, who was patient while waiting for a

book that was finally delivered twenty-three months past deadline.

Liz Gorinsky, who was efficient and diplomatic in coping with all the mess that caused.

Bob and Sarah Schwager, for causing me to write STET fewer times than I can remember on any book.

Ashley and Carolyn Grayson, my agents, who always acted as if this book was about to be delivered at any moment, particularly when talking to me.